ONE NIGHT TO RISK IT ALL

KATHERINE GARBERA

TWIN SCANDALS

FIONA BRAND

D0718800

MILLS & BOON

First Published in Great Britain 2019
by Mills & Boon, an imprint of HarperCollinsPublishers,
1 London Bridge Street, London, SE1 9GF

One Night to Risk it All © 2019 Katherine Garbera
Twin Scandals © 2019 Fiona Gillibrand

ISBN: 978-0-263-27202-4

1219

MIX
Paper from
responsible sources
FSC™ C007454

This book is produced from independently certified FSC™ paper to ensure responsible forest management.

For more information visit: www.harpercollins.co.uk/green

Printed and bound in Spain
by CPI, Barcelona

ONE NIGHT
TO RISK IT ALL

KATHERINE GARBERA

My parents will celebrate their fifty-second
wedding anniversary on Christmas Eve,
so this book is for them.

They've taught me so much about what love
and marriage and family mean,
and I'm so lucky they are my parents.
Love you both very much!

One

Inigo Velasquez lived life at a fast pace and liked it that way. As the youngest and arguably handsomest of the Velasquez brothers, he enjoyed life to the fullest. No tying the knot and settling down for him. Plus, his career as a Formula One driver kept him on the road and away from his matchmaking mama for most of the year.

He had to give his mom credit, though. It took some real determination to arrange a setup at a party on New Year's Eve, one that wasn't even taking place in their hometown of Cole's Hill, Texas. Back home, Inigo was always on his guard for his mom's maneuvering, but tonight they were all the way across the country at the Hamptons home of his brother Alec's baby mama, Scarlet O'Malley. Inigo had mistakenly assumed that his mom's network wouldn't be able to produce any potential bridal candidates this far afield.

He had to give her high marks for finding a woman who was hitting all of his hot buttons. She was tall, probably an inch or so shorter than his own five-foot-ten frame. She had long blond hair with some darker streaks that hung down her back. She wore a chemise-type shift dress that was brilliant sapphire blue and complimented her silvery eyes perfectly.

She didn't let her height keep her from wearing heels, and she was by far the most stunning person in the room. She moved through the well-heeled, moneyed crowd with ease, which made him wonder who she was.

"Mom, you've outdone yourself," he said as his mom came over to him with a glass of champagne in each hand. She handed him one, which he took and knew he'd have to nurse all night. He was already training for the upcoming season, and that meant watching his alcohol intake.

"Thanks, sweetie," she said. "It's really only a glass of bubbly."

"I meant the woman," he said.

"What woman?"

"Are you seriously going to pretend that the only single woman in the room isn't here at your behest so that I accidentally meet her?" he asked.

"Inigo, I didn't invite anyone for you to *accidentally* meet. I wanted my boys to settle down in Texas. But Mo is the only one who married a Cole's Hill girl. Diego divides his time between London and Texas, and it looks as if Alec is going to be doing the same, commuting between New York and home. I want my boys close so I can spoil my grandchildren," she said.

Inigo couldn't believe how he was the only Velasquez brother still single. Diego, his eldest brother, had married British legacy jewelry designer Pippa Hamilton-Hoff. Alec had Scarlet, and Alec's twin, Mauricio, was now engaged to his long-time on-again, off-again girlfriend, Hadley.

"So, she's not for me?" he asked.

His mom shook her head and started laughing. "Honey, it's amazing that with your ego and inflated head you can even get the helmet on at the start of a race."

"Ha-ha, Mom. You know it's not that far-fetched that you'd try to set me up," he said.

"I know. Which girl is it?" his mom asked.

He nodded in the blonde's direction.

His mom whistled between her teeth. "She's a looker. How do you know she's single?"

Inigo tried to play it cool, like he hadn't asked around to find out who she was. But his mom, who was watching him, just smiled and shook her head. "You like her?"

"Don't get any ideas," he warned her. "I have a big year coming up, and I'm focused on being number one."

"I know you are, baby. And your father and I are very supportive of that," his mom said. "But if you like her… maybe you should go and introduce yourself to her."

"I might now that I know you didn't meddle to get her here," Inigo said.

"Might what, son?" his father asked as he came over, putting his hand on his shoulder and squeezing.

"He might go talk to that girl," his mom said. "Here, finish this for Inigo. He's training and shouldn't be drinking."

"Whatever you say, darling," his father said, taking the champagne flute from Inigo's hand. "What a party!

Several people have already confused me with Antonio Banderas tonight."

His mom swiped the glass from his father's hand. "Obviously you've had too much to drink if you think that's what they said."

Inigo smiled at his parents joking around with each other. Seeing them together always made him think of relationship goals. But they had gotten together back when life was simpler. Now the world was faster, meaner and more connected. He had to hustle a lot to stay relevant off the track while still winning races on it. There was no time to find someone and get to know them in the real world the way his parents had.

But someday he did want that…when he was like thirty or, hell, maybe forty, depending on how his career went.

"Which girl are you looking at?" his father asked when his mom spotted one of her favorite Food TV chefs and wandered over. This party had everyone at it, and frankly it was the kind of shindig that he tried to avoid except when his sponsor made him attend.

Sponsors and family. They were the only two things that he ever allowed to pull him away from racing.

"Dad, you can't call women girls anymore," Inigo said. "But she's the blonde in the blue dress over near the French doors."

"You know I meant no disrespect," he said. "Hell, you and your brothers still look like boys to me. Guess it's my age."

"Don't be all aw-shucks with me. If Mom or Bia heard you, you'd be in trouble," Inigo scolded.

"I know. Maybe I'd better go back and find that lady who thought I was Antonio Banderas," his dad said.

"I wouldn't. Unless you want to start the new year with Mom ticked off at you," Inigo said.

"True. How'd you get to be so smart?" his dad asked.

Well, Inigo hadn't been drinking all night, the way his father clearly had, which made everything sharper, but he smiled at his father and winked. "From you."

His father clapped him on the back. "Of course you did. I like your gir—woman. Have you talked to her?"

"Not yet."

"What are you waiting for, son?" his dad asked. "She's alone. Go."

His father gave him a nudge toward the blonde, and at that moment she glanced over at him to see his father pushing him toward her. Their eyes met, and he knew that he was hooked when she shook her head, smiled at him and crooked her finger.

Marielle Bisset had almost skipped tonight's party. It wasn't her normal scene, but her good friend and fellow social media influencer Scarlet had been insistent that she at least make an appearance and meet representatives from some of the brands that she'd been working with. Scarlet had been her mentor for the last six months. And once she'd realized that the other woman was pregnant, Marielle realized this might be the chance she'd been waiting for.

Scarlet had taken Mari under her wing when Mari had come back from a disastrous year abroad. Scarlet had been more than a mentor to her; she'd been really good at teaching Mari how to accept her flaws and own her past mistakes so she could be a better person.

She'd been slowly growing her YouTube channel and working on increasing her numbers so that she could become a style guru like Scarlet, but it was hard to build that kind of influence. Marielle had been doing it for a little over a year now and felt like she was just starting to find her own place in the noisy world of influencers.

She'd come back to the Hamptons and her parents' home after a disastrous affair with a married man that had left her shattered. She shook her head, wishing it were just as easy to shake off how bad she'd felt when she finally realized he was married. She'd been hiding out in East Hampton for the better part of the last five years in between traveling the world and searching for answers about herself. She'd been making peace with her mistakes, keeping a low profile and building her internet-based influencer business. The scandal and hurt she'd caused had left her broken.

Glancing around the room, she locked eyes with a hot guy who was being shoved in her direction by an older man.

He had dark brown hair, but from this distance she wasn't sure of his eye color. He bore a strong resemblance to the older man, who was laughing. She couldn't help but smile at them. It was clear that they had a strong bond—probably father and son.

Her gaze locked with the man's, and she felt a zing go through her. Dang. It had been a long time since she'd felt anything like that. He looked embarrassed, which was cute, so she crooked her finger at him, and he arched one eyebrow at her as he made his way across the room.

"So someone thinks you should meet me," she said. "But you needed a shove?"

"Uh, no, that's my dad. And he's in full-on party

mode," he said, then groaned. "Not that I needed my dad to push me toward you or that I always hang out with my parents."

She just laughed. He seemed so genuine and real that for a moment she wasn't sure he belonged here. "It's okay. Your dad seems like a lot of fun. I haven't seen you at any of the other parties this holiday season, so I'm guessing you're not local."

"No. Texan born and raised. Are you a local?" he asked.

"Sort of. My parents have a house here. I grew up in the city but summered out here," she said. Oh God, she was rambling. But it was totally his fault. Up close she saw that his eyes were a deep, dark chocolate brown and that he had a small scar in his left eyebrow. His jaw was strong and his mouth firm, but he smiled so easily that it distracted her.

"How do you know Scarlet?" he asked.

"She's sort of my mentor. She's been so great about answering all of my questions and helping me to come up with a business plan as an influencer," she said. Scarlet had been the first person to take her seriously when she'd suggested that she wanted to make a career out of social media. Her father had been disappointed that she hadn't landed a husband by now.

But that was her dad. Always making her feel like a disappointment. Not like this dude's dad, who was watching them and smiling in a sweet way. His dad seemed like a really nice guy. Or maybe a silly drunk, she thought as he turned and moved toward the bar. She realized she'd seen him at the bar a few times tonight.

"Your dad is too funny," she said.

"He's a mess. He's just enjoying the fact that all of

his kids are here tonight. Normally at least one of us is away on every holiday, so he's thrilled we all are here."

"That's so cute. Usually it's the mom who's like that," she said.

"Yeah, my mom is a newscaster in Houston, so when we were growing up, she was gone a lot and Dad was the one who did all the school pickups. They are both pretty fabulous," he said. "I'm pretty lucky in that they both made us a priority but weren't too overbearing."

"Must have been nice," she said. As the only daughter in a family of five children, she'd always had a little too much attention from her parents. Her dad had been overprotective when she was younger, but once she was eighteen, he thought that she should find a good man and settle down. He was very old-fashioned about stuff like that.

"What about you? Are you here with anyone?"

"Um, no."

"It might be too forward, but I'm glad you're here and I hope you will be at midnight," he said.

"Nah, I'm happy to be here with you," she said, taking his hand and leading him through the French doors and out on the balcony.

The night air was cold after the warmth of the house, but there were patio heaters stationed every few feet, so it wasn't unbearable. "Why are we out here?"

"I want to kiss you and didn't think I should do that in front of your dad."

He smiled. Damn. He had a really great smile and though she knew she should turn and walk away, there was a big part of her that didn't want to. It was New Year's Eve. Surely she could have one night of fun without it being a big deal, right? One kiss wouldn't hurt.

Right?

* * *

She smelled of summer and sunshine as he lowered his head and their lips met. A zing went through him. Was it a warning? But she tasted good, and her lips felt perfect under his. Her kiss wasn't too wet, and she didn't try to shove her tongue down his throat the way so many women he kissed did.

She held on to his biceps, and he couldn't help himself: he flexed his muscles and was pretty sure he felt her smile against his kiss. He had the feeling that he amused her, which was fine with him, because for the first time in a while, he was with a woman who made him feel like he didn't have to try. He could be himself…heck, after his dad shoving him toward her, he'd sort of had no choice but to just be Inigo Velasquez from Cole's Hill, not the up-and-coming F1 star. As a Formula One driver he was always aware of his visibility and he was always focused on winning. For this one night he wanted to focus on her.

He had one hand lightly around her waist, and his fingers flexed as he slowly deepened the kiss. In the distance he heard the sound of the party guests counting down from ten.

He lifted his head. "Got one kiss in this year. I want you to be the first kiss of the new year too."

"That's why I led you out here," she said, tipping her head back and studying him. Her long hair brushed over her shoulder, and he lifted one hand to twirl a tendril around his finger. It was soft and light, as he expected.

When he heard everyone yell, "Happy New Year," he leaned in, brushing his mouth over hers. "Happy New Year."

She kissed him again. None of the tentative teasing stuff he'd been doing, but full-on kissed him. He pulled her closer into his embrace, wrapping his arms around her waist.

Loving the feel of her breasts against his chest and her hips nestled close to his, he pressed his hand against her lower back as she sucked his tongue deeper into her mouth.

He felt his engine roar to life and knew that he was going to get from zero to sixty in a nanosecond with this woman. But they were in public. At a party. A party his parents were attending.

He stepped back, keeping his hold on her waist but breaking the kiss. She looked up at him, a flush on her cheeks and neck, her breath coming in quick bursts. "What's the matter?"

"I think we should get out of here before this kiss gets out of control," he said.

"Is it getting out of control?" she teased, drawing her finger down the column of his throat and running it around the collar of his tuxedo.

A shiver of pure sensual delight went through him.

He was pretty close to saying the hell with it and leading her to the secluded section of the balcony behind the large potted fir tree. But this wasn't some foreign city after a race. This was his sister-in-law's house, where she had family and friends over, and he knew that he had to be discreet.

But then she leaned in, wrapping her free arm around his shoulders, and he forgot about everything but the feel of her in his arms and her mouth under his. Her taste was addictive, and he had the feeling that he might never get his fill of her.

He skimmed his hand down her back. The satin material of her dress was soft but not as velvety as her skin. He cupped her butt and lifted her off her feet more fully into his embrace. She moaned deep in her throat, and his engines roared to life.

Yeah, she had him firing on all cylinders. She was exactly what he needed tonight. Maybe she was the reason he'd given in to the pressure of his family and come along. He needed this kind of fun. Someone who was here for her own reasons, even if she might be trying to get with him to put another notch in her lipstick case.

Just two people with a strong attraction who wanted each other.

It had been a long time since he'd done this. A little over a year. He liked sex, but women were a distraction and he had been focused on winning. But this was one night. A New Year's gift from the universe.

"Inigo? You out here? Mom needs her New Year's kiss," his sister called from the patio door.

He broke the kiss and stepped away toward his sister, determined to hustle her back inside.

"I'll be right in, Bia. Tell Mom to kiss Dad again. He's definitely in the mood for it," he said.

"He's the one who sent me to find you. Mom won't leave until she's kissed all of her kids."

He heard the woman behind him chuckle and turned back toward her. She wiped his lips with her finger, and he guessed he'd been wearing her lipstick.

"Go on. I'll meet you inside."

He nodded and walked away, still in a sensual haze. The last thing he wanted to do was hang out with his parents, but he knew they were sticklers for holiday rituals.

Bianca linked her arm through his, leaning her head

on his shoulder. "Sorry I had to pull you away from your lady. I think Dad sent me because he knew the boys would tease you endlessly."

"Probably. Thanks for that," he said.

"So who is she?"

He shook his head. "Uh, I didn't ask her name."

"Oh, just went straight for the kiss," Bianca teased.

"Something like that," he said as they reached his parents. He hugged them both and wished them happy new year.

"Happy New Year, Inigo," his father said as he hugged him. "Looks like my instincts were right about you and the lady."

"Dad," he warned his father. His father was usually more subtle than his mom but they both wanted him to find someone and "settle down."

"Just happy to see you smiling off the track," his father said.

"Me too," he admitted.

Then he bade his family good-night and went to find the blonde temptress he'd kissed earlier.

"I don't want to push my luck, but do you want to come back to my room?"

"Yes," she said.

Two

The suite he'd been given at the O'Malley compound, Maison de Houblon, was in a large guesthouse off the pool. It had a great room with a kitchen and living room area and then a large bedroom that had French doors that overlooked the ocean. But tonight, he was more concerned with the view in his arms.

"I don't even know your name," he said.

"Marielle. You?" she asked. There was a lilt to her words, a patrician New England accent that he hadn't really noticed before this moment.

"Inigo," he said.

She leaned back and looked up at him. He wondered what she saw.

"Inigo." She said his name slowly, and he liked the sound of it on her lips.

"Yes, ma'am."

"'Ma'am'? There's the Texas," she said with a wink.

"I'll be honest, you're not going to forget I'm Texan," he admitted. No matter how much he traveled around the world or hung out with the Italian owners of Moretti Motors, he was still a Texas man at heart. He wore designer suits and handmade loafers at all the press events and prerace functions he went to, but in his downtime, when he was at home, he preferred jeans and boots.

"Good. I wouldn't want you to be anything other than what you are," she said, running her hand down his chest, her finger brushing over the studs that kept his tuxedo shirt closed. He felt the warmth of her fingers through the layers of fabric.

"I don't have that ability. In fact, my boss is always telling me to wait five seconds before I respond."

"Why?"

"He keeps hoping that common sense will kick in," Inigo admitted.

"Does it ever?" she asked, running her finger over his bottom lip.

Her touch sent a tingle straight down his spine, making him harden. He pulled her closer, skimming his hands over her hips and holding her loosely. "Nope."

She threw her head back and laughed, and everything masculine in him sprang to attention, demanding he make this woman his. He caught the sound of her laughter with his mouth, kissing her, and feeling alive for the first time in a long time.

He tucked that fact away for later but knew that he was holding someone special. Someone who was making him realize that there was life beyond the track.

He felt her hands between them, her fingers moving methodically. He heard the sound of the shirt studs as they dropped to the floor with a soft pinging noise. He lifted her off her feet and turned, moving backward until he felt the bed behind him, and then he sat down. She stood between his spread thighs, her hands on his shoulders.

"Moving a little fast, aren't you?" she asked in a teasing tone.

"I'm sort of known for my speed," he said, then realized how that sounded. "Not that anyone ever complained."

She just threw her head back and laughed and said, "Did you stick around long enough to find out if they did, speedy?"

"Yes. I'm not a one-and-done kind of guy," he said. It had been a really long time since he'd laughed this much with someone. Spontaneously he put his arms around her body and drew her close, the fabric of her satiny dress scrunching up under his arms. He hugged her to him. Just for a moment he wanted to savor this feeling of lightness. Like there was nothing but fun when it came to this woman.

"What's this?"

"It's just been a while since I've laughed this much," he said. "Thanks."

"You're very welcome," she said, pushing her fingers through his hair and rubbing his scalp as he tipped his head back and looked up at her. "You're different."

"So I've been told," he murmured as her lips came down on his. Their tongues met and rubbed against each other.

She tasted so damned good. He had noted it the first time they kissed, and it was difficult for him to forget. She made him hungrier for more. If hooking up with her made him feel this good, he might have to break his rule about celibacy during the racing season and keep seeing her.

She framed his face with her hands, tipping his head back. The bed dipped as she put one knee on it next to his hips and half straddled him. He fell back on the bed, using his arms around her waist to bring her with him. He liked the way she felt pressed against him from shoulders to waist.

He ran his hands up and down her back, cupping her butt as she deepened the kiss. Though he'd joked about being known for his speed, he'd never been one to rush sex. And it seemed neither was she. She took her time exploring his mouth and moving against him in small subtle movements that made him wish they were naked. But he didn't want to stop kissing her to remove their clothes.

She circled her finger around the back of his ear, rubbing against the side of his neck, which made him so hot and hard that he thought he would explode.

He put his hands on her thighs. Her legs were firm and the skin soft. She wasn't wearing hose, so he was touching her bare skin as he spread his fingers wide and squeezed gently.

She shifted her legs against his as he traced one finger up the back of her thigh. She mumbled something against his lips, but he didn't register the words, just the husky tone of her voice and the way she continued to move against him. Her mouth followed the path of her finger down his neck. His shirt fell open as she moved down his body.

Pushing the hem of her dress up to her waist, he noticed she had on the tiniest black thong. She shifted, kicking off her heels and sitting back as she looked down at his body. He had an intense workout routine to keep in shape. Other athletes didn't always realize the discipline it took to be a driver.

Marielle seemed to like his muscled chest. She pushed the shirt off his shoulders, and he sat up, shrugging out of first one sleeve and then the other.

He had a tattoo on the inside of his left arm that read, If Everything Seems Under Control, You're Not Going Fast Enough. She traced the tattoo and arched one eyebrow as she looked back at him.

"Does everything seem under control?" she asked.

"No, it doesn't," he said, wrapping one hand in her long blond hair and bringing his mouth back down on hers.

He didn't want to talk or think about racing right now. He had been steadily getting better on the track, and a big part of him believed that was because he'd quit hooking up with women, but tonight he didn't want to think about that. It had been too long, she felt too good and it was a new year.

She put one hand between them on his chest. Her fingers spread wide, and her nails scored his skin lightly. He shuddered and felt himself harden further. She eased her hips forward, her center rubbing against the ridge of his erection.

He groaned as his hips jutted up against her. *Oh, damn.* This was going to be harder than he thought. It had been too long since he'd held a woman in his arms, and his body seemed to be on autopilot. Like when he was on the final lap and saw the finish line, he was ready to go. He reached between their bodies, intent on freeing himself, finding a condom and driving himself home inside her.

But the back of his fingers brushed against her underwear, and he felt her heat. She made a little sound at the touch against her intimate flesh, and he turned his hand, cupping her and rubbing just the tip of his forefinger between her legs. She spread her thighs farther apart, and he leaned back to give himself more room as he ran his finger around the edge of her thong panties and then dipped it inside, finally pushing his entire hand into the front of her underwear and caressing her. He parted her, tapping her clit lightly. She moaned, and her fingernails dug into his chest a little deeper. He tangled his other hand in her hair and brought his mouth down on hers.

He kissed her as he continued to tap against her, her hips moving subtly. Then she tore her mouth from his and reached for the hem of her dress, drawing it up and over her head, throwing it behind them.

He saw her breasts, small but perfectly naked, and her tiny nipped-in waist. She reached between their bodies and undid his belt and then slowly lowered his zipper.

"I want you naked," she said.

"Me too. Are you on the pill?"

"Of course I am. I don't like taking chances."

"Me either," he said.

She shifted off his lap, and he pushed his pants and underwear down his legs. By the time he was naked, so was she. She turned back to him, standing there in front of him completely bare, and he took a moment to appreciate how lovely she was. She wasn't built like a supermodel but was more of a real woman. Her legs weren't especially long but seemed just right to him. She had a birthmark on her left side that was shaped like a paint splotch; he couldn't help himself and caressed it, tracing the shape. She had a belly button ring, which he fondled as he used his other hand to draw her back into his arms.

She fell against him, and he rolled over so she was under him. She put her hands on his waist and then squeezed as she ran her hands down his sides. He honestly wasn't sure how much more touching he could handle before he came on her belly, which wasn't how he wanted this to end, so he took her hands in his and stretched them up above her on the bed.

He watched her carefully to see if this bothered her, but she just winked at him. "Maybe I'll let you tie me up later."

His hips jerked forward at the thought and he could only nod; words were beyond him at this moment. He held her wrists with one hand and drew his index finger down her body, starting at her forehead. She had a pert nose that he couldn't help dropping a kiss on as he drew his touch down farther, over her lips and her neck and then around the full globes of each breast. He lowered his mouth to one of her nipples while he teased the other one with his fingers.

Then he moved lower, tasting her belly button ring with his tongue, and felt her undulate against him as he moved still lower. He fanned his fingers out and cupped her, running his finger around the opening of her body and then bringing it up to tap against her clit again. She shifted against him, her legs going wider as he brought his mouth lower, wanting—needing—to taste her. He had to let go of her hands, but he felt enough in control that he thought that would be okay.

He was wrong.

She tasted better than anything he'd ever tasted before. He couldn't get enough. His tongue flicked over her and then his entire mouth ate at her most intimate flesh until she shoved her hands in his hair and held his head to her body as her hips thrust upward against him.

She rocked against him again and again and then called out his name as her orgasm rolled through her.

He lifted his head and looked up her body. Her head was thrown back and her chest was heaving, her nipples tight little buds. Her hips were still rocking slightly, and he knew he'd never forget how she looked right now. He moved up her body, letting his chest brush over her mound and then her stomach and her breasts. He braced his weight with his hands on either side of her shoulders. She opened her eyes, looking up at him with that silvery gaze of hers, but up close her eyes were silvery gray.

"Well, hello there," she said.

"Hi."

She twined her arms around his shoulders and leaned up to whisper directly into his ear. "Are you going to take me now?"

His hips moved against her, the tip of his erection finding her opening. He met her eyes and leaned down to kiss her, letting her taste herself on his lips.

"Yes," he said against her mouth as he drew back his hips and drove himself deep inside her.

She was tight when he entered her, and he waited to let her adjust to his size. She wrapped her legs around his waist and lifted her upper body so that her hard nipples brushed against his chest each time he drove into her. He wanted her passion to build to climax again, but now that he was inside her, it was the same as being strapped into the cockpit of his race car—there was no stopping him. The light had flashed green for go, and he had one objective in mind.

He rode her hard, driving into her again and again, and as he felt the sensation running down his back that meant he was closer and closer to his orgasm, he reached between their bodies, flicking at her clit to help her along. She arched under him, her nails digging into his shoulders.

"Inigo," she cried.

The sound of his name on her lips triggered his orgasm and he started to come, thrusting into her until he was empty and drained. She arched against him repeatedly, and when they were both still, he rolled to his side, lying on his back next to her.

The air in the room was cool compared to the heat of her body next to his. He already wanted to be back inside her. He turned his head on the bed and found she was looking at him.

"Was that slow enough for you?" he asked teasingly.

"Yes, speedy. You were just right," she said, rolling close to kiss him. "Want to join me in the shower?"

She trotted toward the bathroom, and he just lay there staring at the ceiling. His mother always said that fate brought people into his path when they were meant to be there. And he was struggling right now not to make this more than a New Year's Eve hookup.

Honestly, that was all he had time for, but something about Marielle made him feel lighter, made him feel... stronger. Like he could conquer anything.

It could be because it had been more than a year since he'd gotten laid, but he wasn't convinced.

"Are you coming?" she asked, leaning around the door frame from the bathroom.

"Yes, ma'am," he said, jumping off the bed and heading toward her.

It seemed like it might be her and not just sex. But then, one night wasn't going to change his life. His mom might be a big believer in fate, but he'd never seen its proof in his life.

He showered with Marielle, taking his time to wash her, making sure he explored all the places on her body that he might have missed when he'd made love to her earlier. They did it again in the shower and then dried off and curled up in the big king-size bed in the guesthouse. He held her in his arms as she slept and watched her. Tomorrow everything would be different. The holidays weren't officially over until January 2, but he had a session at the simulation track and if this was going to be the year he unseated the current champion, then this night was all he'd have with her.

He watched the clock and held her, pretending for a moment that things were different, but as much as he enjoyed having her in his arms, he knew that he wanted something more from life. He wanted the title of champion, and these emotions she stirred in him would distract him from his goal. Something he couldn't allow.

Besides, if they were really fated to be together, then she'd come back into his life at another time.

He drifted off to sleep just before dawn and only woke when his alarm went off at ten in the morning. Marielle rolled over and looked up at him from under tousled hair. "Why is your alarm going off?"

"I have a family breakfast. Do you want to come with me and meet the gang?" he asked. "Scarlet will be there."

"Yes, I think I would. I better dash out to my car and grab my overnight bag so I have something to wear other than last night's dress," she said.

"Why do you have an overnight bag in your car?" he asked.

"Just in case. I liked to be prepared. If I get too tipsy to drive, I can always stay at Scarlet's," she said as she got out of bed and stretched before pulling on her dress.

"I like that dress," he said.

"I do too, but it's really better for nighttime," she said.

"Agreed. Which car is yours? I'll get your bag," he said. She told him, and he went out to retrieve it.

They got dressed together, which was fun. He wanted her again, but he didn't want to give in to the craving, so he forced himself to make do with a kiss and held her hand as they walked to the main house. But as they entered the house, they didn't exactly receive the warmest of greetings.

"Oh my God. Who invited her?" Bianca said, standing up from her seat as they entered the enormous living area. There was anger in her voice. Inigo wasn't sure who Bianca was referring to at first but noticed she was staring at Marielle.

"What's going on?" he asked his sister.

"I should be asking you that. What are you doing with Jose's mistress?"

Three

Bianca... Jose's ex-wife was here? She hadn't seen the woman in more than five years, and she'd worked hard to put that horrible day out of her mind. The moment she'd discovered her lover Jose was married had been one of the worst in her life. Seeing Bianca now, all the guilt and shame came rushing back. There was something akin to hatred in the pregnant woman's eyes, and the look on Inigo's face made it clear he wasn't too pleased to find out she had this connection to his family.

To be fair, she'd had no idea who Inigo was when she'd slept with him, but now seeing him next to Bianca, she put the pieces together. They were obviously related. And she now vaguely remembered that Jose had mentioned he had a protégé he thought would do great things in Formula One. Was it Inigo?

"I guess I should be going," she said.

"Yeah, I think that's a good idea," Bianca said. "Who even invited you?"

"I'm Scarlet's friend," Marielle said.

She knew that the woman had cause to be upset with her, but she wasn't the only one to blame. Jose had told Marielle he was divorced, and she had been stupid enough to believe him. She soon realized it wasn't his only lie when she'd caught him in bed with another woman—a woman he'd been seeing for years. She'd felt like a fool, falling in love with another woman's husband. Seeing Bianca brought back all of those feelings of self-loathing that she'd hoped she'd moved beyond.

"Scarlet's my sister-in-law," Bianca replied.

Of course she was. "Honestly, I had no idea that you would be here. That part of my life was over ages ago, and I'm not proud of my role in what was going on in your marriage."

More people were entering the room, including Inigo's parents, and then Scarlet and her assistant, Billi Sampson, came in. Marielle looked at her friend, who was visibly pregnant and still looked very sleepy.

"Scarlet, thank you for inviting me last night. I'm afraid I have to run this morning, but I'll be in touch later," Marielle said, walking out of the room.

Inigo didn't try to follow her, which was probably for the best. He had been fun last night, just what she needed to distract her from her own problems. But obviously neither of them had intended for it to be the beginning of a relationship.

Yeah, right.

But she knew that it was over. There was no way she could have any kind of relationship—not that she was looking for one—with the brother of the woman whose husband she'd slept with.

Ugh.

Her mom was always going on about reaping what she sowed, and damn, this was a pretty rotten crop to reap. But this trouble was of her own making. When she thought back to the woman she'd been when she was twenty-one, she cringed. She'd been so shallow. So into her own pleasure and her own life that she had been unable to see past Jose's lies to the family that she was hurting. It wasn't that she was so much wiser at twenty-six, but damn, she was a little smarter when it came to men. Or at least she'd thought she was.

No more hookups with men whose last names I don't know, she thought. *Yeah, let's make that rule one for the new year.*

The engine of her Corvette roared to life. She put the car in Reverse and spun out on the gravel drive as she tried to get away from the house and all the people inside it. But there wasn't a car that had rolled off the assembly line that would go fast enough to take her away from herself.

She had that way of doing this more often than she wanted to. She knew it wasn't her fault—how in the world had she ended up at a party with Jose's ex-wife? That was never supposed to happen. She'd followed the teachings of a well-being guru, who had advised her to write a letter apologizing. The guru had said that would bring forgiveness from the universe.

Marielle thought she needed a refund, because all she could see as she raced down the road was the look on Bianca's face as she'd recognized her, and it certainly hadn't resembled forgiveness.

She pulled into the drive that led to her family's mansion and slowed the car, fumbling on the visor for the garage door opener. She parked the 'Vette next to her father's classic Porsche and sat there for a minute, realizing that she was on the edge of tears.

She took a deep breath, fumbling in her purse for her phone and that meditation app that her brother had gifted her for Christmas. She opened it and closed her eyes, listening to the soothing voice and pretending the heat on her cheeks was the sunshine the app's moderator was talking about and not tears.

But in her heart the truth was strong, and she knew that she hadn't forgiven herself for those long-ago mistakes. Thank God she hadn't run into Jose's son. The little boy his wife had been pregnant with while he'd been telling Marielle that she was his soul mate. If she'd been older…

Or not as dumb, she thought.

This wasn't working. She dashed her hand over her cheeks and turned off the car, getting out and standing there for a minute. She smelled cigarette smoke and looked up to see her eldest brother, Darian, standing there watching her. "I wasn't spying, just giving you space."

"Thanks," she said, walking over to him and taking the cigarette from his hand, dropping it on the ground and putting it out with the toe of her shoe.

"You're supposed to be quitting."

"I know. I didn't take a drag, I was just holding it," he said. "What's up with you?"

"Ran into one of my past mistakes this morning. It's hitting me harder than I expected," she said.

"Why? You know you're not that woman anymore,"
he said.

Why?

She shrugged, but Inigo's face danced through her
mind. She'd liked him. He'd been fun, and he'd made
her feel like she was enough.

"What were you doing with her?" Bianca asked as
she and Inigo watched Marielle drive away.

"She's the girl…the one I told you about last night,"
he said, trying to put together the two images he had
in his head. Jose's mistress had always seemed someone cold and calculating. While he had never seen his
brother-in-law with the woman, he had assumed that
she'd manipulated Jose into the affair. Jose had been
his idol. Inigo had wanted to be Jose when he grew up.
But this…

Marielle hadn't seemed like the type of woman…
who would what? he asked himself. Cheat? Have sex
with a man? She'd been fun, and he hadn't thought of
anything but the heat between the two of them. He had
put it down to a year's worth of celibacy, but honestly
she was hot and sexy and he had wanted her again
this morning. Maybe that was what had caused Jose
to cheat.

"Her? Couldn't you have picked anyone else?" Bianca asked.

Inigo's heart was breaking at the pain and humiliation he heard in his sister's voice.

"I had no idea who she was to you, Bia."

"Fair enough. But I never want to see her again," Bianca said. Just then Derek Caruthers entered the room,
rushing to his wife's side.

"Bianca, are you okay? I'm sorry I wasn't here with you."

"It's fine. I'm glad we're leaving this morning. I'm ready to get back home," she said. "I never thought I'd see her again."

"I'm sorry," Scarlet said. "I had no idea you two knew each other or the circumstances. Did you know?"

She pivoted on her husband, Alec, who just wrapped his arm around her and hugged her close. "Of course I knew he'd had an affair with Marielle. I didn't know you knew her."

Inigo just walked out of the room. He was angry. All of the emotions that he'd felt when Jose had died, and he'd learned the truth, came back. He knew that wasn't a healthy space for him to be in and ignored his father's calls and his brothers as he first walked and then ran back to the guesthouse where he was staying. He changed into his running gear and left the house through the glass doors that led to the beach. He was vaguely aware that it was cold, and a light rainy snow was falling, but he didn't feel any of it.

He only heard the pounding of his feet on the pavement of the path that was empty on this wintry January morning. He concentrated on each step, trying not to allow any thoughts in his head, but it was hard to keep them out.

He had always had a gift for attracting relationships that were toxic, but this had to totally take the cake. He'd found the one woman in the world he really couldn't be with. It would destroy his family if he was with her.

And yeah, it had been a fun hookup, but there was another part of him that wondered if this was his way of making sure that nothing distracted him from rac-

ing. From winning. He'd always been the kind of ath-
lete that pushed everything aside to win. And he was
close to being the champion, which had been his one
goal since he'd started in the Formula One junior program at fourteen.

He also felt the pain of realizing that his idol had feet
of clay. That he was human and real and that he hadn't
been perfect. The cold air felt like a blade in his lungs
as he continued to run, and he veered off the path and
into the small town, where everything was closed. No
one was out this early on New Year's Day.

Just him.

Just the man who had too much on his mind and no
easy way to sort it out. Should he just let Marielle go?
Should he try to get vengeance for Bianca? He couldn't
help it, but that thought had entered his mind. Maybe it
was that he felt she'd fooled him too. She had to know
who he was. But how could she have? He'd been on a
different circuit that year when Bianca had been pregnant and Jose had cheated.

Many times Inigo had wondered if he'd still been
shadowing Jose, would his brother-in-law have thought
twice about cheating?

At the end of the day, was he to blame? He'd pursued winning at any cost, and had turning his back on
Bianca and Jose that year been part of the other man's
downfall?

He had no way of knowing. Jose was dead, and Bianca had never wanted to talk about it.

He stopped running, leaning forward to put his hands
on his knees, his breath still sawing in and out of his
lungs. His exhalations were loud in his head but didn't
drown out his thoughts. He could fix this. Make up

for anything he might or might not have done back in the day.

He could have Marielle and publicly dump her. Would that even bother her? She'd been a married man's mistress.

But even as the thought formed, he knew that it didn't matter. She needed to know that the Velasquez family weren't to be toyed with. The rational part of his mind warned that there was more to the story than he knew. That the "facts" he had came from the dirt that Alec had dug up on her on the internet. Most of the mistresses had been named but Marielle hadn't been on the list.

But he could only listen to his gut and his heart. His heart remembered the paleness of his sister's face as she'd seen him standing next to Marielle. His gut remembered the strident tone that Marielle had used before walking out. His body remembered her twisting under him the night before.

He could have it all. The woman he lusted after and revenge for his family.

Hiding at her parents' house wasn't ideal. The maids were in and out of her room, her mom sent a tray with lunch, and then her dad knocked on her door. And finally, Marielle faked needing to visit a friend having an emergency and left. Her brother was in the garage again when she came downstairs, and she got it. She wished her problems were as easy for the world to see as Darian standing there with an unlit cigarette. But hers were different.

She was the one with a weakness for men and making dumb choices…could that be called addiction too?

She left in a cloud of muddy snow as she sped away

from her problems. There was a wistful sort of regret that engulfed her as she got on the Long Island Expressway and headed back toward Manhattan.

Dang.

This must be how Inigo felt when he was racing. There was a certain freedom from everything but the road and concentrating on the path ahead of her. Maybe she should take up driving professionally.

As soon as the thought popped into her head, she hit an icy patch and her car hydroplaned for a minute, fishtailing wildly on the road. She took her foot off the gas as she saw her life flash before her eyes.

Damn.

She slowed the car and pulled onto the shoulder. Her hands were shaking, and her heart was racing. She didn't want to die. She sat there. The silence in the car made her ears ring, and finally she turned on the radio. "About Last Night" was playing, so she flipped the station and heard Debussy's "La mer." Yeah, classical was good. Just what she needed right now.

She dug into her purse and found her phone. Scarlet had texted her.

Are you okay? I wish you hadn't left like that.

What could she say?

I'm not great. I'm sorry. I could tell I was freaking her out, and you know I'm not good in those situations. I hope I didn't make things awkward for you.

Scarlet and Siobhan had been the first women friends she'd genuinely had in years, and she hadn't wanted to screw it up. But maybe she had. Maybe she should stop trying and just enjoy the train wreck that was usually her life.

You didn't. Well, it was awkward, but I feel like both of you were freaked. If you want to talk, I'm going to be in the city until Friday. Let's have coffee…by that I mean you drink the coffee and I smell it and pretend that I'm having some.

Marielle felt a wave of relief go through her.

Thank you. I'd love that. I'm heading back to New York now. My parents' house was stifling. I'm sorry again for this morning.

I know the feeling. No problem. Can't wait to catch up.

She tossed the phone back into her bag before she asked for Inigo's number. A part of her felt like she should say something to resolve the situation with him, but another part—the smarter part—knew there would be no resolution. She could keep him in her memories as a fun night. And that was all.

Her phone rang, and she glanced at the caller ID. It was her friend Siobahn Murphy, who was the lead singer of Venus Rising. The two liked to party together, and she was always down for a good time. Just what Marielle needed at this moment.

"Hey, girl, happy New Year," she said as she answered the speakerphone and got back on the road.

No more driving fast to outrun her problems. She sat in the slow lane going a respectable speed.

"Hiya. Scar texted me," Siobahn said. "What the hell happened?"

"I'm not sure. I mean, I met this cute guy and he was funny and flirty. Even his dad was funny, encouraging him to talk to me. We kissed at midnight…it was hot," Marielle said. More than hot. It had made her see him as more than a hookup. She had to be honest with herself. She hated the way things had ended with Inigo. But she doubted there was any way back from the current situation.

"Yeah, and then?"

"Then one thing led to another, and I spent the night with him," she said.

Siobahn wasn't fishing for lurid sex details. But there was no way to explain the thing without mentioning that.

"Then this morning he invited me to breakfast with his family, and I knew Scar would be there, so I was, like, sure," Marielle said. Then she walked in and saw Jose's wife staring at her like she was the most loathsome woman on the face of the planet… Maybe she'd skip mentioning that bit to Siobahn. "And…"

"I know. You don't have to say it. I'm in Manhattan. Come to my place. We can eat ice cream or drink wine or do whatever you need. Don't go to your place alone," Siobahn said. "You need someone to remind you that you aren't that woman anymore."

"Thanks," she said. She had changed a lot from who she'd been at twenty-one, and it had been a long hard road with lots of pitfalls. But she had changed. She hadn't made peace with all of her past, but one thing she had made were good friends like Siobahn. She'd been the one who'd introduced her to Scarlet and had started her on this path.

"I'll text you when I'm close."

"I'll be here. I'm eating leftover ham, which isn't healthy, but I'm a bit hungover," Siobahn said.

Marielle had to laugh. She didn't drink like that anymore but remembered those days. She hung up with her friend, realizing that Bianca might never forgive her, but Marielle had to find a way to forgive herself. She couldn't keep beating herself up for old sins.

Not saying it would be easy, but she was going to definitely make that one of her resolutions.

Four

The weather this first week of January reflected Marielle's mood as she left her building on the Upper West Side. It was bitterly cold with a messy sleet and rain falling. The doorman held an umbrella over her head as she dashed to her waiting car. Her driver held the door open as she slid onto the leather seat and the welcome heat. She thanked them.

Scarlet had been true to her word and helped her out despite the fact that it must have caused friction with her new in-laws. But then again Scar knew what it was like to be the center of negative attention. They'd grown up in similar worlds, Marielle thought.

But even career pluses couldn't take away the ache inside when she thought of that encounter with Bianca. It wasn't that she'd really considered Inigo to be a guy she wanted in her life. For all she knew, they might not even be compatible. He might be one of those guys who drank beer out of a bottle and didn't use a coaster…or something like that. But the fact that she didn't get to let it fall apart the way her relationships always did… that bugged her. That had to be what was bothering her.

But she couldn't miss a guy whom she'd slept with one night and that was it.

She wouldn't let herself.

She wasn't that girl.

She had never needed a man after Jose. He'd changed that dream of hers. The one where she met a guy and he swept her off her feet and they lived some sort of fantasy life providing her a Disney Channel–perfect family, not the messed-up one that was hers. But she'd learned that she was better on her own.

Men were fun.

Inigo had been fun.

Until…

But that was in the past and she was moving on. She had an interview with a lifestyle brand that wanted to work with her. She had a manager who had worked hard to get the appointment for her, and she was glad for it. She'd even gone all in and dressed like Blair from *Gossip Girl*. She wanted to look the part of what they wanted. On every influencer account she'd checked out, the look was a mix between Jackie O and *The Official Preppy Handbook*.

The heels she wore were designer, but her manager said if she wanted the work, she needed to make a decision to either flaunt her family name or hide it. She couldn't use it when she wanted to and then drop it when she didn't.

So she'd decided to use her middle name instead

of her last name and pretend she wasn't part of one of America's richest families. She didn't want to rely on the name. She'd seen what it had done to her brother Darian. Holding an unlit cigarette in the garage and looking like a trapped animal. But her brother believed in the family mission statement and would do whatever Carlton instructed.

Marielle and Carlton had never gotten along. As her father's trusted right-hand man, he'd been the one to step in and divert the media attention from her after the affair with Jose had been made public. He'd quieted things down and done his magic to keep her out of the spotlight. But she still didn't like him. He always wanted Marielle and her brothers to present this perfect Kennedy-esque image of family.

They were more like the behind-the-scenes Kennedys. The ones who'd been real and human and made mistakes.

"Excuse me," she said, bumping into a man who had stepped out of a building while talking to the man behind him.

She stumbled, he caught her and she smiled her thanks. He smiled back and then she heard someone clear his throat behind him. She glanced over the man's shoulder and straight into the dark chocolate eyes of Inigo Velasquez.

"Inigo!"

She turned on her heel, but she was already a bit off balance and stumbled for one step before straightening her spine and continuing along the sidewalk.

"Have a good one, Marielle," he called after her.

She lifted one hand and gave him the bird as she

kept walking. She knew he didn't deserve that from her, but she was just ticked off about him and the situation.

She'd almost gotten him out of her head, and of course she'd see him again. It was kind of like the Marielle law. If she never wanted to see a man again, they'd run into each other. That included her father, Carlton and former lovers.

She finally got to the ad agency for her appointment and stepped into the lobby, moving off to the side to compose herself for a moment.

Was it just her, or did Inigo look even cuter than she remembered? His lips had almost lifted in a smile before tightening. She thought for one second he might have remembered the fun they had before he recalled who she really was.

She took a deep breath. None of that mattered now. She pulled her iPhone from her bag and opened the voice memo that Siobahn had recorded for her. She had made up a song for her to remind Marielle of her new path.

Marielle rules the world,
A badass who makes things happen,
Leaving only smiles in her wake.

She smiled and listened to it two more times. Now the song was in her head. Siobahn had used notes that were designed to stick in the listener's mind. And as she tucked her phone away after checking her lipstick, makeup and hair, she heard the song playing in her mind.

She smiled at the security guard and gave him her ID. He raised one eyebrow at her last name, but it wasn't uncommon, so she just kept smiling as he asked her to put her bag on the scanner and then cleared her to go into the building.

Inigo Velasquez was a memory. A happy memory that she had left behind.

Yeah, right.

Dante Peterson punched Inigo on the arm as Marielle walked away. Both of them were unable to tear their eyes off her. How was it possible she had gotten even more beautiful since he'd last seen her?

She gave him the finger, and he almost smiled before he caught himself. She was his family's enemy. He had to remember that.

"Dude…she doesn't like you," Dante said.

"That's not true. She liked me just fine. I'm the one who doesn't like her," Inigo said.

"Sure you are," he said.

"Screw you, Dante," Inigo said. "She's the other woman. The one Jose was cheating with."

"Well, damn. That really sucks."

"Agreed."

"So how do you know her?" he asked as the Moretti Motors driver pulled up and got out to hold the door to the Vallerio sedan. The car was classy, powerful and the hallmark of the vehicles that Moretti Motors made.

"Where to, Mr. Velasquez?" the driver asked.

"We need to go to the Four Seasons," he informed the driver, sliding into the car first with Dante following behind him.

He really didn't have time to think about Marielle. There were some suspicious things going on with the racing team at Moretti Motors, and Inigo had just left a meeting with the team boss. It was believed that someone on one of the teams was sabotaging his car to ensure that Esteban Acola, the top driver on the Moretti Racing team, would win.

They needed someone with entrée into the high-stakes sports betting world who could infiltrate the operation and do some betting to see if their suspicions were correct. And Inigo was now related through marriage to just such a person. Malcolm Ferris was engaged to Inigo's new sister-in-law's sister, Helena Everton. Malcolm had offered to help out if needed and had arrived in New York last night to meet with Inigo today.

Inigo had brought that information to the meeting.

"I really hope that this turns out to be a false lead. I don't want to think of someone on our team betraying us like that," Inigo said.

"Me either. If it is someone, I'm going to beat the crap out of them," Dante said.

"No, you're not. Marco might, but you're not."

Dante laughed. "You're right. So, about the girl."

"The *woman*. What about her?"

"I know there's more to it than that she was with Jose," he said.

"We hooked up on New Year's, and then the next morning I found out. Bianca confronted her, and she left. That's it. I didn't talk to her again," he said. "I'm kind of pissed at her. I don't believe that she didn't know who we were. She even played all innocent like she was shocked."

"To be fair, she might not have realized who you were. You and Bianca do have different coloring."

"How many brothers-in-law of Jose are drivers? I mean, there's pretty much just me," Inigo reminded his friend.

"Fair enough. So what are you going to do about it?" Dante asked.

What was he going to do about it?

He had no idea. The way she gave him the finger, sort of thumbing her nose at him, had made him want to laugh, but at the same time he remembered the look on Bianca's face New Year's morning. That pain and devastation at seeing the other woman. Sure, his sister was happier now married to Derek Caruthers than she'd ever been with Jose. But that wound was still there.

Was there something he could do to even the score? To help Bianca heal and maybe get back a bit of his pride? Because a part of him still wasn't sure Marielle hadn't known who he was when she'd slept with him.

"I don't know. It would be sort of fitting if I dated her and then dumped her publicly. She's some sort of social media influencer or something like that. Scarlet mentioned that Marielle was trying to follow in her footsteps."

"Could you do that?" he asked. "I mean, I know hooking up is fine because you know it's just fun and just one night, but dude, you haven't been in a serious relationship since…have you ever been in one?"

Inigo punched his friend on the shoulder. "No. But that's because I never allow anything to interfere with driving. I don't think she'd be any different."

Dante shrugged. "I don't know. I saw the way you watched her."

"Yeah, right. You were too busy staring at her to even notice me," Inigo said. That was another thing about Marielle: she drew attention the way an engine needed fuel. She seemed to enjoy it too. She dressed to impress. He understood from Scarlet and Bianca that clothing, hair and makeup were all tools in the viral social world. He got that. But there was a part of him that couldn't help feeling that she wanted that online life and didn't care what happened off the web.

"True. She's hot," Dante said.

"She is," he said, as the car drew to a stop. They got out and went into Malcolm's hotel. Inigo tucked his idea of revenge away while he waited for Malcolm to answer the door of his suite. But he liked it.

It would give him a chance to get some closure for Bianca and for himself. Because until that moment that they'd seen Bianca and he'd realized who Marielle was, he'd felt…well, that didn't matter. He wasn't a man who got emotionally involved, as Dante had just pointed out. Soon it would be time for him to focus on the upcoming season, and revenge might help him to get Marielle out of his system for good and keep a clear focus going forward.

Malcolm opened the door and invited them in, but there was worry on his face. Inigo wondered if Malcolm was going to be able to do what they were asking of him. He was just getting over his gambling addiction, and asking him to return to that world was a big favor.

Malcolm wanted to impress his fiancée and prove that the past was truly behind him. Facing his demons head-on was one way to prove it. But when Inigo and his friend from Moretti Motors arrived at the hotel suite, he had doubts.

Helena had gone out to have coffee with a college friend, so he'd been waiting for the men alone. Like all addictions, his sort of flourished when he was by himself. He knew that he could reach out to Mauricio,

Inigo's older brother and his best friend, for help, but at the same time he wanted to prove to himself and to his friends and family that he had this. He wasn't going to keep failing.

"Hey, Inigo, great to see you."

"Great to see you too," Inigo said. "This is Dante Peterson, one of the engineers who works on my team. He's going to be monitoring the input to see if there is any tampering."

Malcolm shook hands with both men and led them to the sitting area of the suite, which overlooked Central Park. The room that Moretti Motors had provided for him was impressive and spoke to the money the company had invested in their Formula One racing program, which didn't surprise him. When men were wagering the kind of money that had been talked about, the stakes had to be high.

"So…what is it that they want me to do?" Malcolm asked after he'd offered both men a drink and they'd declined.

"Place some bets. My teammate and I are going to be using the new state-of-the-art indoor racing simulator in secret today. They want to establish a base time before the public practice to confirm their suspicions about sabotage," Inigo said. "If anyone decides to look into your finances, we are going to funnel the money into an account through Hadley to Helena and then you can use it."

"That's fine. I have my own resources, if that would be better," Malcolm said.

"Let me talk to the Moretti Racing team and I'll let you know," Inigo said.

"Fair enough. Should we be meeting and talking like this?" Malcolm asked.

He had wondered about the same thing, but because they were related by marriage, no one thought that it would arise suspicion. "For now, I think it's okay. When you go to place the bet tomorrow, you should say that we are related by marriage and that I was bragging about being really fast this year. Like you sort of have the inside track," Inigo said.

"Are you a braggart?" Malcolm asked.

"He does think the world revolves around him," Dante said.

"Ha. Not really. I mean, I am a good driver, and I'm not going to pretend that winning isn't my focus. And we have put together a plan that is bound to deliver."

"That's all I need. Should we have dinner in public so that the saboteur can see us socializing?" Malcolm asked. He wanted Helena by his side through this process as much as she could be. She was the one who was keeping him strong, and he didn't want to let her down.

"I'll let you know later," Inigo said. "I'll text you."

The two men left a few minutes later, and Malcolm walked around the empty suite. This was why he'd started gambling in the first place, to give Helena the luxe life. He made good money as a Realtor in Cole's Hill, but he wanted her to have this kind of life. And he hadn't wanted to have to wait until they'd been married five or ten years. He wanted to give it to her from the beginning.

Instead he'd lost their savings and almost lost her. He walked to the windows to stare out at the skyline, but all he really saw was himself sleeping in his car and avoiding the love of his life because he had fallen so far down. He hadn't been able to find a way out of it until she'd stepped in and demanded to know what was going on.

He'd told her reluctantly. It had been difficult to lie to Helena. He'd been in love with her since the moment he'd seen her that first day of high school. Sure, he'd known her before that, but when she'd walked into AP US history, he'd really seen her for the first time.

Everyone had said that high school crushes don't last, but there had always been a bond between the two of them. They'd dated and gotten engaged believing the future that they wanted would be easy to achieve. But Helena's family was seriously wealthy—a ranching family that had been in Cole's Hill for a long time. And Malcolm had always known that he was going to have to work extra hard to give her the life—

"I'm back," Helena said, walking into the suite and interrupting his thoughts.

He turned and smiled at her. She wore one of those knitted hats with a faux fur pom-pom on top. Her cheeks were pink from the cold. She was so beautiful his breath caught in his chest.

She was his. The doubts that had plagued him weren't quieted, but they sort of subsided for a moment. He couldn't lose her. He'd do whatever he had to in order to be the man she needed him to be.

Not an addict who gambled away all of their money, but a man she could be proud to call her own.

"Babe?"

"Yeah?"

"You okay?" she asked, putting her purse on a chair and coming over to him, wrapping her arms around him and resting her head on his chest.

"Yeah. I am now," he said, holding her. He felt the cold that lingered on her jacket and on the tip of her nose when he bent down to kiss her.

Holding her centered him. His addiction sponsor had warned him about turning to another person or thing to replace gambling, but in his heart, he knew that holding Helena and relying on her made him stronger.

And he didn't regret that.

He lifted her into his arms and carried her into the bedroom to make love to her. That always centered him and made him remember why he was staying strong.

Five

"Thank you, Inigo, for coming with me. I really wanted to get a few cute things for the baby while I was here. I'm not sure I'll be coming back to Manhattan for a while after the birth," Bianca said as they left Bonpoint and stepped out into the heavy foot traffic on Madison Avenue.

He held his four-year-old nephew Benito's hand and all of his sister's bags as they walked up the street. On a certain level, this shopping trip was his way of apologizing for sleeping with Marielle. He'd never meant to hurt his sister, and he knew that seeing Jose's former mistress on New Year's Day had upset her.

"Not a problem. I love spending time with you and Benito."

"Me too, *Tío*," Benito said. He was holding a small wooden replica of the first Moretti Motors Formula One car.

"But you hate shopping," she said. "Don't deny it. No man wants to spend hours looking at children's clothing."

"Honestly, it was a nice distraction this morning. I have my first time trial in the new simulator, and I would have just been going over setups and running the track in my head if I hadn't come with you. And I pretty much did that last night, so we're good."

She laughed. "I'd forgotten what it was like to be in that life. Jose was like that, always thinking about the tracks and the setup. He'd wake up in the middle of the night and jot down notes for his engineers or sometimes even call them," she said.

There was a note in her voice that he didn't recognize, but he did know this was the first time that he'd heard Bianca talk about her deceased husband without a layer of bitterness. "He was very demanding. But that was what made him the best."

"Was it?" she asked.

He glanced down at Benito, who wasn't paying them the least bit of attention. "What else would it be?"

"I don't know. Maybe the lifestyle, the women, the attention from the paparazzi—you know how he ate that up."

Jose had been the kind of person who commanded attention wherever he went, not unlike a movie star or a famous rock and roll singer. There had been something about him that just drew every eye in the room. Inigo hadn't been surprised that women were drawn to him; he knew men were too. He'd been charming and funny and had a way of making each person he spoke to feel as if they were the only one who mattered.

But Inigo had been surprised that Jose hadn't been

loyal to Bianca. How had he read that wrong? There had been a feeling of sincerity in his brother-in-law that Inigo still couldn't mesh with the reality of what he'd learned after Jose's death.

"He did," Inigo said at last. "Do you want to talk about her?"

"No. I never want to discuss that. You know she wasn't the only one," Bianca said. "Just the last one."

He had known that. He'd learned it from his tech-genius brother, Alec, who had dug deep on the internet to find all of the details so that there would be no more surprises for their sister. He got all the dirt that Jose had hidden from them and laid it bare. There would be no more surprises from beyond the grave.

"He was such a bastard," Inigo said but then shook his head. Jose hadn't been, though. For all his faults, he'd come across as a great guy.

"It would have been easier if he had been," Bianca said.

As they continued up Madison nearing the famous Ralph's Coffee that was part of the flagship Ralph Lauren store, he could see a crowd of people. "I wonder what that is."

"Me too," Bianca said. "I love the energy in the city. It's so different from Cole's Hill."

"Definitely. At home the only crowds are at the Bull Pen on Friday night."

"So true," she said. "Can you see who it is? I wonder if it's someone famous."

Inigo maneuvered around people trying to get a glimpse of the person and stopped in his tracks as he saw the familiar long silver-shot blond hair and silvery-gray eyes. Marielle.

"It's no one famous," he said.

"Oh, it's probably just someone you don't recognize. Maybe a Kardashian."

"It's not. I know who they are," Inigo said, trying to steer Bianca away from the crowd. But his sister was stubborn and elbowed him.

"Stop it, Inigo. You're being silly. I want to see who it is," she said, moving closer.

He wasn't going to physically keep her from seeing Marielle. After all, she was pregnant and needed to be careful. But his sister had definitely inherited their mother's mule headedness.

She made her way forward, and the crowd shifted. He knew the instant his sister saw her. Her back stiffened, and she turned away, walking back toward him. "You did know who it was."

"I did. I wasn't sure..."

"Don't worry. I think I've had enough of the city. Can you get me a cab?" she said, reaching over and taking Benito's hand.

He nodded and lifted his arm to hail a cab. Two women walked by them as he did so.

"I love her. She's got the best life and advice. I want to be Mari when I grow up. She's really got it together."

His eyes met his sister's, and he saw the color drain from her face.

"Bia—"

"Don't. Please don't say anything. I hate that she's Insta-famous and that people want to be like her," Bianca said. The cab pulled up, and he opened the door. He helped Benito into the back seat first and then turned to hug his sister. She seemed smaller now, less in command, and he hated that.

He felt someone watching him and looked up to see that Marielle had noticed them. She lifted her hand to her lips and blew them a kiss. She had no shame. Not a shred of remorse over what she had done to Bianca.

Marielle was very pleased with the meeting she'd had. She tried not to look smug as she left the building on Fifth Avenue, but it was hard. The day was cold and gray, and after the way her new year had started, she had felt the same. But she was shaking it off. She decided to stop by Ralph's for coffee.

She posed in front of the famous Ralph's sign for a selfie and shared it with her followers with a tease that she had big news coming before going inside. A few of her followers spotted her and came over to pose with her and to chat. She was enjoying the moment a lot; this was something she'd never thought she'd find for herself. She texted Scarlet to thank her for recommending her for the meeting and then her manager to make sure he knew the terms she'd negotiated with the brand.

She glanced up to see Inigo and his sister staring at her. Jose's son was with them, but he was engrossed in the toy in his hand. Bianca turned away, and Inigo followed her to hail a cab. Marielle felt some of her happiness ebb away, and as Inigo hugged his sister and looked at her, she realized part of what she felt was guilt—but also defiance. So she lifted her hand and blew them a kiss before turning and walking away.

Coffee would cure all of her problems, she thought as she joined the line in Ralph's. A moment later someone entered the shop and got in line behind her.

"I'd ask if you are following me, but you were here first," Inigo said from behind her.

She turned around and looked into chocolaty-brown eyes. He stood there looking better than he had a right to. "Shouldn't you be in Europe training for the upcoming season?"

"Nope. Moretti Racing built a new facility on Long Island and we're using it for the preseason training. They're trying to get a foothold in the US market and nab up-and-coming drivers before they commit to NASCAR."

"Just my luck," she said.

"You say that like I did something to you," he said. "I'm not the one at fault here."

She shook her head. "Gentlemanly of you to point that out."

She gave the barista her order, paid and then stepped away from Inigo. Why had she even bothered to speak to him? She should have ignored him.

But how could she?

She wanted him to accuse her of being a homewrecker so she could defend herself. Tell him how Jose had said he was divorced. How Jose had made it sound like he was the victim. But really, what would that help? She'd been seeing a married man. The fact that she'd thought he was divorced didn't really matter, did it?

Carlton had told her to stay away from married men when he'd stepped in to fix the PR nightmare she'd created. And her father had backed up Carlton's warning with a solid disinheritance threat if she didn't toe the line.

Inigo stepped over to her, and she rolled her eyes as he arched one eyebrow at her. "Would you like to join me?"

"Why?" she asked.

"So we can say goodbye properly. We never had the chance," he said.

She thought about it for a minute. He was right. If they ended this the way they should have on New Year's Day, then maybe she'd be able to forget him and move on. She was of course already moving on, but the part of her that kept thinking that she didn't have to would get the hint.

"Sure," she said.

"Why don't you grab us a table and I'll get our drinks," he suggested.

"Sounds good," she said, scanning the seating area for a free table. When she spotted one, she moved quickly to grab it. She sat down and took an antibacterial wipe from her handbag and cleaned the table.

Inigo set their drinks on the table before sitting down across from her. He stretched his legs out under the table, brushing against hers. She shifted around, crossing her feet under the chair so he wasn't touching her.

She wasn't doing this again. She couldn't. She'd hooked up with him once, and that was okay, but now... knowing who he was? Nah, she didn't need that kind of trouble in her life.

"So..." she said. She'd never been good at leaving something alone. If she had a scab, she picked at it. Not that she was saying that Inigo was like a scab, but the way he made her feel was similar. Her skin felt too tight when she was around him. Like she had an itch that couldn't be scratched. Part of it was sexual, but a bigger part was just the mélange of emotions he stirred in her.

"So, you and Jose, huh?" he asked.

She put her arms on the table, holding her coffee

cup loosely in her hands. Of course they were going to have to talk about Jose. "Yeah. Do you really want to discuss that?"

He turned away from her and she noticed he had a strong jaw, especially when he clenched it. "No. I don't. I just don't get it."

"What's to get? He was funny and charming. He told me his marriage was over," she said. "I believed him."

"He was funny," Inigo agreed, ignoring the rest. She really didn't blame him.

"Yeah. How well did you know him?"

"He was my mentor. I started racing karts when I was thirteen. The next year he started dating Bianca, and he sort of took me under his wing. I thought…well, it doesn't matter, but his death was hard on me. Then after he died, I learned about the thing with you. It was like losing him again," Inigo admitted.

She could tell he hadn't meant to tell her that last bit. But it really drove home the fact that the two of them shouldn't be doing this. She wanted closure and not friendship, yet his pain mirrored her own. She had been betrayed by Jose as well—not that Inigo would see it that way. But the truth was she'd had an expectation that Jose was an honest man.

"I'm sorry. I miss the fun person I knew. Not the other guy that I learned he was later," she said.

She put her hand on Inigo's where it was clenched on the table. He looked over at her, and she couldn't read the expression in his eyes. That troubled her. Had she said the wrong thing? Hell, when didn't she?

"I'm sorry too," he said. "I wish you hadn't known him."

"I'm not," she said. Without Jose she would never

had gotten the wake-up call she needed to figure out what she wanted for her life instead of following the script of what everyone expected her to do.

Her response surprised him. He thought she'd have said she wished she hadn't been the other woman, but she seemed pretty okay with it to him. The idea of revenge stirred again in the back of his mind. He thought back on his sister's pale face, which served as a strong reminder of how much Marielle had hurt her. He wanted to think he wasn't petty and base, but every time he tried to be the better man, it came back. He didn't need the distraction, which Dante had been quick to point out, yet at the same time, when would he have a chance for payback like this again?

"I'm surprised. I'd think being with a married man—"

"It wasn't like that. You more than anyone know how it is on the road during the season. I was a cup girl. I was traveling around with the teams, and we met. There are the drivers who don't have sex at all, and then the others who are always looking to get laid."

She was so blunt. Her words were the truth. He'd seen it himself as he walked through the trailers. He was aware of the women with hot passes waiting to see who was looking to get lucky. Some of the drivers even believed if they had sex right before a race it improved their performance behind the wheel. Esteban was one of those men. It definitely hadn't hurt him behind the wheel.

"I guess the lives of the families back home don't matter," he said glibly. Why had he sat down with her?

A part of him wanted to believe she was more than

she seemed. More than Bia had made her out to be. He couldn't help remembering their night together in the O'Malleys' guesthouse. It had been special.

"It's a different world. You know it doesn't feel like real life," she said.

"Hmm. That's interesting. For me it's where I'm most at home and more myself than anywhere else," he said.

"You would say that. You're a driver. You probably don't feel alive unless you're going three hundred miles per hour. You're not human like the rest of us."

"Not human?"

"You know, you're like a demigod moving that fast. Not paying attention to anything that gets caught under your tires and blown toward the side of the road."

"You don't know me," he said. "Some drivers might be that way, but I'm not."

She shrugged, taking a sip of her coffee. He noticed her lipstick left a mark on the side of the cup. She was like that mark on the cup, but on his psyche. Their one night together was bright red.

Had it been a fluke? He wished he could easily figure that out. If it was, then he could walk away. Should he try it again? What the hell?

He wondered if it was the lack of sleep or just his nerves at the thought that someone might be working to actively keep him from winning. Or if it was her crystal-gray eyes watching him like a dare. Causing him to stop weighing the consequences and teasing him into taking what he wanted.

And he did want her.

But then he thought of that smug look on her face when she'd said that during the racing season regular rules of decency didn't apply. It wasn't that he normally gave a crap about how people behaved unless it affected him, but she'd hurt Bia. That kind of thinking had been responsible for hurting his sister.

He couldn't let her get away with it. She might find someone else to hurt by her actions. He wasn't holding himself up as some sort of moral police—he knew he had flaws—but he couldn't just walk away after she'd said that. She wasn't even taking responsibility for her own culpability in the affair. She'd pretty much said that since drivers have big egos, it was Jose's fault.

He wasn't letting Jose off the hook, but he was dead, so there wasn't much that Inigo could do about that.

"I don't know you," she said. "I did sort of like you, though."

"Did?" he asked. If he was going to make this work, he had to let go of showing her he was pissed and at least try to be charming. The only thing was, when he tried to be, he never could pull it off.

"Well, you haven't been very nice today," she said.

"You gave me the finger," he said. He could still picture her hand in the air as she walked away from him.

"You thought it was funny, didn't you?" she asked.

He had. "I don't know what to do with you."

She tipped her head to the side, and her long blond hair flowed over one shoulder. She pouted at him with those full lips for a second and then said, "You did okay when we were in the bedroom."

Immediately he felt a jolt go through him. "We got along pretty good, didn't we?"

"Uh-huh. Was it just a one-night hookup? I mean, before you found out about the thing with your sister, did you think we'd see each other again?"

Wow. That was the million-dollar question. If he said

no, he'd come off like a douche, and if he said yes, he'd seem like a sap who had placed an emotional price on their night together.

"I don't know," he answered as honestly as he could. "I liked you, and I wasn't ready to think about more than spending the day with you."

"Fair enough. So, are we going somewhere from here? Or is it so long?" she asked.

"You're very blunt," he said.

"I am. It's just that when I expect things, they never turn out like I think they should. If I ask and still get disappointed, I've got no one to blame but myself."

Six

Marielle had always lived her life in the nothing ventured, nothing gained mind-set. Scarlet's late sister, Ivy, used to call it the "leap and end up with scratched knees" motto. Either way, Marielle wasn't one to hedge her bets. More than once it had netted her something she hadn't expected. And she couldn't regret that. One of the things that she'd been running from when she'd left home to be a trophy girl in the F1 was her safe, boring life. Though her mom seemed happy with her life as Mrs. Bisset, Marielle had wanted more. Or at least some adventure before she became a Mrs.

"Blame is a tricky thing," he said. "It always seems to imply regret to me."

She smiled and couldn't help it. She wanted to make him out to be just like Jose and the other drivers she'd met during her year on the F1 circuit, but he was different. It wasn't just the way he made her feel like she was going to explode if she didn't touch him. Or the way he made her wish she could just drown in his deep brown gaze for an afternoon. It was something more. She'd venture to say that he got her, that he understood where she was coming from. But she couldn't be certain of that yet.

"Do you have many regrets, speedy?"

He shook his head. "Nope. I always go full out, and if it doesn't work out...well, then, at least I tried."

"Me too," she said.

He shook his head. "I don't want to like you."

"Well, there you have it."

She shouldn't have been surprised that his words hurt her a little, but she was. She knew that she was persona non grata in his eyes. That she'd crossed a line that most decent people thought shouldn't be crossed. But at the same time, she had just felt like he got her. Apparently, she was wrong.

Shocker. *Not!*

She pushed her chair back and started to stand up, but he caught her hand in his. "I'm sorry. That was an asshole thing to say."

"It was."

"The thing is, I do like you. You keep surprising me, and I know that I shouldn't be sitting here with you, but I am. And I don't want you to walk away angry."

She tugged her hand from his. She got what he was saying. But this was complicated. And honestly, not the kind of thing she needed right now. It had been fun to flirt with him and pretend that coffee could lead to something more, but this was Inigo Velasquez. The brother-in-law of Jose Ruiz. She'd made herself a promise when that relationship had ended.

No more Formula One drivers. No more men who were so used to moving through life at blinding speed. No more.

So why was she lingering?

She should grab her bag and walk out of here with a haughty toss of her head.

Instead she was looking into those big brown eyes and searching for something that she knew she wasn't going to find. That she had told herself she didn't need and that she could live without.

"Let me buy you dinner to apologize."

"Hmm…let me think about it," she said. She reached into her bag and pulled out one of her business cards and handed it to him. Then she grabbed a second one. "Here's my contact information. Write yours on here."

She handed him the extra card and a pen and watched as he wrote in a hasty scrawl. He passed the card back to her, and she tucked it into her coat pocket before smiling at him and turning away.

She zipped up her coat as she walked through the busy coffeehouse to the door. She told herself she wasn't going to look back, but when she walked by the tables, she couldn't help herself. He was staring down at the card with her contact details on it. She shook her head, thinking she didn't understand him at all.

She hailed a cab and gave them her brother's brownstone address without a second thought. She needed someone to talk sense to her. Girlfriends were good for telling her what she wanted to hear, but Darian would tell her the truth whether it hurt or not. He'd always been good about that.

She got out at his Upper East Side address, then hurried past people on the sidewalk and up the stairs to let herself in. As soon as she did, Bailey came to greet her.

The large St. Bernard came barreling at her, barking his hello. She braced herself as he went up on his back legs to greet her, licking her chin as she turned her head.

"That's what you get for not knocking," Darian said.

"Sorry, Dare. I was afraid you might be out back staring at a cigarette and wouldn't let me in," she said, rubbing Bailey behind his ears until the dog was satisfied and trotted back down the hall to his master.

"When you come out swinging, I know you're not sure of something," he said.

"When am I ever sure?" she asked. "Please tell me that one day I will not be this big hot mess."

"Mom seems to think so," he said. "But so far I haven't seen anyone who has it together."

"Not even you, big bro? You're a political strategist. You look good on paper and you know how to make everyone else look good too," she said.

"All of the Bissets look good, Mare. So, what's up?" he asked, leading the way into his den. She could tell he'd been working, because he had a can of Red Bull next to his laptop. He gestured for her to sit down on the leather couch and when she did, he sat next to her.

"Uh, um, I ran into Inigo Velasquez again. We exchanged some words, and he invited me to dinner. I know I shouldn't go," she said.

Then she looked at her older brother, who leaned back, crossing his arms over his chest. "I shouldn't, right?"

"Tell me everything," he invited.

She did, pouring it all out. The stuff about Bianca and how it had made her feel like pond scum, but how she'd responded by blowing them a kiss, which made

Dare wince. She told him about liking Inigo, giving him the bird, having coffee and getting lost in his eyes.

"Mare, I don't know how you do it, but God knows you could make walking across the street into something complicated," he said at last.

"I know. What should I do?" she asked him.

He considered it for a while, and she got fidgety. The fact that she had come and asked for advice was probably all the indication she needed that she shouldn't go out with Inigo.

"Go. You'll regret it if you don't."

"I might regret it if I do," she said.

"Well, then, you might as well give yourself something to regret," he said.

Getting into the simulator and putting on his helmet at the Moretti Racing facility forced Inigo to remember what was at stake. Last night he'd been drinking ice water and using the Peloton in the house he'd rented that was only a few miles from the facility. He'd been thinking about the text message he didn't receive from Marielle.

But that was a distraction.

Revenge.

Who did he think he was? Machiavelli?

Marco Moretti was in town. Right now, he was standing in the booth next to Keke Heckler. Both men were legendary drivers and had built the Moretti Racing program from the ground up. Inigo had been ecstatic when they'd asked him to be a part of the team three years ago. And they'd taken him from middle-of-the-pack finishes to the top ten. But he craved the championship.

There was no room for revenge in a winning driver's psyche. He knew that. Dante had been funny in the car, but the truth was his friend and head engineer for his team had a point. He should only do things that improved his time and his racing.

"How does the cockpit feel?" Marco asked. He spoke very good English, but the hint of his Italian upbringing was there in every word.

"Good," Inigo said, adjusting his shoulder straps. The cockpit he was sitting in mirrored the custom-made interior of his actual car. The seat had been molded to fit his body and had been placed at the exact length from the steering wheel and pedals that he liked. He twisted his head and shoulders, popping his neck before he settled into the seat.

They were running the Melbourne course, which would be the first race of the season. He closed his eyes and reached through all of his memories to the Melbourne race last year. He remembered the atmosphere and the people. The weather and the day. He wanted to be in the right mind-set.

"I'm ready," he said.

"Good. We're set up too," Dante said.

The simulation had him on a qualifying lap, so he waited, watched the lights, and when they hit green, he hit the gas. When he drove, there wasn't time for anything else except the track. He didn't think when he drove—he reacted. He became one with the car and drove like the machine was an extension of his body.

He pushed everything from his mind but couldn't help remembering the feel of his hands on the curves of Marielle's hips. The car reacted the same way she had, responding to his every touch. He continued the course, coming up on the finish line as everything in him was narrowing down to the track, the touch, the sound of the engine. That first lap time would be recorded, and he kept driving knowing they wanted the best of three and would get an average.

The team of engineers who worked on his car were recording every detail. There was even someone who was monitoring his heart rate to see if it increased as he powered through the turns.

"Good time. Take a break and we'll set up for another run," Dante said through the speakers. "The team noticed a slight hesitation in the engine. We want to tweak that."

"Okay," Inigo said, getting out of the simulator. He walked over to the area where Marco and Keke stood.

"I like what I'm seeing," Marco said. "I have a good feeling about this year for you."

"Me too," he admitted to his boss.

Keke rubbed the back of his neck. His once blond hair was now streaked with gray, but the forty-seven-year-old former driver was still fit and sharp. "You're all in for training, right? No outside distractions?"

He nodded. Where was Keke going with this? "Always. I don't drink, work out and try to keep my focus on the track."

"Good. That's really good. I hate to bring this up," Keke said.

"Why?" Marco asked. "If you have a concern, you should mention it."

"I am mentioning it," Keke said. The men had been teammates and were good friends—at times the dynamic reminded Inigo of his relationship with his brothers or Dante.

Keke turned to him. "My wife mentioned she heard a rumor that you were linked with the up-and-coming lifestyle guru Mari."

"Damn," Marco said, looking at Inigo. "I wanted to rib him about turning into an old woman, but is that true? You've always been about no women during the season."

Keke's wife was the former swimsuit model Elena Hamilton. Elena had turned to designing swimsuits after her modelling career had ended and was one of the top designers for athletes now.

"It's…it's sort of true. We hooked up on New Year's Eve," he said. "I don't see it going anywhere."

Especially since she hadn't texted him back about dinner. Was he thinking about that, about being stood up, and not about the revenge plan he had for her? Not very Machiavellian of him, was it?

"Good. I don't know her," Keke said. "But wasn't there something with her and a driver where she was the trophy girl?"

"Woman," Inigo said.

"What?" Keke asked.

"Women don't like to be called girls," Inigo said. "She was a trophy woman."

Marco started laughing. "Good luck with that. Elena and my wife, Virginia, have been trying to bring him into the twenty-first century."

"Hey, I didn't mean any disrespect," Keke said.

"I know," Inigo said. "Force of habit."

"Fair enough. You know I don't give a crap about your personal life, so if you want to date or hook up with a different *woman* before every race, that's up to you. Just make sure it enhances your racing profile. You are sharper this year, and we think you could win races and actually be in contention for the championship."

He heard what Keke was saying. He had nothing but respect for both him and Marco. These two knew what it was like to race and win, and Inigo wanted that. But he also wanted to make Marielle pay for how she'd made Bianca feel. "I will. Nothing is more important to me than winning."

"That's what we like to hear," Marco said.

Dante and his team finished up on the simulator, and Inigo got back in to take another test run. This time he pushed the thought of Marielle further out of his mind and concentrated on the track. On beating his previous time. And he did it.

Marielle saw the call from her mom and hit Ignore. She had a feeling that Darian might have let slip some of the details of what was going on in her life. Normally her mom wasn't the touchy-feely type, but she'd called every day for the last week. The family usually communicated through a chat app with Carlton, who kept everyone's calendars. So she knew it wasn't an emergency.

And she didn't want to talk to her mom. All of her life Marielle had been struggling to get out from under her mother's shadow. She'd been the perfect hostess and wife. Everyone always wanted to talk to Marielle about her mom and her mom's style. She looked effortlessly chic, and Marielle's own manager had more than once suggested she could grow her followers more easily if she'd just embrace the classic Bisset style, but she didn't want that.

Who wanted to feel like the only reason they were successful was because of their mom? Not her. But more than that, she and her mother hadn't ever really gotten along. Marielle was pretty sure that was due to the fact that her mom didn't like to share attention from the men in the family. Or at least that's what her psychiatrist had hinted at.

She didn't know. But when her mother called again five minutes after the last call, Marielle answered.

"Hey."

"Hello, Marielle," her mother said. Her mother had gone to a boarding school in Switzerland and had retained a somewhat understated European accent despite the fact that she'd been living in the United States for the last thirty years.

"What's up?"

"Straight to the point as always," her mom said. "I heard through a friend that you're becoming a very popular influencer. Your name showed up on a list of those I should invite for the Bridgehampton Winter Classic."

"Wow. That's great news," she said. "Of course, I'll come."

"The odd thing is that you aren't on there as Marielle Bisset, you are listed Mari-Marielle Alexandria."

"I know. I didn't want anyone to think I was representing our family," she said. "You've mentioned a number of times that I'm not always great at that."

She heard her mother sigh. "That's only the truth. Even Carlton agrees."

"I know," she said. He'd told her on many occasions.

"Aside from that…how are we going to handle this? Do you want me to pretend I don't know you?"

She hadn't thought that far ahead when she'd started her account. "No. I think people who have known us both for years will think that's silly. I won't publicize it on my account. Do you think that would work?"

"I don't know, Marielle. This is very odd. Let me discuss it with your father and Carlton, and I'll get back to you. For right now I'm going to put you down as a maybe on the list."

"Mom, this is a huge event for influencers. It would hurt my career not to be there," she said.

"I'll take that under consideration," she said. "I'll let you know later today."

Marielle hit the disconnect button before she said something she'd regret later and slammed the phone down on the table in front of her. She couldn't deal with this. All of her life she'd been struggling to find a way to be the woman she wanted to be and now that she was so close, her name was once again standing in her way.

She so wished she'd been born Marielle Smith or Jones or anything other than Bisset.

Her phone buzzed, and she saw it was a group message from Carlton requesting a family meeting to discuss "the M problem."

"The M problem?" she said out loud to her apartment. Of course they'd need a meeting for that.

She texted back she was out of the country. And she intended to be.

Her phone rang a minute later. *Darian*.

"Mar, what is going on?"

"Mom found out that I'm doing the social media influencer thing and doesn't know if I should be invited to events she's on the committee for. She actually asked if she should pretend not to know me."

"Oh, that's—"

"Messed up. But hey, it's me," she said.

"I'm not going to allow this. I'm going to speak to Dad about it," Darian said. "You know if you went to him, she'd have to back off."

"I do know that. But I also know that if I do, she'll be a total witch to me every time I see her," Marielle said. "I'm just not sure how to play this."

"Don't play it. Come to the meeting and just say this is what you are doing. It'd be ridiculous not to associate with you regardless of the name you use," Darian said. "I know that our brothers will agree with me."

"Zac definitely will, but he's training for the America's Cup and doesn't mind ruffling feathers because he's not around to suffer the consequences. Logan might feel differently since he has to see Dad every day. And who knows what Leo will say?"

"Trust me," Darian said. "I'll talk to them and we'll present a united front. Come to my place tomorrow night at six. I'll have it all worked out."

"Aren't you supposed to be working on some big campaign strategy?" she asked, loving her big brother for stepping in but knowing she shouldn't rely on him to do this for her.

"I can do both, kiddo. Just be here tomorrow night."

"I will be," she said. "Love you, Dare."

"Love you, too."

She hung up with her brother, and a moment later he responded in the group text that they were all unavailable. Immediately her sibling chat group lit up with her other brothers wanting to know what was going on. Darian just said he'd explain everything at six at his place. Zac said that he would join by video chat, but it was cutting into his training time.

It had always struck her how odd it was that all of

the Bisset siblings spent more time away from their parents than with them. Even though Mari had been crashing at their family home in East Hampton, she'd made sure to arrange it so she wouldn't have to spend too much time with her folks.

Seven

Marielle still hadn't texted Inigo back. Instead she was hanging with her bestie, Siobahn Murphy. Siobahn had been the lead singer for Venus Rising since she was fourteen. The band had been comprised of older members and they'd been put together by a producer who... was no longer with the band. Marielle and Siobahn had met at a party at the Royal Bahamas club when they were both eighteen. They'd been young, had too much money and both of them had a simple goal: live life to the fullest. For Marielle she'd just wanted to not be like her parents and her older brothers. It wasn't much of a goal, but it had worked.

Looking at both of them now, eight years later, it seemed that life had certainly not worked out the way either of them planned. Siobahn was fresh off a breakup; her ex, a singer-songwriter, had immediately eloped to Vegas with one of her dancers. It had almost broken Siobahn, who had truly loved Mate.

Sitting in Marielle's apartment eating vegan pizza on a Friday night wasn't what they had envisioned for themselves at twenty-six. They should be owning it. But sometimes Marielle thought this was owning it.

Her mom hadn't tried to speak to her again after Darian had sent his last message to the group chat and Marielle was relieved but also a little sad. Would it kill her mom to act maternal to her for once?

"Ugh. I don't really like this cauliflower pizza crust," Siobahn said. "Just got an invite to the Polar club. Want to check it out?"

"Yes. I was just thinking we should be out on a Friday night... I need to meet someone and hook up so I can wash away my last one," Marielle said. She wouldn't have admitted that to anyone other than Siobahn, but her friend understood.

"Me too. Mate is posting pictures of him and the wife on his yacht. Last year that was me. And I hate that I still care, but..."

"Let's go. We're going to find some hot guys, hook up, and then we'll both be in a better state of mind," Marielle said.

"Let's do it," Siobahn said, following her into her bedroom, which had a huge walk-in closet that Marielle had spent a year designing and having built.

She'd sort of retreated to her apartment and spent a lot of time redoing it. That was how she started her social media channel, just working on the apartment and working through her issues at the same time.

They raided her closet and both came away with outfits that suited them. Then she called down to her driver, Stevens. Technically he was Darian's driver, but Dare hardly ever used him. Her brother liked to walk so he could eavesdrop on conversations and hear what was really on people's minds. He used that information when plotting strategy for his clients. He really was too good for this world, she thought, not for the first time.

He could be tough when he had to, but he always put everyone else first. *Especially her.* She needed to figure out how to deal with her mom without involving him.

Someday.

"Girl, we are going to own it tonight," Siobahn said as she snapped a selfie of the two of them.

Twenty minutes later, seated in the VIP section of Polar, Marielle wasn't too sure her plan for the evening was the best one. Sure, there were a lot of guys who seemed to be willing to hook up with her, but she just felt…they weren't doing it for her. She couldn't help comparing each man to Inigo. She wasn't trying to, but she'd notice that one's jaw wasn't as strong as his was. That another one's eyes weren't as warm and chocolaty. That yet another suitor didn't smile at her smart-ass comments the way Inigo did.

He wasn't the man for her. She knew this. So why was every guy not as good as him?

That ticked her off. She was headed to the bar to get a couple of shots of tequila, which always made even the most mediocre of evenings better, when she heard a familiar Texan drawl. She stopped and glanced around, and there he was. The very man she'd come here to forget—and failed.

Was it karma?

She'd decided to move on and couldn't because…

they weren't done with each other, she thought. He glanced over in her direction, and their gazes met. His face tightened for a moment, and then he shook his head.

He lifted his hand and crooked his finger at her, and she stood there and started laughing. It didn't matter that they weren't perfect for each other. That the world was never going to be a place where they could be a couple because of her past actions. He got her.

She walked toward him, and he moved away from the high table where he'd been toward her.

"How is it that the one woman I'm trying to forget I keep bumping into?" he asked.

"Karma. I've just decided it's karma. I'm not sure if it's good or bad or what," she admitted.

"Karma, eh? Sure, I'll go with that," he said. "I promised myself I wasn't going to sleep with you again, but you look so damn hot in that…is that even a dress?"

"Of course it is," she said. They were both trying so hard to avoid fate, she thought, but there was no way they were going to be successful.

"Dance with me, Inigo. Let me put my hands all over you and we can pretend that it will be enough until midnight, when we both have to leave and go home to our real lives."

"Is that what you said to Jose?" he asked.

And it was like a knife right in her heart. "No, it's not."

Surprised at how deeply that had hurt, she turned and walked away from him. She was used to jabs from the media, from her mom, but Inigo had surprised her. He definitely didn't get her if he could say something like that to her.

* * *

Inigo almost let her go, but he wasn't an asshole—as much as that comment had made him sound and feel like one. The thing with Jose was harder to shake than he wanted to admit. And he was in the club trying to forget Marielle, but then there she was.

He had to force his way through the crowd to her. She was seated in the VIP area, but luckily the club's owner was an F1 fan and the bouncer knew him. The man lifted the rope and let Inigo through, but as he got closer and saw her face, he knew he should just apologize and leave.

His thoughts of revenge were a distant memory at this point because he'd never witnessed the aftermath of his senseless tongue before, and he definitely didn't like what he saw.

Her friend noticed him before Marielle did and came at him with attitude and probably more than a bit of violence on her mind.

"I'm a total d-bag. I know it," he said as she approached. He recognized her as the singer Siobahn Murphy, not just because everyone knew who she was but also because she'd been in Cole's Hill for a month with Scarlet a few months ago. His sister liked her.

"You really are. Wait, aren't you Bianca's little brother?"

"I am."

"I guess it's safe to say that every family has assholes," she said.

He started to argue, but she interrupted him.

"Don't. I know you're mad, and you might feel slightly bad about what you did to her, but she deserves better. No one is perfect—you might want to remember that."

"I know that better than most. Listen, I shouldn't

have said it, and I need to apologize, but not to you. So, either sit down or go and do your thing."

Siobahn raised her eyebrows at him. "You've got five minutes and then I'm intervening, and trust me you aren't going to like that."

Siobahn walked past him, and Inigo realized that while he and Siobahn had been talking Marielle had composed herself. She looked bored and beautiful, but he felt like maybe he could still see the hurt in her eyes. That she wasn't really ready to talk to him.

But this wasn't something that he could let go.

"I'm sorry," he said as he approached her booth and slid onto the bench across from her. "I have no excuse except that I guess it bothers me that I want you so much when I know that I can't have you."

She didn't say a word, just shook her head. And he guessed he didn't deserve anything more than that.

"The truth is—"

"I don't care," she interrupted. "I thought you were someone…that doesn't matter now. Fine, I heard your apology and I accept it. You can leave now."

Leave now.

He should do just that. He'd seen what happened when he hurt her, but she had been quick to move on. Would he even be able to make her feel bad if he dated her and broke up with her in a public way? Also, could he stop himself from falling for her? It was harder than he had imagined. There was something about her…

He'd told himself there was no way he could be with her and that wasn't just talk to keep himself from getting involved during the racing season. He legitimately couldn't be with her.

But he'd hurt her, and he hated himself for that. He'd

meant to remind himself that she couldn't be his, and probably he'd sealed his fate. Ensured she'd never look at him with that heady cocktail of lust and affection again.

"I could. But I… I can't. I just don't want to leave it like this. Every time I try to fix this, I seem to be making it worse. And believe me when I say that's not how I normally operate."

She almost smiled. He saw her lips twitch. Aware that the clock was running before her friend came back and kicked him out of Marielle's life, he knew the next few seconds were very important. But his whole life was measured in seconds. In making snap decisions and trusting his instincts. He felt time warp around him the way it did when he was driving. He knew that whatever he did next would decide if he spent more time with this woman or lived with regret the rest of his life.

His pulse was racing, but he felt calm. He was in his element, and unlike earlier, when he'd been riding hormones, he was ready for this.

"I want to believe you, but you keep letting me down," she said.

"I feel like I know the answer to this. But will you give me one more chance to prove I'm not that guy?" he asked.

She chewed on her lower lip, and it was the first thing he'd seen her do that revealed her nerves. Even the night they'd met, she'd been cool and composed. It was the first time he saw that she was real. That underneath the sassy comebacks and quick smiles there was a hell of a lot more going on. He had to fix this and leave, he thought.

"Until midnight," he said.

That was his last offer. He liked her on a level that made no rational sense to him. She was a distraction, the last woman he should be chatting up, but at the same time, he couldn't just walk away.

"Dance with me," he said. "One dance, and if you still don't want to give me another second, I'm out."

"Dance with you? Isn't that what I suggested?"

"It is, which is why I'm hoping you have an interest in either forgiveness or humiliating me on the dance floor."

She shook her head. "I'm not like that."

"Give me a chance to get to know you. I'll stop saying dumb things…well, maybe that's too big of an ask, but I'll try to stop."

She laughed, and he felt it all the way to his core. His racing vision left, and he was once again just a man sitting across from a gorgeous woman, knowing that if she said yes, he was one lucky bastard and he should work hard to not screw up anything else this evening.

"Yes."

Marielle felt like she'd had too much to drink. She knew she shouldn't be dancing with him, not now. Not after what he'd said. He'd shown her who he really was, and she had to remember that. But it was too bad that her hormones hadn't gotten the message. She was still attracted to him. He had a sweet smile that was sensual at the same time. It was his mouth. That damned perfectly formed mouth of his that had made her say yes.

Now she was swaying to the music under the strobe lights of the club, pressed close to him because of the crowd on the dance floor. The energy was electric, and she felt it pulsing through every inch of her. Inigo must

too, she thought. He had his hand on her hip, and he un-
dulated against her. He knew how to move.

She was trying to remember that he said stupid
things, but honestly at this moment all she could think
about was getting him alone and getting him naked
again.

A part of her acknowledged that she wanted to walk
away with the upper hand this time, not be the one left
shattered by the morning after, but another part didn't
give a damn about any of that. She was hot and horny,
and she wanted this man. Inigo was the only one who
could satisfy her tonight, and after a long week where
she definitely had more lows than highs, she was going
to take what she wanted.

The music changed to an old Pitbull club song, and
Inigo jumped in the air pumping his fist. He leaned
over, wrapping his arm around her, pulling her into the
curve of his body. "I love this song."

She could tell. The beat was sensual and hot, Cuban
beats with the Miami heat, and Inigo moved to the
music like it was flowing through him. His hands were
soft on her hips, urging her to find the same movements as he had. She stopped thinking, stopped analyzing and let the music consume her the way that it had
Inigo. She sank deeper into the curve of his body. She
felt his hips against hers and his hands sliding up and
down her sides. She felt the ridge of his erection grow
against her and twisted her hips to rub against him.
She let her head fall backward so that her hair brushed
against his shoulder, and she felt the warm exhalation
of his breath against her neck a moment before his lips
touched her skin.

She shivered with sensual delight, and it was all she

could do not to grab his wrist and lead him to the VIP bathroom.

But she wasn't that woman. Not tonight.

Or was she?

What was wrong with having fun and enjoying a moment like this one? She knew how rarely they came along.

She turned in his arms. His eyes were heavy lidded as he danced and watched her body. She put her hands around his shoulders and moved against him. Their eyes met, and she leaned up to kiss him. His mouth against hers was firm yet also soft at the same time. Better than she remembered.

How was that even possible?

His tongue rubbed against hers as he held her to him with a hand at her hip. They moved together to the music, and she knew she was never going to be able to just walk away from this man.

There was something about him that... *Stop*. She made her mind cancel that thought. This was a hookup— they could both walk away guilt-free and then get back to their real lives.

He lifted his head, breaking the kiss, then put his hands on either side of her face and leaned down, kissing her harder and deeper, sending a pulse of need and desire through her. Her breasts felt heavier, needy, and her center was moist and aching for him. She shifted to rub against his erection, and he broke the kiss again, this time putting his hands on her hips as he maneuvered them both through the crowded dance floor. As soon as they were out of the throng of people, he led her to a quiet hallway and stood in front her, sheltering her body with his as he put one hand on the wall next to her head.

"I want to take you back to my place. No thinking about who we are or anything like that. Just us. One night only."

She almost smiled at the way he was trying to be a good guy. His erection was hard and rigid pressed against her hip. His voice was raspy and raw with need. And he couldn't stop touching her. His finger rubbed up and down the column of her neck. She stood there caught in the sensual web that they were both weaving around each other and knew there was nothing she could do but say yes.

"Where do you live?" she asked.

"Central Park West," he said.

"I'm closer. Let's go to my place," she said.

"Perfect. I have a driver," he said, moving his hand from the wall and reaching into his pocket, which drew her attention to his groin. She caressed him through the front of his pants as he hit a button on his phone and sent the message.

He groaned as she rubbed the tip of his erection, then took her hand in his. "I want to do this when we are alone and I can get you naked."

"Me too," she said. "I need my bag and then I can go."

He led her back to the VIP area and stood by the velvet ropes as she went and grabbed her bag. Siobahn was gone, but there was a note from her friend on her phone that she'd come back if Marielle needed her to.

She texted she was good and didn't mention Inigo. He was her dirty little secret tonight—just as she suspected she was his.

Eight

It took them longer than Inigo anticipated to leave the club, because he couldn't keep his hands off her. There was a sort of haze over him right this moment. All he could see was Marielle. Her lips were wet and swollen from his kisses. *Damn.*

He leaned in to kiss her again. The bouncer held the door for them, and they were caught between the warmth of the club and the snow and sleet falling outside. Inigo pulled her into his body to protect her from the elements. She put her hand on the side of his neck, tipping her head slightly, and he knew she wanted to say something, but her lips were too tempting to resist and he kissed her again.

He wasn't aware of anything but Marielle. He tucked that fact away to examine later, because he knew that she was the first person to bring on that focus he normally reserved for racing.

"Mr. Velasquez," his driver said, clearing his throat.

He pulled his head from Marielle's and glanced at the driver, noticing he had opened the door. He took her hand and pulled her quickly across the sidewalk through the snow toward the waiting Moretti Motors Vallerio sedan. She slid easily into the back seat, laughing as she sat down and slipped on the leather seats.

He climbed in after her, lifting her off the seat and onto his lap.

She felt chilly from the snow and sleet, and he cuddled her close to him while she ran her fingers through his hair. "You have snowflakes on your eyelashes."

"Do I?"

"You do," she said. "Close your eyes."

He did as she asked and felt the warmth of her breath against his face before she kissed both of his eyes lightly and then settled back onto his lap. "There you go."

He opened his eyes. Their gazes met, and he felt his pulse start racing again. He didn't want to have a quickie in the car. He wanted to make love to her properly. To take his time with Marielle, because maybe if he got her out of his system he could move on. No more rude potshots at her and no more lust that he couldn't control.

He was used to control, and he hated that she made him feel like he had crashed his car and was rolling over and over, like nothing in the world was solid and he was holding on trying to find his center.

With Marielle he was simply holding on to her. And he felt his grip on her was tenuous at best. He should be scared, but instead he was turned on and excited. He couldn't keep his hands off her and she didn't seem to mind, moving to straddle him on the back seat of the car. He held her to him as she deepened the kiss and he clutched at her backside, bring her closer to him as he shifted his hips underneath until he could rub the ridge of his hard-on against her center.

She rocked her hips, moving over him with the kind of pressure that made his pants too tight and made him want to just say screw it and take her here and now.

He moved his hand under the hem of her dress and felt the cold skin of her upper thigh. He rubbed his hand up and down, each time coming closer to touching her center. It was hot and moist and beckoned him. He remembered how hot they had been for each other the last time. If it was even possible, it seemed he wanted her even more now.

He felt the pulse in his erection where it was trapped too tightly in his boxer briefs, and when he pulled his mouth from hers, turning his head hopefully to see something that would distract him, he just met her gaze.

That cool gray gaze of hers was hot, like the heat in the cockpit of his car when he was driving. And the excitement he felt as he approached the finish line, this felt like a victory. He had never thought he'd have her in his arms again. But here she was.

He wanted to make this last. Needed to find his much-lauded self-control.

"What are you thinking?"

"Don't come in the car," he said without thinking.

She threw her head back and laughed. "Damn, speedy. I was thinking, *I hope he comes in the car.*"

"Marielle, darling, you are pushing me to the very edge of my control," he admitted, burying his face in the crook of her neck.

Which was a big old mistake, because she smelled so good. How could perfume be sexy? On her it was.

"Well, then, I'll have to see what I can do to push you past it. I want to see you when you aren't thinking and analyzing everything," she said.

"I'm not sure that's a smart idea," he said.

"I thought we'd decided this wasn't our most intelligent decision," she said, shifting on him to run her finger down the side of his jaw to his mouth. She drew her finger over his lips, and he felt it as if she were caressing his groin.

He groaned and shook his head, sucking her finger into his mouth. He needed to take charge but every time he did, he saw the finish line and he wanted... Marielle and this entire night to last as long as it could.

The car pulled to a stop, and he glanced out the window. They were at his place.

"We forgot to give the driver your address," he said.

"That's okay. We had a nice ride."

The door opened, and a rush of cold air came in, doing nothing to cool him down as he got out and reached back to offer his hand to her. He nodded to the driver, and as Marielle stepped out, Inigo scooped her up in his arms, carrying her toward his building. She wrapped her arms around him, and he lowered his head to kiss her as he stepped into the lobby.

Inigo had never been much of a playboy when it came to women. He liked women and had been on his fair share of dates, but driving was the focus of his life, and no woman had ever held a candle to the rush he got when he was behind the wheel.

His brother had commented that maybe he hadn't

met the right woman, and for the first time Inigo understood where Mo had been coming from. Marielle was different; everything with her was more pronounced. When he kissed her, he felt a jolt that was beyond just sexual and maybe…maybe that's why he'd been trying to justify being with her.

Trying to make it into some sort of revenge scheme so he wouldn't have to admit that she did something to him that no other woman ever had.

Keke and Marco had been circumspect, but Dante hadn't been as nice. He had warned Inigo that it was one thing to get his rocks off with a hot chick but another to have his bosses discussing it. He knew Dante's career was tied to Inigo's winning as well.

Everyone on the team had a vested interest in him winning. So he couldn't let sleeping with her be a distraction.

She wrapped one leg around his thigh as she put her hands in his hair and deepened the kiss. He groaned. He could give himself all the mental warnings he wanted to, but there was no way he was walking away from her tonight.

He couldn't.

He wasn't even tempted to, if he were being completely honest with himself. He carried her down the hall to his apartment and then lifted his head from the kiss, shifting her in his arms and setting her on her feet next to the door.

He used his thumbprint to unlock the door and opened it, stepping aside and gesturing for her to precede him into his place.

She stepped into the foyer of his apartment, and he reached around her to flick on the lights. He closed the door behind them and watched her as she kicked off her heels and slowly walked down the marble-tiled floor toward the living room.

She stood at the base of the curving staircase, her hand on the mahogany railing, her head tossed back. "I like your place, speedy. Is your bedroom up here?"

His throat felt tight as he closed the distance between them, remembering the feel of her body pressed against his in the club. He wanted her. Maybe more than he wanted to win at Melbourne, which should have jarred him, but for tonight he ignored it. Tomorrow he had to get this attraction for her under control but for tonight… nothing mattered except this feeling and this moment.

She crooked her finger at him, and he groaned as he slowly moved up the stairs toward the landing.

Her thick blond hair fell around her shoulders, and the thin slip dress she wore clung to her curves as she reached behind her and drew the zipper down. He stood beneath her on the stairs watching as she lowered it and her skin was revealed. She had a small tattoo on her left shoulder that he hadn't noticed the first time they'd been together.

He took the steps two at a time to catch up with her. Wrapping his hand around her waist, he pulled her back against him and used his teeth to pull the thin spaghetti strap down her arm. He could see the design of her tattoo more clearly now. It was a serpent wrapped around an apple that had a big bite taken out of it.

He traced it with his finger. "What does this mean to you?"

She shook her head, her long blond hair brushing against the backs of his fingers. "Sinner. Mostly I got it to annoy my mom, but I also knew that I couldn't keep pretending to be something I wasn't."

Sinner. The word echoed in his mind and shook him. Was she as blasé about the affair with Jose as she'd seemed? Or had it cut her deeper?

He stopped thinking about that. He drew his hand down her shoulder blade; her skin was soft and smooth. He felt her shiver under his caress, and she shifted around to face him. As she did so, the dress fell farther down, revealing the curve of her nipped-in waist.

He lifted her off her feet again and carried her down the hall to his bedroom. He hit the light switch with his elbow as he entered and put her on her feet in front of the king-size bed. She smiled up at him.

"What's got your engine roaring?"

He groaned. "Really?"

"I like a good pun," she said with a wink.

"That's not a—"

She let her dress drop to the floor, so she was now standing in front of him wearing just a tiny pair of bikini panties and that smile of hers that would tempt any man to follow her.

He couldn't think. He reached for her breasts. He was rock-hard and on fire for her. Each breath he took smelled of her perfume, and his heartbeat seemed to be saying her name. *Marielle. Marielle. Marielle.*

He put one hand on her waist to draw her to him, but she wedged her hand between them, her fingers going to the buttons of his shirt, slowly undoing them. He watched her for a minute then realized he had a nearly naked woman in his arms.

She touched him in a way that made him feel like the only man in the world. Her eyes were heavy lidded as she leaned forward, kissing his neck as she drew her nails down the center of his body. Blood rushed through his veins, pooling in his groin and making him even harder as she caressed her way down his body.

Her fingers were cool against his skin as she pushed the shirt off his torso. He shrugged out of it and drew her into his arms, enjoying the feel of her naked breasts against him.

A growl was torn from him when her hot mouth brushed over the column of his throat. She took her time nibbling her way down his neck to his chest, biting his left pec, which made him jump in surprise. She looked up at him, her gray eyes sparkling. "Too much?"

"Not enough," he said, his eyes narrowing as he reached down to undo the fastening of his pants and give his erection more room. Her tongue brushed his nipple, and gooseflesh spread over his chest and back. His hips jerked forward, and she reached out, pushing her hand into the opening of his pants, rubbing her palm over him.

He ran his hands over the length of her naked back. He wanted to believe that his excitement was just because it had been so long since he'd been with a woman, but he knew that this was more about Marielle. She was forbidden fruit. His boss had mentioned her by name, his sister hated her and his best friend thought she was trouble.

But he couldn't resist. He'd always been the sensible Velasquez, but had that all been an illusion? Was it simply because he'd been going too fast to realize that he was just as impulsive as his brothers?

Marielle wasn't shy when it came to touching him, and he loved it. Bracing herself with her hands on his shoulders, she slowly traced each of his ribs before moving lower.

Part of him wanted to let her do whatever she wanted, but another part of him was aware that this was only the second time in a year that he'd had sex, and he was on edge. His control wasn't as great as it once had been. She rubbed her fingertip along his belt, tracing it around his waist and then coming back to the lowered zipper. He sucked in his breath and held it until she winked at him.

She took the shaft of his erection in her hand, stroking him through his underwear. He felt his erection jump and a bit of moisture form on the tip. He wasn't going to make it much longer. He tugged her into his arms, holding her so that her bare breasts brushed against his chest.

Leaning back on the bed, he used his hands to part her thighs and drew her down on his lap. He pushed his underwear down to free his length and then shifted his hips until he felt her warmth against his tip.

He knew he should get a condom on, but for this moment he wanted to savor the feeling of her heat against his naked shaft. He stretched to reach the nightstand and took out a condom, handing it to her.

Then he lifted her up with his arm around her waist and tugged her panties off her body. She settled back on his thighs, tearing open the condom and putting it on him.

She straddled him and he put his hands on her waist, drawing her down. He tried to let her set the pace, but she was in the mood to tease him and he was already on the knife's edge. He cupped her buttocks and drew her down hard as he thrust up inside her. Driving himself all the way into her body, he held himself there.

She gripped his shoulders with her hands, her nails digging into his skin as their mouths met. Her nipples were hard points and he pulled away from her mouth, glancing down to see them pushing against his chest.

He caressed her back and spine, scraping his nails down the length of it. He followed the line of her back down to the indentation above her backside.

She closed her eyes and held her breath as he fondled her, running his finger over her nipple. It was velvety compared to the satin smoothness of her breast. He brushed his finger back and forth until she bit her lower lip and shifted on his lap.

She moaned a sweet sound that he leaned up to capture in her mouth. She tipped her head to the side, immediately allowing him access to her mouth. She stayed like that, straddling him so that just the tip of his erection was inside her.

He scraped his fingernail over her nipple, and she shivered in his arms. He pushed her back a little bit so he could see her. Her breasts were bare, nipples distended and begging for his mouth. He lowered his head and suckled.

He held her still with a hand on the small of her back. He buried his other hand in her hair and arched her over his arm. Both of her breasts were thrust up at him.

He wouldn't let this be about anything other than the physical. One night for revenge, he'd thought, but this was the second time they'd been together. And revenge wasn't on his mind.

She rocked her hips, trying to take him deeper, and he knew the time for teasing was at an end.

He gave her another inch, thrusting up into her sweet, tight body. Her eyes were closed, her hips moving subtly against him, and when he blew on her nipple, he saw gooseflesh spread down her body.

He loved the way she reacted to his mouth on her. He sucked on the skin at the base of her neck as he thrust all the way home, sheathing his entire length in her body. He knew he was leaving a mark with his mouth, and that pleased him. He wanted her to remember this moment and what they had done when she was alone later.

He kept kissing and rubbing, pinching her nipples until her hands clenched in his hair and she rocked her hips harder against his length. He lifted his hips, thrusting up against her.

Her eyes widened with each inch he gave her. She clutched at his hips as he started thrusting. She held him to her, eyes half-closed and her head tipped back.

He leaned down and caught one of her nipples in his teeth, scraping very gently. She started to tighten around him. Her hips moved faster, demanding more, but he kept the pace slow, steady. Building the pleasure between them.

He suckled her nipple and rotated his hips to catch her pleasure point with each thrust. He felt her hands clenching in his hair as she threw her head back.

He varied his thrusts, finding a rhythm that would draw out the tension at the base of his spine. Something that would make his time in her body, wrapped in her silky limbs, last forever.

He tensed, blood roaring in his ears, as he felt everything in his world center on this one woman.

He called her name as he came. She tightened around him and he looked down into her eyes as he kept thrusting. He saw her eyes widen and felt the minute contractions of her body around his as she was consumed by her orgasm.

He rotated his hips until her hips stopped rocking against him. She wrapped her arms around his shoulders and kissed the underside of his chin.

He wanted to believe that nothing had changed, but he knew that everything had. Revenge had seemed like the only solution until now. He was starting to care for Marielle, seeing beyond the woman who'd hurt his sister to the woman who was vulnerable and sexy—and everything he hadn't realized he'd been looking for.

Nine

Not sure if she'd stayed or left, he was almost reluctant to get out of bed. But he had never been the sort of man who hid from anything, so he did. He used the bathroom and then heard piano music downstairs. The living room of his apartment had a baby grand piano because Bianca had said it would photograph well when *Urban Living* magazine did a spread on him. He pulled on his Moretti Motors sweatpants and a T-shirt and went downstairs more quickly than he normally did, skipping his set of morning reps.

There she was, standing over the piano, her fingers nimbly picking out the melody of a classical piece that he struggled to identify. He was pretty sure it was Debussy, but his musical leanings were more toward rap.

"Morning," he said.

She turned and smiled at him, backlit by the lights in the hallway that led to the kitchen. Her long silvery-blond hair was loose and hung over her shoulders. She wore one of his shirts, her long legs bare. His gut clenched. He'd meant for last night to be the last time they were together. Both of them were on the same page as far as that was concerned. But this morning there was none of the awkwardness that had dominated their other morning after.

The music stopped, and she glanced over at him. Her eyes were sleepy, but she flashed him a smile. "I hope I didn't wake you."

"You didn't," he admitted. "I have a testing session I need to get to. I wasn't sure you'd still be here."

"I was going to leave but didn't want to slink out. We didn't say goodbye last time. And this time…well, I thought we needed that. To make sure it's officially ended," she said.

"Definitely," he agreed. "Do you need some clothes?"

"My assistant is bringing some stuff over for me," she said. "I don't think I'd look as good in your sweats as you do."

He smiled at the way she said it. She was keeping things light, and he would do the same. "Bianca keeps some clothes here."

"I don't want to wear your sister's clothes."

"Of course not." Clearly, he needed coffee. That had been…the wrong thing to say.

"Coffee?" he asked her.

"Do you have green tea?"

"I think I might have some. I'll go and check," he said, moving farther into the living room, walking past her into the kitchen. As soon as he was in the kitchen, he let out a breath he hadn't realized he was holding.

He still wanted her.

How was that possible?

Last night should have cured him of the desire for her. But to be fair, what guy could resist Marielle wearing his T-shirt and playing the piano? It was so sexy and sensual, and it literally took everything in him to keep from walking back in there and seducing her on the piano bench.

He went to the big espresso machine he'd been gifted last year when he'd done an ad for the company and flicked on the button to start the warm-up process. Then he realized he had no idea where his housekeeper might store tea.

He started opening up cabinets and then stopped. She wasn't playing anymore, and he knew his comment about Bianca had affected her. He didn't need to do anything more than get her some tea—if he could f-ing find it—and then go to training.

He finally found the cupboard stash of tea. It was a mahogany case he'd been given when he'd done the fastest qualifying lap at the Singapore Grand Prix last year.

He walked back to the living room, where she was sitting at the piano but looking at her phone. Her shoulders were slumped, and to him it seemed like she'd gotten bad news.

"You okay?" he asked.

"Yup. Jim dandy," she said. "My dad always says that. No idea what it really means."

"My dad says things that I really don't get too," Inigo said, coming over to her. "I found this. Any tea in here excite you?"

She took the case from him and set it on the bench beside her, finally opening it up and looking through the selection. She handed him a tea bag, and he took it, along with the case. "When did you learn to play the piano?"

"Starting when I was six. One of my brothers showed an aptitude, and my parents thought I might enjoy it too. I think they thought we'd be this famous classical duo for a while. But Leo lost interest when he hit puberty. Apparently, girls were more interesting than piano."

Inigo smiled. "And you stopped?"

"I was the add-on child, so it seemed best," she said.

"Add-on?"

"Sorry. I'm dealing with some family stuff and feeling like a total bitch about them," she admitted.

"I'm sorry too. Want to talk about it? Or should I just go and get your tea?"

She looked over at him. "Why do you have to be a Velasquez?"

He sat down next to her, putting his arm around her shoulder and hugging her close for a minute. "I don't know," he said, then after a moment of silence, continued. "Tell me about this thing with your family," he said. "It will make us both stop thinking about each other."

"I don't think it's going to work that easily."

He used his knuckles on the black keys to play the one thing he could, the riff on "The Knuckle Song." And she smiled, as he hoped she would. "We won't know if we don't try."

"Fair enough," she said. "My dad had an affair two years before I was born. He was a prominent congressman, and the identity of the young aide he'd had the affair with was found out—it was a big scandal everywhere. My dad realized he could be 'that cliché mid-life crisis guy.' That's how he puts it. Like that explains everything. Darian, my oldest brother, said that it changed Mom. I've always been her consolation baby. I showed how my parents got back together and proved to the world that they were still solid."

* * *

She shouldn't have brought up the circumstances of her birth. Not to Inigo. But she was feeling down, and in this sort of mood she got destructive. And it wasn't like he was thinking of her as anything other than his booty call from last night. Even if they wanted it to be more, there was no way. He'd confirmed that when he'd sat down next to her on the piano bench.

Playing the piano had started her down this path—or maybe it was waking up next to him. She would deny it out loud, but she'd slept better in his arms than she had in a long time.

"That's horrible. I'm sure that's not true," he said. "When you were a kid, it might have seemed that way to you, but your parents love you."

She started laughing. "How would you even guess at that? Do you think you know them from articles and TV documentaries?"

"No. I'm just basing it on my own parents. When I was a kid, I thought that they liked my twin brothers best because they always got the most attention. It was only as I aged that I realized they needed the most attention. The rest of us were pretty self-sufficient. Diego has always been more at home with horses than people. Bianca was into fashion and her own thing, and I had racing."

Marielle looked over at him. He was an odd contradiction—at times brutally honest and then sweet. She wished she were wrong about her parents but she knew she wasn't, given that her mom was still very reluctant to even invite her to events she was in charge of. The thing was, 85 percent of the time Marielle didn't care about what her parents thought. She was busy doing her own thing, and so were they. It was just when she needed something…did they ever come through for her without giving her a hard time? If she could just say screw it to her mom and not attend the events, it would be much easier.

"That's nice, but I really am a reminder that he cheated and she wanted to leave. But he talked her into staying. I was supposed to make things better between them…but my mom had a difficult pregnancy and birth. She also didn't like having a daughter as much as she thought, and everyone was surprised that my dad took an interest in me. He hadn't really spent a lot of time with the boys when they were babies…anyhow, that just made it worse with the two of them. And they did a shit ton of press after my birth because Carlton—he's Dad's head of staff—thought it would help in the polls."

Inigo just stared at her, and she realized that she'd laid too much truth out there. But she got tired of lugging it around, and this morning her guard was down.

He didn't say anything. He just pulled her into his arms and hugged her closely to him. "God, what a mess."

She smiled.

He'd said just the right thing. Again.

Why couldn't she have met him instead of Jose all those years ago?

But she hadn't.

"It really is. You already know the worst side of me, so sharing it with you doesn't seem so bad."

"I'm glad. Despite everything else, I'm glad we had this night together."

She nodded and looked away from him, back at the keyboard. "Yeah, me too."

"Why were you thinking of them?"

She shook her head. She wasn't going there. Not with Inigo and not this morning. They were essentially strangers with the hots for each other, and that was good enough. She decided she'd done enough soul baring for now.

"Who knows," she said. "So…what exactly does a testing session entail?"

"I'm trying out different cockpit setups at the facility. My engineering team has made some adjustments from my last run in the simulator. We load up the different tracks and then the weather conditions and my placement to see how I react to different variables."

She shifted on the bench, tucking one leg underneath her as she studied him. "That's fascinating. When I worked for F1, I really never knew much of what the drivers did when they weren't at the track."

"Yeah, there's a hell of a lot more involved than just getting behind the wheel. Some of the technical stuff fascinates me, and because I'm good friends with one of the engineers I know more about that part than some drivers. But most of it is over my head. I mean, I tell them what I want the car to do, and they make tweaks either here at the facility or in the trailer at the track and the car is adjusted. It's cool."

She smiled. He was so cute when he was getting all nerdy about cars. Mentally she slapped herself. She couldn't fall for him. They could never be friends. There was too much heat and too much baggage between the two of them for that to ever happen.

"So, you want your tea?" he asked after a few minutes.

"Yes," she said as her phone pinged with a message. "My assistant is downstairs with my clothes."

"Great. I'll let the doorman know to let her up."

"Him. It's PJ."

"Okay," Inigo said and hit a button on his smartphone to let the doorman know that her assistant was okay to come up. He slid off the bench and stood there for a minute.

"I liked your piano playing. No matter why you learned, it's part of you, and you shouldn't deny it."

Then he left to go back into the kitchen, and she could only watch him leave. And firmly remind herself this time their goodbye was for good.

Inigo wasn't surprised when he got to the Moretti Motors testing facility to see that Dante was already behind his computer working away. Matteo was running a circuit on the Melbourne track, and both of the bosses were observing from their conference room. He'd heard that Malcolm had been invited out to the track so that when he went to place his bet those running the betting ring would think he had inside information.

Inigo rubbed the back of his neck. The dancing and the sex with Marielle had completely zoned him out. He was so chill right now that he wasn't sure if he was going to be good behind the wheel or not. Normally he was tense and focused. But this chill feeling wasn't that bad.

"Inigo, hop in the cockpit and let's see if this setup is working for you."

He walked over and started the process of buckling himself in. He put on his helmet and then flexed his fingers, cracking his knuckles and gripping the steering wheel. He heard everything his engineers were saying as they cued him up. Then he waited for the green light and took off on the simulated track. His instincts were more heightened then they had been the last time. The car seemed an extension of him, and he moved through each turn and curve with ease. He kept accelerating, and he knew he was having the drive of his life. He didn't question it—he just did the laps. When he stopped, there was silence on the headset.

"Guys? How was it?"

"Good…damn good. We need to check a few things," Dante said.

Inigo got out of the simulator and noticed that everyone was working at their monitors. Had his chill attitude made him drive like a rookie? Had that drive of his life really been a huge mistake?

"How'd it go last night?" Dante asked when Inigo walked over to him.

"Good, man, the best," he said. "What's up with my time?"

"We are still checking a few things. I've sent my data over—we should hear something in a minute," Dante said, spinning around to face him. "So last night was good…guess you gave up the revenge thing?"

"Yeah," he said. "I mean, it's not like I'll see her again. Last night…was goodbye."

Dante just chuckled and shook his head. "If anyone else said that to me, I'd call them a liar, but I know you have ice in your veins when it comes to women."

"I'm not cold," Inigo said.

"Dude, you are. And that was envy you heard. I wish I could be more like you," Dante said. "Relationships are messy, but you always skate right by them. And it's not like the women you hook up with hate you later. They're cool too."

Inigo wasn't sure he liked the way Dante was describing him. He couldn't argue with his friend because his description was spot-on, but he didn't know if that was the kind of man he wanted to be.

"Yeah, lucky me," he said, feeling some tension seeping into his Zen attitude.

Marco came into the room with Keke behind him. Both men had a look on their faces that Inigo hadn't seen before. He felt nervous. Hell, why had he slept with Marielle last night? His celibacy during the racing season had sort of been his way of making sure he stayed in the right headspace to race. Of course, last night he hadn't been thinking about the season or his time.

It had all been Marielle.

Which had felt so damned good at the time, but now, in retrospect, he regretted it. Maybe it was because he knew she was forbidden fruit, or maybe it was just that he didn't like to have anyone walk away from him. He was always the one who left, he thought, but with Marielle it had been different.

"Inigo, we want you to drive again. Your time was faster than Matteo's and the best you've ever done," Marco said, his Italian accent slightly more pronounced than usual.

"Whatever you did last time," Keke said, clapping him on the shoulder, "do it again."

"Yeah, okay. I can do that," he said. But now he was worried he couldn't, and he knew that was going to mess with his mind. He stepped away from everyone, turned his back on the room and remembered the way Marielle had been when he'd left her this morning. She'd still been sitting at the piano playing some classical song as she'd watched him leave.

Leaving had been hard; he'd wanted to go back and make love to her right there on the piano bench. He felt that chill feeling sweep over him again. He was getting back to that numb mind space where he was able to feel physically sated from the night before but with that tiny tinge of excitement that he could have her again tonight.

He didn't bother to let doubt or anything other than that calm but edgy feeling fill him as he turned and walked over to the cockpit of the simulator. Everyone stepped back and let him do his thing. Even the engineers who helped strap him in didn't speak to him. They were used to drivers and their rituals. Inigo flexed his fingers and cracked his knuckles as he always did and then put his hands on the wheel.

There was no room in his mind for doubt, and as they counted down to starting, he let go of everything that didn't serve the course. He became one with the car the way he always did, felt the road underneath the wheels even though it was just a simulation. As he maneuvered around the track with ease, the car responded to him the way Marielle had last night. Every touch was strategically placed to keep the car purring and doing exactly what he wanted it to do.

When he stopped and got out of the simulator, he looked over at Marco and Keke, who were standing at Dante's station. Both men let out a whoop, and Inigo knew he'd done it again.

But it wasn't just him…it had been Marielle. The woman he'd mentally and of course literally said goodbye to looked as if she were the key to him driving and posting the fastest time of his career.

Well, hell.

Ten

Malcolm left the Moretti Motors facility and drove back into the city after texting the bookie he'd been dealing with for the racing bets. He then pulled off on the side of the highway and texted his best friend, Mauricio Velasquez. Mo called back instead of texting.

"Hey, what's up? You said you were going to be in New York for a few more days?" Mo asked.

"Yes. The Moretti thing is really blowing up. I thought if you had any clients you wanted me to meet with while I was here, that might be a good thing. I need to keep my focus and remember that gambling isn't paying my bills, my job is."

"Got it. I'll send you some information. Actually, there's a property I'm trying to get that's in Hadley's old building. One of her neighbors owns it. I think Helena met her once, and of course she knows all about me, so she doesn't want me to be her agent even though I'm licensed to sell in New York—but she's ticked at what I put Hadley through, but she'd probably talk to you. Got time to do that today?" Mo asked.

Mo and Hadley had been through a lot. At a certain point, Mo had hooked up with someone else while still texting Hadley he wanted her back. She'd come back to town to surprise him and found another woman in his bed. She'd broken up with him on the spot and moved to New York before Mo had realized he was an idiot to let her slip away and set about winning her back once Hadley had moved back to Cole's Hill.

"Yes," Malcolm said. "I definitely do. I don't want to be lingering with the bookie looking at the racing form and thinking I could use the money to get rich quick."

"Good. You doing okay?" Mo asked. "Inigo can find someone else if you're not sure you can handle it. It hasn't been that long since you stopped."

Was he doing okay?

No.

Hell, no.

But his fiancée and her family had asked him to use his expertise—which was also his weakness—to help them, and he wasn't going to let them down. Nothing had compared to how he'd felt when he had let Helena down the first time. He'd promised himself he'd never do it again.

And this was nothing. Just a little walk through fire, but hey, he could handle this. He needed to prove to himself that he was stronger now. That he wouldn't fall again. Because Helena wanted the whole enchilada with him. Kids, golden anniversary, growing old together. He couldn't fall back into his old habit. He needed this.

To prove to her and to himself that he had really conquered this.

"Yeah, I'm good. I just needed to talk. Sometimes it's good to get out of my head," Mal said.

"I know what you mean. Talking to you and to Hadley is what keeps me from giving in to my anger...but honestly, I'm mellower now than I've ever been in my life. My dad thinks it's because of Hadley. He said getting laid regularly does that."

Malcolm laughed. "Your dad is too much."

"He really is. I hope I'm still having fun when I'm old like him."

"Goals right there."

They both laughed, and then Mo asked, "Seriously, you okay?"

"Yeah. I am. With Helena here, and talking to you, it keeps me clear. Helps me stay in the real world, not that gambler's red haze where it seems like one bet could make me a tycoon."

"A tycoon? Seriously?" Mauricio asked.

"Yeah. Like the Monopoly dude," Malcolm said, feeling much more normal now. "That's why I got into real estate."

"You know what? Me too. I mean, it helped getting that house in town to fix up the summer between my freshman and sophomore year in college, but once I started flipping houses, I realized how much money could be made with a good eye."

"You definitely have the eye," Malcolm said. He did appreciate all that Mo had taught him about real estate. He had been floundering at the agency he'd worked at before Mo had brought him on board. He never could forget what his friend had done for him.

He'd given him focus and a chance to become the man he wanted to be. A man Helena could be proud to call her own.

"You do too. I'm glad to have you on my team," Mo said. "I'll send that info over. Let me know if you need anything else."

They hung up, and Malcolm got back on the road. It was good to know that this favor for Moretti Motors wasn't the only thing on his plate today. He needed his real job and real life around him.

Helena was waiting for him in the lobby when he got back from Moretti Motors, and she rushed over to him as soon as she saw him, hugging him and then stepping back to look up into his face.

"How'd it go?"

"Great. Straightforward and easy," he said. "Do you feel up to coming with me to meet a real estate client? It's an apartment in Hadley's old building. I thought afterward you could show me that bagel place you and Hadley always rave about."

She nodded. "Yes. I'd love to. Are we staying in New York for a while?"

"No. One more night and then we're heading home. But this is a client who probably won't deal with Mo because she knew about the drama between him and Hadley."

"Ah. His womanizing ways catching up to him."

"Something like that," Malcolm said. It felt good to have Helena by his side. He was worried when he saw how concerned she'd been. But seeing the way she kept giving him glances when she thought he wasn't looking just drove home the point that she still wasn't sure of him.

He felt that tension start in the back of his neck. Sometimes it was really hard not to feel as if Helena and her entire family were judging him. He knew he came from the poorer side of town. And Mr. Everton had made it clear that marrying his daughter wasn't a shortcut to the country club set. Which was fine, since that was something Malcolm had never aspired to. He just wanted to live with the woman he loved.

She slipped her hand in his.

"I don't know if I could do what you're doing," she said, going up on tiptoe and kissing him. "You have way more courage than I do."

Her words were a balm for his soul, and he let them soothe the tension away.

Marielle had texted Darian and told him never mind, she'd handle her mom and Carlton without him. He'd only responded that he was there if she needed him, but she was pretty sure she wouldn't. After she'd spilled her guts to Inigo, she'd realized how much of that childhood resentment she'd been using to feed her journey as an adult. She'd been making choices for a long time just to annoy her mom.

It was like she was still jumping in the pool yelling, *hey, Mom, watch me*, to a woman who would rather sip her martini and gossip with her friends. She'd had such a feeling of clarity when she'd left Inigo's place that it had been almost like a weight was lifted from her.

It would be nice to use her family connections, but she didn't need them. She'd been very content with building her influencer career based on doing the things she loved. The things that suited her. It would be a huge shortcut to have her mom invite her to her top-tier events, but at the same time, it wasn't the end of the world if she didn't.

When she got back to her apartment, she had to prepare and write a series of posts. Her photographer was coming over just after lunch to do a photo shoot for a sponsored post that she'd be running next week. The sponsor was the luxury jewelry brand House of Hamilton. They were trying to promote their name to a younger crowd and, in the words of the PR manager, home in on the blue box market.

Her phone pinged, and she saw it was a message in her Snapchat group from Siobahn.

Did you hit it last night?

Yes. It was good. Not like it could have been.

I'm in the studio until six. Can you hang out?

Maybe. I have a call in to my mom. I need to go and see her. You down for a drive to the Hamptons?

No. But when you're back ping me.

She set her phone aside and went to fill up her water bottle, and when she came back, she saw that Siobahn had sent another message that said if she needed her, she'd go with her.

She smiled to herself. She'd always felt so isolated by her feelings of inadequacy, which in retrospect had made her easy pickings for a man like Jose. She felt like she didn't deserve a man who was free to be hers, so that was what she'd attracted. And it would be easy to place the blame on her mom, but the truth was whenever she'd been presented with two choices, she always leaned toward the one that would cause the most grief for her parents.

Her phone rang, and she saw it was her parents' house phone in the Hamptons. She took a deep breath before she answered the call. She felt the tension in her shoulders, and that knot in the pit of her stomach appeared as it always did when she thought of speaking to her parents...or worse, Carlton.

"This is Marielle," she said, using the manners and etiquette that her mother had drilled into her as a child. She always introduced herself. Her mother thought it was the height of arrogance for someone to assume they knew who you were.

"Hello," her mom said. "I'm afraid we have a dinner party scheduled for tonight, but I'm coming to the city for a luncheon and could meet you for coffee at Ralph's after. Let's say three o'clock. Would that work for you?"

Her mom's tone was quiet, as if she wasn't too sure of what Marielle's reaction would be. It was one of the few times she could remember her mother suggesting the two of them do something together and alone. "Yes, I can do that."

"Great. I'll add you to my calendar. See you then," her mom said, ending the call.

Marielle set the phone down and thought about her mom. She didn't really seem like she wanted to change, and Marielle knew she had to be careful not to project onto her mother the feelings of the relationship she wanted. Her therapist had helped her realize that.

Ugh.

Why did life have to be so complicated?

The doorbell rang, and she heard PJ answer it. A moment later he came in with a vase of pink peonies. "For you."

"Wow. Very nice. I wonder who they're from?" she asked. Maybe the brand she'd met with the other day.

She pulled out the card once PJ went back to his tablet to answer some DMs she had received. He screened most of them and provided answers she'd already written to her most commonly asked questions.

She opened the card and saw the printed message.

Thanks for last night. Would you have dinner with me tonight? I'd like to discuss possibly seeing each other again.
Inigo

She read it, then reread it.

What the hell?

They'd already discovered they were oil and water—they didn't match. It didn't matter that they went up like flames when they were together. This dance they were playing with each other had to end.

Yet she didn't want to say no.

She sort of did want to see him again. He had made her see her world in a way that she'd never looked at it before, and though a part of her felt like she was using him, another part was eager to see what would be revealed if she spent more time with him.

Dinner at his place sent a certain message. Exactly the one he wanted her to receive—that he was happy to hook up, but that was it.

He shoved his hand through his hair.

This had stupid written all over it.

But he needed to see if sleeping with Marielle was making him faster. Marco had seen a picture of him and Marielle from the night before when they'd been getting into the car. Apparently, the paparazzi had been watching the door. He couldn't remember anything but wanting to be alone with her.

Marco had said that he'd had a woman change his driving: his wife. Which made Inigo reluctant to continue anything with Marielle. He hadn't said anything to his boss about the fact that she had been Jose's mistress. But Dante had looked up his times later, and they'd notice a slight uptick.

Now that he thought about it, it made him feel sort of sick. Was he really using her because he thought she'd made him faster?

The simple answer was yes. The championship had eluded him for too long. But he also knew that he couldn't just use her. He had to be clear about his intentions.

God, he felt like his dad. Was it an old-fashioned sentiment? She wasn't looking for a ring from him. She had her own thing going. She didn't need him, did she? Sex was just that—sex.

Why did he feel a knot in his stomach at the thought of that?

She'd been different from the beginning. He couldn't say it was just because he'd ended his self-imposed celibacy. It was more than that.

This was something else. Once again he felt that tension at the back of his neck that warned him this might not be as straightforward as he wanted it to be.

But he wasn't willing to let go of her if it meant winning.

He'd sent flowers, and she'd agreed to come to dinner. He had ordered from one of his favorite restaurants, and they had sent over a sous chef to prepare and serve the food in his dining room that overlooked Central Park. The city was blanketed in snow from a cold snap, and as he looked out the window, he almost had to pinch himself.

Driving had given him this life. It wasn't like he had grown up struggling. He'd had nice things; his father was a horse rancher and he'd grown up in a world of wealth and privilege. But this was different. He'd earned this. This was his.

His phone vibrated with a message from the doorman that Marielle was here. He texted to send her up and then alerted the chef that they would be ready to eat in thirty minutes or so.

He went to the door to wait for her. She arrived a few minutes later, her hair pulled into a loose ponytail low at the back of her neck. It wasn't one of those messy buns that so many women wore these days. She had on a pair of skinny leather leggings and a soft-looking sweater that hugged the curves of her breasts and made it damned near impossible for him to look away. But he finally did.

He smiled when she waggled both of her eyebrows at him.

"I thought we'd decided last night was goodbye," she said, walking into his apartment.

"Plans change," he said. He was thrown into doubt about whether to tell her that she'd made him faster.

He was a mess right now. What if it wasn't her? He'd been really focused over the last year.

Dante had warned him that he was going to have to be careful about attributing too much to Marielle.

"They do. So…"

"I have a private chef making dinner for us, but can I get you a drink?" he asked.

"Are you drinking?" she asked. "I thought you were sticking to ice water during the racing season."

"I am. Well, pretty much all the time. Plus, my brother Mauricio has a short tempter, and I found when I drink, I do too. And I saw how destructive that was for him…so I avoid it whenever I can."

"Fair enough," she said. "I'm fine with soda water and a twist of lime."

"Coming right up. If you want to have a seat by the fire, I'll bring the drinks," he said.

He'd lit a fire in the fireplace, thinking it would be more romantic than sitting on the couch with *SportsCenter* playing in the background. But maybe that would have sent a different message. He realized he was standing at the bar looking down at the limes that the chef had prepared earlier and wondering how he'd ever thought he could get revenge on her. He couldn't even find a way to tell her about how she'd affected him at the test today.

He felt like some kind smarmy dude even thinking about how he would suggest that they hook up so his times could keep getting faster.

"Inigo?"

Startled, he spilled some of the soda water he'd just poured as he turned to her.

"What's going on?" she asked. "I've never seen you

move this slow before or be so jumpy. You're usually moving faster than the speed of light and smooth as hell."

He handed her the drink after he wiped the glass down with a napkin. "I have a proposition for you."

"Ooh. I'm intrigued. Is it an indecent proposal?"

He felt his face flush. She threw her head back and laughed. "Okay, let's hear it. Though I have to be honest and tell you that if you offer me less than a cool million, I'm going to be insulted."

She always surprised him, never reacting the way he expected. "Money would sully what we have."

He felt like he was getting some of his mojo back. She made him feel calm…well, horny as hell, but calm inside. And he had to wonder if that was all he needed from her. But why would he turn down sex if she agreed?

Eleven

Once again he had surprised her, but really, should she have been? They were both dancing around the attraction between them, neither of them wanting to admit that there could be anything more than sex.

But could there be?

"So...no money," she joked. But what did he want? She wondered sometimes why she never found a normal guy who just wanted to chat on a dating app and then meet for a meal. Instead she had this...something she wasn't sure she actually minded.

"I feel like it might be better to talk about over dinner. I had a plan," he said.

"But that's not going to work," she said. "You can't bring something like this up and then let it go. That's not how this works. You said you had a proposition for me."

She'd been told she was too blunt. Her aunt Tilly

had warned her more than once to slow down and let
her tongue catch up with her mind. It never hurt to give
something a thought or two before she blurted it out.
But that didn't really suit her. It never had.

"Um, so, today at practice I clocked the fastest time
I've ever had. We did it three times to see if it was a
fluke. There was a new setup, but that isn't enough to
get the kind of speed I got out of the simulator today.
It was everything coming together for me. And I think
that was because of last night," he said, turning away
from her to look out the window.

She lived on the other side of the park, and their
views were different. She moved over to stand next
to him.

He had just articulated what she'd felt today. Sex had
been sort of a detox of all the junk that had been plagu-
ing her lately, and she wouldn't mind trying it again.
But she knew from the past when she had tried to justify a relationship—the one with Jose—it hadn't really worked. She feared what she had with Inigo would
quickly become something different than what had happened last night, especially since there was still bad
blood with his sister.

"I had a moment of clarity today too. I think it was
talking to you that made it possible."

"I want to do more than talk," he said sardonically.

"I figured," she said. "But that helped me. You gave
me some perspective that I hadn't been able to find before this."

"So we can hook up for me and talk for you," he said,
then shook his head. "That sounds even crazier out loud
than it does in my head."

She had to agree it did sound crazy. "I can't go on the Formula One tour with you."

She wasn't going back there again. All of those cities were tied to memories of Jose and now tinged with the fact that he'd been playing her the entire time. She didn't want to have to deal with that. Not now that she was sort of getting herself back on track.

Inigo rubbed the back of his neck, turned to put his drink on the bar and then walked back over to her. "I don't even know if you're what is making a difference in my driving."

"So?"

He shook his head. "I don't know. I had a vague idea of what I was going to suggest, but being here with you, there's no way I can do it. There's something douchey about saying to a woman, *hey, let's hook up so I can see if sex is making me better at my job.*"

She couldn't help the smile that broke across her face. She shook her head. This. This was exactly why she was here in his apartment, despite the fact that he had said some truly mean things to her in the past and would probably do so again. He was unpredictable and at the same time so honest...which was why she knew he'd say something to her again that would hurt. He didn't have that bullshit filter that most of the men she dated in the past had. The one that allowed them to say things to her that she'd believe even though they were lying.

"No, you can't say that. But I'd be willing to try it again," she said. "I like you, Inigo. We can't ever have a relationship, because as much as I don't like Bianca, she's your sister. But the sex is good, you're funny and I enjoy being around you."

He tipped his head to the side, studying her for a few

minutes. It felt longer than waiting in the line at Ralph's during rush hour. She had no idea what he was hoping to find in her expression, so she tried to look neutral and then started to feel self-conscious. She ended up just turning to stare out the window. Snow was falling, and from up here it looked peaceful. Like being inside a snow globe.

From up here she could have one of those picture-perfect lives—the one that her followers on social media thought she had. She reached for her phone. But the reflection off the plate glass didn't make a good photo.

"What are you doing?"

"Waiting for you and trying to figure out if I can capture the pristine snow falling on the city. From up here it seems…"

"Ideal."

She nodded. Ideal. That was a good word.

"So are we doing this?" she asked.

"Let's have dinner and then decide," he said. "When you mentioned Bianca, it made me realize that I hadn't thought of how this would affect anyone but you and me."

"We are the only ones who have a stake in this," she said. Was his sister really going to be mad that he was dating her? Probably. Marielle would be ticked off if one of her brothers had dated a girl that had cheated with her ex. She sighed.

"Okay."

Dinner was good, but honestly, Inigo wasn't in a frame of mind to savor it. He wished he'd stuck to his plan, but instead he had sat awkwardly across from Marielle thinking about the dumb-ass way he'd propositioned her. He'd meant to be smoother about it. To be Mr. Charming for once in his life. He should have called Diego. His older brother was good at knowing the right thing to say.

But he didn't really want to let his family know that he'd been sleeping with the woman Bianca hated. Over and over as they ate the meal, that was all he could think of. Marielle was working hard, trying to keep the conversation going, but he knew he was giving her nothing. Just one-word answers and long drawn-out silences between topics.

He'd never been this awkward with a woman.

His phone vibrated in his pocket, and he took it out to see that Keke was downstairs and wanted to come up.

"Uh, one of my bosses is here," he said to Marielle.

"Okay," she said. "Do you want me to leave?"

"No. I've been so horrible, I need a chance to make it up to you. Let me see what he wants," Inigo said.

He texted that it was okay for him to come up. "At least we will have someone to help make conversation."

"Yeah. I had no idea that I would ever work this hard to talk about nothing," she said.

"I'm sorry. It's not like me to say something inappropriate to a woman and then totally shut down," he said.

"I know. I get it. We really shouldn't be doing this. It doesn't matter if you think I'm the reason you drove faster today. Given our connection through Jose, we can't ever do this," she said.

"I know. I had forgotten," he said. "I mean, not really. But when I see you, Marielle, I don't think about Jose or the past. But it is there."

Before she could answer, he heard Keke's hard knock on the door and went to answer it. The German stood there with a big grin on his face, filling the doorway. Next to him was his wife, Elena.

"Sorry to stop by unannounced, but I had an idea that I wanted you to think about tonight," Keke said, coming in. He glanced over at the table and saw Marielle then looked back at Inigo.

"You have a date?"

"Yes, I do," he said.

"See, I told you to call first," Elena said. "Nothing can sway him when he starts thinking about racing," she added to Inigo.

She brushed past Keke and walked over to Marielle. She introduced herself and then suggested that they take a bottle of wine and get comfy. "It's supposed to be date night. Our first in three months, but Keke...well, racing is his first love."

"Woman, you know I love you more than racing. But Inigo and I need to discuss this. I promise we won't be more than thirty minutes."

"I've heard that before," Elena said, then looped her arm through Marielle's and led her to the sofa in front of the fireplace.

"Sorry," Keke said, turning to him. "But this is important. Remember how we changed the setup on the second run today?"

Inigo nodded, but his attention was divided between Keke's explanation of how he could shave possibly up to a second more off his time by shifting at a different moment and watching Marielle pour two glasses of wine for herself and Elena.

Keke kept talking, but all Inigo could hear was the women's laughter. Finally his friend and boss put his arm over Inigo's shoulder. "You okay?"

"Yeah," he said. He'd just spent the evening trying to convince himself that Marielle was the key to winning and now…he was getting the message that maybe he hadn't thought this through. His gaze drifted over to the women, and Keke noticed.

"It's not always easy to balance racing and a woman," Keke said. "Elena had her own thing, which made it easier for us. Is she the woman that Marco mentioned?"

Inigo turned away from them, walking to his den area, and Keke followed. "I wonder if today was a fluke."

"That's why I'm here. One of the strengths that I had as a driver was the ability to analyze not just the car and the setup but also my physical well-being. What was going on in my head and my body. I stopped by so we could work through that," he said.

"I had spent the night and morning with Marielle," Inigo said. "You know I've been careful about keeping myself focused on driving and not allowing anyone to distract me, but she's different."

"Good. That's the kind of thing you should log," he said, reaching into his jacket pocket and pulling out a small journal. He put it on the desk between them. "This is my journal from the year I won the championship. It's got everything in there. Even the stuff I did wrong. I wasn't on my A-game that year, but I was happier than I'd ever been before, and I think some of that joy translated behind the wheel."

Joy.

Not sex. Inigo flipped open the journal and glanced down at it. Keke was very detailed, outlining everything from the moment he woke up. He detailed his sex with Elena too, which Inigo didn't want to read about. But when he flipped the page, he saw that Keke had then described how he'd felt when he qualified for the race.

"I went back at the end of the race and underlined the things I thought helped me," Keke said. "Marco thinks this is all mumbo jumbo, but racing has never been just about the machine. The driver has as much to do with it. And I think you are on the verge of finally understanding what that means."

"I agree," he said. "Thanks, Keke. I think this will help."

"Good. That's what I was hoping to hear," the other man said, clapping him on the back. "Marielle can make you into a better driver, but watch the balance, because some women can become the kind of distraction that no man wants."

Marielle had more fun with Elena and Keke than she expected to. She'd been exposed to many drivers in her year as a trophy girl, but it had been different than this quiet evening at home. They ended up playing cards with the other couple, and she saw a different side to Inigo. He was relaxed but a little on edge at first, which made sense given that Keke was a former Formula One champ and his boss, but as the evening wore on, he started to loosen up.

Elena had given her some advice about dating a driver. Marielle appreciated it, but it also made her realize that many people didn't know about her affair with Jose. Carlton had done a nice job of covering it up. At the time she'd been ticked off that he'd stepped in, but thinking about how Elena and Keke might have treated her if they knew, she was glad.

And it drove home the fact that if she was going to

keep doing this, even just as some sort of friends-with-benefits thing, she needed to make amends with Bianca. She was starting to really care about Inigo, but she had to be careful because she had a way of ruining even the simplest relationships.

"We should be going. I told the sitter we'd be home by eleven," Elena said. "Thank you for helping salvage our night."

"You're very welcome," Marielle said. "I really enjoyed it."

"Me too. You've got my number, so text me. We can have lunch or coffee," Elena said.

"I will," she said when Elena leaned in to kiss her cheek before she and Keke left.

When the door closed behind them, Inigo leaned back against it. "That was unexpected."

"It was. I think they saved our evening," she said.

"I think so too," he said. "Listen, I think I was wrong to suggest we hook up so I can improve my time. I don't want that to be the only reason we are together."

"Me neither," she said. "But honestly, I don't see a way for us to be together. I mean, I'm lucky that they didn't know I had been with Jose, but that is bound to come up at some point. I don't want that to affect how everyone sees you."

He shook his head and then rubbed the back of his neck. Something she realized he did when he was trying to figure out what to do. They were both caught between the past and this thing between them. It had almost been easier when it had been just sex. But tonight had changed that. She felt like they were becoming friends, and she couldn't hurt a friend.

She had so few, and each of them was cherished. She

had to admit this was the first time she'd met a guy who made her feel this way. That didn't mean she was going to pursue it. In fact she was pretty damn sure she was going to walk away.

She had no idea how to handle him. She reflected on their evening with the older couple. What she'd seen between Keke and Elena was different than anything she'd experienced before. She liked it, but they were very domestic and that wasn't where she was in her life. She'd pretty much decided that marriage wasn't for her. And could she be satisfied with anything less? Would he?

He'd just asked her to hook up, so she guessed he'd be happy with much less.

"It's too bad that we can't just…never mind," he said.

"What? Don't turn shy on me, speedy. You've never hesitated to say what's on your mind."

He shrugged. "I was going to say sneak around, but I don't think either of us would enjoy that."

"No," she said, turning away from him and walking back to where she'd left her bag. She didn't want to be his secret lover. She'd done that before. "I think this really is goodbye."

She turned to face him and then walked over to grab her coat and the container of leftovers the chef had prepared for her before he'd gone home for the evening. She put on her coat as Inigo stood near the door watching her as if he wasn't sure what to do.

But she was taking herself out of this equation. She'd had enough of this world. That confidence that had come from her early-morning discussion with Inigo was all she needed to make herself move on. This was fun right now, but history had taught her that it would become toxic in no time at all.

"I hope you continue to post those faster times," she said. "I think this year is going to be a good one for you."

She leaned over to kiss his cheek, but he turned his head and their lips brushed against each other. She deepened the kiss without thinking, thrusting her tongue into his mouth as she angled her head to grant her more access. She put her free hand on the back of his neck and enjoyed every second of the kiss before she stepped back.

"Good night."

She opened the door and walked away without looking back. She knew she'd made the smartest decision in her history of dating. Though she had a few twinges of regret thinking she could have hooked up one more time with him, she knew in the end this move had been the best one for her.

Her sleep that night was restless, and she dreamed of Inigo's touch on her body, waking in a fever for him, but that was something she was going to have to live with.

Twelve

"Thanks for adjusting your schedule to mine," her mom said as Marielle showed up for tea at the Waldorf the next afternoon. Their plan to meet at Ralph's yesterday had fallen through when her mother's lunch ran long. But she never missed a chance to stop by the Waldorf when she was in town, so this was the perfect chance to catch up.

"Not a problem," Marielle said, sliding into the chair across from her mother. "I'm sorry that things got so out of control the other day on our call. I know that your events have a certain standard to them, and I realized that I don't want you to compromise anything to include me."

Her mother leaned back in the chair, her eyes narrowing a bit. "I'm not sure if you are serious or not."

"I am," Marielle said. "The thing is, if you included

me with the other influencers, it would be a nice bump in my profile, and I think it might bring me some more luxury brands as sponsors. But at the same time, it wouldn't hurt me to build my following and work to increase my numbers on my own."

Her mom nodded. "Your social media handle was on the list of influencers that the charity thought should be invited, so someone thinks you are ready to move to the next level."

"I'm glad to hear that. I know you haven't had a chance to see what I do on social media," she said. "Maybe you'd like to accompany me to an event, so you can observe me interacting and see how I translate the event to my followers."

Her mom seemed surprised for a split second before she hid it. "I'm not sure that my schedule will accommodate that. I've had a look at your social media sites and really like what you are doing with those stories. I was surprised at how real it felt when I watched it. I liked what you did with your posts about New Year's Eve."

"Thank you," she said. "Most of that was Scarlet's idea. She's been mentoring me as I'm working to learn the right way to build my followers. She said to be authentic but also make sure to put limits in place. She's kind of a trailblazer when it comes to this. She started out with her reality TV audience and has been growing it since then."

Marielle didn't mention that she hadn't had a chance to talk to Scarlet since New Year's Day, when the thing with Bianca had happened. She wasn't about to tell her mother about that. Her mother had liked Jose when Marielle had brought him home that one time, but when he had died, and her parents had realized that Jose was married, they'd been horrified. Especially her mom, who had been cheated on by Marielle's father.

Her therapist had asked if she'd had the affair to make a statement to her mother. Had it been a passive-aggressive move? But Marielle couldn't make that connection. Other than wanting to be as different from her mother as she could be. She knew she couldn't bring that subject up at their meeting. Maybe later she'd talk to her mom about the fallout on New Year's.

"That's really nice of her. She's on my list as well. Perhaps you two could come together. Many people know that you're friends, and I think that would be a nice workaround for the situation. You and I can be ourselves without having to make a public statement about being mother and daughter. Would that work for you?" she asked.

It was more than she'd hoped for, and Marielle nodded. "Thank you."

"No problem. I was impressed that you didn't go to Dare to solve this for you. I thought about that a lot after your call. I know that there are times when our relationship has been strained, but coming to me on your own really meant a lot to me."

"Me too," Marielle said. "I recently met someone who made me look at myself in a new way, and it really has helped me a lot."

"I'm glad to hear that. Who is it?"

She wasn't prepared to talk about Inigo and had surprised herself that she'd even mentioned him. "Just a man who was at Scarlet's party. He was funny and charming, and he saw me not as Marielle Bisset but just as a woman. Does that make any sense?"

Her mother laughed and nodded. "More than you

can know. It's nice to just be a woman every once in a while. Reminds us of who we are when we aren't in the spotlight that follows your father around."

"Exactly," she said. They finished having tea, and her mother gave her a hug before she left. Marielle was about to get in a cab when she felt someone watching her. She glanced up to see that it was Elena, Keke's wife. She smiled and waved.

"How do you know Juliette Bisset? I've been trying to get a meeting with her to see if she'll use my swimsuit line at her summer Hamptons party, and she always says no."

"She's my mom," Marielle said.

"She is? You seem so…different. God. Listen to me. I think I've spent too many hours with this one," Elena said, lifting a cute little toddler into her arms. The boy had white-blond hair and Elena's striking eyes. He smiled at Marielle, and she smiled back.

"It's okay. My family is complicated, and so is my mother. I've spent my entire life trying to not be like her, so it is a compliment of sorts."

"I'm glad to hear that. When I first started modeling, I didn't speak English, so everyone thought I was a frosty bitch. It took a long time to shake that image. I guess what I'm saying is that I completely get what it's like to have people think you are one thing and knowing it's not you."

"Thanks, Elena."

"You're welcome," she said. Marielle had that feeling again like she had turned a corner, and she liked it. She'd had a meeting with her mom and hadn't ended up saying something she'd regret later. No matter what else happened, she owed Inigo for that.

* * *

Inigo's times weren't as good as they had been the day before, and he wanted to blame it on the evening he hadn't spent with Marielle. But he knew it was just because he wasn't connected to driving today.

And now he had another problem. Bianca had seen the picture of him and Marielle kissing as they got into the car the other night. She'd texted him first thing, but he hadn't responded.

Marielle had been right when she'd said there was no way they could have anything together. He knew that. But he also wondered if there were some way that Bianca could meet her...and then what? His sister was never going to see Marielle as anything but Jose's mistress. She'd never know that crazy sense of humor she had that always made him laugh.

Nor should she have to. Bianca had struggled to find her happiness, and she was truly in a good place with her marriage to Derek. Her son, Benito, had happy memories of his daddy because Bianca hadn't wanted to take that from him, and she was expecting another child.

They were doing well. And Inigo, who'd spent so much time going after what he wanted and not really considering how it affected his family, wasn't going to be the one to rock the boat.

"What is going on today?" Marco asked, coming over to the simulator. "Take a break and get your head on right. If you drive like this, we'd be better to send Keke's three-year-old to the race."

He nodded. "Sorry. I'll do better next time."

Inigo walked out of the simulator room and hurried into the small room that had been set aside for him.

There was a couch where he'd tossed his duffel bag when he'd arrived this morning. He took out his phone, accessing his playlist, and as he did so the empty notebook that Keke had left for him fell out. He picked it up, grabbed a pen and started writing down everything.

The mixed feelings he had about letting Marielle go. How what he'd learned about Jose was making him question so many things that he'd always taken for granted. How he could have known the man as well as he thought and never realized he was cheating on Bianca.

And he had never suspected it. He hadn't seen Marielle or any other woman, but it had been clear when Jose had died that there had been many women.

He thought about what Keke had said. Joy had been what helped him drive better, but joy didn't seem like something that Inigo could easily access. Instead he thought of the day before and that chill feeling that had swept through him when he achieved his best times. He knew that it had been the sexual satisfaction that had started it. He closed his eyes, leaning back against the wall as the playlist switched to the songs that had been playing in the club when he'd danced with Marielle. Pitbull, as always, sang the soundtrack to his life, and now Inigo pictured Marielle in his arms on the dance floor.

He remembered the faint smell of alcohol and sweat and her fresh flowery perfume. How she'd felt as her body had brushed against his.

He took several deep breaths and pushed out all the baggage that came with being with her and stood up. He just wanted to remember how he'd felt in that one moment with her in his arms.

He remembered how she looked as he'd made love

to her. His body shuddered with the memory of how perfectly she fit him.

He walked back into the simulator room and nodded to Dante, who was lounging against his workstation. Dante called for everyone to get into position as Inigo walked to the simulator and got in.

Immediately he felt a difference in his performance. He had no idea if his time would be as good as the day before, but he realized that he was figuring out something about himself. The driving couldn't be separate from his life. He couldn't isolate himself from the world in order to drive faster. Until now, he'd cut himself off from women, drinking, family time. While he wasn't going to start drinking again, maybe it was time for him to start living. To find a way to blend the two.

The way that Marielle had done for him. He knew it hadn't been her intent, but she'd forced him to see the link between racing and his family. When he stopped and got out of the simulator, he glanced over at Marco.

His boss nodded and gave him a thumbs-up sign. "Better. Keep doing that. Whatever it is that you did at the end. That is the key for you. My brother needs me back in Milan, so Keke will stay and send reports to me. I like the way you are improving, Inigo. For each driver, the key to winning is something different. It's not something that I can tell you or even Keke, for all his wisdom, but to me it seems as if you are getting closer to that."

He nodded. "I am. I'd like to take a few days off over the weekend to go home. My sister is close to delivering her baby, and I'd like to be there for that."

Marco took a deep breath and shook his head. "Will it interfere with your driving?"

"Honestly, I think it might help it. I need to keep living. I've been too isolated, and it isn't really helping me to win."

"Okay. You're from Texas, right?"

"Yes. Why?"

"I'd like to see you out on a track getting some real-world practice. I'll have my assistant see if you can get some time at the track in Austin. Sound good?"

"Sounds perfect," he said.

Marco left, and Inigo realized for the first time since he'd started racing, he felt comfortable being a driver. He'd always thought the approach he'd been taking would bring him the results he wanted, but it hadn't.

Not until now. Not until Marielle.

Two days later Marielle was at a party at Siobahn's to celebrate the release of her latest single. Marielle had done a live video and her followers loved it, then she'd taken a break and was sitting in a quiet corner trying not to do a search on Inigo. She missed him. Yet at the same time, she was trying to remind herself that she didn't need him.

"Hey. Do you mind if join you?" Scarlet said.

She was in her second trimester and had a cute baby bump but still managed to look like the hellion she'd always been.

"Sure. How are you doing?" she asked as Scarlet sat down next to her.

"I'm good," she said, rubbing her stomach. "I wanted to see how you were. I know that things didn't end so well on New Year's Day. I haven't had time to call... well, that's not true. I wasn't sure what I was going to do at first. Alec and his family see you as some sort of femme fatale and think you should have a big scarlet letter on your chest."

Hearing what she already knew said out loud was like a little wound to her chest. It hurt, but it also made her angry. "Whatever. It's not like I want to be in their lives."

"Well, not all of their lives," Scarlet said.

She nibbled on her lower lip, turning her head to the side. Yeah, not all their lives. Just Inigo's. "That's over."

"Is it? I saw a photo of you two not that long ago on TMZ. And honestly it was that picture that made me realize that Alec was being stupid. I mean, you two were really into each other. And why shouldn't you have a chance at that? Why should I be mad at you for something that happened before either of us knew the Velasquez family?"

Marielle couldn't help smiling at the way Scarlet said it. She put her arm around the other woman, hugging her. "Thank you. That has to be one of the nicest things anyone has ever said to me. It means more than you know to hear that. I don't think Inigo and I will ever be together, but still it's nice to know you had my back."

"No problem. As troublemakers, we have to stick together," she said. "Plus, Siobahn read me the riot act. Her point was, since when did I let past mistakes define how I look at a friend. I know you regret falling for Jose's lies, and if Bianca ever met you she'd realize that you beat yourself up for that still."

Marielle had to laugh. Siobahn was still down on guys after her ex had married someone else mere weeks after dumping her. "She sees the world from a unique vantage point right now."

"That doesn't mean she's wrong," Scarlet said.

"Don't let her hear you say that. It will go to her head."

"Whose head?" Siobahn asked, coming over and sitting down next to them.

"Yours."

"My new single rocks, doesn't it?"

"It's a revenge song… I think when Mate hears it, he's going to lose his shit," Scarlet said. "Wish there was a way to see his reaction."

"Oh, there will be. He's doing red carpet for that movie he wrote the soundtrack for. I'm sure it will come up," Siobahn said.

"How can you know that?"

"I was on a morning radio show this morning and hinted it was about him without saying it," she said. "Life is good."

Marielle knew that feeling. It was hard having your heart broken and feeling so low. Though she wasn't the kind of person who wanted some kind of public humiliation for her exes, she understood why Siobahn did.

"How's things with the race-car driver?" Siobahn asked. "You could have brought him."

"We're not together," Marielle said. "It was a hot mess when we tried to figure out how it would work, and we both walked away. It's better."

"I saw you two—"

"Don't, Siobahn. I know you mean well, but there's no way that we can be together. My life is finally not the cray-cray show it always has been," Marielle said.

"Fair enough. I just know you. You looked like you were starting to fall for him."

"Probably all the more reason for us not to be together," Marielle said. "When has love ever ended for any of us in anything but disaster?"

"Uh, excuse me. I'm rocking happily-ever-after," Scarlet said.

"You are. You're the exception that proves the rule. Siobahn and I can't chance it. We might jinx you," Marielle said.

"You won't jinx me. But I do like the idea of you getting you right before you add a man to the mix. For me I had the pregnancy, so I had no choice but to figure out how I could make it work with Alec. And you know, I'm glad I didn't have too much time to think about it. That man might make me crazy sometimes, but I've never felt so happy and in love in my entire life. And he actually loves me."

"Of course he does. He'd be an idiot not to," Siobahn said.

Marielle hung out with her friends for the rest of the evening, and when she went home, she told herself that the empty apartment didn't bother her. She was strong and independent. She didn't need a man. In fact, she'd never really needed anyone else. But that didn't mean that she didn't miss Inigo.

He had a way of making her laugh at nothing. She stood at the window and remembered standing by his, seeing Central Park from the other side. Tonight, there wasn't as much snow, but she wasn't looking at the park. Instead she tried to see all the way to the other side and the man she was trying to convince herself she didn't miss.

Thirteen

Breakfast at Peacock Alley in the Waldorf Astoria was both elegant and refined. Inigo had never been before, but Marielle knew the maître d' and had gotten them a table that was out of the main dining room and quiet. She looked different than what he'd come to expect today. She was still herself, but she'd braided her long blond hair and a few tendrils had escaped to frame her heart-shaped face. She smiled easily, but he could still see some signs of tension in her expression.

He felt it too. Accidentally running into her at Ralph's when they'd first reconnected had been one thing, but this…he was now back to toying with an idea he wasn't sure he could commit to.

Revenge had been an idea that he'd toyed with but his heart wasn't in it. As much as he thought Marielle needed to be brought to see how badly she'd hurt his sister, he couldn't stay away from her. He was in the crosshairs of a dilemma like he'd never experienced before. He'd always prided himself on being a man who put family first, but here he was with Mari. Again.

He'd finally answered Bianca's texts. To say his sister was upset about the TMZ photo of him kissing Marielle was an understatement. She had gone into brutal detail about what had happened with Jose. Now Inigo was torn. Part of him was still so angry about how Bianca had been treated by Jose and his mistress. But another part of him looked at Marielle and had a hard time making the connection between any viciousness on her part and the hurt and guilt that were in her eyes so often when she spoke of Jose.

He needed answers, which was why he'd asked Marielle to meet him even though they'd agreed not to see each other anymore. He had to ascertain if she was the heartless other woman or Jose's victim. He'd seen Jose use his charm to soothe angry race officials and tempt fans over to their team. He'd been larger than life and Inigo had been in awe of the man. He had wanted to be like him when he grew up. But now...

Feet of clay, he thought.

"I'm not sure I've ever been with a guy and not talked for this long," Marielle said. "You're very serious this morning."

"Got a lot on my mind," he said. "And I was checking out this place. Not many restaurants like this in Cole's Hill."

"My family has been coming here for Sunday brunch for years. We have a history with this place. After we eat, I'll show you the portrait of my paternal grandparents with the former owners that hangs in the owner's lounge."

"I'd like that. Is family important to you?" he asked, as one of the waiters poured him some coffee.

"I'd like to say no, but that's not true. As much as I try to do things to shock my parents, I do love them," she said.

"Was the affair with Jose something to shock them?" he asked.

She tipped her head to the side. "Are we going to talk about that again?"

"I think we have to," he said. He'd always been direct, and he couldn't imagine that he was going to change now. He wanted to understand her. To try to reconcile the lover who'd been in his bed on New Year's Eve and the woman he'd learned she was the morning after.

"Of course I wasn't doing it to shock my parents. It was because I thought I loved Jose," Marielle said with a shrug. "I never would have gone into that relationship if I hadn't believed him when he said his marriage was over."

"Do you regret the affair? Now that you know about Bianca?" he asked.

She picked up her mimosa and took a sip. "How can you be asking me this? I already told you how much shame I feel."

"Bianca saw a picture of us kissing when we left the Polar club the other night, and she isn't happy. She's been telling me more about what happened," he asked.

"Is that so? Well, you should just remember that there are two sides to every story," Marielle said. "Not that I blame her at all. But he lied to both of us."

Inigo felt the slow burn of anger. The fact that Marielle seemed to have no shame about her actions made him realize that his attraction was a mirage. He might be seeing something in her that wasn't real.

Sex. He had to remember it had been a year since he'd gotten laid before Marielle. Maybe that was responsible for his obsession with her.

"I'd think you'd have some regret. She was pregnant."

"I can't control anyone other than myself. I was upset and broke things off when I realized that Jose was lying to me," she said. She chewed her lower lip and looked away from him. "He made me promises as well. But he wasn't a man of his word."

That didn't jive with the Jose he knew, but Inigo had realized after his mentor's death that there was a lot about him that he'd never known. He'd only seen Jose's talent as a driver and knew that if he wanted to be the best, he needed to emulate what he saw.

On the other hand, he didn't feel as if he knew Marielle at all. She seemed so callous toward Bianca and took no responsibility for the outcome of her affair. That affair had devastated his sister. Inigo wondered if someone treated Marielle that way, she'd finally be able to find some empathy for Bianca.

And worst of all, Inigo still wanted her. Could he have her? Or was avenging his sister the right course after all? He'd been so worked up after his call with Bianca that he hadn't even thought about how all this might impact his racing.

"Did you only ask me to lunch to discuss the past? Because if so, we're done here," Marielle said, shifting in her chair as if she were going to get up and leave.

"No, I want to discuss the future," Inigo said, stopping her. "I need you back."

* * *

Marielle showed up twenty minutes early to her dinner date with Inigo, which wasn't like her. She almost had her driver circle the block a few times so she wouldn't be early and realized she was nervous.

What did it matter?

He was just a guy.

She hadn't been able to resist when he'd asked to spend more time with her. She scolded herself for giving in to temptation and knew that the situation with Bianca meant that it wouldn't last. But she couldn't lie to herself. She'd missed Inigo. She had to see where this went, even if it didn't end well.

She glanced at her phone and decided she could play this off if she used it for her social media channel. Her manager had noted that her live videos were the things that really got the most views.

She took a deep breath and then asked the driver to stop. Living her best life on social media was always easier than her reality.

The restaurant Inigo had chosen was very popular, and there was a line outside. There had been a light snow falling, and it was almost too perfect. It was the kind of wintry evening that was made for romance. There were some carriages lined up to take couples through Central Park, and she used them as the background, adjusting her position to find the best light for her video.

Then she took a deep breath and turned on the live video feed. She waited a moment for the feed to start and then smiled at the camera.

"Hello, everyone. This is the perfect night for romance and wintry fun. I am in Central Park waiting for my date, and this light snow has started to fall. For a long time, I saw snow as something to be avoided. I always used to worry that it would ruin my hair, make it frizzy, or that the snow would leave wet stains on my clothing."

She tipped her head back and let the snowflakes fall on her face. She'd been so shallow.

"Now when I think of all the moments like this that I never let myself enjoy, I regret it. I was so obsessed with getting the perfect picture to share, with making sure that everyone thought I had a better life than I did, but the truth is, I wasn't living it. I was staging it, and in the end I wasn't a very happy or nice woman. I hope that if you are watching this, you will get out tonight. Go and enjoy the evening wherever you are and don't worry if it's not perfect. If your hair is a little frizzy or your boots get muddy, that doesn't matter. Are you with the person you love? Someone who makes you laugh? Or even just on your own, enjoying what the evening can provide?"

She noticed that people were watching her, and she just smiled as she twirled in the snow. "Don't let anyone steal your joy tonight."

She turned off the camera and walked back toward the restaurant. That's when she saw Inigo standing a few feet away wearing a black wool coat. He was watching her. She knew she didn't look as good as she had earlier; she could feel the cold on her face and imagined her cheeks and nose were probably red. But the snow and the magical atmosphere this evening had taken away her nerves.

Just letting go of perfection was bringing her a satisfaction she hadn't been able to find before this.

"Hello, speedy. Looks like I beat you tonight."

He smiled at her and didn't say a word as he walked over to her and took her in his arms to kiss her. The kiss was warm and passionate and everything that she wanted but had never had.

She saw the flash of the paparazzi bulbs behind him and wouldn't have minded for herself, but this wasn't something that Bianca needed to see. The fledgling relationship she was trying to build with Inigo didn't need the added attention. But she wished she could just ignore them and revel in the fact that for the first time in her life, she was being deliberate in her actions. She wasn't staging her world to seem as if she was living a good life—she was actually enjoying it.

And this man.

This improbable man that she shouldn't be kissing at all. But he was perfect for this night.

She put her hands on his face and deepened the kiss. Then he tipped her back, not breaking the kiss, before lifting his head and looking down into her eyes. "Might as well give them a good pose for their photos."

"Might as well," she said, hoping that she wouldn't regret being so public with Inigo. But it was different, and in a way this suited her brand, her lifestyle that was a mix of luxury and authenticity.

She took a deep breath and felt something shift deep inside her soul. Some place that had been barren and cold for the majority of her life no longer felt so cold or alone.

He twined their fingers together and led her toward the restaurant. She was aware of people watching them, and she realized that for the first time she was the center of attention not because she was outrageous.

"You are such a cute couple," an older lady said to them.

She glanced over at Inigo to see how he took that comment and noticed how satisfied he seemed. Maybe this was more than sex. Maybe.

After dinner Inigo was still not sure how to proceed with Marielle. She was funny, irreverent and sometimes would do things that shocked and turned him on. Like when she ran her foot up his leg to his crotch as he was giving the waiter his order. And when his voice dropped an octave, she just winked at him.

But at the same time, there was Bianca and what Marielle had done with Jose. Was Marielle the shallow, callous woman she'd seemed to be in that situation? Should Inigo be the brother who was there for Bianca this time instead of the one who was…well, oblivious to what was going on?

But Marielle had him in a sensual daze. He'd found his own hand up high on her thigh as they'd shared a decadent dessert. And when he paid the bill and led her outside to the waiting car and paparazzi, he didn't think about Bianca or revenge. In a fevered state, he'd pulled Marielle into his arms, his hand sliding under her coat to hold her to him as he kissed her the way he'd wanted to since the very beginning of the meal.

The flashbulbs of the paparazzi who had been following them around brought him out of his sensual haze. He lifted his head and looked down into Marielle's upturned face. He went back to how he'd felt before talking to Bianca this week. He couldn't follow through on his callous plan. He couldn't hurt Marielle the way he'd intended. His tit-for-tat idea of hurting her after making her fall for him wasn't going to bring him any solace or give his sister the peace she needed.

His family were going to see these photos, but he would have to deal with the consequences. Before he might have used them as part of a plan to publicly dump and embarrass Marielle, but now he had no intention to.

"What's going on, speedy?" she asked once they were in the car.

Her nickname for him almost made him smile. "I can't keep doing this. I think you and my sister need to talk."

She shifted completely off his lap and turned to stare out the window. The lights of the city illuminated her reflection, and what he saw made him realize how difficult this was going to be.

"Why? What purpose will that serve?" she asked.

"I like you, Marielle," he admitted. "And it's not just because of my times behind the wheel. I don't want this to be just hooking up. But it can't be anything more unless you and Bianca…come to some sort of understanding."

"Understanding?" she said, turning to face him. "I didn't go after her husband… Jose hit on me. He told me his marriage was over. I don't think I owe her anything."

"She's never going to see it that way," Inigo said. He was being torn apart by this. How could Marielle not see that?

"I don't care," she said. "I'm not saying I haven't made mistakes in my life, but I'm done apologizing for being alive."

"That's not what I'm asking you to do," he said. This wasn't going the way he'd hoped. "Forget I mentioned it."

"How can I forget it? It's always there between us. As you said, there is no way to move past this. The one who could have made this right is dead. We both only know what he told us."

She had a point, but Inigo knew there wasn't a way for him to continue in this relationship with her and not hurt his sister. She lowered the divider between the front and back seats. "Could you take me to my place?"

She rattled off her address, and the driver switched lanes to head toward her place. She put the privacy barrier back up. "I think we need a break to figure out what to do next."

He nodded. "I'm going to Texas to do some training at the track in Austin, and then I'll be back here in February for a week before we leave for Melbourne."

"I'm going to concentrate on my career too," she said. "It's finally starting to take off, and as much as I enjoy this, I want to see what I can do with that."

"Fair enough," he said. "I'll get in touch when I'm back in town."

"Okay."

They were silent for the rest of the drive, and when the car pulled up in front of her building, she put her hand on his arm to stop him from coming around to open her door. "Let's just say goodbye now. It's been fun."

Fun?

"Okay."

It was all he could say. He could think of many ways to describe their time together, and fun wasn't one of them. It had been so much more from the moment he'd spotted her at Scarlet's New Year's Eve party. But now it was over. No matter what they'd both said, this was a forever kind of goodbye. And he was just going to let her leave.

Maybe if it was the end of the season or if he had a win under his belt, he would have made a different choice, but he just sank back into the leather seats of the Vallerio sedan and watched her walk away in the slush.

All of the romance of the evening was gone. No more softly falling snow, no more surprise kisses. No more Marielle.

She entered the lobby of her building without a backward glance, and his driver eased back into traffic, taking him toward his home. He let his head fall back and tried to reassure himself that everything was for the best and this was the good life. But it didn't feel like the good life. It felt like he'd made a mistake. But at the same time, what else could he do?

She couldn't see her way to make peace with Bianca, but was that why she'd left? Or was it that she didn't care for him? He might have been pushing for something she simply didn't want.

When he got to his building and went into the lobby, Dante was waiting for him. They had planned to meet at his place to go over the latest results of his sessions at the facility. He was glad to see his friend and head engineer. Work was what he should be focused on.

"Do you have time to talk?"

"About the new setup?" Inigo asked. He needed to talk about racing and get his head off of Mari and those thoughts of what could have been.

"Uh, yeah, of course, what else would I want to talk about?"

Dante seemed a little strange but then started talking about the changes in the cockpit setup and the engine, and Inigo relaxed. Maybe he was being oversensitive after dealing with Mari. After hearing her dismiss what they had as just fun when Inigo was beginning to think he wanted much more.

Fourteen

"Hey, um, Inigo, this is Derek... When you have a moment, could you please call me? There's something I'd like to discuss with you. I'm on call and have surgery this morning, but you can leave a message on my cell or with my assistant. We really need to talk."

Inigo saved the message. Worried something was wrong with Bianca, he dialed Derek's number, but it went to voice mail.

"Hey, Derek. Call me when you get this? I'm leaving my phone on and I'll have one of the engineers get me if I'm in the simulator."

He hung up, rubbing the back of his neck. Worry about his sister was at the front of his mind. He'd been hoping to talk to Bianca about Marielle. Though she still hadn't shown any regret for being Jose's mistress, Inigo was falling for her. He wanted her in his life, but he knew that would never happen if he didn't find a way to make peace between his sister and Marielle.

His timing was bad, though. Bianca was in her last trimester, and if Derek had called, it had to be bad news. He texted his dad to ask if Bianca was okay. He was so nervous, he saw dots dancing in his eyes before his dad's response reached him.

Hiya, son, we had dinner with her last night and she was fine. Do you know something? Should I go over to her place?

His parents would know if something was wrong related to the pregnancy. Maybe Derek was calling about something else. He twirled his phone in his hands, trying to decide how to respond to his dad.

I was just checking in but didn't want to bother Bianca.

How's the training going?

Really well. The new facility is nice. We are going to head to Melbourne at the end of February.

Mom and I want to see you before then.

I will make that happen. I'm coming to Austin for some practice laps. See you then. Love you.

Love you too.

"Inigo, you ready to try this new setup?" Keke asked.
"Yeah. Sorry about that," Inigo said, walking over

to Dante's desk, where Keke waited. Both men had a new configuration up on the computer monitor. "Dante, watch my phone. My brother-in-law left me a voice mail on my last run, and it sounded urgent. If he calls again, will you answer it and then pull me out of the simulation?"

"Is it about your sister?" Keke asked, putting his hand on Inigo's shoulder and squeezing.

"I'm not sure. I just don't want to miss another call. She's not in labor and there is no emergency my parents know about, but that doesn't mean anything," Inigo said.

"We've got your back on this. Can you clear your mind?" Keke asked.

He nodded. He wasn't going to allow anything to keep him from another good run. He had noticed that as his relationship—could he even call it that?—with Marielle had developed, he'd been finding a way to clear his head and drive faster. Part of it was focusing on the remembered feel of her in his arms, but a bigger part was just that she cleared his head. Even with the complications of her past with his sister, she gave him something to look forward to that he hadn't had before.

He took his run. Technically he knew he'd done everything right, but he was also pretty sure that his time wasn't that great. When he got out of the simulator and saw the looks on Keke and Dante's faces, he knew his gut had been right. They both just told him to take a break and come back after he'd spoken to his brother-in-law.

Inigo went outside. Late January on Long Island wasn't exactly balmy, but he needed the brisk air to help clear his head. He was worried about Bianca, half in love with Marielle, unsure how to bridge the gap between the two women and what it would do to his driving this season if he didn't get it sorted out.

The easiest thing would be to break it off with Marielle, but he knew he couldn't do that. He no longer just saw the smiley, sexy persona she presented to the world. Instead he saw the woman beneath the surface. The woman who was struggling to get past her mistakes. He could sympathize with her.

Racing had always commanded all of his time and energy, so he hadn't had the misspent youth that his brother Mauricio or Marielle had, but without racing, would he have been any different from them?

His phone finally rang, and he almost dropped it when he went to answer it.

"Derek?"

"Yes, sorry to bother you when you are working, Inigo, but I need to talk to you," Derek said.

"Go for it."

"We saw the new pictures of you and that woman online, and they showed up in the *Houston Chronicle* as well. Bianca is shocked and upset by this, especially since she'd already talked to you about the earlier photos," Derek said.

"She's really pissed, isn't she?"

"Yes, she is, and I don't blame her. I know it's not my place to talk to you about who you're seeing, but is it possible to not do this now?" Derek asked. "Even as I hear myself saying this, I feel stupid. But you know your sister. She's freaking out, and that's not good for the baby or for her. And she's my world…"

He sighed. Maybe there was no choice but to stop kidding himself that he could be with Marielle. He had never wanted to hurt his sister, and there was the complication of being with a woman who made him feel the same burning excitement outside of the track that he did on it. It was hard to handle.

Betraying Marielle would put distance between them. It would definitely put an end to whatever was going on between them, and he wouldn't have to worry about how trying to have a relationship with Marielle would affect his racing season. But hurting her? Could he live with that? Then again, could he live with himself if he brought a woman that his sister couldn't endure into their family? He had started something in ignorance, never guessing that love would hurt like this.

"I know that. I promise you that this relationship isn't what you think it is. I'm not seeing her anymore. It was…doesn't matter. I'd never hurt Bianca like that and turns out neither would Mari." He couldn't really say that was the reason she'd broken things off with him but he was going to frame it that way.

There was silence on the phone. His heart ached even saying those words, but he knew he needed to do something.

"Inigo, I don't think that's what Bianca would want."

"What does she want?" he asked Derek.

"I'm not sure she knows herself," Derek said. "It would be easier if Jose were still around to talk to. I think what hurts her the most is she never got closure."

"I agree. Jose left behind a mess and we're all still dealing with the wreckage," he said.

"True. Will we see you before you leave for Melbourne?"

"Yes, I'm hoping to come home when Bianca gives birth and mix that with a training session that Moretti is sending me to Austin for," Inigo said.

He hung up a minute later and turned back to see Dante standing there. "So, how's things with your sister and Marielle?"

"Not good. The press keeps running the picture of that kiss even though we haven't seen each other in a while. Bianca is upset by it and I can't do more than walk away. Everything is a damn mess."

"Did you walk away?" Dante asked.

"Reluctantly," Inigo admitted. "Why?"

Dante shrugged. "I might have said something in the bar the other night about Jose and Mari and your sister."

"What do you mean might have?" he asked. This didn't sound good.

"I can't recall the entire night. I remember someone asking me about Mari and I know I said something about the stuff you told me when you were talking about revenge. Dude, I'm sorry. I hope I didn't screw up royally."

"Hell."

"I know."

"Listen, whatever happens, it's on me. I shouldn't have been talking to you about it," Inigo said. He owned his mistakes, unlike Jose who'd just run from them as fast as he could.

"You trusted me," Dante said. "I should have had your back."

He nodded and just turned away. "Want to talk about racing instead of women?"

"Yes. In fact, I think from now I'll stick to cars. I understand them much better than women."

Dante just patted him on the shoulder and led the way back into the building to talk about the setup for the car. Inigo spent the afternoon trying to concentrate on driving in the simulator, but his heart wasn't in it. He thought about the pain in Derek's voice and the hurt he might cause Marielle if he didn't figure it all out. He realized he'd looked at love like a child. He'd thought he could play around with a complex woman and walk away unscathed, never realizing that he could be hurt by this too.

He finished his laps, and his time was slightly improved, but not enough to make him or Keke happy. Marco was due back tomorrow, and everyone was on edge, wanting to see some major improvement from him.

He got in his car and drove not toward his house in the city but out toward the Hamptons. He needed an escape, but he knew that the road wouldn't take him away from the weight that was heavy on his shoulders.

He turned around at the first exit and headed back toward New York. The traffic was heavy, and by the time he parked his car in the garage under the building, he was irritated with himself and with Marielle. If she'd been willing to meet him part way, this wouldn't have happened.

He walked into the lobby and saw the paparazzi waiting. Some of them were stringers for online gossip websites like TMZ and E! They wanted a story, and were out for blood.

"Is it true that you are involved with Jose Ruiz's mistress?"

Inigo froze, staring at the man who'd asked the question. How had he known? Marielle had never been named in the press. Dante had said he had mentioned it at a bar when he was drunk…who had he been talking to?

"It's Marielle Bisset, right?" the reporter persisted.

"I can't—"

"Can't or won't? Your sister was his wife, right? How did you end up with the same woman? Does she just really dig drivers?"

"Stop with these questions. That's an insult to me and to her. She's not into drivers."

He walked past them toward the elevators.

"But she was Jose's mistress, wasn't she?"

Inigo clenched his jaw to keep from responding and just waited for the elevator doors to open. Once he got inside, he hit the number for his floor. When the doors closed, he punched the paneled wall. He didn't know what kind of story they were going to run. He should call Marielle and his sister and let them both know what was going on.

But at the same time, he didn't want to talk to either of them. He knew that no matter how he sliced it, he was responsible for this. He shouldn't have ever gone on a second date with Marielle. He should never have slept with her and started to care about her. He should have left her alone instead of falling in love with her.

And now he'd never have her. There was no way back from this kind of story.

But how had they found out about Jose? He hadn't told anyone… Was it Dante's slip of the tongue? He was the only one Inigo had told the whole story to. He knew it wasn't Bianca, Derek…or Marielle. It seemed a far stretch that Siobahn or Scarlet would have let the story out. The only other person who knew the details was Dante.

He punched in his lead engineer's number.

"Did you talk to the press?" he asked as soon as Dante answered.

"What are you talking about?" he asked.

"Marielle and Jose. Did you leak that?" he asked point-blank as he entered his apartment and threw his keys against the wall with enough force to leave a mark.

"I must have. I mentioned I was drunk and I know that's not an excuse. I'm so sorry. I never intended for any of this to happen."

"I get that. But I'm going to have to try to fix this… damn, my nephew doesn't know about his father. I know he's only four. But someday he's going to google his name, and this is going to come up. Bianca's going to have to read about it again and be humiliated. And Marielle, who had started to set herself up as a life-style influencer, is going to have to start over. How can I fix this?"

"I thought you and Mari were done."

"Hearing these questions and wanting to protect her has shown me that we're not," Inigo admitted, realizing that he'd been running from his feelings since that moment. He should have known there wasn't a fast enough speed to get away from this. He loved Marielle, and he wished there was some way he could fix this for her.

"Have you seen the news?" Marielle's assistant asked as he walked into her room at 5:00 a.m. He smelled of snow and aftershave, but his hair was standing on end as if he hadn't brushed it. She realized he'd probably doused himself with the scent on the way out of the door. He was usually so well groomed that it was surprising to see him so unkempt.

"What? No. It's an ungodly hour. What are you even doing here, PJ?"

"You need me," he said, sitting on the edge of bed

and fumbling around in the covers for the remote control. He pointed it at the TV, which was always tuned to E! "I would have brought you something to drink but, girl, I didn't want to stop on my way over. This is crazy."

Puzzled, Marielle turned her attention to the broadcast. "Breaking news this morning that upcoming social media influencer Living with Mari is actually Marielle Bisset," the entertainment news anchor reported breathlessly.

"That's not too bad. It was bound to come out at some time," she said. "It's not like it was going to take a lot of digging to find that out."

"Keep watching."

"Though her channel is one that promotes both good deeds and clean living, we have learned that she was the mistress of a married Formula One driver Jose Ruiz for the nine months that his wife, Bianca, was pregnant. Not sure how that meshes with her mission statement but given that she's a Bisset, not entirely surprising. Within social circles she is known for being a wild child and is rumored to be her father's favorite. I think we all remember that her birth followed his infamous affair nearly thirty years ago."

What the hell?

Marielle pulled the covers over her head. A sick feeling was developing in her stomach. This was stuff that shouldn't be coming out now. She rolled to her side, hugging her pillow to her stomach, and wished she was the type of woman who could cry. But she never had been. She couldn't even get too angry, because they hadn't reported anything that was untrue.

But how had they found out?

"Is my phone blowing up?"

"Yes," PJ said. "Want me to handle it today?"

"I don't know. I need to talk to my parents. I don't know how they'll want me to handle it," she admitted.

"Bisset's current beau, Formula One driver Inigo Velasquez, had no comment," the announcer was saying.

"Please turn that off."

PJ did as she asked and then handed over her phone. "It's your mom. Or do you want me to handle it?"

She took the phone from him. "Mom."

"Marielle," her mom said. "How are you?"

She almost cried then. Thank God her mom was always the first to go into crisis mode. "Freaking out. I thought that thing with Jose was buried. I have no idea how it got out. I'm sorry they led with me being a Bisset."

"That was their mistake. Carlton is on his way to your place, and I will be leaving the Hamptons shortly. We are going to come out swinging. Do you have any idea who could have leaked this?"

"No. I mean, there are only a handful of people alive who know about me and Jose," she said.

"The wife. Didn't you say you'd seen her recently?"

"I did," Marielle admitted. Bianca had been mad and hurt, but she had also been pregnant and had a four-year-old son to think about. For the life of her, she couldn't imagine Bianca leaking this to the press.

"Would she do this?" her mom asked.

"I don't think so," Marielle said. "Would you have done it? Years later, would you bring up the woman Dad did his thing with?"

"No. I hate her. I don't even want to hear her name mentioned," her mom said. "I don't want to rule out the wife, but we'll put her at the bottom of the list. What about the driver you were seeing?"

Inigo? "He's her brother. Surely he wouldn't do that."

"Would he have had a reason to?"

"I don't want to believe that he would, Mom. I mean, we stopped seeing each other to avoid hurting anyone else."

"Okay. But he's still on the list. Who do you know who might be jealous of your success? You have sort of gone big since Christmas," her mom said.

Marielle couldn't think of anyone. But just hearing her mom defending her and helping her to figure this out meant more to her than she could say. Her mom was still talking about influencers who'd tried to get invited to her event when Marielle started crying. It didn't matter who had leaked the negative information. For the first time in her life, she was being treated as a Bisset, not as a mistake or a consequence of her father's misdeeds. And she hadn't expected it to affect her as deeply as it was.

"Thank you, Mom."

"You're very welcome. I know we haven't always seen eye to eye, but for someone to come after you now is not right. I'm a very powerful woman, and when I find out who it was, they will be very sorry they messed with me. Now don't respond to anything until Carlton gets there. He's bringing a PR person who specializes in dealing with this kind of situation. Is your assistant there?"

"Yes, he is."

"Let him answer the door and go out and get whatever you need. Stay put until we get there. We'll take care of this," her mom said.

She hung up a moment later, and Marielle turned to PJ. "Mama is finally protecting her little cub," he quipped.

"She is. Who do you think would do this?"

She was trying to think of anyone who would want to harm her career, but this felt really mean-spirited— she hoped that it wasn't anyone she knew well. She wasn't too sure that she wanted someone in her life who would do that.

"I have no idea, but we will find out," PJ said.

Fifteen

Inigo didn't really look at his phone screen as he answered the video chat. He'd left a bunch of messages for Marielle wanting to explain and apologize to her, but she wasn't talking to him. In fact, her family PR man had texted him and told him to stop calling.

"What did you do?"

"Nothing. This wasn't me," Inigo said to Bianca, but his sister wasn't having any of it. She'd video called him, and he could tell she was visibly upset.

"There are reporters in Cole's Hill…that hasn't happened since Hunter got married. No one is happy about it and everyone—I mean everyone—is giving me looks like, *that poor girl*. I went from being someone everyone envied to someone they pitied overnight."

"I think you're exaggerating," Inigo said, noticing as the words left his mouth that Derek was moving his hand across his throat as if to tell Inigo to shut up. He realized that he'd said the wrong thing.

"You think I'm overreacting?"

"No," he said in a rush. "That's not what I meant. Listen, Bia, I didn't do this. Someone on my Moretti Motors team leaked it. Back on New Year's Day I thought that I would make things right by trying to get revenge for you. But once I got to know Marielle, I couldn't… That doesn't matter. She won't even take my calls. I've got Alec looking into it. He can find even the smallest trace of information on the internet. I'm sorry for all the trouble this is causing you and Marielle. For what it's worth, I know Jose lied to her too. She didn't know he was still married when she was seeing him."

Bianca's mouth got tight, and then she nodded. "You're right. It is a big mess. But we're going to make sure the person who caused this trouble will never meddle in my business again."

"You bet we are. But are you okay? How's things with the baby?"

"Fine. I'm fine. The baby is as stubborn as Derek and refusing to come out. They are going to induce on Friday," she said.

"I love you, Bianca. I'll be there on Friday if I'm still welcome. I'm truly sorry for all of this."

"Of course you are welcome, you're my baby brother. And it's not your fault, Inigo," she said. "And as much as I wanted to blame Marielle, it's not hers either. We are both still dealing with Jose's crap even though he's been dead for years. Of course, it's embarrassing to have the world know he cheated on me, but I have a good life with a man I love very much, and I'll get over it."

He smiled as Derek hugged his sister and then kissed

her. They had what he wanted. What he'd hoped to find with Marielle, he was realizing. He had made a million excuses for why she affected him so much. She was hot; it had been so long since he had sex; she got him because they weren't trying to impress each other. But the truth was he loved her. He'd probably fallen for her the minute she'd caught him staring at her while his dad shoved him toward her.

"How's Marielle handling this?" Bianca asked after a long pause.

"I don't know. She's not talking to me."

"Oh, Inigo," Bianca sighed. "Why? What happened?"

"I couldn't keep on seeing her… It doesn't matter," he said. There was no way that he was telling his sister he'd broken up with Marielle to keep from hurting Bianca.

"Was it me? Did you let her go because I demanded that you stop seeing her? I'm sorry. I know I was freaking out, but now all this mean-spirited gossip has reminded me how much better my life is now. And I bet Marielle's is different too. I remember that she was twenty-one when she was with Jose. I should have been mature about this."

"Thanks, Bia, that means the world to me. But the issue with Marielle is mine to fix. And you were a victim of Jose's lies and Marielle's gullibility."

"Well, fix it," Bianca said. "Do you love her?"

He just shook his head. "I don't know how to fix this."

"If you love her, you should go to her and tell her you're an ass and she was right—"

"Let me handle this," Derek said, taking the phone from Bianca.

"You think you know more than me?"

"No, but I'm a guy, and I know what it's like to have to woo back a stubborn woman," Derek said.

"Stubborn? *Moi?*"

"Yes. Now go," he said, kissing her and pushing her out of the room.

Inigo wasn't sure that Derek had any advice that would help him. He'd screwed up in his own special way. Derek was more mature, maybe even a little old to be dishing out advice to him.

"Dude, I appreciate it, but I got this."

Derek just laughed and shook his head. "You got this? Tell me what you plan to do."

"Figure out how to spin the leak, then take care of it," Inigo said. "Once everything dies down, then I'll text her and try to get back together."

"You're an idiot," Derek said.

"Hey."

"I know I'm not your brother except by marriage, but I meant that in the kindest way possible. You can't let any time pass, Inigo. Go to her. Tell her what's in your heart and make sure she understands you want her by your side."

He looked at Derek. Would that work? "What if she says forget it?"

"Then you take a few days and go back again. Mo knows what I'm talking about. Your older brother did this again and again with Hadley until she was ready to forgive him. I'll tell you something I have learned from your sister. The deeper the hurt, the more you need to make sure she knows how deeply you love her. If you can't do that, if you don't feel as if you can't breathe when you think of the rest of your life without her, then let her go."

Inigo nodded. He did feel like that. As if without her by his side the rest of his life would be the blur that the world was when he was driving three hundred miles per hour. "Thank you."

"No problem. If you need anything I'm here."

"Thanks, Derek. Keep me posted about the baby," he said, ending the call.

He needed a plan.

The beach was deserted in late January as Marielle and her mother walked along the shore. After her mom had fought her way through the lobby of her building filled with paparazzi, she'd decided they needed to be isolated on the family's twelve-acre home in the Hamptons. It had been three days since they had come back here. Marielle was still recovering, and also wallowing in the love and affection her mother was showering her with.

They'd left the house earlier, as Carlton and her father were having a meeting to determine what the best course of action was. In the past she'd have been tucked up in her room feeling scared and guilty, but not today. Marielle realized for the first time what it meant to be a Bisset and have her family behind her. She'd spent the majority of her life trying to shake off her name and her association with them. But letting Carlton take over the entire mess had been a blessing.

Siobahn had driven her out to her parents' house and stayed for two days before she had to get back to New York because she had another single coming out. Her brothers had all rallied around her, and her father was getting the Bisset legal team ready to ruin the life of whoever had leaked the information—something that

Marielle really couldn't get behind, because at the end of the day the gossip was true.

Her mom had been the biggest surprise. Ever since they'd come back out to the Hamptons, they'd spent long hours walking together on the beach. Her mother didn't talk much, she just held Marielle's hand and listened. That relationship—that bond—was something she'd never realized she'd missed until now.

On today's walk, her mom let her talk about Jose and the affair and urged her to try to figure out her feelings for Inigo. Then she just calmly said, "You were a girl who made foolish choices, but now you're a woman. Make wise choices. I had to face my part in your father's affair all those years ago. I'm not saying it was my fault he cheated. That's on him. But…this is the complicated part… I sort of liked it that he was gone and not in my business with the boys. He used to fight a lot with Leo, and I hated that."

"He's still so hard on Leo," Marielle agreed. "Why is that?"

"They are too alike. I don't know what was in Jose's head, and he's not here to explain it to us. My only advice to you is leave it in the past. It's out there, so it can't hurt you any longer. You have a career that will survive this," her mom said.

"Thanks, Mom," she said at last, hugging her mother.

"Now about Inigo…"

"What about him? His sister isn't ever going to forgive me," she said.

"Is that all that is keeping you apart?"

Was it? He had a busy life and schedule. He'd asked her to give him a chance at a relationship, but she'd never been good at them. She really was better in short doses. Inigo's sister made things complicated, but it was the thought of hurting Inigo that kept her from reaching out.

She might have fallen for him, but he saw her as a possible good-luck charm, someone who could help him win. What if she no longer could do that? What if…what if she wasn't enough?

"No," she admitted to her mom. "It's me. I'm not sure I'll ever be enough for him."

"Does he make you feel like you are less?" her mom asked. "I don't know him at all. I did ask around and heard some encouraging things, but that's never the same as knowing a man intimately. Out of the public eye, life is always different."

Marielle linked her arm through her mom's. "He's never made me feel less than. In fact if I'm being completely honest, he sort of makes me feel like it's okay to be the real me. You know what I mean?"

Her mom tipped her head to the side, studying her. "The real you?"

"Yes," Marielle said, realizing how true it was. "You know how I can sometimes do things without thinking them through…well, Inigo just goes with it."

She stopped walking, as it dawned on her that she'd said no to being in a relationship with him not because she was unsure of him but because she was unsure of herself. She couldn't trust that he could really like her. And she knew a lot of that stemmed from not liking the woman she'd been. But since New Year's—since the night they'd first been together—she'd been changing. Some of it had started before all that, when she'd stopped pretending to have a good life and started sharing more honest posts on her social media channel.

Inigo had seen the real her.

And he liked her.

"Good. That's what I like to hear. I'm not supposed to tell you this, but he's called every day since the story broke, and he wants to see you," her mom said.

"Why aren't you supposed to tell me?"

"Carlton said it would be better if we had no contact with Jose's wife's family," her mom said. "Your father agreed, but I wanted to talk to you first. I'm not saying he won't back you—you know your father would give you the moon—just that he wasn't sure if this Inigo was worthy of you. And frankly, neither was I."

Worthy of her?

She couldn't help the tears that burned her eyes and blinked to keep them from falling. For the first time in a really long time, maybe ever, she felt her parents' love. She wasn't that consolation baby anymore. She wasn't the daughter they didn't want but had needed to move away from scandal. And it meant more to her than she'd thought it would.

Her mom hugged her close and then wiped her own eyes. "I'm sorry it's taken us so long to have this conversation."

"Me too," Marielle admitted.

Inigo hadn't liked going to his brothers for advice, but that's how it had worked out in the end. He'd had no choice. He'd flown to Cole's Hill to be there for the birth of his niece, Aurora, and ended up having a family discussion on how he could win back Marielle. Derek's brothers were there as well, so he'd gotten way more advice than he could use. His brother Mauricio and Nate

Caruthers had both agreed he needed to get Marielle naked and in bed as soon as he could.

"Remind her how good you two are together—unless you aren't? Is that the problem?" Mauricio had asked.

Which had led to some good-natured fighting.

Derek and his brother Alec had both reminded him to be honest and speak from the heart. Ethan had joked that at least they knew no one was coming back from the dead, which Inigo had to be honest was a complete relief. Ethan's wife's former fiancé had been presumed dead after a plane crash but then it turned out he'd survived. His return had forced Ethan to admit he loved Crisanne and wanted her for himself not just to console her because of what she'd lost.

Finally it had been Diego on the private plane from Cole's Hill back to New York who had offered him the best advice. "Take her back to the beginning. Show her how much you love her and what it means to you that you met her. It's not easy being vulnerable to a woman, but if she knows she's your heart…it makes everything easier."

So here he was in the O'Malley mansion with only their house staff, waiting and hoping that Marielle would accept Scarlet's invitation to an imaginary party. Scarlet had agreed to set Marielle up.

He had asked the staff to direct her to the large ballroom that overlooked the ocean where he'd first seen her. He waited for what felt like hours before he heard the peal of the doorbell, which he hummed along to, realizing it was the O'Malley Beer jingle. Then he stood there tensely waiting. He heard the sound of heels on the marble in the entryway. He hadn't realized he was holding his breath until she stopped in the doorway of the ballroom and he exhaled in a rush.

Her long, silvery-blond hair hung around her shoulders. She'd pushed her sunglasses up on top of her head, which held her hair back from her heart-shaped face. Her lips were full, tempting, reminding him of how long it had been since he kissed her. Her silvery-gray eyes watched him warily, and he reminded himself getting her here had only been step one.

"Seems like someone lied to me about the party," Marielle said. She stayed in the doorway watching him.

"I asked her to do this," Inigo said.

She stood there for a few more moments while he just tried to figure out what to say. How could he make things right? He realized all of the advice that everyone had given him wasn't helping. He didn't want to screw this up but was very afraid he would.

"Why am I here, Inigo?" she asked.

"Firstly, it's my fault that everything came out about you and Jose. I want to apologize for that," he said.

"You leaked it?"

"No. But I had mentioned it to someone on my team and he spilled it—accidentally but still…"

"Not Keke?"

"No, never. Elena really likes you, and so does Keke. He would never hurt anyone," Inigo said.

"Good. I liked them too," Marielle said. "Thanks for clearing that up. You could have left a message with that information."

"I could have. But Carlton told me to stop calling and texting," Inigo said. "And I'm not going to. I didn't invite you here today for that. I just wanted to clear it up before I told you…well, what I want to tell you."

He felt really hot. Like his entire neck and torso were covered in sweat, and she still just stood there watching him.

"I'm listening."

Oh, God. Could he do this? Tell her he loved her? But he knew he had to. He couldn't keep moving through life at Mach 1 and hoping that when he finally slowed down he'd have someone waiting for him.

He had rehearsed some romantic-sounding things but now standing here, drenched in his own sweat, they were gone.

"I love you."

God. He'd blurted it out, just sort of yelled it across the room.

"What?"

"I'm messing this up," he said, tugging at the collar of his shirt and crossing the room to her. He stopped when he was a few feet away, because he caught a whiff of her perfume and it made him remember how her entire body felt in his arms.

"I love you, Marielle. I wanted you to come back here because this is where I started falling for you that very first night when you crooked your finger at me."

"You did?" she asked, arching one eyebrow at him. "Your dad had to shove you toward me."

"Only because I knew that once I went to you, you would be forever in my heart. It took me a long time to realize that, but it's the truth. I love you."

She gave him a sort of sad smile. "But unless I'm wrong Bianca isn't going to be too thrilled to have me in your life and I don't blame her."

"She's—"

"No, we can't ignore her feelings on this, Inigo," she

said. "My mom told me she still hates the woman my father had the affair with all those years ago, and Mom never has to see her. How would it be fair to Bianca for me to be in her life?"

"I was afraid you would feel that way," he admitted. "You have such a good heart. Bianca wanted to come with me today, but she's just given birth and travel is out of the question," Inigo said. "But she sent this video message for you."

Marielle blinked at him, then shook her head. "What?"

"Just watch the message and then we can talk," he said, handing her his phone.

She looked at him, hesitating a moment, before pressing the screen to start the video.

"Marielle, I'm sorry I couldn't be there to talk to you in person," Bianca said in the video. "While your affair with Jose was a shock to my system and something that was devastating when it happened, I've moved on to a rich life surrounded by a family that I love. If I know anything about Inigo he wouldn't have continued to see you if there wasn't something special in you. I'm not saying you and I are going to be besties starting tomorrow but I would like to get to know you better. I forgive you."

The message ended and Marielle let her hand holding the phone fall to her side. There were tears in her eyes as she looked back over at him.

"Thank you for this," she said.

"You're welcome. I love you, Marielle, and there is nothing I won't do to get you into my life. That is, if you want me."

She crooked her finger at him.

He closed the distance between them, stopping when

they were only a few inches apart. He was waiting but his heart was full of hope.

"I love you too, Speedy," Marielle said.

He lifted her into his arms and kissed her. It didn't matter when they both knew it, just that they had admitted their feelings for each other.

"I know it won't be easy, but I want… I want us to spend the rest of our lives together. We can figure it out as we go along," he said.

"I like that idea," she said.

Epilogue

One year later

The past year of Inigo's life had gone by at a fast pace. He'd won several races during the Formula One season and had finished in the top five. Keke and Marco were both overjoyed with that result and were looking at ways to improve for the coming season, but everyone agreed he was on the right track. Everyone had said that his happiness off the track had brought him the results he'd never been able to achieve by himself.

Dante had left the Moretti Motors team and gone to work in MotoGP. After revealing that he'd been drinking the night of the leak with Curtis Hemlin, another engineer on the team, an investigation had been launched. It turned out, Curtis had been the one leaking Inigo's times to the bookies. Curtis had been fired and was under criminal investigation. Malcolm's undercover gambling had helped them get the proof they needed that Curtis was the saboteur. Dante had offered heartfelt apologies to both Marielle and Bianca, and Inigo was glad the other man had found a fresh start.

Malcolm and Helena had been married in the fall; practically the entire town of Cole's Hill had been there. Malcolm had written his own vows and made Helena and all the women in attendance swoon at his promises to be his own man and try to avoid temptation. Malcolm really seemed to be a new man after all he'd been through.

Most surprising of all, his sister and Marielle were becoming friends. Once the ugliness of Jose's behavior was out in the open, the two women were both able to move past it. Which was more than Inigo could have hoped for.

Now he couldn't help watching Marielle across the room at Scarlet's New Year's Eve party. The last year had been a busy one for her as well. She'd been honest about her affair with Jose, and that had won her more followers because she'd told the truth. She'd taken on more brand work, and Inigo was in awe of how she managed everything.

He noticed her height, as always, but also the way her hair hung down her back. The dress she wore was one of those shimmery shift dresses she favored, leaving the majority of her back bare. Inigo had taken advantage of that all evening, loving the feel of his hand on her bare skin.

The edges of her tattoo were visible. She'd had a tiny race car added underneath the poison apple. She no longer thought of herself as a sinner, she'd told him, now that they were living together in their truth.

Tonight he hoped to ask her to be his wife. The last year had tested them, and they'd found their own way of living together while he traveled around the world and trained and she worked. He was already talking to Keke. In a few years, after he'd won a championship, he hoped to retire from driving and move up into management at Moretti Motors.

"Sweetie," his mom said, coming over to him and handing him a glass of champagne. "I had hoped I wouldn't have to tell you this, but it's time to ask Marielle to marry you."

"Mom."

"I thought you'd do it last year when you were both home for Thanksgiving," she added.

"You can't be in charge of this," he said to her.

"In charge of what, son? You know your mom only has your best interests at heart," his father said as he came over, putting his hand on his shoulder and squeezing.

"I do," his mom said. "You need to put a ring on Marielle's finger. She's not the kind of woman who will wait forever."

"Listen to her, son," his father said.

"I love you both, but I will do this when I'm ready," he said, hugging them. He walked away, a bit irked that they were pressing him on the very night when he intended to propose.

He'd had the ring for three months now, an exquisite bespoke piece that his sister-in-law Pippa had designed for him and had made at House of Hamilton, the royal

London jewelers. He'd been waiting for the right moment and knew that it was tonight.

Marielle glanced over at him and waggled her eyebrows, then she crooked her finger at him, beckoning him toward her. He moved slowly across the room, and then when he was a few feet from her, he went down on one knee.

She just stared at him.

"Are you doing this?"

"I am," he said. "Marielle, you own me heart and soul, and I can't imagine my life without you by my side. Would you please do me the honor of marrying me?"

The music had stopped, and everyone had turned to stare at them, but he had eyes only for her. She was the only one here who mattered at this moment, and she knew it.

She nodded. "Yes!"

He got to his feet, took out the ring and put it on her finger. He lifted her into his arms and whispered against her lips, "I love you."

She put her hands on either side of his head and kissed him back long and deep. "I love you too."

Applause broke out, and their families all came over to congratulate them. Inigo's life had always seemed better as he'd raced through it, not letting anything touch him. But he knew that it had been empty without this woman he loved by his side.

* * * * *

TWIN SCANDALS

FIONA BRAND

To God, who 'so loved the world, that he gave his only begotten Son, that whosoever believeth in him should not perish, but have everlasting life.'
—*John* 3:16

Many thanks once again to
Stacy Boyd and Charles Griemsman.

One

Ben Sabin tossed the keys of his Jeep Cherokee to the parking attendant standing outside the sleek new Messena resort in Miami Beach. After picking up the guest key card that had been left for him at the concierge desk, he strode through the foyer, past the entrance to a large reception room where groups of elegant guests were sipping champagne and eating canapés. He was almost clear when a well-known gossip columnist made a beeline for him.

"Ben Sabin." Sally Parker couldn't hide her glee as she positioned her cell to video him. "Did you know the Messena twins are here? Although how could you not, since they've been resident in Miami for the last three months."

Ben's jaw tightened. Even though he'd known all of that information well in advance, his response was sharp and visceral, which didn't please him. He should have been over his fatal attraction to spoiled heiress Sophie Messena by now.

And it wasn't as if he didn't know what the likely outcome of a liaison with a woman like Sophie would be. At age nine he'd a had front-row seat to the breakdown of his parents' marriage, which had literally petered out when his father's Texan oil wells had dried up. He could still hear his father bitterly commenting on how failing to find more oil had cost him his marriage. All Ben had been able to think as he'd watched the rooster tail of dust kicked up by Darcy Sabin's departing car was that he had lost his mother.

Then six years ago he'd found himself in his father's predicament when his beautiful, wealthy fiancée had left him within twenty-four hours of a financial crash that had almost bankrupted him.

Years of hard work and calculated risk later, and after an inheritance that had made him an overnight billionaire, suddenly he was back. At least as far as Sophie Messena was concerned.

Sophie Messena. Tall, lithe and athletic, with the kind of slow, fluid walk that would have turned heads even if she hadn't been gorgeous.

Caught once more in the crosshairs of a woman who seemed more interested in his share portfolio than in who he really was, for Ben, the decision to walk away from the one night they had spent together had been a matter of self-preservation.

But the press had seen things somewhat differently, courtesy of a neat publicity stunt Sophie had pulled a few days later, which had made it look like *she* had dumped him.

Irritatingly, Sally Parker was still keeping pace with

him. His flat "no comment," as he strode toward a bank of elevators, seemed to fall on deaf ears.

"It's not the twins, plural, that you're interested in, though, is it? I hear that you and Sophie Messena were once a hot item, despite the fact that yesterday you were heard to say…now let me get this right." She frowned and smiled at the same time, as if she was having trouble remembering the headline she'd splashed across multiple social media accounts just hours ago. "Hmm… that the twins are 'empty-headed and spoiled and that any man would have to be brain-dead to date either of them.'"

Ben came to a halt. Keeping a tight leash on his patience—a patience that had been forged by time in Special Forces, then honed by years spent in the hard-edged construction industry—he stabbed the call button for the high-speed private elevator that led directly to Nick Messena's penthouse office. His gaze rested on the flashing numbers above the sleek stainless-steel door that indicated the elevator was on its way.

He had not said those words.

If he had, it would mean that a year ago *he* had been brain-dead and that he still was because, despite walking away from Sophie, nothing had changed: he still wanted her.

He hadn't said the words, but he had a fair idea who had. The brief conversation he'd had on the way to the airport with his new, brilliant but opinionated business manager, Hannah Cole, was the only possible source of the comment. Clearly it had not been a private conversation.

The gossip columnist, oblivious to the fact that she was being ignored, leaned on the wall. A cat-that-got-the-cream smile played around her mouth. "Strange then, to use a euphemism, that you *did* 'date' Sophie Messena. Now, a year after she ditched you, you're involved in a business deal with her brother, Nick, and gorgeous Sophie is also in town. So, what's really going on, Ben? Seems to me you just can't stay away."

The doors finally slid open. His expression remote, Ben stepped into the elevator, swiped the key card and punched the button for Nick's office. Seconds later, he was propelled several stories up to the penthouse. As he stepped into the hushed foyer, Hannah, who had once worked as a PA for his late uncle Wallace, and whom Ben had inherited along with Wallace's multibillion-dollar construction and real estate business, stepped forward and checked her watch. "You're *almost* late."

Ben lifted a brow. Hannah was middle-aged, plump, wealthy in her own right and possessed of a dry, no-nonsense sense of humor. Sometimes he wondered if he had made a mistake in employing someone who didn't need the job and knew just a little too much about him and his checkered family history. But after years of dealing with the tensions of younger, ambitious managers, Hannah's bluntness worked for Ben. "I ran into some interference."

"Let me guess," Hannah grumbled as she moved in the direction of Nick's office, "the Messena girl?"

Ben pushed back the cuff of his jacket and checked his watch. "The one I'd have to be brain-dead to date?"

Hannah gave him what passed for an apologetic glance, although it was so brief he almost missed it. "Sorry about that. I should have waited until we were out of the taxi before I made that comment."

Because the taxi driver had clearly taken the quote straight to the press, no doubt for a healthy cash payment.

"You shouldn't have said it, period. I haven't seen Sophie for a year."

Though the very last time he had seen her was still indelibly imprinted on his mind. Her ridiculously long lashes curled against delicately molded cheekbones. Dark hair trailing down the sleek, elegant curve of her naked back. The one slim arm flung across his pillow as she slept.

Sophie Messena had in no way looked like the A-list party girl she was purported to be, and that was what had fooled him. There was a cool directness to her glance, a clear intelligence and a habit of command that should have annoyed him but which he had found more than a little fascinating...

Hannah stopped and pinned him with her brown gaze. "You want my opinion? You should have picked another time to sign this contract. One when Sophie wasn't around. The fact that you chose a time when she *would* be around says something. You're supposed to be getting into bed with The Messena Group, not Sophie Messena."

Ben repressed the urge to pinch his nose. He remembered a time, pre–Sophie Messena, when the conversations he'd had with business colleagues were about managing risk, contractual obligations, closing out deals and headhunting the right people. Now everyone seemed to have an opinion about his dysfunctional love life. "There's a new deal to be signed, and this resort is the last project I managed for Nick before I left Messena Construction. I need to be here."

Hannah made a rude sound. "And that's another thing. If you get tangled up with Sophie Messena again, Nick is going to react. Big-time. You can kiss any future deals goodbye."

She trundled past the receptionist's desk and started toward an open door at the end of a broad corridor. As Ben strolled toward Nick's office, he noted the lineup of Medinian oil paintings that decorated light-washed walls. The paintings, all from the Mediterranean island of Medinos, were old, priceless and very familiar, because Ben had seen them on a daily basis when they had adorned the office of Nick's Dolphin Bay Resort in New Zealand.

Despite the Messena family leaving Medinos and most of them settling in New Zealand, their connection to Medinos was still strong. The abiding theme of battle-scarred warrior ancestors was hard to miss, the message clear: don't mess with Nick Messena *or his baby sisters.*

Hannah was right, he thought grimly. Nick had overlooked his sleeping with Sophie a year ago because, like everyone else, he thought Sophie had ditched him, *and* that it was over. Ben was pretty sure Nick had actually felt sorry for him. But if Ben got involved with Sophie again, the gloves would be off. He would have to either cut ties with The Messena Group or marry Sophie Messena.

Given that it would be a cold day in hell before he would make his father's mistake—a mistake that had led to suicide—and marry a woman as calculating and career-obsessed as Sophie Messena, he would be crazy to take the risk.

Ben stepped into Nick's swanky office and lifted a hand to Nick and John Atraeus, who was some kind of a distant relative and, now, Nick's new business partner. As he joined them out on the terrace, he took in the tropical heat, the balmy air and impressive view of Miami as it flowed around the coastline, glittering softly in the night. Broodingly, he conceded that he *could* have picked another time to meet. Like tomorrow morning, for example, when John and Nick, who were both here for the launch party, would still be around.

But the truth was that, a year on, he was no nearer to forgetting about Sophie than he had been when he had walked out of his hotel suite in Dolphin Bay, leaving her asleep in his bed.

He still wanted her, and the frustration and restless dissatisfaction that had followed that one night had somehow managed to nix his love life completely.

Just to admit that annoyed Ben. It meant he was still affected by the kind of obsessive, addictive desire he had decided would never rule him again.

The problem was, he had tried abstinence. That hadn't worked, so he had tried dating, specifically women who did not look Sophie. That hadn't worked, either, because none of the pretty blondes he had dated had truly interested him.

Which left one other strategy to get Sophie out of his system. A crazy, risk-taking option that was the military equivalent of picking up an unstable, unexploded bomb.

Getting gorgeous, fascinating Sophie Messena, back in his bed...just one more time.

Hell would freeze over before Sophie would allow Ben Sabin close to her again.

Sophie Messena took the elevator of her brother's newest resort down to the ground floor. The only reason she was here tonight was for the express purpose of confronting Ben for his horrible behavior in sleeping with her a year ago, then ditching her without so much as a word.

Sophie tensed at the thought of seeing Ben again.

He was six feet two inches of broad, sleek, muscular male, his dark hair cut short, his jaw tough, with the kind of cool blue gaze that regularly made women go weak at the knees.

But not her. Not anymore.

Tonight she was determined to exorcise the last dregs of the fatal attraction to Ben that had dominated her life for two-and-a-half years. Finally she would be able to move on.

It would be over.

Forcing herself to relax, she exited the elevator and strolled into the foyer with barely a hitch to her stride and with a smoothness it had taken weeks of physiotherapy and repetitive exercises to achieve. A faint stiffness was still discernible in her lower back, courtesy of the dislocation injury she had sustained when her SUV swerved off one of Dolphin Bay's narrow country roads eleven months ago.

That was three weeks after Ben had left her bed following their one tumultuous night together. She had thrown away his brief note thanking her for a "nice" time.

Nice.

As if leading up to that night, there hadn't been eighteen months of a sultry, electrifying attraction that had made it difficult for her to think about anyone but Ben Sabin. Not to mention the frustrating encounters that had fizzled into nothing, before she had finally made the desperate decision, on Ben's last night in Dolphin Bay, to go out on a limb and seduce him.

She stopped opposite the reception desk near an alcove decorated with palms at which she had arranged to meet her date for the night. She checked her watch.

He was late, which was annoying because it was imperative that she not be seen alone tonight.

For an unsettling moment, she had trouble remembering her date's name. It wasn't until she spotted him walking toward her that it came back to her. Since she had met Tobias, a broker who worked for her banker brother, Gabriel, only a couple of times, and both of those times only in passing, when he had been out on a date with her twin, Francesca, maybe that wasn't surprising.

As she greeted Tobias, the knowledge that she was just minutes away from seeing Ben, made her jaw tighten.

One year ago Ben had walked out on her. Three weeks after that she'd had the accident. Her body had recovered physically. Now, tonight, she would test the mental and emotional healing she hoped she'd achieved after untold hours of very expensive therapy. If the assurances her therapist had given her were anything to go by, she should now be completely immune to him.

Frowning, Sophie scanned the room—which was thronged with a glittering array of guests, local business people and, of course, media. Her stomach tightened ever so slightly when she caught the back of a dark head. By the time the man turned, she had already dismissed him; he was tall enough to be Ben, but his hair wasn't cut short and crisp, and his shoulders were too narrow. Not broad and sleek and muscular from the time Ben had spent in the military, followed by years of hands-on construction work and long hours working out in his private gym.

She took a deep breath and tried to relax, but in the instant she had thought the man was Ben, her heart had raced out of control and adrenaline had shot through her veins. Now, instead of being relaxed and cool as a cucumber, as she had planned, she was terminally on edge.

"Do you want to, uh, dance?"

Sophie remembered her date for the evening, Tobias. Now an ex-boyfriend of Francesca's, he was tall, dark, muscled and handsome. He looked super hot but, unfortunately, Sophie couldn't seem to drum up anything beyond polite interest for him. With any luck, when Ben showed up, he would see her with Tobias and jump to the conclusion that the few passionate hours Sophie had shared with Ben were ancient history and that she was now very occupied with her latest guy.

"Maybe we can dance later." She sent Tobias an encouraging smile. When Ben arrived it would definitely be good to be seen on the dance floor with Tobias, preferably slow dancing to something romantic.

Linking her arm through Tobias's to make sure they were seen as a couple, she steered him in the direction of the bar, asked for a glass of sparkling water and took a sip. Anything to distract her from the attack of nerves that had come out of nowhere. Nerves she shouldn't be feeling because she was *over* Ben.

"Drowning your sorrows?"

Sophie almost choked on a swallow of water as Francesca waved at Tobias, who had stepped away to speak to an elderly couple. For a split second, Sophie had had trouble recognizing her own twin. "You've dyed your hair blond."

Francesca signaled to the barman that she would like a glass of champagne. "Britney Blonde Bombshell. Do you like it?"

Sophie studied the silvery blond color, which was struck through with honey streaks and darker lowlights.

On a purely aesthetic level, she could appreciate that the beach-babe effect was gorgeous, but dying her hair blond held no appeal for her. To put it bluntly, she wouldn't be seen dead with blond hair, probably because every time she saw a picture of Ben on social media, he had a blonde clinging to his arm. "It's...different."

Francesca shrugged. Though identical in appearance with Sophie, she was the polar opposite in terms of personality. "You know me, I like change."

She sipped her champagne. Her gaze restlessly skimmed the packed dance floor as if she was looking for someone. "Right now I feel like I need to be a little more...definite in my personality. More like you. I love your dress, by the way. You always look so cool and in control in white."

Francesca glanced down at her own red silk wraparound dress with its starburst pattern at her midriff. She frowned. "Maybe I should try wearing white."

Sophie set her drink down with a clink. "You don't wear white."

White was Sophie's designated color. It was a twin thing. From around the age of six, when their brains had finally developed enough that they realized the adults were dressing them like robot clones, all in the name of twin cuteness, they had rebelled. There hadn't been a discussion, just a moment of shared outrage, then, somewhere in the midst of the weird, developing alchemy of being twins, a tacit understanding that they needed to dress differently. Sophie had chosen whites and neutrals; at a stretch she would wear pastels or dark blue. Francesca had gone straight for the hot, wild colors. They had maintained discipline for years with the result that no one ever confused them, although Francesca, with her bolder look, had had to get used to the evil twin jokes.

Francesca's chin firmed. "I'd wear white if I got married."

"Married?" Sophie frowned. "Lately, you're not even dating."

And she realized that, in itself, was strange. Francesca, who was a free spirit in contrast to Sophie's ultra-ordered, perfectionist, control-freak existence, usually had a man in tow. None of them ever lasted very long unless she chose to keep them as friends, as she had with Tobias. Since Francesca was softhearted, endlessly forgiving and hated hurting anyone, she had a very long list of male friends. The difference in their personalities was also the reason that Sophie was the CEO of her own fashion retail company, while Francesca preferred to operate as head fashion designer for their own brand. "What's going on? Have you met someone?"

Francesca ran a fingertip around the rim of her champagne flute. "I'm not sure. Maybe. I've got…you know, one of my *feelings*."

Now Sophie was worried. Francesca, aside from being outgoing and too compassionate for her own good, was strongly intuitive. Sophie had learned, along with the rest of the family, to pay attention to Francesca's "feelings" even though she didn't understand where, exactly, they came from.

A case in point had been when their father had been killed in a car accident years ago. It had been Francesca who had woken their mother up and raised the alarm, insisting there was something wrong. An hour later the wrecked vehicle had been found. It had been too late to save their father, but from that day on they had all paid attention to Francesca's premonitions.

Francesca took another sip of champagne and stepped away from the bar, her attention once again focused on the colorful, shifting crowd. "I just feel that tonight I could meet that special someone."

She smiled, although the smile seemed over-bright and a little taut, as she deposited the half-empty flute back on the bar. "Fingers crossed. So far Miami has been a complete washout where men are concerned." She grinned at Tobias, who was now leaning against the bar, arms crossed over his chest, a rueful expression on his face. "Except for Tobias! Mind if I borrow your date for this dance?"

"Be my guest," Sophie muttered, her concern for her twin evaporating as she spotted a tall broad-shouldered figure in the crowd. A sharp tingle shot down her spine. He turned, and her attention was riveted by the strong, faintly battered masculine profile, courtesy of the fact that his nose had once been broken, and a rock-solid jaw. It was Ben.

His gaze locked with hers for a searing instant. Her heart sped up, making her feel suddenly breathless, and, out of nowhere, an irresistible thought surfaced. Maybe, the business he was conducting with her brother aside, Ben was here for *her*. Maybe, after a year of separation, he had finally realized that what they had shared had been special.

Dimly she recognized that this was not the reaction she should have after months of therapy designed to reposition her thinking. She was supposed to be focused on choosing the best for herself, not setting herself up for disappointment again.

All of that was swept away in the sudden realization that Ben was not alone.

Sophie stiffened. Somehow, she hadn't expected him

to be with someone. She had thought that, because her life had ground to a halt while she'd processed the hurt of rejection, he would also be affected in some significant way. That he might even be missing her, or regretting leaving her without a word, without even a phone call—

Her jaw tightened. Of course, that presupposed that Ben had a heart.

Her gaze settled on the woman who was pulling him onto the dance floor. She looked young, barely out of her teens, with tawny blond hair piled in a messy knot, a short turquoise silk dress skimming her curves, a tattoo on one slim shoulder and outrageously high heels.

Sophie's breath came in sharply. She was only twenty-seven, but looking at the young, vibrant thing in Ben's arms, she suddenly felt as old as Methuselah and, with her simple white designer dress and low, strappy shoes, just a bit…boring.

However, if she was "old," then Ben, who was thirty, was ancient and practically cradle snatching.

Though Sophie knew she should drag her gaze away, seeing Ben with the gorgeous blonde made the shock that he had found someone else burn deeper. Even worse, it successfully cheapened the one night they had shared. A night that, for Sophie, had been singularly intense and passionate and seemed to signal the beginning of the kind of deep, meaningful relationship she had thought she might never experience until Ben had strode into her life.

Blindly she turned back to the bar. She was aware of the barman asking her a question. Champagne? Drawing a breath that felt impeded because her throat seemed to have closed up, she dredged up a brilliant smile. "Yes."

Her fingers closed on the chilled flute. The first sip helped relax her throat, the second made it possible to feel almost normal. Probably because she was focused on something other than the fact that Ben was not the honorable man and exciting dream lover—the dependable, prospective husband—she had foolishly imagined him to be. Instead, he was as shallow as a puddle and a rat to boot. He had utterly betrayed her trust, and the whole situation was made worse by the fact that she had naively given herself to him.

Not that he had noticed that she had been a virgin the night they had made love. That tiny fact had seemed to bypass him completely.

When she had realized he had no clue, she'd felt an odd moment of disconnect, which she should have realized was a *sign*. Then the warmth of the night and the heady excitement of lying in Ben's arms had kicked in, and she had dismissed the impulse to tell him. She'd had too many years of warily skirting relationships to let her guard down so easily, and Ben had a formidable reputation with women.

Now she was glad she hadn't told him the truth, because clearly Ben lacked even the most basic insight into the female psyche. Her virginity was not something she had bestowed lightly. It had been a gift of trust that she had not wanted to see trampled. Sophie had decided that, until they had established an actual relationship, telling Ben that she had been so picky that she had waited making love *until him*, had seemed too acutely revealing. It would have put her at a disadvantage, and given him entirely too much power.

Finally, she had so *not* saved herself for him. Sleeping with Ben had just…happened.

She took another sip and checked how much champagne was left in her glass. She hadn't had that much, maybe a third, but she was already feeling the effects. Not a happy buzz exactly, but the tightness in her stomach had gone and she was definitely starting to feel more kick-ass and in control.

However, the champagne also seemed to be having another effect. Without the normal careful editing of her emotions, the memories were flooding back, bigger, brighter and more hurtful than ever, which was… disappointing. She had gone to a great deal of effort to bury them beneath long work hours and an extremely busy dating life with men who did not remind her of Ben. She took another sip.

Sophie glanced back at the dance floor, which was a mistake, because once she fixed on Ben she couldn't look away. Now that the initial shock of seeing him with another woman had passed, a weird jagged emotion hit her square in the chest, making it hard to think, making it hard to *breathe*.

She knew Ben had been dating up a storm; that he had been running through women like a hot knife through butter, because one of the gorgeous blondes he had dated and who was now obviously obsessed with him kept posting photos of them together on a popular social media account. Whenever Sophie needed to remind herself just how big a rat Ben was, all she needed to do was check Buffy Holt's feed.

But this was the first time she had seen him with a new lover in the flesh.

Another punch of raw emotion caught her, the fierceness of it making her go hot, then cold, then hot again. Her jaw clenched at the horrifying realization that she was jealous.

Her fingers tightened on the champagne flute. She

didn't think she had ever been jealous before. However, she had heard enough about the emotion to understand that the taut, burning anger and explosive desire to do something off-the-wall, like confront Ben and wrench the pretty blonde from his arms, were classic symptoms.

With careful control, she set the flute down on the bar, deciding that it wasn't helpful to have any more alcohol. The few sips she'd swallowed had already flipped the lid on a Pandora's box of thoughts and emotions.

Jealousy.

She needed to hit her head against the nearest wall because that meant that somehow, despite every effort, Ben was still important to her. Reaching for calm, she picked up her half-drunk glass of sparkling water and threaded her way to the dance floor. The pretty blonde was now nowhere to be seen, and Ben was standing alone on the edge of the dance floor.

He half turned as she approached, a sleek cell phone held to one ear. Dimly she noted that the call was probably the reason he had ditched his date. Because with Ben, business *always* came first.

His dark blue gaze connected with hers. His lack of surprise at seeing her informed her that he had known she would be here and he had come to the party, anyway, *with another woman*. She suddenly knew what the phrase "a woman scorned" meant, because that described exactly how she felt.

"Sophie." He lifted the phone from his ear. "It's good to see you—"

A sudden image of the brief note he'd left her after their one night together made her see red. "Don't you mean *nice*?"

She'd had time to think as she approached him. She didn't fling the water because chances were, she was so angry most of it would miss him. Instead, she stepped close and upended the glass over his head. Satisfyingly, water also cascaded over his phone, with any luck killing it.

"Just so you know," she said crisply, "I'm not a glass half-empty kind of girl."

Two

Sophie registered the stunned silence punctuated by the motorized click and whir of a high-speed camera, and the flash of multiple cell phone cameras. All documenting the fact that she, a person who hated scenes, had just made a very public, very messy scene *with the man she had slept with—and who she was supposed to have dumped—a year ago.*

Face burning, feeling quietly horrified, she turned on her heel, walked back to the bar and returned the empty glass to the barman. She managed a cool smile, then made a quick exit out onto the terrace, which led down to a gleaming pool and beautiful gardens. Behind her, she was aware of the hubbub of noise as waiters scurried to clean up the water on the floor so that no one would slip. She was going to have to apologize to them, and to Nick, who would go crazy because she'd made a scene at his launch party.

She reached the secluded far end of the terrace, which was shaded with large, lush potted palms. Gripping the railing, she stared down at the glowing turquoise pool. The sound on Ocean Drive registered. The screech of tires, as if someone had just braked, followed by the long blast of a horn spun her back just over eleven months, to the accident and her last encounter with Ben.

Not that she had been thinking about him when her SUV had skidded on the loose piece of metal on a country road, then rolled down a gully choked with vegetation and trees. She had been focused on a future that did *not* contain him.

Happily, the airbags had deployed and the safety belt had done its job, but the two full revolutions down the shallow bank had battered her SUV. Worse yet, the seat belt had repeatedly cut into her torso and stomach, leaving a deep bruise and placing an extra load on her spine at vertebrae T11 and T12.

When the SUV had stopped, it was miraculously right side up. After the airbags had deflated, she found herself enclosed by dense brush and staring at the gnarled branches of a tree, which meant she was invisible from the road.

Her handbag, gym gear and bottle of water, all of which had been in the back seat, were now strewn around her in the front of the car. Her nose was stinging from the water bottle hitting her face while the car had been doing its tumbling act.

Not a problem. But the instant she reached for her handbag, a sharp pain in her right wrist and one in her lower back made her freeze in place. A quick inspection of her wrist suggested it had probably taken a hit from both front and side airbags when she'd automatically thrown up her arm to shield her face. It was straight but already swelling, which meant it was sprained not broken. Since she'd had a broken arm as a kid, she knew the difference.

She had no idea how bad the back injury might be. She didn't think it was too serious because she hadn't lost any feeling anywhere, but it was starting to throb, and she knew enough from the first aid course she'd done, and from her mom, who had trained as a paramedic, that you didn't mess around with spinal injuries. The injuries meant she couldn't afford to try to exit the SUV herself and climb up to the road.

Luckily she had her cell phone with her, which she suddenly loved with passion because it was going to connect her with the good, safe world out there.

She also knew exactly where she was, so at least she could take charge of getting rescued.

Moving carefully, so as not to twinge her back any more than necessary, she retrieved her phone from her bag.

Normally, she would ring the emergency services number, but since her mother, who had trained as a paramedic after Sophie's father's death and volunteered for the local ambulance service, it made sense to kill two birds with one stone and ring her.

Annoyingly, she was forced to use her clumsy left hand because her right hand was out of commission. Instead of getting her mom's number, she scrolled too far and found herself staring at Ben's.

A sharp, stabbing pain replaced the throb in her back, and she realized she had tensed. The hand holding her phone jerked, and her thumb must have moved on the screen because suddenly the phone was dialing him.

She wasn't even supposed to have his number, because when he'd walked out on their one night together and disappeared overseas, he hadn't given her any contact details at all. She'd had to stoop to getting the number off her brother, Nick's, phone.

A split second later, his deep, cool voice filled the cab. "Sophie? Why are you ringing? Is something wrong?"

Shock and mortification held her immobile for long seconds, along with the realization that for Ben to know it was her calling meant he must have her number—and she hadn't given it to him.

It registered that his voice sounded more gravelly than usual, as if she had just woken him up. She probably had, since he was living half a world away, in Miami.

A sudden image of Ben sprawled in bed, of his bronzed shoulders and broad chest a stark contrast to white sheets, made the breath hitch in her throat. She cleared her throat, which felt suddenly tight. "Nothing that you can help with."

"Are you sure? Babe, you sound…odd."

Babe.

He had only called her that once before, while they had been in bed. He certainly had no right to call her that now! And she was *injured*. She shouldn't be lingering on the phone talking with him. What she needed was an ambulance. Suddenly the weird desire to keep Ben with his dark velvet voice on the line was gone and she was *back*. "You're in Miami, I'm in New Zealand. There's no way you can help me." She hurriedly added, "Not that I need help from you with *anything*."

Her jaw tightened at the fact that she had almost let him know that she was, actually, in need of help, a situation that was unthinkable, since she would rather crawl through the scrub and up the bank with her injured back and sprained wrist than accept any help Ben Sabin might care to offer.

"It's been *nice* talking to you," she said smoothly, "but I didn't mean to call you. Igloos will be melting in the Arctic and polar bears sunning themselves in Central Park before it happens again. It was a misdial."

With a stab of her thumb—this time deadly accurate—she terminated the call.

She scrolled through her contacts and succeeded in contacting Luisa Messena. With her mom and help on the way, she tried to relax. But the instant she didn't have anything to do, all she could think about was Ben. Embarrassed heat flooded her that she had actually *rung* him, which was at the top of her list of things not to do.

On top of that, the fact that he'd somehow gotten hold of her number and had never bothered to contact her made her mad, which was not good, because it meant she was obviously still harboring sneaky feelings for him.

While she was at home convalescing, her mother, who had figured out that she was struggling with lack of closure around her "relationship" with Ben, had suggested she have counseling and had recommended a therapist. Sophie hadn't thought she would like the process, but she had taken to it like a duck to water, because the therapy had put the power back in her hands.

What she had felt for Ben was past tense and controllable. She did not have to feel disempowered by what he did or did not do. She was free and empowered to make her own choices.

A distant flash of lightning jerked her back to the present, and to Nick's party, where, once again, she had managed to utterly embarrass herself.

The breeze lifted, blowing loose strands of hair

around her cheeks. She was on the point of leaving and returning to the room Nick had reserved for her at the resort when a sense of premonition tingled down her spine. *Ben.* Her breath hitched in her throat, and for a crazy moment she wondered if she was experiencing one of Francesca's feelings.

When she turned, he *was* there. The terrace lights glanced off the clean cut of his cheekbones, emphasizing the intriguing shadows beneath and highlighting the solid line of his jaw. He shrugged out of his jacket, which had water stains down the lapels, and tossed it over the wrought iron railing. The white shirt he was wearing was wet all down the front and plastered across his chest, making him seem even broader and more muscular than she remembered.

He dragged long fingers through his damp hair and wiped moisture from his chin. His gaze connected with hers. "I guess I deserved that."

Sophie tried not to notice the way Ben's skin glowed bronze through the wet shirt. She remembered the pretty blonde.

Stomach tight, she glanced past Ben's shoulder. There were a few people strolling around the terrace, but none of them looked remotely like the girl with whom Ben had been dancing. "Shouldn't you be looking after your date?"

He dragged at his tie, which she was gratified to see was also soaked. "I don't have a date. That was Ellie, the daughter of my business manager. And before you ask, my business manager is also female, but fifty-something and happily married."

Though Sophie wanted to stay angry and distant and cold, relief flooded her. A little desperately she reminded herself that Ben was still a rat, just not a big

enough rat to bring a date to a party at which he knew
she would be present.

"What makes you think I need to know anything
about the women in your life?" She cleared her throat,
which felt tight. "You're free to date who you want,
just as I am."

Ben's gaze zeroed in on her mouth as if he had picked
up on the extra huskiness of her voice, the one sign she
couldn't control when she was upset. It was a reminder
that he knew her too well.

Normally, when it came to men, it was easy for Sophie to keep them at a safe distance. But Ben had, literally, become part of the family for eighteen months,
turning up for Sunday lunches, sharing celebrations and
spending hours sailing with Nick. He had even been invited to family weddings and christenings, all of which,
she now realized, had slowly worn away her defenses
and changed the way she had thought about him.

She had begun to think of him as possible husband
material.

He leaned back against the terrace railing, arms
folded across his chest. "According to social media and
the tabloids, *you* haven't exactly been lonely."

She stiffened at his clear reference to the guy she
had flaunted in front of the paparazzi as her new man
just days after Ben had walked out on her. Since then,
she had kept up a steady stream of handsome escorts—
most of them Francesca's friendly exes—just to hammer
home that she did not miss Ben in the least.

"So, who's the lucky guy tonight?" Ben's gaze narrowed. "He looks familiar."

Probably because Ben had seen him when he was
dating Francesca. Warmth flooded Sophie's cheeks. For

a heart-pounding moment she tried to remember the name of her date. "Oh, you mean, uh—Tobias."

Ben's expression seemed to sharpen even further. "Tobias Hunt, of Hunt Security?"

Offhand she could not remember Tobias's surname; he could be from the royal line of Kadir for all she knew. She had met him for only the third time this evening, and all she had was a phone number and a first name, both of which Francesca had supplied. "We've only just started dating," she said smoothly.

Technically, this was a first date, even as she instinctively knew it would also be the last, because Tobias, despite his masculine presence and good looks, was an oddly lackluster companion.

"So, not serious yet?"

"Not so far." She met his gaze squarely. "Tobias and I are just good friends. Not that it's any of your business."

For a disorienting moment Ben's gaze burned into hers. "It used to be my business."

Sophie's heart pounded in her chest. In a moment of clarity she realized that Ben was suffering from the same kneejerk reaction that had affected her when she had seen him dancing with the young blonde; he was jealous. If he was jealous, that meant that he did still feel something for her, something real enough that it had lasted through a year of separation. She even had the sense that he was on the brink of saying that he was sorry he had walked out on her and that he wanted her back. Then his expression seemed to harden and he broke their eye contact.

She thought grimly that he was regretting the momentary lapse. And suddenly her rage was back, which was a relief, even if she was beginning to feel like Dr.

Jekyll and Mr. Hyde. "As I recall, we didn't exactly *date*. We slept together one night, then you disappeared."

His brows jerked together. "You have to know that I didn't intend to sleep with you that nigh—"

"And that's supposed to make me feel better? That you slept with me *by mistake*?"

"It wasn't a mistake. It was the night of my farewell. I was leaving for Miami, with no plans to come back to New Zealand. That's not exactly great timing for starting a relationship."

Though wanting to stay furious because it felt so much stronger and more empowering than feeling dumped, Ben's use of the word "relationship" literally took the wind from her sails. It meant he *had* been thinking about her in relationship terms. Although, clearly, he had not been thinking very hard. "We had chemistry for months before that—"

"Babe, if I'd made a move on you earlier, that would have meant we would have been dating. Then I would have been answerable to Nick."

Babe. There it was again. A secret thrill she absolutely did not want to feel coursed through her. Obviously, where Ben was concerned, she was more vulnerable and needy than she had thought. The fact was she could not afford to weaken because he had called her babe...as if he still saw her as girlfriend material, as if they still had an intimate connection. "What does Nick have to do with any of this?"

Ben leaned on the railing beside her, suddenly close enough that she could feel the heat of his skin. His clean masculine scent teased her nostrils, spinning her back to the one night they had spent together and the heated, addictive hours she had spent locked in his arms. Out of nowhere, the intense awareness that, a year ago, had burned her from the inside out was back.

His gaze touched on hers, and for a fractured moment the air turned molten and she had the crazy thought that Ben was just as affected as she.

"Nick was my boss," he said flatly. "When he knew I was interested, he spelled it out chapter and verse. Unless I was ready to make a commitment, as in marriage, I should leave you alone."

Sophie's startled gaze clashed with Ben's. The word "marriage" was faintly shocking. It also invested what Ben had just said about Nick with the ring of truth. When it came to the Messena women, Nick and her other three brothers—Gabriel, Kyle and Damian—were territorial and overprotective. It was the kind of medieval, macho behavior that gave her warm fuzzies and a wonderful sense of security when she did need protection. She knew that, hands down, if anyone tried to bother her or touch her when she didn't want to be touched, he would have to deal with four large, muscled brothers and their version of the law of the jungle.

The downside to the Messena men was that they could be macho and controlling, and could totally overstep the mark by interfering with her life.

The reasons for Ben's abrupt departure and lack of communication were starting to come clear, although not entirely. "Nick can be overbearing, but that still doesn't explain your behavior *after* you slept with me." No apology, no phone call, not even a text message explaining why he didn't want to stay in contact, just that shabby little note thanking her for their night together...

Ben shrugged, his expression remote and unapologetic. "Like I said, I was leaving for the States. I was taking on a new business. There was no way I could afford to start a relationship."

Relationship. There was that word again. Despite her determination to not allow Ben to affect her, the fact that he *had* seen her as potential relationship material, but in the wrong time and place, was quietly riveting. It raised the possibility that, maybe, there could be a right time and place.

Still, Sophie knew that timing and geography weren't the only issues with Ben. From her online research she knew that he had also been burned by a past relationship and now seemed chronically wary of commitment.

Previously, she had dismissed Ben's past. He was a big boy; he should be able to get over a broken engagement. However, that had been a serious mistake, because commitment was obviously still a problem.

The moment she had realized he'd had her number when she had been sitting in her SUV at the bottom of bush-choked gully burned through her again. "You had my number. You could have phoned me."

"If I'd done that we'd be right back where we are now." Ben's gaze seared her.

With slow deliberation, he picked up her hand and threaded her fingers with his. Heat shimmered from that one point of contact, making her heart pound and her stomach tighten. Memories she had worked hard to bury flooded back. Ben's mouth on hers, heat welding them together as they'd lain together in his bed. The intense emotion that had poured through her with every touch, every caress, along with a bone-deep certainty she had never experienced before and which had been the reason she had consented to sleep with him in the first place. The uncanny conviction that after years of disinterested dating, she had finally found The One.

With a jerky movement, she withdrew her hand.

Ben pushed away from the railing and dragged off his tie as if it was suddenly too tight. He draped it over the railing next to his jacket. His brooding gaze dropped to her mouth. "I didn't call you because I didn't think you were serious about wanting a real relationship."

She frowned. He could only be referring to the fact that she was naturally wary and standoffish when it came to relationships and that it had taken her eighteen months to admit to him that she found him crazily attractive. "It's not as if I'm in the habit of having one-night stands!"

He shrugged. "I was also not in a position to offer any kind of commitment."

Sophie met Ben's gaze squarely. She could barely concentrate on Ben's struggle with his emotional past when she was coping with her own very present struggle and the startling revelation that he still wanted her. "You could have asked me what *I* wanted instead of talking to Nick. It's not as if my brother is any kind of a love doctor."

To put it succinctly, Nick had had a serious issue with commitment, which had been resolved only when the woman he had married, Elena, had taken a risk on him and he had ended up falling for her hook, line and sinker. It had just taken some time.

Suddenly all the breath seemed to be sucked out of Sophie's lungs. Elena and Nick's relationship had been a bumpy affair, but Elena had persevered and she had won out in the end. Sophie believed that Elena had won Nick because what they shared had been real and true in the first place. But the relationship could easily have failed if Elena hadn't taken the initiative and risked herself by sleeping with Nick in unpromising circumstances. *Twice*.

Sophie took a deep breath and tried to stay calm, which was difficult because her mind was going a million miles an hour. Usually she was guarded, logical: smart. She did not let emotion carry her away. She did not try to *win* a man, especially not an alpha male like Ben, because alphas were dominant and predatory and they preferred to do the hunting.

But this was different. They were on a darkened terrace, with the perfumed night pressing in around them. Heated awareness pulsed through her as she grappled with the dangerous knowledge that Ben still wanted her.

It wasn't love, not even close.

But it was a start.

If Elena had worked with Nick—who, let's face it, had been an extremely unpromising boyfriend—Sophie could work with Ben. In that moment a world of possibilities opened up and a year of wallowing in victimhood was gone. She was back to her normal ultra-organized, controlling self with a project to manage, and that project was Ben Sabin.

She closed the distance between them. "Let's not worry about the commitment issue right now," she said smoothly, her palms gliding over his shoulders.

Three

A jolt of pure sensual awareness hit Ben with all the force of a freight train. But, as Sophie wound her arms around his neck, he also couldn't help noticing the odd expression on her face, as if she was assessing him for a position in one of her successful luxury fashion stores. As if he was an employee with hidden potential she was determined to unlock.

Keeping a tight leash on his control, he stared down into a face that had fascinated him from the moment he had first seen Sophie two-and-a-half years ago. He had just taken the job as construction manager with Nick. With liquid dark eyes, cheekbones to die for, a firm chin and a distractingly husky voice, Sophie Messena was drop-dead gorgeous in anyone's language.

He was also aware that it was not just how Sophie looked that attracted him, because she had an identical twin who looked and sounded exactly the same. And he didn't feel a thing for Francesca.

When he was near Sophie, something happened. It was like being plugged into an electrical outlet; every cell in his body tightened and all brain function stopped. She could have a bag over her head and he would still recognize her.

"I thought you didn't want this," he ground out, "that you weren't a glass half-empty girl."

And it was a fact that, with Sophie, half a glass was all he could afford to offer. As mesmerizingly attractive as she was, she was exactly the kind of pampered, spoiled rich girl on the hunt for a wealthy husband or a trophy affair he usually went out of his way to avoid.

Six years ago when he had established his first construction business, he had done the one thing he had promised himself he would never do, after being caught up in the messy breakup of his parents' marriage: he had fallen for a rich man's daughter. Even knowing the pitfalls, he had worked to attain her and to hold her. Then, when a financial crash had almost bankrupted him, Melissa had walked the same day. She had handed him back his engagement ring and smoothly told him that she could never marry someone poor. To rub salt in the wound, within the week she had moved in with an extremely wealthy and older business competitor.

Since then Ben had worked hard to rebuild his finances, climbing corporate ladders as he managed construction for other firms. In that time his experiences with women had done nothing to change his mind. He knew how it worked; money married money.

Sophie, who had been born with a diamond-encrusted spoon in her mouth, wouldn't have looked at him twice if he hadn't been successful. And the stakes had recently gotten a whole lot higher. When he had started working for Nick Messena, there had been an eighteen-month period during which Sophie had kept a cool distance despite the attraction that had sizzled between them.

A year ago, he had inherited a multibillion-dollar construction and real estate business and Sophie Messena had slept with him. He had to consider that her main focus wasn't him, personally, but his inheritance.

It didn't feel that way right now, though. She lifted up on her toes and fitted herself against him as if their last passionate encounter had been just hours ago and the past year of separation hadn't happened. Close enough that there was no way she could miss exactly how much he still wanted her.

"I've changed my mind," Sophie murmured, a husky catch to her voice.

Ben's body tightened on a powerful surge of desire. Maybe he could have kept his perspective, he thought grimly, if he hadn't seen her on Tobias Hunt's arm. Something fierce and primal had risen up inside him. And it had only grown worse when he learned who Tobias was. Ben's cool, controlled plan to seduce Sophie Messena in order to put to rest the fatal attraction he had so far failed to shake had crashed and burned.

If Hunt had been one of the normal run of men Sophie had been dating—soft, manicured men who took orders and drove desks—Ben could have maintained his aloofness. However, there was nothing ordinary or even remotely domesticated about Hunt despite the fact that he had spent several months working for Gabriel Messena, presumably to gain experience with playing the financial market. Aside from being the scion of an international manufacturing conglomerate, which, among other things specialized in high-tech military equipment, Hunt was ex-military.

Even though Ben was aware that he was being seduced, his hands, of their own volition, settled at her
hips, pulling her closer still. There was his problem, he
thought. This encounter with Sophie was following a
familiar, conflicted pattern. He couldn't resist her, and
he couldn't trust her.

But damned if he'd stand tamely aside and let Hunt
move in on her.

Sophie's gaze was oddly considering, giving him
the inescapable feeling that he was being evaluated in
some way. She brushed her lips against his, sending a
rush of heat through him that tightened every muscle
in his body.

"About that glass," she said huskily. "Half a glass
will do for now."

Francesca stepped out onto the terrace and stopped
dead. Sophie was kissing Ben Sabin, and it was not just
a casual peck.

For long seconds she was frozen in place, not knowing what to do. Usually, Sophie was extremely careful
with men. She almost never let any of the men she dated
so much as kiss her. Francesca knew for a fact that Sophie had not slept with anyone until Ben. She also understood why Sophie was so picky.

Ever since their father had been killed in a car accident with his alleged mistress, Sophie had been frag-
ile about relationships. Maybe that was because Sophie
had always had an unusual character. She tended to be
black-and-white in her thinking. When it came to trust
it was all or nothing. Added to that, she had been Daddy's girl, then the father she had adored had tipped her
world upside down by betraying her twice. The first
time by dying, the second by apparently having a mis-

tress, which Sophie had viewed as an utter betrayal of the entire family.

Consequently, when it came to relationships, she practically interviewed a potential date before she committed. Then she micromanaged the "relationships" because she hated anything unscripted or creative happening.

The droves of men who fell for her didn't understand what they were letting themselves in for. It was like watching an assembly line, with no hope that any of them would make the grade.

Until Ben.

A little anxiously Francesca skulked in the shadows of a large potted ficus, trying to stay out of sight. She was glaringly aware that with her platinum-blond hair, it was terminally difficult to hide because she practically glowed in the dark. She tucked herself more firmly behind the plant, ignoring the discomfort as a branch scraped her jaw and caught in her hair. Her stomach tightened as one kiss morphed into a second, then a third.

Seconds later, Sophie took Ben's hand and led him down the steps into the garden. Francesca had to steel herself against rushing after Sophie. The only thing that stopped her was that Sophie seemed to be taking the lead and not Ben She frowned, tossing up whether or not to call Sophie and try to talk some sense into her. Although, given the way they had kissed, she didn't hold out much hope!

A faint sound made Francesca straighten with a start. She almost died on the spot when she realized that the person who had busted her for spying on Sophie was the guy she'd had a crush on for the past couple of years, John Atraeus. She attempted to shuffle out from behind the tree but a strand of hair had caught on a branch of the ficus.

She pulled on the strand, which stayed stubbornly tangled.

"Wait. Let me do that." John stepped close enough that she could feel the warmth of his body, smell the tantalizing scent of his gorgeous cologne. His jaw brushed her forehead, sending a hot zing of awareness through her as he worked on the silky strand, which was so blond it still startled her.

"All done." His gaze met hers for a long moment, then he frowned. "Damn. What have you done to your jaw?"

She registered the faint sting, touched the area and felt the dampness of blood. She vaguely remembered a scrape from one of the branches, but she had been so intent on worrying about Sophie she hadn't paid it much attention.

As she stepped away from the tree, John produced a snow-white handkerchief. She stared at the beautifully folded linen and embarrassment burned through her, along with an uncharacteristic thread of panic. This was not the way it was supposed to be. She had wanted to be cool and sophisticated, more like Sophie, less like Jane of the jungle with pieces of tree caught in her hair. "I can't use that."

John glanced around the terrace, which held a few scattered groups of people. "The only entrance to the bathrooms is inside, which means you'll have to walk back through a party crowd that's crawling with media." He lifted a brow. "If you'll hold still for a second or two, I'll press the handkerchief against the cut until it at least stops bleeding."

Horror struck Francesca at the thought of how many

media personalities and reporters there were, every one of them with a camera and longing to catch her looking bad. "Okay."

Another half step, and he tilted her head slightly to one side and pressed the folded handkerchief against her jaw. Francesca knew she should be concentrating on how happy she was to have a practical solution to fixing her face, but with John's fingers firm on the sensitive skin of her jaw and the clean scent of him in her nostrils, all she could think of was that finally, even if it hadn't happened exactly as she'd planned, she was close to John.

John lifted the pad, refolded it, then pressed it against her skin again. His breath feathered across her forehead, and for a long, dizzying moment she wondered what would happen if she closed the oh-so-tiny gap between them, clutched the lapels of his jacket, went up on her toes and kissed him on the mouth.

Taking a deep breath, she met his gaze boldly, but in the instant that she made the quarter step toward him, a vibrating sound emanated from his jacket pocket.

"That'll be the call I was waiting for." Leaving her holding the handkerchief, John stepped away, cell held to one ear.

Francesca teetered, just a little off balance. She had actually been on the verge of kissing him. Her cheeks burned even hotter. Had he noticed? she wondered. In any event, she no longer had to die wondering why John had been on the terrace. He had not come looking for her as she had hoped; he had been waiting for a call.

Feeling embarrassed and flustered because she had been a split second away from humiliating herself completely, Francesca remembered her jaw. She found her compact and peered at the scratch, which was absurdly small yet had bled quite a lot. Luckily, her dress was red and, thankfully, the pressure had worked, stopping the bleeding. Refolding the once pristine handkerchief, she stuffed it in her clutch and resolved to launder and return it to John. Probably by post.

A few paces away, leaning on the wrought iron railing, one hand thrust casually in the pocket of his narrow dark pants, phone to his ear, John was speaking not in English, but in liquid, totally sexy Medinian.

Francesca knew she should cut and run now, before she did make an utter fool of herself. Instead, she lingered near John, while she soaked in the liquid cadences of his deep voice and the romance of a language that their families shared and which she now wished she'd made more of an effort to learn.

Using the excuse of needing to tidy herself before she went back to the party as a reason for staying out on the terrace, she extracted another twig from her hair and tossed it into the midst of the tree branches. Searching through her beaded evening bag, she found a comb and began running it through her hair with slow, systematic strokes.

When her hair felt smooth and sleek, she deposited the comb back in her bag and snapped the clutch closed. As she did so a thought made her mood plummet. She was probably wasting her time waiting out here with John. Even though his last flame, a gorgeous blonde model, was finally out of the picture, and there did seem to be a momentary vacuum of blondes, it was entirely possible that John had brought someone else to the party.

Every other time she had been at the same social event with John, he'd had a beautiful girl on his arm.

She didn't know why she hadn't considered that possibility before now.

Feeling both annoyed and depressed, she dragged her gaze from the mouthwatering cut of John's cheekbones and the intriguing hollows beneath, the totally sexy dimple that flashed out as he grinned. She scanned the terrace, half-expecting to see his beautiful new girlfriend waiting for him.

Suddenly, changing her hair color to blond so she could level the playing field and give herself a fighting chance seemed a little desperate. She had been certain that the attraction she felt was mutual, but now her thinking seemed horribly flawed and any hope that she would finally end up in John's arms practically nonexistent.

John terminated the call and straightened away from the wrought iron railing. He slipped the cell back into his jacket pocket, and suddenly nerves she normally never felt with a man kicked in.

She was used to being in charge, to picking and choosing and being the one who said no. But for reasons she could not quite pin down, John Atraeus was important. Every time she bumped into him, she got the *feeling*, and tonight it was stronger than ever, tingling through her like an electrical charge and reaffirming a conviction that had stayed steady for almost two years: that John Atraeus belonged to her, and she to him.

John glanced at her hair, a faint frown of puzzlement making him look even more handsome. "So, why were you hiding behind the ficus? A new life as a private detective?"

"Just looking out for my sister. She's with someone who—well, I'm not so sure he's good for her—"

"Ben Sabin. He's hard to miss."

Francesca's fingers tightened on her clutch. For some reason John seemed disposed to stick with her and talk, which was putting her on edge. Was he just being friendly? Or did he mean something more by it?

Now that she finally had the one-on-one time with him she had craved, contrarily, all she wanted to do now was hurry back to the room Nick had reserved for her at the resort, find some chocolate and try to pretend that tonight had never happened. "What about you?" She rubbed her palms over her upper arms, which now felt slightly chilled. "I'm guessing this is a work visit, since I saw you in Nick's office."

As soon as the words were out, she wished she could snatch them back because it sounded like she had also been spying on John.

John lifted a brow, informing her that that was exactly what he'd thought.

He shrugged. "You'll know soon enough, anyway. Your brother, Ben and I decided to go into business together on Sail Fish Key. We finalized the agreement tonight."

John's attendance at the launch of Nick's new resort now made perfect sense. She already knew that Ben, who owned the largely undeveloped Sail Fish Key, had gone into partnership with Nick to complete the build on a luxury resort that his uncle had started before he died. All the nearly completed resort needed was a retail complex, which was where Atraeus came in. He had made billions building luxury malls and securing high-end brands to populate them.

Determined to make her escape before she embarrassed herself further, Francesca forced a bright smile. "Well, thanks for the rescue, but I think I'll have an early night—" And try to get hold of Sophie on her phone before she made another dreadful mistake with Ben.

"Why did you change this?" John picked up a strand of her hair, preventing her from stepping away.

Fiery awareness zinged through Francesca, making her heart pound. She could have prevaricated, could have shrugged and kept the conversation light, but she was suddenly aware of an intensity in John's gaze that seemed to go beyond a mere interest in her hair color.

A pulse pounding on one side of John's jaw riveted her attention. She realized that he was as nervous as she. Suddenly her plan to try to save Sophie from her fatal attraction to Ben—a plan that she instinctively knew had little chance of succeeding—went on the back burner. Sophie was going to have to look after herself!

She had come here tonight to take a risk on John Atraeus, and that was exactly what she was going to do. Lifting her chin, she met his gaze boldly. "I changed it because I thought you liked blondes."

He wound the strand of hair slowly around his finger, taking a half step closer as he did so. "I like brunettes, too. I've liked you for a long time, but you've always got some guy in tow."

Francesca's gaze dropped to that riveting pulse along the line of John's jaw. "I've got a lot of...um...friends."

"Just friends?"

"No one serious." She met his gaze, drew a deep breath and took the final revealing plunge. "And I don't have a date tonight."

The words rushed out, creating a curious moment of silence during which she wondered frantically if John was now going to draw back and stop flirting with her because he *was* with someone.

Instead, he released her hair, picked up her hand and linked his fingers with hers. The glint of masculine satisfaction in his dark gaze made her heart beat even faster. "Ditto. So, what do we do next?"

Heat and sensation poured through Francesca from that one small point of contact. John didn't have a date, and she was now very clear on the fact that he *was* attracted to her.

Relinquishing his hold on her hand, she stepped close enough that she could feel the heat of his body. Lifting up on her toes, she rested her palms on the hard, pliant muscle of his broad shoulders. His swiftly indrawn breath sent pleasure cascading through her.

Finally, after two years of wanting and dreaming about a man who was always off-limits because he was with another woman—and of hoping for the kind of incandescent love that seemed doomed to remain only in her dreams—it seemed that she and John were finally going to be together.

Feeling as giddy as a teenager, she looped her arms lightly around his neck. "Let's start with a kiss."

Four

Sophie pulled Ben into the hotel room Nick had booked for her. The second the door clicked closed and they were finally alone together, her nerves kicked back in. Up until this point she had been on autopilot, following her natural instinct for managing a situation. She had made the executive decision that they would make love and, accordingly, had brought Ben to *her* room. En route she had gone to the trouble of ordering champagne, which should get here any moment.

Not that she really felt like any more alcohol. But an elegant, frosted bottle of champagne would set the scene nicely and cue Ben that this was not just about sex, as it had clearly been the last time.

A year ago she had made the mistake of allowing emotion to sweep her off her feet. She had been so captivated by what she was feeling that she had stopped thinking and simply reacted. Consequently, Ben had taken the lead and in his usual no-frills masculine way, he'd bypassed romance. They had ended up in bed within moments of entering his suite, which had been totally exciting but, in retrospect, a serious mistake. She had allowed him to sweep her off her feet; she had allowed him to make all the decisions. This time, things were going to be different.

In terms of creating a positive starting point for a relationship that wouldn't hinge only on wild, crazy, fabulous sex, the fact that she had managed to slow things down and bring some order to the process felt like progress.

She sent Ben a brilliant smile, but now that they were alone she felt slightly panicky. Her management skills had carried her this far, and now she was aware of a powerful and undermining emotion she didn't often experience: vulnerability. Maybe that was because when they had made love before, even though it had been significant and special for her, Ben had treated the event as a one-night stand and nothing more.

A knock on the door provided a welcome relief to the tension that had sprung up between them, and the churning feeling in the pit of her stomach, *as if she was on the verge of making another terrible mistake.* Determined to ignore the attack of nerves and get the seduction back on track, Sophie opened the door and directed the attendant to wheel the trolley into the sitting room. The festive pop of the champagne cork and the fizz of an expensive vintage as it was poured into two flutes was a welcome distraction.

Still on edge, not least because after a year she was actually on the verge of making love with Ben again, Sophie tipped the attendant and hustled him out the door. Taking a deep breath, she strolled to the trolley, picked up both flutes and handed one to Ben. She cast around for something to say that wasn't clichéd and that would mask her nervousness. There was really only one option. They would talk business until the awkwardness dissipated, *then* she would move things into the bedroom. She gave Ben the kind of neutral professional smile that usually worked to smooth the way with her clients. "So— here's to your new business venture in Miami."

Ben froze in the act of taking a sip of his champagne. "Nick told you?"

His gaze had cooled perceptibly, which was not the reaction she had expected to what had been a fairly safe conversation opener. Sophie set down her own flute without drinking any champagne. "Nick mentioned that he and you were going into partnership on a resort development on Sail Fish Key. I presumed that was why you were here."

"I'm surprised he mentioned it, since we've only just signed on the deal tonight."

Suddenly Sophie understood why Ben was being terse. Contracts and partnerships were a sensitive business, so naturally he would not want the information to become public until everything was signed and sealed. "As it happens, this afternoon I dropped in to discuss a business venture of my own with Nick. I saw the partnership agreement on his desk so, naturally, I asked him about it."

Ben's brows jerked together. Actually, she'd had to pry the information out of Nick, which had been no easy task.

"*You're* doing business with Nick?"

Sophie's chin came up. "Hoping to be."

Filled with the sudden conviction that any chance at a relationship with Ben was rapidly evaporating, Sophie decided it was time to dial things up a notch. Relieving Ben of his flute, she boldly rested her palms on his chest. The thud of his heart was disturbingly intimate.

She took a deep breath, her pulse racing. "I've been trying to get Nick to let me establish retail outlets in all of his resorts, but he's being typically cagey."

Ben's hands came to rest on her waist, the heat of his palms burning through the thin silk of her dress. As pleasurable as it was for Ben to touch her, frustratingly his hold prevented her from closing the last small gap between them.

"That would be because Nick's brought in John Atraeus to handle the retail."

Sophie's gaze jerked to Ben's. Any thought of seduction was abruptly wiped from her mind. "John Atraeus? Why wouldn't Nick have told me that?"

"Probably because the partnership deal was only agreed this week and wasn't official until we signed tonight."

Sophie swallowed her disappointment and a strong jolt of annoyance. She had wanted to establish her own chain of stores in Nick's properties. He hadn't made her any promises, and she had known she might be biting off more than she could chew since her business was still in its growth-and-development stage, but still…they were family. He should have told her he was planning on getting Atraeus to manage that side of the business.

Ben's gaze seemed to drill right through her. "Does that…change things?"

For a split second Sophie thought he was suggesting that now she knew Atraeus was the one who held all the power over the retail side of the business, she would change her mind about sleeping with Ben. As if she was only sleeping with him to close a deal!

The instant the thought surfaced, she dismissed it.

Aside from being a horrible thought, it made no sense because their chemistry went way back and they had made love before without any hint of a business connection. Besides, how could Ben possibly think financial calculation had anything to do with their relationship now, when just an hour ago she had emptied a glass of water over him?

Clearly she had jumped to a completely wrong conclusion. Ben was probably just concerned that Nick's decision had killed the mood completely and that, with her business scheme in tatters, she would no longer feel like making love.

Relief nixed the crawling tension that had gripped her. With an effort of will, she clamped down on her annoyance that Nick hadn't seen fit to tell her about his plan and thus save her the embarrassment of finding out secondhand. She forced a smile. "Why would Nick's deal with John Atraeus change anything? My business proposal is still on the table. All that's changed is that I now have to deal with John instead of Nick, which could work very well for me."

Ben's gaze was oddly neutral. "Of course. Atraeus has a portfolio of high-end malls."

"And designer franchises," she murmured absently, reaching up to cup the tough line of Ben's jaw. "A business connection with John could allow me to go global a lot faster."

Ben's hold on her waist loosened. For a disorienting second she thought he was going to step back. Her reaction was kneejerk and fierce, surprising even herself. Her arms coiled around his neck, bringing her in close enough against Ben, that his muscular heat seemed to burn right through her.

She was breathlessly aware that for the first time in a year—since the last time she had been in Ben's arms—she was feeling too much, revealing too much. But the fact was she couldn't bear it if Ben cooled off and walked away now. Despite all of the distance and issues, the confusion and the hurt, despite the fact that she couldn't quite trust him, Ben *mattered*.

Her forehead grazed his jaw. The roughness of it against her tender skin sent a sharp pang through her. His arms closed around her, steadying her, pulling her in even tighter against him, and the closeness of the contact, the knowledge that he did want her after all, made her almost giddy with relief.

In that moment she realized how much she had missed Ben despite her efforts to move on from that one night together, despite how annoyed and hurt she had been. She realized how much she wanted him despite everything that had gone wrong. She breathed in, her nostrils filling with the clean, masculine scent of his skin. "Why are we talking business?"

"Damned if I know," he muttered, and then his mouth came down on hers.

Heat and excitement poured through her as they kissed, making the blood rush through her veins, making her skin seem tight and unbearably sensitive.

Her fingers curled into the hard muscle of his shoulders as she lifted up, angling her jaw to deepen the kiss. Long seconds later, he broke the kiss, only to close his teeth over the lobe of her ear.

She fumbled with the buttons of his shirt, baring an enticing strip of muscled torso. Simultaneously, she felt the zipper of her dress glide down her spine. The delicate silk of her dress loosened and slid from her shoulders to puddle around her feet. Ben shrugged out of his shirt, drew her close for another kiss and then, shivering seconds later, deftly dispensed with her bra.

Her breath came in sharply at the intimate heat of skin on skin. Then Ben bent and took one breast into her mouth. Time seemed to slow, stop as heat gathered and coiled...

"Oh, no, you don't," Ben muttered. "Not yet." The world went sideways as he swung her into his arms. She wound her arms around his neck, dimly aware of her shoes sliding off her feet and dropping onto the gorgeous hardwood floor as Ben strode toward the bedroom.

The dazzling light of the sitting room chandelier changed to the muted shadows of the bedroom as he deposited her on the king-size bed. As she sank into the soft mattress, the crisp coolness of the linen coverlet was faintly shocking against her overheated skin, making her feel suddenly vulnerable and exposed despite the fact that she wasn't quite naked. Dragging a corner of the coverlet over herself, she watched as Ben stepped out of his trousers. The lights from the pool area directly below her balcony glowed through gauzy drapes, flowing over his broad shoulders, muscled biceps and washboard abs. Sophie was abruptly riveted. In a business suit Ben was formidable, but naked he possessed a primitive beauty that was breathtaking.

As he sheathed himself with a condom, she suppressed an odd pang of regret. Ben was behaving responsibly; she *wanted* him to wear a condom. But a crazy, impulsive part of her—the part she usually kept tightly under wraps—noted his easy control, as if he was not quite as affected as she.

The instant the thought surfaced, she dismissed it as wild and idiotic. She should be happy that Ben was so controlled and pragmatic. Making love without protection went with trust and commitment, marriage and babies. They hadn't reached that point *yet*.

And the last thing she wanted was for Ben to discover how inexperienced she was. If he found out that this would only be the second time she had made love, that he had been her only partner, and that she had instigated lovemaking both times, it could make her appear needy and overly committed. Given his problem with commitment, it might even scare him off.

A sudden flash of how she had felt a year ago when she had awoken to find herself alone in a rumpled bed stiffened her resolve. Taking a deep breath, she dismissed memories that were still stark and vivid and which, irritatingly, had refused to fade. She had turned a corner in her thinking and was looking to establish a fresh start, a new beginning, for them both. This sudden attack of jitters was just her type A, control freak personality reminding her that she hated taking risks.

The bed shifted under Ben's weight as he joined her. His gaze traveled the length of her body, which was now enshrouded by the stifling but gorgeous white coverlet. He frowned. "Did I miss something here?"

"Nothing's wrong." Sophie dismissed the attack of nerves, forced a smooth smile and dispensed with the cover. "You took too long."

With deliberate movements, she pushed Ben flat on his back and straddled him. Bending down, she kissed him slowly and thoroughly on the mouth.

Taking the initiative felt exhilaratingly bold and empowering. The last time they had made love she had felt swept along, swamped by the sensations that had assaulted her and the intensity of her own emotions.

Excitement zinged through her as she registered that, this time, things would be different.

This time *she* was in control.

Five

Ben's hands settled on her waist, holding her in place as the kiss deepened. Relief spiraled through Sophie. They seemed to be back on track. Now she just needed to stay focused on reminding him of the powerful chemistry that had bound them together from the first and which had endured despite his walking out on her a year ago. She needed him to wake up and see her as precious, to value her and *want* a relationship; to do what he did in business and ruthlessly pursue her until she finally said yes.

The thought that she might actually say yes to a proposal of marriage from Ben startled her enough that she froze in place. Somehow her thoughts had raced ahead, possibly because she was used to "visioning" for her company and had seen the potential in Ben. The plain fact was that Ben had a lot of catching up to do before she would ever consider him for the role.

Ben's gaze was wary. "What have I done?"

"Nothing…yet." She ran a hand down his chest, then lower, her confidence building at his reaction to her lightest touch. "I'm hoping that's about to change."

A split second later, he rolled, his weight pressing her down into the mattress. Feeling his fingers hook through the waistband of her panties, she lifted her hips so he could draw them down her legs. Her breath came in as she felt him lodge between her thighs.

"Is this fast enough for you?" he muttered, his gaze locked with hers as he slowly slid home.

She reached for breath as she adjusted to the shape of him. "I'd say it's…just about right."

Sophie grasped his shoulders and tried to breathe, tried to control the exquisite sensations that poured through her as he withdrew and pushed deep again. But breathing was difficult as pleasure, heated and un-bearable, gripped her. The aching sensation low in her belly coiled and tightened, then splintered, spinning her into the night.

Long minutes later Sophie roused to the slow stroke of Ben's fingers on her back. The sensations that had been so overwhelming stirred through her again, tight-ening every muscle, every cell of her body. Ben, who was propped on one elbow, bent and kissed her on the mouth, taking his time. This time the lovemaking was slower, languorous, the pleasure so intense and pro-longed that when she finally climaxed, tears squeezed from beneath her lids. She knew it was dangerous to feel too much, and dangerous to let Ben see how much he affected her. But she couldn't help herself because in a curious, inexplicable way, making love with Ben felt like coming home.

* * *

Bright moonlight beamed through the curtains, rousing Ben.

He noted the time on the digital clock on the bedside table. It was a little after four. Sophie was half-sprawled against him, her head on his shoulder, one slim arm flung across his chest as if even in sleep she wanted to hold on to him.

But he knew that the desire Sophie was feeling was ephemeral and would soon be displaced by the reality of her wealthy, privileged and high-powered life. The Messenas were old money, and with his rough military and construction background, he had no place in their world despite his recent inheritance.

It was a reality he knew well, because he had seen the dynamic play out with his parents. Despite the passion that had driven them together, they had been a mismatch, the brash cowboy who had struck oil on his dustbowl of a ranch, and the cool, sophisticated heiress who had left when Ben's father had gone broke. The fact that his own engagement had followed the same pattern had only burned the truth in deeper. As gorgeous as Sophie was, as much as he wanted her, he was once bitten, twice shy. They were the kind of mismatch he could not afford in his life, again.

Plus, as beautiful and feminine as Sophie was, he knew she possessed the same kind of ruthless, entrepreneurial qualities her brothers possessed. The fact that she had initiated a seduction tonight and then started talking business in the middle of it more or less proved the fact that she had ulterior motives. The only honest thing they had shared was the sex, and that had been spectacular.

Brooding, he took in the way the silvery moonlight,

diffused by gauzy drapes, flowed over her cheekbones, highlighting her faintly imperious nose and finely cut mouth, and investing the silken lashes that feathered her cheeks with an added, fascinating sense of mystery. Lying naked in tangled linen sheets, Sophie had a timeless beauty that tugged at him as if in some indefinable way she was his.

Ben rebuffed the romantic notion; it had no place in his practical, pragmatic life. And there was his problem, he thought. He had come to the party tonight with the express intention of putting an end to his obsession with Sophie Messena. A part of him had hoped that when he saw her he wouldn't want her, that he could put the stubborn attraction behind him and move on.

That notion had evaporated in the first moment. One turn of her head, a glimpse of her level dark gaze and gorgeous cheekbones, and he had been gone.

When she had tipped the glass of water over him, his fate had been sealed. Sophie's jealousy had hit him like a kick in the chest, igniting an instant response. Her seeming hurt had fooled him…until she had started talking business. The second she had begun probing into his business affairs, reality had reasserted itself. He had hoped that spending another night with Sophie would be enough to get her out of his system, but the grim fact was that nothing had changed. Somehow, he had once again gotten caught in an obsession with the type of woman he had sworn off.

It was a mistake, but at least now he knew it had to end.

He fought the urge to draw her close, which would be fatal. Considering his track record with Sophie Messena, he wouldn't be able to stop himself from making love to her again. Instead, he gently disentangled himself, eased from the bed and padded through the suite retrieving his clothes. He dressed then let himself out and made his way to the room he had booked for the night.

After a quick shower, he called the concierge and arranged for his Jeep to be delivered to the front entrance of the hotel. As he strode across the foyer, he found he couldn't walk away cold this time. On impulse, he paused at the concierge desk. The instant he arranged for two dozen deep red roses to be delivered to Sophie in the morning, he sensed he was making a mistake. A mistake he had made once before, when he had sent flowers to a business partner's daughter as a simple thank-you for being his date at a work dinner.

Since then, Buffy Holt had pushed the social agenda, inserting herself into Ben's meetings with her father and making it clear she wanted a relationship. She treated every social event Ben had attended with her father as a date, and had repeatedly contacted him online and through his business numbers and email addresses. She had even gotten hold of his cell phone number and kept messaging him. He believed the term was stalking.

Not that Sophie would stalk him, he thought; she had too much class for that. She would ditch him,, like she had a year ago.

That fact should please him *Once he could forget how good it had felt to have Sophie back in his arms.*

Sophie turned over in bed and burrowed into the softness of a down pillow. She was caught in a dream, a delicious, tender dream where Ben was smiling and relaxed and holding her, pulling her close for another kiss.

Automatically, half dreaming, half awake, she reached for him, and found…nothing. Her eyes flickered open. The soft light of dawn flooded the room, illuminating tumbled sheets and a lone shoe on the floor. She drew a breath, but even before she turned her head on the pillow, she knew she was alone.

Her heart began to pound. She drew another deep breath and attempted to calm down. Just because Ben wasn't in the bed didn't mean he had gone, as in *gone*. He could be in the bathroom or the sitting room. Maybe he was even out on the terrace, taking one of his business calls and being careful not to wake her. Dragging the sheets back, she retrieved the robe from the back of the bedroom door and shrugged into it. Her stomach tensed as she surveyed the room. Ben's clothes were gone. But if he was outside, of course he would be dressed.

She checked the bathroom, which was empty. The towels looked fresh and undisturbed, which meant Ben hadn't showered. Feeling suddenly sick to her stomach, she turned to leave. As she did so the huge mirror over the double vanity threw her reflection back at her, momentarily riveting her in place. Her hair was tousled, her mouth soft, the robe gaped to show a faint abrasion on her collarbone where Ben's roughened jaw must have scraped across her skin.

Jerking the door closed, she walked into the sitting room and then out onto the terrace, which was also empty. She did another circuit of the rooms, looking for a note, something, *anything*.

Grabbing the phone she rang down to the concierge desk. She didn't know for sure if Ben was booked in here; he could have just planned to attend the party and leave. But if he was staying the night, maybe he had simply gone to his own suite to shower and change?

When she was put through to Ben's suite, a surge of relief made her legs feel as weak as noodles.

The phone rang for a period of time, then switched to the answering service. Sophie hung up, took a deep breath and called the concierge again. Her voice was husky and a shade too flat as she asked if Ben had checked out. She had to wait while the concierge spoke to another staff member. He finally came back to the phone and apologized. Apparently, Ben *had* left in the early hours and, because he was a guest of Mr. Messena and no payment was required, the night staffer had failed to check him out.

Sophie thanked the concierge and fumbled the phone back into its cradle. Feeling like an automaton, she sat down on one of the comfortable couches and stared blindly at the beautiful suite. Her gaze lingered on the waiter's trolley with its bottle of champagne and the two flutes, both barely touched. Jaw tight, she pushed to her feet and wheeled the trolley toward the door. Parking it to one side of the small foyer, she yanked the door open, only to be confronted by a bellhop carrying a huge bunch of long-stemmed red roses.

Surprise registered in the bellhop's gaze, then he grinned and handed her the roses. Sophie stared at the lavish bouquet, feeling as if all the air had been punched from her lungs. Roses, especially red roses, were a gift of love. Had she had gotten things totally wrong. Perhaps Ben hadn't ruthlessly ditched her, after all, *for the second time.*

Maybe he'd had to leave because of some emergency, and there would be a note tucked in among the flowers? Feeling utterly confused, she told the bellhop to wait. Placing the gorgeous blooms on the coffee table, she quickly found her bag and extracted cash to tip him.

After he had wheeled the champagne trolley out into the hall, she closed the door and turned to stare at the roses. Her heart was pounding, which was faintly scary because the reason Ben had sent them shouldn't matter so much. She was used to controlling relationships, setting the boundaries and terminating them when they didn't work out. She had thought long and hard before she had slept with Ben the first time. This time the process had been somewhat more rushed, but in the end she had stayed true to herself. She had weighed the pros and cons and made the decision to risk sleeping with him a second time.

A quick search of the roses revealed no thoughtful note that might explain why he had left in the night without a goodbye.

Checklist, she thought grimly. Ben had left before sunup without an explanation and without the courtesy of leaving either a phone number or an address. The fact that he knew that she had his phone number and probably knew where he lived didn't count; this was about manners. This time he'd had the decency to send flowers but the roses were depressingly devoid of scent and, though beautiful, weren't even her color. Somehow that seemed symptomatic of everything about her nonrelationship with Ben. If he had known anything about her at all it would be that she liked perfumed flowers and *white* roses.

Faint sounds out in the hall signaled that housekeeping was doing the rounds. Picking up the roses and holding them at arm's length, Sophie opened the door to her suite and gave the bunch to a tired-looking woman who was collecting room service trays that had been left outside of the suite opposite. When her face lit up, it somehow took the sting out of Ben's gesture, which was patently devoid of anything but the most caveman-like acknowledgment that they had spent a night together.

Sophie returned to her room, her gaze automatically sheering away from the rumpled bed. She took a quick shower, then wrapped herself in a thick white towel as she combed the tangles out of her hair. She froze as she noticed a pink mark on the side of her neck, as well as the one on her collarbone. Both were clearly scrapes from Ben's stubbled jaw, testament to the fact that she had just had a night of steamy passion with…someone.

Jaw taut, she dressed quickly in white jeans and a loose, pale gray boatneck cotton sweater. She dried her hair then took care of the marks on her neck and collarbone with dabs of concealer.

When she was finished, she could no longer see the marks, although that didn't change the fact that she knew they were there. After applying light makeup and pinning her hair up into a loose knot, she stared at herself. She looked pale but composed, and disorientingly the same, as if she hadn't just made a second horrendous mistake with Ben.

And she was still the same, she thought a little fiercely. Sleeping with Ben—being ditched by him a second time—had not changed anything about her. She had taken a calculated risk; it hadn't worked out. Life moved on. She would take what positives she could from the experience. Next time she would be smarter about men: she would be smarter about Ben Sabin.

She did not know what on earth had attracted her to him in the first place. She must have been stark, staring crazy. Maybe it had been some kind of hormonally driven primitive desire to mate with a strong alpha male that had temporarily hijacked her brain? And, let's face it, she had been brought up surrounded by the ridiculous amount of testosterone from four older brothers, so it made sense that on an instinctual level she would naturally tend toward the same kind of difficult, dominating male. Or maybe it was that, at twenty-seven, her biological clock was ticking and Ben had just happened to be around at the time? Whatever the reason, her usual radar for detecting what she called URM— Untrustworthy Rat Men—had failed.

She searched through her small traveling jewelry case and found the diamond studs her brothers had given her as a twenty-first birthday gift. The studs, made by her favorite designer, were deceptively simple. The stones were flawless and glowed with a pure white fire. They were a gift that signified love and thoughtfulness, because they were exactly what she would have chosen herself. More than that, they were a gift that, every time she wore them, made her feel loved and valued. It was a reassurance she desperately needed now.

With methodical precision, she fitted the gorgeous studs to her ears, then, driven by a desire to exit the suite and the hotel as quickly as possible, she threw her things into her overnight bag and checked her watch. Francesca had given her a lift because it hadn't made sense for them both to drive out to Nick's resort, so she was dependent on her sister or a cab for transport. It was a little early for Francesca, who hated getting up before ten on weekends, but Sophie decided to call anyway. The first call went through to voice mail, as did the second and third.

Feeling frustrated but now desperate to leave, Sophie hooked the strap of her tote over her shoulder and stepped out of the suite, wheeling her small case behind her. As she strolled toward the elevator, the doors slid open and she glimpsed a tall dark guy, his back to her as he waited for a woman with a stroller and two toddlers to exit. For a fractured moment, her mind said it was Ben, that he hadn't left after all, but it wasn't Ben, not even close.

The stranger's gaze connected with hers as they descended to the lobby. She caught the flare of masculine speculation but by now totally off men, Sophie stared straight ahead. When the elevator came to a stop she stepped into the gorgeous marbled foyer, and tried Francesca's phone again. This time she got a response. Relief at hearing her sister's voice made her feel the tiniest bit shaky. "Good, you're up," she said as smoothly as she could manage. "I was hoping we could leave soon. Like now."

"Leave?" Francesca's voice sounded muffled, as if she'd just been dragged from a deep sleep. "I thought we'd agreed to stay for lunch with Nick."

"Something's come up. I need to get back to my apartment." She had to squash the urge to confide the whole sorry story, which was weird because normally she was the strong one and it was Francesca crying on her shoulder.

"You sound a little strange. Is everything all right? Don't tell me you and Ben—"

"I'm *fine*, and it's nothing to do with Ben."

"I thought you and he—"

"You thought wrong. He left…last night." Which was only the truth.

"So you're okay, that's good." Francesca smothered a yawn. "Look, can you take a taxi? I'm tired. You might not have had a late night, but I did. A *very* late night, if you get my drift."

Sophie caught the low timbre of a masculine voice in the background and froze inside. Francesca was with someone, and evidently, despite the fact that the sun was up, he was still there instead of skulking off under cover of darkness.

She swallowed to keep the sudden huskiness from her voice. Until that moment she hadn't realized how much she had been counting on the simple, uncomplicated comfort of being with her twin. "No problem. I'll see you later."

Slipping her phone into the back pocket of her jeans, she made her way to reception, which was now packed with tourists all wanting to check out or join a tour group that was assembling in one corner. A frustrating ten minutes later, she finally reached the desk and checked out. As she handed over her key she saw the familiar figure of John Atraeus, who was joining the adjacent queue.

He stared at her as if he was having trouble figuring out which twin she was.

"Sophie," she said helpfully, and his face cleared.

"I know Francesca's got blond hair, but even so, you're...amazingly alike."

"Apart from the hair, we're identical. Although, in terms of personality, we're poles apart."

He grinned and shook his head. "The first time I ever met you both, I got that."

Sophie hesitated. Now was the perfect time to extend the conversation and start steering it in the direction of business. Normally, that was exactly what she would do. But, after last night, all she wanted was to go home and do something—anything—to help get her balance back. With a shrug, she waved and headed for the door.

When she got outside there was a line of people waiting for taxis. Feeling more and more stressed and upset by the minute, she parked her bag and waited. Seconds later a sleek Mercedes slid to a halt by the curb. John Atraeus collected the keys from the valet and placed his bag in the back seat. He caught her gaze and lifted a brow. "I'm heading into town if you want a lift."

She hesitated, but only for a moment. "Why not?"

Still feeling emotionally bruised by her encounter with Ben, Sophie was happy to relax in the passenger seat and let John do the talking. He was staying in town another night because he had a crucial meeting with a high-end group of franchises that were looking for a new home after the retail chain they were with had collapsed. If he could sign them, he could extend his reach into the uppermost end of the luxury market.

He hadn't mentioned the group's name so when she did, and said she had heard about the trouble they were having, he gave her a startled look.

She shrugged, still feeling curiously flat and divorced from a conversation that, normally, she would find fascinating because it was part of *her* business.

John braked for a stoplight then accelerated smoothly through the intersection. Sophie caught the flash of what looked like a delivery van veering toward them on John's side. She opened her mouth to warn him, although she didn't need to because John had already braked. Even so there was a sickening thud and she was knocked back in her seat by the airbags deploying.

A little grimly, she noted this was the second accident within a year. She wondered if there was going to be a third.

The car was stopped and the airbags had deflated, but that wasn't what concerned Sophie. John appeared to be unconscious. Unfastening her belt, she leaned over to check him. Because Sophie's mother was a trained paramedic she had made sure that both her daughters knew all the basics.

John was breathing steadily but didn't respond to Sophie's voice or a mild shake, so he was definitely unconscious. Not good. There was a lump forming on the side of his head, so it seemed clear he had taken a hit from something, either the airbag or the buckled driver's side door.

Someone wrenched her door open and helped her out. She reached for her phone, but the woman who had helped her waggled her own phone at her. Emergency services were on the way.

Six

Two hours later, Sophie was still stuck waiting at the emergency room. Before she had gotten into the ambulance with John, she had collected all of their things and rung his rental car agency, which had arranged to have the car towed. While she waited for the doctor to finish with John, she had gotten out her phone and tablet and caught up on some correspondence. Since it was Sunday, there had been no use making any business calls, so she had spent the time revising the business proposal she had given Nick, and which she would now have to present to John.

As she did so, Ben's words from last night came back to haunt her. "*You're* doing business with Nick?" As if it was inconceivable that Sophie was playing with the big boys and cutting deals at the level that Ben and Nick operated.

She did not want to think about Ben, but the hours

they had spent together kept pushing back into her mind, making it hard to concentrate on anything else. She kept picking through every moment of last night, trying to work out where things had gone wrong.

In retrospect, business had been the absolute wrong topic of conversation. It had not been the icebreaker she had hoped it would be. By choosing the subject, she guessed a part of her had wanted Ben to understand that she wasn't just a pretty rich girl who strolled into her big brother's office occasionally. She had hoped he would notice that she had aspirations and a *life*, and that life included a vibrant, growing business she had built from the ground up. Instead, Ben had seemed to cool. It was almost as if her business success had made her less attractive to him.

Sophie frowned. She did not want to think that Ben found intelligent, successful women unattractive, but it was a conclusion she had to consider. Especially since she had easily discovered online that the woman he had once been engaged to had been a wealthy socialite who had, by her own admission, enjoyed lunching, shopping and overseas travel.

Since then, nothing much in his dating career had changed. She knew because she had checked. When he did take time out of his busy schedule to date, the women he was photographed with were usually beautiful socialite types who did nothing more strenuous than charity work or a little modeling.

A small but significant thought struck her. They had also all been blonde, even down to his previous fiancée. Why hadn't she seen that? Or that all he seemed to want was a pretty, decorative girlfriend who was just around at strategic times—like at night.

Speaking of blondes, it suddenly occurred to her that

the reason Ben had had to leave so suddenly could be
another date with Buffy. Feeling instantly annoyed by
the thought, she looked up Buffy's most trafficked social media page. She hadn't checked it for a couple of
weeks, because she had been so busy putting together
the business proposal for Nick, but the instant the page
opened she realized how big a mistake that had been.
Buffy's interest in Ben had escalated exponentially and
suddenly her page was all about Ben.

Sophie no longer had to die wondering why Ben had
left her bed in the early hours of the morning, because
Buffy knew. Apparently, Ben had arrived in New York
on the redeye flight that morning in order to be there
for a mega-important charity event, *with* Buffy.

She scrolled through posts, a number of which she
hadn't seen. Ben, despite a heavy work schedule, apparently taking time out to be with Buffy at the opening of her father's new building in Manhattan; Buffy
on-site at one of Ben's construction projects, wearing
a hard hat. Buffy in a skimpy bikini that showed off
a number of edgy tattoos, posing with Ben on her father's superyacht.

Sophie closed the app abruptly. She hadn't taken the
Buffy thing seriously because Ben had dated a number of women during the past few months, and Buffy
with her rock-chick tattoos and piercings just hadn't
seemed to be his type. But maybe tattoos were Ben's
thing? Also, Ben had extensive business dealings with
Buffy's father, Mathew Holt, which further explained
the Buffy connection. The clincher had been that Buffy
had a habit of sensationalizing her social media posts,
some of which had turned out to be "fake news."

Was Buffy's relationship with Ben fake or real? From

where she was standing now, it was beginning to look disturbingly real.

Pushing to her feet, she stalked to the end of the corridor and stared down at the parking lot outside. Her heart was pounding and, as hard as she was trying to stay cool and composed, misery kept pulsing through her in waves.

She was beginning to understand just how big a mistake she had made in sleeping with Ben. She had sidelined her normal clinical approach and had allowed frustrated desire to color her decision. Using the strategy Elena had used to net Nick hadn't worked because of one basic flaw that now seemed glaringly obvious: what had worked with Nick would not necessarily work with Ben. She knew that Ben was liked and respected by her brothers and honorable and trustworthy in ways that counted with men, but for reasons she only partially understood, he was not that way with women.

Sophie paced some more, ending up near the public restrooms. On impulse, she went into the women's room and stared at her reflection in the mirror above the basin. Her hair, pinned in its loose knot, was so dark it was close to black. Her eyes were also dark, her features fine, bordering on delicate—except for her chin, which was firm. Even to herself she looked just a little too incisive and direct to be truly pretty, and there was not a hint of cheesecake.

Reaching up, she drew the pins from her hair and let it fall around her face in waves. The look was softer, but only just—it wasn't going to fool anyone, least of all herself. Soft, cheesecake prettiness was just not her, and the thought that she had, even for a moment, considered trying for it was…annoying.

Tucking the loose strands of hair behind her ears,

she returned to the waiting room. She could not believe how blind and stupid she had been. There was no way she could, or would, ever fulfill Ben's clichéd male fantasies. She could never be the kind of woman he clearly desired, who lunched and shopped and was pretty and biddable.

And pigs would fly before she would *ever* dye her hair blond or get a tattoo.

She glanced at her phone and frowned. Francesca had not called, texted or messaged her on Snapchat. That wasn't unusual, since she and Francesca didn't live in each other's pockets, but she had half expected Francesca to check up on her about Ben again. Although, given that Francesca had wanted to sleep late, then stay and have lunch at the resort, maybe she had just gotten busy and they would catch up later.

A door opened off to the left, and John, looking deathly pale, walked through with the doctor.

He waved a prescription. "Mild concussion. Painkillers and rest."

The doctor, a middle-aged Indian woman, smiled at Sophie. She had x-rayed John just in case. Since nothing was broken and he had seemed lucid and alert, all he needed were painkillers. However, obviously assuming they were a couple, she advised Sophie to keep a close eye on John through the next twenty-four hours and to call the hospital if she was at all concerned.

Relieved, Sophie called a taxi and rounded up their baggage, which the emergency room receptionist had helpfully offered to store behind her desk.

Ten minutes later, the taxi driver loaded their luggage and Sophie climbed into the back seat with John. She hadn't enjoyed being involved in yet another accident, but it had been oddly therapeutic to be needed and able to help.

John, who looked surprisingly normal since the telltale lump was mostly hidden by his hair, gave the driver the address of his hotel.

He attempted a smile. "Hey...thanks, Francesca."

"I'm not Francesca." She caught the flicker of confusion in his gaze.

"Then you must be the other twin—uh, Sophie."

Sophie gave John an assessing look as she fastened her seat belt. "Of course I'm Sophie. But you already knew that because I told you my name back at the hotel."

The taxi hit a speed bump. John winced at the jolt as the taxi accelerated out of the hospital parking lot into traffic. "Hotel? That would be the Messena resort."

"Of course. You were there last night." She suddenly felt as if she was talking to a child. "Don't you remember?"

"Last night?" He frowned. "I know I was supposed to sign a deal with Nick—"

"Which you did. Then you stayed the night. I know that because I met you in the lobby this morning. It was crowded, there was a line for taxis so you offered me a lift into town."

He let out an oddly relieved breath. "So that's how you came to be with me. I thought it might have been because..."

It dawned on Sophie *exactly* what John had been thinking. "What on earth made you think I might have slept with you?" She caught the taxi driver's gaze on her in the rearview mirror and lowered her voice. "Do I look like the kind of woman who casually sleeps with men she barely knows?"

"Uh, no." He shook his head and winced. "No, you

do *not*. Look, I'm sorry, I don't know why I even imagined we might have slept together. It was just that, for a minute there, I had this…weird feeling. But you're right, we hardly know one another."

"Good." She sent John another steely glance to completely squash any idea that she might be even remotely interested in him now or any time in the future. "I'm glad we got that sorted out."

She could not explain why John Atraeus was a nonstarter for her. He was nice, but he was just not her type. Unfortunately, she seemed to be attracted to difficult, dominating, untrustworthy men.

She took a deep breath and made an effort to relax but the conversation with John had shoved her right back into the rawness of hurt. She was now crazy angry that she had slept with Ben, and unfortunately John had gotten the brunt of it.

The taxi slowed to turn into the drop-off zone in front of John's hotel then came to a halt because there was a line of taxis. Sophie frowned when she identified a TV news van parked directly outside the entrance.

She glanced at John, who had tipped his head back on the headrest and closed his eyes. "Does the doctor know you're suffering some memory loss?"

John gave her a wary glance. "She asked me what day it was, but she forgot I was wearing a smart watch."

She frowned. "So how far back can you remember?"

John straightened as the taxi maneuvered into the forecourt. He peered at the hotel entrance as if the light hurt his eyes. "I remember checking in here yesterday morning and having a couple of business meetings. After that…? Nothing, until I came to in the car."

"Do you remember you've got a meeting this afternoon?"

He checked his watch, tapped on an app and muttered something under his breath. "How do you know about the meeting?"

"You told me not long before we had the accident."

"Even though I know the date, I keep thinking it's Saturday. Damn, I really did lose a day." He searched in his pocket and came out empty. "I don't have my phone. I must have left it in the car."

"Your phone's here." She fished it out of her handbag. "Unfortunately, the screen's shattered. I found it on the road. I think someone might have driven over it."

John stared glumly at the phone, then tried to activate it. When the screen remained blank, he gave up. "It doesn't matter, I know the details of the meeting—the time and the address—which is kind of weird when I can't seem to remember a thing about the last twenty-four hours."

Sophie paid the driver and kept an eagle eye on John as he slowly exited the taxi. She'd had a concussion once as a child when she had fallen off a horse. She could still remember the sickening thud as she'd hit the ground, colors shifting across her vision, then the headache to end all headaches. She had walked on eggshells for days.

A bellhop arrived to collect their cases, greeting John by name. Within a matter of minutes they were in the swanky lobby of one of Miami's most expensive hotels. Sophie noticed a sign directing press conference attendees to the launch event for a prominent technology company's newest generation of smartphones, and her stomach sank. That meant media, and lots of it.

As they waited at the front desk to get a spare key, because John thought he had probably left the room key in his car, Sophie glanced around. Her stomach sank as she recognized a familiar face: Sally Parker, a well-known journalist who had been at Nick's launch party last night, and so had probably witnessed Sophie pouring water over Ben. If she saw Sophie with John Atraeus now…

Face burning, Sophie tried to keep a low profile as John got the room key, but as they turned from the desk, John, who was moving a little woodenly, stumbled over the case of another guest. Afraid that he would fall and hit his head again, which would be incredibly dangerous for someone who was already injured, Sophie grabbed his arm. She had meant to steady him, but John, with his solid weight, ended up pulling her off balance. As he straightened, he steadied her, both hands wrapped around her upper arms.

"You sure you don't want me?" Despite his pallor there was a glint of humor in John's gaze.

"Positive." The motorized whir of a camera made Sophie tense as she quickly released herself. Not fast enough, she thought, as she caught the expression on Sally Parker's face.

Great. She could just imagine the tagline. *Sophie Messena on Man Rampage.* Or more probably, *Sophie Messena Dangles New Man in Ben Sabin's Face.*

She felt her blush deepen as memories flooded back. When Ben had ditched her a year ago, she had felt so hurt and betrayed she had deliberately let it drop to a prominent columnist that they were dating. A few days later, she had gone to a charity ball with a new man. The media had howled for a whole week about Ben being ditched.

Knowing Parker, she would resurrect the old story and play it again, and frame this one as a trashy love triangle.

As much as Sophie disliked that kind of media coverage, it occurred to her that maybe, after being abandoned by Ben a second time, a second fake, sensationalized story about her and another man was not such a disaster.

It wasn't something she had planned—*this time*—but it had worked for her before so why shouldn't it work again? When Ben heard that she had been snapped with John while en route to John's hotel room—just hours after she had slept with Ben—he would once again understand that *he* had been categorically dumped.

With calm deliberation, Sophie looped her arm through John's as they walked to the bank of elevators. "I've been thinking." She hit the call button. "Head injuries are tricky things. You probably shouldn't be alone, just in case there are complications—"

"Complications?"

"Let's not go there." She smiled briskly. "I've had a concussion. The headache tends to stick around. The painkillers are probably going to make you sleepy, which means you're going to have trouble concentrating. You should reschedule your meeting—"

"Not possible. They're Japanese, there's an interpreter. They're only in town one day, so it's a one-shot deal."

The doors slid open. Sophie waited until the elevator was shooting upward. She gave John a crisp look. "In that case, I've got a proposition. As it happens I speak a little Japanese. I'm happy to help you get through your meeting and, if you need it, I'll even stick around for the night to make sure you're okay. Strictly as a friend."

By the time Sophie had gotten John to and from his meeting at a hotel that was, thankfully, just a block away, he was as white as a sheet. As they waited for the elevator in John's hotel, Sophie noticed that Sally Parker was still staked out in the lobby. She decided that it was time to do some damage control in terms of her family, before the media story broke.

The most effective way to do that was to call her mother and give her a heads-up that she was spending the night in John's hotel room strictly on a medical basis. That way, if Nick or any of her other brothers heard anything, she could always refer them to their mother, who would calm things down.

Predictably, when Sophie called and mentioned the accident, Luisa jumped to the conclusion that Sophie was hurt. When she finally calmed down, she insisted on personally talking to John to check for herself whether or not he should be in a hospital.

Apparently, John received a favorable prognosis. He handed the phone back to Sophie. At that point she braced herself for the inevitable conversation about why Sophie was looking after John.

Avoiding John's interested gaze, Sophie attempted to keep her voice neutral and breezy—to completely ignore the fact that a media storm was brewing—and just relay the main points. "John's in business with Nick. He gave me a ride back from Nick's resort launch party this morning, and, as it happens, I've been wanting to pitch a business proposal to him."

Not that she was going to pitch the business proposal right now for two very good reasons. Atraeus was sick and weak, and it would be tacky to take advantage of him. Plus, she was in his hotel room. They both knew she was just helping him out, but it didn't matter. Discussing business while in John's personal space was crossing a line.

There was a small silence. "Nick told me he was going into business with Atraeus, which is fine. He seems a nice boy. A shame about Ben, though."

Even though she had braced herself for it, Sophie's stomach tightened at the mention of Ben. "You know about Nick's deal with Ben?"

"It's a bit hard to miss when it's being hash-tagged all over the place, along with that other stuff some journalist *apparently* overheard him saying—"

Luisa stopped midsentence, which in itself was unusual. Sophie could feel herself tensing more. When she spoke her voice sounded flat and husky even to herself. Betrayal, suspicion and anger seemed all tangled up. Part of her wanted to spill all of the hurt, but the other half of her would rather die than do something so wimpy.

She took a deep breath and let it out slowly. "So, what, exactly, has Ben been saying?"

Thoughts about what he could possibly have said that was bad enough that her mother didn't want to relay it cascaded through Sophie's mind. It had to be something personal. She immediately dismissed the idea that Ben would kiss and tell. As dysfunctional as their relationship—if she could even call it that—had been, he had always been discreet.

She had been the one who had lost her temper and made the silly mistake of deliberately telling the media that they were a couple, then publicly "dumping" him a few days later by dating someone else. In terms of revenge, it had come back to bite her because no one had believed she had been deeply hurt except for Francesca. The uniform response from her family had been polite interest tinged with disappointment. Worse, she was pretty sure Nick had even felt sorry for Ben, hence the

infuriating situation of Nick going into business with
Ben, the real villain of the situation!

"I shouldn't have said anything," her mother said
quickly. "You know what reporters are like, and Ben
did seem to be such a nice boy. It's probably all made
up, anyway."

Sophie's frustration ratcheted up another notch over
the fact that her mother would actually take Ben's side
in anything. "*What's* made up?"

There was a loud noise in the background, which
Sophie instantly identified as a helicopter.

"That's Gabe." Her mother's relief was palpable as
she mentioned the name of Sophie's oldest brother.
"He's down from Auckland for a few days with the
family. Sorry, honey, I've got to go. Talk to you later!"

A loud click in Sophie's ear signaled the end of the
conversation. Sophie stared at the phone for a long moment then checked online to see what her mother was
talking about.

Seconds later, she stared in disbelief at the headline
of the story—by the same reporter she had run into in
the lobby of John's hotel.

According to Ben, "Any man would have to be brain-
dead to date either of the Messena twins."

For a split second John's luxury hotel suite, with its
white sun-dappled walls, paved, leafy terrace and perfectly harmonized furniture, winked out to be replaced
by a red mist.

She checked the date of the article. It was the day of
the launch party, which meant Ben had made that insulting statement before he had slept with her.

She didn't know if that was better or worse.

Either way, it pointed to the fact that Ben wasn't
just a rat; he was a chauvinistic, insensitive predatory

rat with manners from the Dark Ages. She shoved her phone back in her handbag and walked out onto John's overlarge patio. She stared blindly at the gorgeous view of the wide curving beach with its gentle breakers flowing in off the Atlantic Ocean. It would be light for a couple more hours and there were still bright umbrellas stuck in the sand. Because it was a Sunday, whole families were relaxing on the beach, and kids were playing with buckets and spades.

The view was bright and cheerful, even idyllic, and out of nowhere she found herself fighting off tears because the scene made her feel lonely and isolated, as if her life—as busy and successful as it was—was empty.

Even though she knew the sense of lack of a lover or a husband came from Ben's rejection of her, that didn't stop it hurting. She drew a deep breath, attempting to dismiss and discredit a need she didn't want to be so crucially important.

Because wanting anything—or anyone—too much made you vulnerable. It meant you had to trust, and for Sophie the whole issue of trust was tantamount to running smack into a stone wall. It had been the death of countless relationships, usually on the first date.

The irony of it was, until she had met Ben, she had never been able to put her finger on what it was that her previous dates had lacked. When she had attended a beach barbecue her brother was throwing and had met Ben for the first time, his masculine confidence and easy air of command had made an instant impact. She had realized that what she was looking for in a date—and a possible husband—had come from her environment, from her brothers and the father she had lost when she was young.

Frustratingly, they were all things that were not polit-

ically correct, like the protective kind of masculine behavior that had irritated her and hemmed in her life for
years. She had gotten into the habit of examining and
discarding her dates when they were not right, but she
was equally aware that if she didn't, her brothers would
shoo her suitors away. Her brothers were usually low-
key about it, but if they knew she was seeing someone,
one of them—whoever was free—would make a point
of dropping in at her apartment before she got picked
up, or would turn up at the restaurant for the express
purpose of eyeballing her date. She had even gotten
used to her brothers' heavy-handed tactics because she
knew it was their way of saying they cared about her.

The problem was, she thought, that when you were
brought up with wolves, you tended to be like them.
It was also a fact that if she ever did choose a guy, he
would have to be able to hold his own with her brothers since *she* wouldn't accept anything less.

Which was why Ben had blindsided her, *and* her
brothers, and why on some sneaky, instinctive level
she realized that she had chosen him. He had the kind
of tough, alpha masculine qualities she had been un-
consciously looking for, and he had them in spades.

In theory, she should have been able to trust him.

Fiercely she wiped away the moisture that had
burned behind her eyes and finally spilled through.
Turning her back on the sun and heat of the beach, she
walked inside, closing the doors to preserve the air-
conditioned coolness.

She checked her watch and then looked over at John.
It was going to be a long night.

Seven

Eyes grainy from too little sleep, Ben got off his return flight from New York to Miami and strode through the arrivals lounge. Even though he knew he should be checking his emails to make sure there were no changes to his scheduled meetings, he found himself flicking through the news feed on his phone.

A headline from a tabloid stopped him in his tracks. "Eeny, Meeny, Miney, Who? Sophie Messena Chooses Atraeus."

On some level he was aware of people flowing around him, the annoyed glance of a businessman as his bag caught the edge of Ben's briefcase. He tapped the link. A photograph of Sophie Messena in a clinch with John Atraeus filled the screen and the bustling noise of the airport dropped away.

He scrolled down. Apparently, Sophie and Atraeus had spent the night at Atraeus's hotel suite. The lovebirds had ordered room service so they could stay in.

Weirdly—because there had been no champagne—a bucket of ice had been delivered along with the food.

Sound and movement seemed to rush back at him, twice as loud and more garish than before. Little more than twenty-four hours since he had gotten out of Sophie Messena's bed, and she was already with someone else. And not just anyone else. Sophie had been clear on the fact that she wanted in on the retail deal on Sail Fish Key, and John Atraeus was the only one who had the power to open that door for her.

Taking a deep breath, Ben unclenched his jaw. Grimly he wondered what had happened to the cool logic that had underpinned almost every decision he had ever made about his relationship with Sophie, except on two notable occasions when they had ended up in bed.

His attention was drawn back to the photo, particularly the expression on Sophie's face, which the photographer had zeroed in on. Her head was tilted back, the pure line of her throat exposed, her gaze intense. She looked as if she was about to kiss Atraeus, as if she couldn't get enough of him.

Fiery tension gripped him. He had no problem identifying what he was feeling. He was jealous. Crazily, burningly jealous.

He didn't like the fact that she had found someone else. He liked it even less that that person was Atraeus, because in his mind Ben had claimed her. A year ago, to be precise.

And he couldn't forget that a year ago, she had found a new someone else within a week. If he hadn't been thousands of miles away, and committed to the complicated process of picking up the reins of his uncle's sprawling business empire, he would have gotten the next flight back to New Zealand.

Instead, he'd had to content himself with doing some homework on the guy, and the next time he was back in New Zealand, he had made it his business to track Xavier Tate down.

A grin relieved some of Ben's tension. After a few pointed questions, Tate had caved. Apparently, Sophie had picked him up at a club and cut a deal. She would introduce him to her brother Gabriel, who ran the family bank. In exchange, Tate had done what he was told. He had escorted Sophie for a week and made it look like he was her new boyfriend. Tate had sworn up and down that he hadn't touched Sophie, that she had been crystal clear on the fact that if he so much as tried to kiss her, the deal was off.

Ben had let him live.

Ben had also concluded that the dates and the media hype, so soon after he had left, had been Sophie's way of covering up the fact that he had hurt her.

That was one of the reasons he had wanted to see her again. A part of him had always wondered if he had been wrong about her, that somewhere in the midst of the addictive, fiery attraction, there had been a glimmer of true emotion.

The other reason was that he hadn't been able to forget her, period.

Ben stared at the photo of Sophie and Atraeus, then with an abrupt movement he closed the page. Until that moment he hadn't understood how fiercely possessive he was of Sophie.

As he made his way toward the exit, he brooded over his obsession with Sophie, the edgy tension that gripped him every time he thought about her, the knee-jerk desire, not just to claim her, but to take her, first from Hunt and now from Atraeus. And all of this, despite knowing from hard, personal experience that, at a foundational level, their relationship wouldn't work because money lay at the center of it.

He registered that, in a weird way, his own hardline, alpha personality was working against him in this. At some instinctive level, from the first moment he had seen her, he had been fixated. He had chosen Sophie, and it seemed he couldn't simply unchoose her. He had spent the past year trying to neutralize what he could only describe as a fatal attraction.

Two days ago, all it had taken was one glance across a room to know that he hadn't succeeded. Jaw tight, he decided he needed to form a strategy to once and for all nix the attraction.

Now that he was irrevocably linked with Sophie through the business deal with Nick, she would be on the periphery of his life for some time. He needed to find a cure, a way to unchoose Sophie.

Although how he was going to achieve that he didn't know.

He was about to drop his phone into his pocket when it buzzed.

He noted the number and reluctantly answered the call, which was from one of his business partners.

The conversation was short and to the point. Malcolm Holt would be at the investors' lunch on Sail Fish Key as arranged, only he was bringing his daughter, Buffy, with him. Apparently, Buffy was very much looking forward to seeing him again.

Ben hung up and stared bleakly out the terminal window. He couldn't help reflecting that life had been a whole lot simpler when he had been a financial nobody working for Nick Messena. Now, in the space of two days, he had given in to the temptation to make a second, steamy mistake with Sophie Messena—a woman who hadn't wanted him until he had become a billionaire—and discovered that forgetting her wasn't so easy after all. At the other end of the spectrum he had Buffy Holt, an extremely wealthy young woman he had only ever dated because of his connection with Mathew Holt. Buffy had made no bones about the fact that she had chosen him and wasn't willing to take no for an answer.

Telling her no wouldn't have been a problem if her father was willing to be reasonable about Ben's disinterest. Unfortunately, Holt, an oil and real estate billionaire who had underwritten a major chunk of the Sail Fish Key project, had a reputation for being difficult. He had made no bones about the fact that he wanted his daughter to have *everything* she wanted, including Ben.

As much as Ben hated to admit it, there was only one way out. He needed a date for tomorrow. It was short notice, so he checked with Hannah. Unfortunately, her daughter, Ellie, had flown out that morning so no dice there. He thought about asking Nick if one of his staff might do it, but discounted the idea. Holt knew Nick and had stayed at his hotels. Chances were he might recognize one of the women. In any case, he would sniff a fake a mile off. Ben needed someone who was confident in the kind of rarified social strata in which Holt moved, someone who could believably be his date and whose very presence would shut down both Holt and his daughter.

Sliding his sunglasses onto the bridge of his nose, Ben walked out into the compressed heat of another steamy Miami day. He found the keys to the Jeep, unlocked it and placed his overnight case on the rear seat. He walked around to the driver-side door, tossed his briefcase onto the passenger seat, waited a few seconds to let the hot air out of the vehicle, then climbed behind the wheel. Adjusting the air-conditioning, he drove out of the overnight parking lot and accelerated into traffic.

The article about Sophie and Atraeus came back to haunt him as he drove. He stopped for a red light, his fingers tightening on the wheel. The problem was, a part of him couldn't believe that Sophie had jumped beds so fast.

Added to that, he knew what the reporter who wrote the article about Sophie and Atraeus was like. If Sally Parker ever stumbled over the truth, it would be a bona fide miracle.

Ben accelerated through the intersection but, seconds later, he did something he almost never did: he changed his mind.

Instead of taking an exit for the east side of town, he headed for Sophie's office, which was downtown, located directly above her newest boutique.

Minutes later he pulled into a parking space. The address was upmarket but nothing like the rarified, high-end luxury of an Atraeus Mall. Although, he guessed, after sleeping with Atraeus, Sophie's ability to access premium retail space would no longer be a problem.

He stepped into the air-conditioned building, checked the list of businesses and headed for the second floor. Within minutes he found Sophie's office. His jaw tightened as he took in the sleek neutral space with its luxe linen couch and spare designer coffee table, the avant-garde art. His gaze was drawn to a silver sconce on the wall that had an antique, faintly battered look. From its very simplicity, it looked like it could have once belonged in an ancient villa, maybe even one of the crumbling monasteries on Medinos.

Nick had once told him that Sophie had a passion for

Medinian objects, to the point that she regularly spent time poking around in secondhand shops, and brought pieces back from family holidays on the island, sometimes even forcing him to take the overflow from her luggage.

The fact that he remembered Sophie was sentimental about the Mediterranean island from which the Messena family had originally come was unsettling. It signaled that he was thinking about her too much, that he was sliding back into the old obsessive behavior he had sworn off.

He checked his watch. The reception desk was vacant, probably because it was lunchtime. Not prepared to give up, he found an open door.

Francesca pushed to her feet, her expression wary. "If you're looking for Sophie, she's out."

And just like that, he knew he had made a mistake coming to Sophie's office in the hopes of finding out she hadn't actually slept with John Atraeus. "With Atraeus."

A sharp clatter was followed by a muffled, distinctly unladylike word.

Francesca retrieved the cell phone she had just dropped, her expression oddly pale as she checked the screen. "John, uh—" she flushed and shook her head "—went back to New York. Sophie's in Miami, somewhere."

Ben frowned at the cell in her hand. "Is it broken?"

Francesca's gaze clashed with his. "It's not the phone that's broken. *That's* got a shockproof case."

Ben had the sudden conviction the conversation was operating on two levels. "So, you haven't seen Sophie?"

Francesca set the phone down on the desk. "She isn't exactly keeping me in the loop at the moment. I haven't seen her since Saturday night."

Which was unusual. From everything Nick had told him, as well as Ben's own experience of the twins, normally they were so close they were practically a double act. "So it is true. Sophie and Atraeus are together."

Francesca's brows jerked together. "If Sophie spent the night with him, then, yeah, you can pretty much guarantee they're together."

The confirmation sent tension spiraling through Ben. It was jealousy, stark and primitive. The very fact that he was jealous meant that he was no longer in danger of sliding back into obsessive behavior when it came to Sophie Messena: he was already there.

"Is there something wrong?"

His gaze snapped back to Francesca's. "What could possibly be wrong?"

"For a moment you looked...weird."

Like he wanted to catch a flight to New York and tell Atraeus, point-blank, to leave Sophie Messena alone?

Francesca's phone made a pinging sound as if a text had just come in. She stared at it as if it was a bomb about to explode, checked the text, then put the phone down, all the color, once again, gone from face. "If this is to do with business you can leave a message for Sophie. Although I thought it was Atraeus who was handling the retail from now on."

"I don't need to leave a message." He had what he had come for: verification that Sophie and Atraeus were a couple.

Half an hour later, Ben turned into the driveway of what had been his uncle Wallace's beach house—or rather mansion—and which was now his home base. The driveway had been repaired and the grounds restored to their original elegance but the old house still needed work. Given Wallace's wealth the place should have been pristine but following his "great disappointment" Wallace had become something of an eccentric. Despite his business savvy, his personal life had collapsed around him when his wife Solange had run off with a lover. The divorce settlement had meant Wallace's first real estate company had had to be sold, leaving him with a large house, which Solange hadn't wanted, and just enough cash to start again. Feeling broken and betrayed, Wallace had sworn off women, taken some crazy risks with real estate that had paid off massively and had managed to die a rich, lonely old man.

It was not a fate that Ben intended to share, despite the fact that it looked like he was headed in the same direction.

Extracting his overnight bad and briefcase from the Jeep, he walked inside, flicking lights on as he went. His footsteps echoed, owing to the fact that Ben had given away most of Wallace's dated furniture to charity and the place was in the throes of renovations. Consequently, most of the downstairs rooms were freshly painted but empty. In a month or so the flooring should be finished, and the new furnishings would go in. The emptiness hadn't bothered him too much until now because he had been doing so much travelling, but he was looking forward to having a real home once again. Tossing the cases down on a couch, he opened French doors and walked out onto a patio that had spectacular ocean views. He stared across an expanse of lawn at the wild stretch of beach and the crashing waves and was instantly spun back two-and-a-half years to Dolphin Bay, New Zealand, and the first time he had seen Sophie Messena.

Nick had thrown a barbecue for him down on the beach to welcome him to the firm. Sophie had arrived

partway through, dressed in white jeans and a neutral
shirt, her dark hair coiled in a loose knot. Compared to
the other women at the party, who were mostly dressed
in bright, skimpy dresses, she had seemed low-key and
sophisticated. One assessing glance from her dark eyes,
and he had known things were going to get complicated.

The conversation with Francesca that afternoon replayed itself in his mind.

When he had met Sophie for the first time, he had
also met Francesca. They had looked strikingly alike,
except for the way they dressed and wore their hair.
Francesca had looked bright and cheerful in a jungle-
print dress, her hair loose. He had felt an instant hot
punch of attraction for Sophie and absolutely nothing
for Francesca, except a basic recognition that she was
beautiful, pleasant and, for want of a better word, nice.

That hadn't changed. As gorgeous as Francesca was,
he didn't react to her at all. She could have been his
sister.

Intellectually, he knew the difference was all to do
with personality. Something about Sophie got to him.
Whatever it was, Francesca did not possess it.

Ever since Ben had walked away from Sophie a year
ago, he had steered clear of dating anyone who looked
remotely like Sophie. Clearly, that tactic hadn't worked.
Now it occurred to Ben that desensitization—spending
time with someone who looked a lot like Sophie—could
be the key to "unchoosing" Sophie.

In which case, Francesca could be the ideal date
he needed for tomorrow. She was gorgeous, available,
wealthy in her own right, and she would handle both
Buffy and Malcolm Holt with ease.

He found his cell phone, looked up the number and
made the call. Francesca picked up. She was in the mid-

dle of a meeting, but to his surprise, agreed to meet him for a drink, even naming the place.

With grim satisfaction, Ben terminated the call. If he could convince Francesca to be his date at the Sail Fish Key lunch, with any luck he would be killing two birds with one stone.

He would be free. Free of the pressure to date Buffy Holt, and free of his obsession with Sophie Messena.

Sophie finally made it home to her apartment at around two in the afternoon, following an interview with a prospective store manager for a new property she was opening in Fort Lauderdale.

John had left on an early flight, which had been something of a relief. As nice as he was, she had found out fairly quickly that they did not have much in common apart from a possible business connection.

The sudden ringing of her landline was startling, mostly because almost no one had her number. People rang her cell. It was Francesca, and she sounded oddly breathless.

"Can you meet at Alfresco at six?"

Sophie frowned. Francesca's apartment was a few streets north of hers. Alfresco was a restaurant and bar situated about halfway between their apartments, so it was easy for them both to reach on foot. "What's the rush?"

"I thought we could have dinner. And, by the way, Ben…uh…called in at the office looking for you today."

Sophie's fingers tightened on the receiver. Suddenly her heart was pounding so hard she could barely breathe. Thoughts cascaded through her mind, including the crazy conviction that, despite everything that had happened, Ben did want her. That, somehow, she had gotten things totally wrong and he hadn't actually walked out on her.

She didn't know what could possibly have happened, but maybe there had been some kind of emergency, and now she had ruined things utterly because he would think she had slept with John.

But if there had been an emergency, why hadn't Ben tried to call her or leave a message? He had her number; he could call her any time he wanted.

Her heart rate flattened out. No, she hadn't gotten it wrong. Ben had not been able to leave her suite fast enough. And the bunch of red roses that had arrived with no note had underlined that fact.

"I don't get it," she said coolly. "Why would he do that?"

"Maybe because you spent the night with him," Francesca said crisply. "When I told him you weren't in, he left."

Sophie tensed. "How did you know I spent the night with Ben?"

There was a small silence. "I saw you kissing him at Nick's launch party, out on the terrace, then you disappeared. It was an easy bet that you spent the night together."

Heat warmed Sophie's cheeks. She vaguely recalled that there had been a few people on the terrace, but there had been no one close, and she and Ben had been at one end and in the shadows. She had thought they had been reasonably private and discreet. "Why didn't you say anything to me about it?"

There was an awkward silence. "Did you really expect me to? The scene near the dance floor was pretty public. And there were a dozen or so people out on the terrace when you kissed Ben, including that gossip reporter Sally Parker. When I walked outside looking for you, it seemed clear that you'd gone after Ben to get him back."

Another wave of embarrassed heat flared through Sophie. She felt like crawling away to hide in a very small, very dark corner, because Francesca was absolutely right. Sophie *had* been trying to reclaim Ben. "Does Nick know?"

"He knows about the kiss and, like everyone else on the planet, he knows you spent the night with Atraeus."

It registered that Francesca sounded a little strange, her voice flat and cool, almost as if she was angry. Sophie frowned. "What's wrong? You seem upset—"

"I'm fine! Why would anything possibly be wrong with me? I'm the happy one who always floats along on the surface and who never has dramas or gets hurt or ditched."

Okay, so Francesca was definitely angry about something. Probably that, after all of the advice and counseling she had given Sophie—and after Sophie had vowed and declared that she was finished with Ben—Sophie had turned around and slept with him again. She rubbed at her temples, which had tightened with a niggling stress headache. "Look, maybe we should forget the restaurant. We're both tired. I haven't had much sleep, and I need a shower—"

"Nick also wants to come along. He's stuck with clients until five thirty, so he's suggested six o'clock at Alfresco."

Even though she had been braced for it, Sophie's stomach tightened. Of all her brothers, Nick was probably the most opinionated and stubborn. Usually it didn't matter, but this time her private life had gotten entangled with Nick's business. The potential was there for him to think she had slept with both of his new business partners, and *that* he wouldn't take lightly.

"If it's any consolation, I don't think he knows you slept with Ben."

Relief made Sophie feel suddenly weak. She sat down on a chair, her mind racing. She loved her family to pieces, but her brothers—especially Nick—tended to be medieval in their thought processes. When it came to their sisters and sex, if they'd had their way, she and Francesca would have died virgins.

It was way too late for that scenario, but that didn't mean they wouldn't be upset. Calling Luisa Messena had been a way of short-circuiting the storm, but it was a fact that if Nick thought she had slept with Ben again, let alone John, it wouldn't be long before he was knocking on her door demanding an explanation. It would take a major event to distract him.

When she'd impulsively decided to stay with John, she hadn't thought about Francesca's possible reaction, or Nick's. All she'd wanted to do was get past the horrible feeling of being ditched by Ben for the second time, of somehow being lacking in the qualities that attracted a mate, of being essentially unlovable. And to make sure Ben understood that *he* was forgotten.

Now it looked like Francesca thought she'd spent nights with both Ben *and* Atraeus. And who knew what Nick thought. "Look, it's not what it seems. I admit, I wanted to get back at Ben, and spending the night with John seemed the perfect solution. He's tall, dark and handsome and the media love him, so from that point of view he seemed perfect. Plus, he was obviously in need of some TLC—"

"*He* suggested you spend the night with him?"

The niggle at Sophie's temples sharpened. "Not exactly. I admit I had to twist his arm, but in the end it was win-win for us both. Especially since—"

"Spare me the details." There was a tense silence. "Does Mom know?"

Sophie frowned again. No doubt about it, Francesca thought she had a thing for John, otherwise why ask the Mom question? It was an unwritten rule that all of the Messena siblings only ever told Luisa Messena about a date when it was someone who was a possible husband or wife. So far she had only ever told her mother about one guy: Ben, and look how that had worked out.

Suddenly, she was over the inquisition and Francesca's complete lack of support for her when usually she was a reliable shoulder to cry on. And completely over the idea that she was unpopular and couldn't sustain a love life. "Mom's cool with it," she bit out. "As a matter of fact, I called her from the hotel."

"I guess if Mom's happy," Francesca said flatly, "then I should be happy for you."

"You don't need to be happy for me! John and I aren't in a relationship. He's likable enough but he's a bit like that guy I dated the other night, what's his name...?" Sophie's brows jerked together. "*Tobias.* Not really my type. I didn't even mean to spend the night with John, but that reporter Sally Parker was in the hotel foyer and I was in a state of shock because—" She stopped; suddenly her chest was banded so tight she could barely breathe. "Ben walked out on me," she muttered huskily. "Again."

There was a brief, vibrating silence. "I thought you were over him! You said you wouldn't have anything more to do with Ben."

Ridiculous tears burned her lids at the concern in Francesca's voice. Until that moment the conversation had been stilted and tense, almost as if they had fallen out, which was crazy. "I was stupid enough to change my mind."

"Then you spent the night with John Atraeus."

"Like I told you, that was just a convenient arrangement. We were just helping each other out—"

"Well, just so you know, Ben's asked *me* out on a date. And I'm thinking of saying yes!"

The sudden dial tone indicated Francesca had hung up.

Shock reverberated through Sophie. Replacing the phone in its cradle, she stared bleakly at the wall for long seconds. Francesca was now dating Ben? In what world could that happen?

Francesca had only ever tolerated Ben because of Sophie. Even then, she couldn't count the number of times Francesca had told her to forget about Ben because she had a feeling about him, because he was a bad risk. Because of all the men Sophie had dated, Francesca liked him the least.

Snatching up the phone again, she called Francesca, but it was busy. Frustrated, she terminated the call, found her cell and called Francesca on that. The call went through to voice mail.

Placing her cell on the coffee table, she began to pace. She wondered whom Francesca was calling? Ben?

An odd sense of disorientation gripped her. She felt like her whole world had been tipped upside down and shaken. Every cell in her body rebelled at the idea of Francesca and Ben together. It just didn't compute.

She found herself staring at an oil painting Francesca had painted and given to her as a gift. It was a large vivid abstract, with slashes of red, orange and bright turquoise that somehow fitted perfectly with Sophie's minimalistic decor and, through some kind of curious alchemy, made everything work.

The contrast of the vibrant painting with Sophie's restrained decor seemed to sum up their relationship. Francesca was creative, Sophie was more about numbers and organization, but they complemented each other. Beyond family, they were best friends.

And they did not date each other's boyfriends.

Or at least they hadn't until Francesca had undergone a Jekyll and Hyde transformation.

Sophie hadn't wanted to go out again, but now wild horses wouldn't keep her from that restaurant. Out of sheer habit, because she was the one who usually took care of details like booking restaurant tables, she called Alfresco. Six o'clock was a busy time, because a lot of people called in there after work. If she didn't book, they would end up having to wait for a table.

A waitress Sophie knew quite well answered. When Sophie made the reservation, Alice checked the computer and came back to her. "No need, Francesca booked the table, but for five, not six. Do you want to change the time? Because if so, I'll have to call her to confirm—"

"No, five is fine. Thanks!" Sophie hung up. Her stomach felt tight and her head was thumping. She paced a few steps and found herself staring at her reflection in a mirror. Her cheeks were pale, her eyes dark, and there was a pulse beating along the side of her jaw, which only happened when she was ultrastressed.

There was only one reason for Francesca to be at Alfresco a whole hour earlier than she had arranged with Sophie and Nick. She was meeting someone else. And that someone else had to be Ben.

Francesca had said on the phone that she was thinking of saying yes to Ben, which meant that she hadn't agreed to date him yet. Meeting him secretly at Alfresco could only mean she had decided to go ahead with the date, because if she was saying no all she needed to do was phone or text.

Sophie checked her watch. Her stomach tightened. It was almost five now. For the space of a few seconds she couldn't decide what to do next, which was so infuriatingly not her. Then a weird kind of calmness took over. She could be wrong. Maybe Francesca wasn't meeting, or dating, Ben.

And maybe pigs could fly. Either way, she needed to know.

Adrenaline pumping, she dragged the pins from her hair, strode into her bedroom and quickly changed into cotton jeans and a white camisole top. She checked her reflection in the mirror and frowned. If she was surveilling the restaurant, it followed that she didn't want to be seen, so it made sense to avoid wearing her signature white.

She quickly changed into a pair of olive green linen pants that had been a mistake purchase, and a taupe shirt that also happened to have matching blocks of olive on it. It struck her that together the pants and shirt looked uncannily like camouflage, but she didn't have time to change again. Besides, the whole point was to blend in and not be seen.

She brushed her hair out so that it swung loosely around her shoulders then found a ball cap in a neutral color and dragged it down over her brow, tweaking the bill so it shaded the top half of her face. She put on sunglasses and grinned. Her own mother wouldn't recognize her. Checking her watch and muttering beneath her breath because now she was late, she slipped on casual sandals, grabbed her handbag and headed for the door.

Dealing with Nick wasn't going to be easy; he was difficult on a good day but she could manage him. It was the possibility of Francesca making a play for Ben, meeting him behind her back, that was making her see red.

That would happen over her dead body.

Sophie may have made a mistake with Ben twice, but he was *her* mistake and no one else's.

Eight

Sophie parked her SUV in a space half a block short of Alfresco, so that if Francesca was meeting Ben she would be able to see her approaching from the opposite direction. As she turned the ignition off, a muscular four-wheel-drive Jeep cruised slowly past. She caught a glimpse of tanned cheekbones and a tough jaw and froze. It was Ben, looking remote behind a pair of dark glasses.

Her mood plummeted. If Ben was here, then Francesca had to be meeting him.

She considered ducking down but decided against it. She was pretty sure Ben didn't know what her vehicle looked like. Plus, she was wearing the ball cap, so it wasn't likely he would recognize her anyway. When she caught the movement of his head, as if he was checking out something in the rearview mirror, she stiffened, then common sense kicked in. He was looking to park, so of course he would check for traffic behind him.

Nevertheless, she slunk down a little lower in her seat and watched until his Jeep pulled over, just a few spaces ahead. Seconds later, without looking in her direction, he strolled into the restaurant. Letting out a relieved breath that he hadn't seen her after all, she checked her watch. Now that the air-conditioning was off, the SUV was heating up. She noticed a heavy buildup of dark clouds, which accounted for the increased humidity.

As the minutes ticked by and she didn't spot anyone remotely resembling Francesca walking into Alfresco, she pondered what to do. Maybe it was a huge coincidence that Ben was here, but how likely was that? She had to conclude that Francesca had arrived early and was already waiting inside for him.

That conclusion should have been enough, except that a stubborn part of her wanted absolute proof; she needed to see them together. Grabbing her handbag, she stepped out into the breathless heat, locked the SUV and started toward the restaurant.

As she walked along the sidewalk, the sun was blotted out by a large purple cloud, and thunder sounded in the distance. But the threat of a cooling downpour didn't seem to make any difference to the air, which was hot and compressed and humid, opening every pore.

She reached the restaurant and took out her phone, pretending to be absorbed by the screen as she surreptitiously checked out the diners visible in Alfresco's windows. Frustratingly, Ben and Francesca were not there, which meant they were seated farther back, possibly even in the shady little courtyard out back.

Perspiration coated her skin and trickled down her spine as she tried to decide what to do next. She undid a button of her shirt and flapped the damp material in an effort to create a cooling draft. She longed to rip the cap off and throw it away. But now that the initial surge of hurt and anger had passed, her usual clarity was returning. She had come this far; she wasn't going home without proof. She needed to see Ben and Francesca together.

Large droplets of rain made the decision for her. She was going in. If Ben and Francesca saw her then, that was a risk she had to take. As she neared the front door of the restaurant, an unexpected solution presented itself. A large group of young people who were seated outside, alarmed by the impending downpour, now wanted to be reseated inside. She let them dash into Alfresco ahead of her, then stepped into the foyer directly behind them. To any casual onlooker, she hoped it would appear that she was with them.

She had kept her sunglasses on, which made things a little dim, but even so she saw the back of Francesca's head almost immediately. She was alone. A cautious wave of relief went through Sophie. Francesca had her laptop out, which meant she was probably working on a design project, something she sometimes did in cafés. Although that didn't mean she wasn't also meeting Ben.

A waitress was in the process of showing the chattering group ahead of her to tables when she saw Ben step in from the rear door, which led to the courtyard, and slide into the seat opposite Francesca. He had a cell in his hand, which meant he had probably just stepped outside for a few minutes to take a private call. As he sat, his head came up and his gaze locked unerringly with Sophie's.

For a split second she froze like a deer in the headlights, then a whole raft of feelings hit: confusion, humiliation, hurt. When she had seen Ben with the anonymous blonde at Nick's launch party, she had been coolly, quietly furious. But this was different: Francesca was her *sister*. Ben had crossed an unforgivable line.

Pulse pounding, she turned on her heel and walked outside. Still on automatic pilot, she threaded her way through the now vacated outdoor tables. Cool air laced with droplets of rain hit her as she headed for her car. She dragged off her sunglasses and dropped them in her bag. She was within sight of her SUV when thunder detonated overhead. Glad that she had thought to pack a small umbrella, she retrieved it from her handbag and flipped it open. Seconds later, torrential rain crashed down.

Ben's gleaming black Jeep loomed out of the blanket of rain. She deliberately gave it a wide berth. Some preternatural instinct made her glance over her shoulder. She glimpsed the unmistakable figure of Ben as he stepped out of the restaurant.

Her heart slammed against her chest and she quickened her pace. She vetoed the thought that he was coming after her. He was probably just heading to his Jeep. After all, he had only glimpsed her in a darkened foyer, and she had been in disguise and wearing sunglasses. How could he possibly have known it was her?

And why should she be worried if he *had* recognized her? She wasn't the one who was sneaking around. All she had wanted to do was confirm whether or not her twin was meeting with her ex-lover. *She* had done nothing wrong.

Annoyed with her panicked overreaction, Sophie forced herself to relax and slowed her pace to a sedate stroll. Ben might have a lot of sterling attributes, but the last she'd heard he did not have supernatural powers.

Ben called her name.

Adrenaline pumped. Sucking in a deep breath, Sophie kept her nerve. If she didn't respond, but kept walking as if the name Sophie meant nothing to her, maybe Ben would think he was wrong and give up.

Her SUV loomed through the steady rain. Fingers shaking annoyingly, she found the keys to the SUV and deactivated the lock.

A distant clap of thunder signaled that the short, violent squall was moving away. The heavy rain ceased as suddenly as if someone had turned off a tap.

With controlled haste, she put the umbrella down. Another step and her fingers closed around the handle of the driver's side door, but her heady moment of triumph that she had avoided Ben was cut short by his deep voice. "Damn, it *is* you."

She yanked open the driver-side door of the SUV, but before she could climb behind the wheel, a hand curled briefly around her wrist, almost stopping her heart.

She spun, outraged that Ben had touched her, even if he had released her almost immediately. She glared at him, noting with grim satisfaction that while she was relatively dry, he was soaked, his black T-shirt plastered to his shoulders and chest and water dripping from his hair. But soaked to the skin, he somehow managed to look larger and edgier than usual.

"Did I give you permission to follow me, or touch me?" She rubbed her wrist to underscore the severity of the touching transgression. "The short answer to both questions is no."

Ben's gaze was cool and disconcertingly direct. "What are you doing here? Now?"

She shook out her umbrella and tossed it on the back seat. "Not that it's any of your business, but I, too, have an arrangement to meet Francesca."

Gratifyingly, a faint hint of color burned on his cheekbones. "I thought that was at six."

She extracted her phone from her bag and placed the bag on the passenger-side seat. "So, I'm early."

"Way early. You were already parked when I arrived—"

She spun and glared at Ben. "Meaning what? That I'm spying on you? What makes you think I would even *want* to spy—"

He lifted the cap off her head. "The way you're dressed, for a start."

Embarrassed heat burned through her as she snatched the damp cap from his fingers and tossed it onto the back seat along with the umbrella. So much for going undercover. "Last I heard you aren't a member of the fashion police."

She should leave. The problem was, arguing with Ben was addictive and oddly satisfying. Until that moment she hadn't realized how furious she was with him.

She met his gaze squarely. "And what would you know about how I dress, or actually, anything about me at all? We've dated twice. In actual fact, they don't even count as dates, because you never asked me out. I just happened to be there, and it was just casual sex, which is horrible to think of when you were the first—"

His gaze sharpened. "The first what?"

Her jaw locked, but there was no point trying to cover up what she had almost said, because she could see by his expression that he knew.

Ben felt like he'd just been kicked in the chest.

When he spoke the words rasped out of him. "Are you telling me that, a year ago, before we made love, you were a virgin?"

Sophie's expression became smoothly blank as suddenly as if a blind had dropped. She glanced at her watch. "Well, this has been fun, but I need to get moving."

And right there he had his confirmation, because if Sophie hadn't been a virgin she would have made very sure he understood that fact. Instead, she was trying to fob him off, as if he was an underperforming employee or one of her dates whose services she no longer needed.

With the revelation that Sophie had been a virgin, suddenly, a number of puzzling details fell into place. Sophie's touch-me-not manner and the formidable reputation she had garnered for preselecting, vetting and controlling her dates. It might also explain how from the time they had first met, it had taken eighteen months of simmering attraction and cool distance before they finally did go to bed.

He was beginning to understand why Sophie had been so angry with him when he had walked away a year ago. At the time he had thought she had set out to seduce him because he had just inherited a fortune, but that was the kind of move a more experienced woman undertook. Understanding that she had been a virgin put a whole new slant on what had happened.

He considered that she could have intended to use her virginity to ensnare him, but he instantly discarded the thought for the plain fact that she hadn't ever told him she was a virgin.

Added to that, Sophie had never tried to place pressure on him, and with the financial power wielded by her brothers and their business connections, she could have. Instead, she had done the exact opposite. The instant he had walked away, she had set about publicly and effectively ditching him, to the point that even Nick had commiserated with him. The clincher was that, even when they had slept together the other night, she hadn't mentioned the fact that she had been a virgin the first time they had made love.

If he hadn't come after her now, he doubted he would ever have found out. Sophie would have closed up and cut him out of her life, the way she had before.

But now he did know, and the knowledge changed everything.

He was beginning to understand that, unlike a lot of the women he had dated over the years, what you saw with Sophie was only the tip of the iceberg. He was also beginning to understand that the more she felt, the more closed off she became. Getting to know Sophie Messena was like peeling an onion, and the layers were fascinating and frustrating. In a curious way, it made sense of his obsession, because if Sophie had been easy to figure out, he would have walked away without a backward glance.

The ring tone of a phone cut through the sound of traffic and the distant rumble of thunder. Giving him a cool glance, Sophie dug her phone out of her bag and half turned away to take the call.

Ben caught the name *John* and every muscle in his body tightened. It had to be John Atraeus, and Sophie's lowered tones, her attempts to keep the call private, confirmed it. She repeated a date and a time, which were instantly recognizable to Ben because he had received a courtesy invitation for the opening of Atraeus's new mall complex in Manhattan on that date. If he didn't miss his guess, Sophie had just agreed to go as Atraeus's date.

Over his dead body.

The fierce surge of possessiveness that accompanied the thought was clarifying.

He had spent the past few days, *the past year*, attempting to dismiss what he felt for Sophie. She was too high-maintenance, too problematic and, with her wealth and connections, she reminded him of his ex-fiancée. Nothing about Sophie's cool elegance or sharp business focus had suggested that she was even remotely capable of fulfilling his own need for a relationship based on emotional warmth and family values. Now, in the space of a split second, everything had changed.

"That was Atraeus."

Sophie's fiery gaze clashed with his. "It was John. Not that it's any of your bus—"

"Atraeus is all wrong for you. You'd be bored within a month."

She shoved the phone back into her bag. "What you know about me would fit on the back of a postage stamp. Just because I made a mistake and slept with you doesn't mean you can have an opinion, or interfere in my love life."

Ben crossed his arms over his chest. "I talked to Atraeus a couple of hours ago, when he forgot to join a conference call we'd arranged. He told me about the car accident *and* the amnesia."

Sophie leveled him with a chilly gaze. "And your point would be?"

"You didn't sleep with him. Just like you didn't sleep with that other guy."

"Which other guy would that be? In the last year I've dated quite a few very attractive men. I'm pretty sure the number stands at around twelve, not including John."

"That's a lot of one-night stands."

Sophie's brows jerked together. "I don't do one-night stands."

And with that statement, a vital piece of information clicked into place. "But you did with me," he said softly.

Sophie seemed to freeze in place. "Sleeping with you was a mistake. Both times."

But she had slept with him, when he was suddenly certain that she had not slept with anyone else, yet.

Atraeus had been a smoke screen so far, just as the guy she had dated a few days after their first night together had been a year ago.

After talking with Atraeus, he had done some checking online. It hadn't taken long to discover that most of the men Sophie dated had only lasted the one date. The overwhelming picture was of Sophie organizing her social life by picking safe, controllable men for various occasions. Probably by interview, he thought.

The knowledge that Sophie had only ever been his settled in.

Just minutes ago he had been caught in the grip of obsessive desire. That hadn't changed. What had changed was the raw surge of possessiveness that was now part of that desire.

And the knowledge that if he didn't claim Sophie, John Atraeus—with his reputation for running through beautiful women—would.

In that moment something shifted and settled inside him. Yesterday, all he had wanted to do was purge himself of his obsession with a woman he thought was driven by cold practicality and *his* bottom line. But in the space of a few minutes everything had changed. Sophie Messena was complex, intriguing and unexpectedly vulnerable, and he wanted her back in his arms and in his bed.

And Sophie Messena wanted him. Nothing else explained the fact that she had slept with him, twice.

But getting seriously involved with Sophie Messena could have only one outcome: marriage.

He had been on the verge of canceling his date with Francesca tomorrow, but he decided to stay with the program for two very good reasons. If he took Sophie with him tomorrow and Buffy made a play for him, Sophie would go nuts, and the last thing he needed was a scene. Added to that, he needed some time to figure out how this was all going to happen, because getting involved with Sophie Messena would send ripples through every avenue of his life, personal *and* business. That left him still needing a date to neutralize the pressure Holt was applying for Ben to cement *their* business relationship by marrying his daughter. At this point, the way he saw it, he couldn't afford to cancel the date with Francesca.

A last remnant of the storm whipped hair across Sophie's face. She hooked a glossy strand behind one ear and shot him a defiant gaze. "Shouldn't you be getting back to Francesca?"

The satiny tumble of dark hair around her shoulders, when normally Sophie's hair was pinned smoothly back, spun Ben back to the last time they had made love. It made him abruptly aware of the mistakes he had made with Sophie and the need to soften his approach. With Atraeus in the wings, he also had to think about staking some kind of claim. It was a complete about-face, but finding out that Sophie had been a virgin, and that she had only ever belonged to him, had changed the rules.

His gaze locked with hers. "Did you get my roses?"

She looked briefly confused. "What roses?"

"The ones I sent after Nick's party."

She frowned, tilting her head slightly to one side as if she was having trouble remembering. "I seem to remember some flowers arriving. Were they from you? I couldn't tell."

Ben guessed he deserved that since he hadn't enclosed a note, but that didn't change the fact that, suddenly, he was ticked. "Were you expecting flowers from someone else? Atraeus, for example?"

"If Atraeus—*John*—sent me flowers that would be none of your business."

Ben's jaw locked. "Atraeus won't be sending you flowers."

And the gloves were off. Her eyes shot dark fire as she stepped closer and jabbed a finger at his chest. "I don't see why it should matter to you one way or the other."

Sophie was so close he could feel the heat from her skin, smell the delicate, exotic scent of her perfume, see the dark shadows beneath her eyes as if she hadn't slept. Join the club, he thought, and his control shredded.

Catching her hand in his, he spread it against his chest.

"This is why."

He took a half step forward, and a split second later, his mouth came down on hers.

Nine

Sophie's response was hot, conflicted and instant.

She should be utterly rejecting the soft brush of Ben's lips; she should be pushing him away. She was hurt—he had hurt her—and she was angry, with a passionate, burning anger that he just didn't seem to get.

But then he didn't get her. Because if he did, he wouldn't have treated her as if she was some kind of convenient bedmate. A disposable lover without vulnerabilities and needs, who wouldn't be wounded when he walked away.

But the very fact that Ben had been upset at the notion that Sophie might have considered the flowers came from John Atraeus, even knowing she hadn't slept with him, had filled her with a weird pulse of hope, because the words had been possessive, even jealous.

But how could that possibly be? That would mean that she mattered to him, that he cared. And if he cared, why had he walked out, twice? And why was he dating Francesca now?

Her fingers wound into the damp fabric of his T-shirt. If she still had access to the gorgeous bunch of red roses he had sent her she would have flung them in his face, then ripped the tender, velvety soft petals from the stems and stamped them into the ground.

She didn't have the roses, but she did have Ben. Anger and passion twined together as she found herself lifted up on her toes. Grasping his shoulders to drag him closer, she angled her jaw to deepen the kiss, all of which underlined the problem she had with Ben: she was a possessive, jealous lover, and she hated it that he should want anyone but her.

Ben muttered something low and flat. His arms closed around her, pulling her in tight against him. Heat swept through Sophie and with it a hot, piercing ache. Her arms clamped around his neck, and a sensual shiver swept her as her breasts flattened against his chest, the nipples pebble-hard. She felt the firmness of his arousal.

Dimly she registered that Ben's arousal should ring alarm bells. It shouldn't turn her on and she shouldn't adore the feel and taste and scent of him, especially not when he was planning on dating Francesca tomorrow.

Ben lifted his mouth long enough for her to gulp in a mouthful of humid air. Sophie was vaguely aware of movement, one step, then two, and the brush of warm metal at her back, the solid weight of Ben pressing her against the side of her SUV.

His muscled thigh slid between hers, intensifying the heated ache low in her belly. It was the point at which she should have said no, planted her palms on Ben's chest and pushed free. But the knowledge that he would stop in a heartbeat, contrarily, made her want the exact opposite, because in her heart of hearts she had always hated that Ben was so cool and controlled that he could step away from this—from *her*—unscathed. She needed him to want her, to feel *something*.

She must have stiffened slightly, because Ben lifted his head, his gaze locked with hers. "Do you want me to stop?"

In response she slid one palm down over his abdomen and cupped him through the taut denim of his jeans. He muttered something low and flat. A split second later she found herself hoisted up so that her feet dangled a few inches from the ground. Reflexively, she clutched at Ben's shoulders, hanging on for dear life as he moved against her, once, twice. She dragged in a damp lungful of air and clamped her arms around his neck, holding him closer still.

They were fully clothed, damp fabric dragging over skin. The sun was out now, burning through the thin cotton of her top, reminding her that they were practically making love in broad daylight in a public place, but it didn't matter. Desire shivered and burned, coiling tight as he moved against her a third time and heat and sensation exploded inside her.

For a long, endless moment time seemed to stand still. Her pulse was pounding, and she could feel the fast, steady thud of his heart. She couldn't believe she had just climaxed, in broad daylight. But in some distant part of her she was also aware that while she had lost control, Ben hadn't.

The honk of a horn flipped her eyes open. Steam rose in wispy tendrils off the road and sidewalk, wreathing cars and turning the air into a steam bath. Ben's hold loosened as a car swept past, spraying water.

He stepped away, his gaze watchful. "Are you okay? I didn't intend to—"

"Make love to me in broad daylight, in the street?" Sophie straightened, glad of the support of the SUV "Or make love to me, period?"

Feeling flustered and embarrassed, she yanked down her shirt, which had ridden up, baring her midriff. As she did so, a car pulled into a space behind Sophie's SUV. A young couple exited, glancing at them curiously.

Ben frowned at the street, which, now that the rain had stopped, seemed to be filling with people. "We can't talk here." He extracted his phone from the back pocket of his jeans. "I'm in town for the rest of the week. Why don't we meet for lunch?"

Her chin came up. That did not sound like an invitation to Sail Fish Key tomorrow, and right now that was the only date she was interested in. "I'm free all day tomorrow."

His gaze connected with hers and held it for a long moment. "I'm not. How about the day after?"

For long moments, Ben's clear refusal to give up the date with Francesca didn't compute, because she had thought that, after the heart-stopping intimacy they had just shared on the street—the fact that she had actually climaxed in broad daylight—he would choose her.

She stared at the obdurate line of Ben's jaw, the red mark on his neck that she must have made. For a wild moment she actually considered asking him not to take Francesca to Sail Fish Key, to take her instead, but that would be begging, and she had to be better than that.

She drew a deep breath. One thing seemed clear. She was tired of beating herself up by staying on hold for a man who simply did not want her enough and could not commit. That was victim behavior.

And she absolutely refused to compete for Ben with her own sister.

Out of nowhere a curious calm settled on her. Somewhere in the back of her mind she recognized it for what it was: a bona fide Messena trait. She had seen it in her grandmother, who had been a formidable businesswoman with an exceptional intellect. Very occasionally, the cold, scary eyes surfaced in her brothers when they had to make unpopular decisions that were set in stone.

With measured movements, she snagged her sunglasses out of her bag and put them on. She would not allow a doomed fatal attraction to ruin her life.

She had to completely eradicate any idea that she could take charge of Ben and make him fall for her by having sex with him. It hadn't worked, *twice*. Make that two and a half times. She had to face the fact that it might never work with Ben, so trying to apply the tactics her sisters-in-law had used on Nick had been flawed, totally impractical reasoning.

There was only one viable decision.

She had to finish with Ben. Forever.

She met Ben's patient gaze and tried not to be mesmerized by the fact that his T-shirt was plastered to his chest and abs.

"Thanks for offering me a real, live date some time when it suits you," she said with steely sweetness. "But I think I'd rather fling myself off the nearest cliff and die a watery death in the Atlantic Ocean than attempt another date with you."

Feeling abnormally calm, Sophie drove back to her apartment. As she stepped in the door, she texted Francesca that she would be a few minutes late. Francesca texted back to say no problem, Nick was going to be late, too, so she would rebook for seven.

Walking through to the bathroom, Sophie dragged off her damp, rumpled clothes and threw them in the laundry basket. She never wanted to see those particular items again.

After a cooling shower, she changed into a white camisole and a pair of loose white linen pants. Five minutes to apply makeup and fix her hair in a loose knot, and she was ready to go.

It wasn't until she walked into Alfresco's that her calm began to disintegrate. She was early and the first to arrive, so the waitress showed her to one of the tables out front.

While she was waiting, instead of checking Buffy's social media pages the way she usually did in her downtime, Sophie decided to check up on Francesca. What she found was interesting. Normally Francesca posted multiple pics of whomever she was currently dating, but there were no snaps of Ben. Even more telling, there was not one mention of him. In terms of Francesca's online social life, Ben did not exist.

Which all seemed to confirm that Francesca didn't even particularly like Ben. As far as Sophie knew, she wasn't attracted to him, either. Francesca's type was Ben's polar opposite; someone who was kind, friendly and open, and who possessed manners.

Something was definitely off.

The clincher for Sophie was that for Francesca to break their pact to keep their hands off each other's guys by dating Ben meant that something had happened that Sophie was not aware of, or Francesca was being pressured in some way.

She closed the page and slipped her phone back in her bag. Seconds later, Nick arrived, still dressed for the office and looking harassed.

A pretty young waitress materialized, delivered glasses and water, and dropped menus in front of them.

Nick handed his back, and said curtly, "Thanks, I won't be staying."

Francesca hadn't yet arrived, but Sophie knew what she liked, so she went ahead and ordered the tapas and the homemade lemonade for which the café was justifiably famous.

Nick waited until the waitress had left before giving Sophie a blunt look. "You know what I'm going to say."

Nick had his stern look on, but it was a fact that he never scared her. She had seen him at age eleven, chubby, with glasses. That was twenty or so years ago, but still… "If it's about John Atraeus, don't bother. There is no relationship. There is no problem."

He sat back in his chair and folded his arms across his chest. "And Ben?"

She kept her expression bland, all the while wondering exactly what Nick had heard. "Ditto."

"That's not what the media are saying."

Deciding to completely ignore what the media might be saying about her and Ben, she briefly told him about John's head injury and the meeting with the Japanese businessmen.

Nick shot her an irritable look. "Why didn't you ring me? I would have helped him out, without the headlines."

Sophie studied Nick's set jaw. He had a thing about car accidents, because years ago he had been the first on the scene of the fatal accident that had killed their father. The accident, and the loss, had stunned them all, but Nick had always been haunted by the fact that he had not gotten to his father in time to help him. "I was on the spot. It was no problem to help John."

"That's the second accident in the past year," he growled. "And you didn't tell me about the first one, either."

"You were out of the country at the time. Besides, I wasn't badly hurt, just a sprained wrist and a couple of bruised—"

"I know exactly what happened to you. Aside from the wrist, you had a few minor cuts and bruises and an injury to your lower back that was serious enough that you were lifted out in a stretcher and helicoptered to Whangarei Hospital. You spent two nights in the hospital before insisting that Francesca help check you out, in a wheelchair, your arm in a sling, against doctor's orders. I read the traffic police report. The only thing that saved you was the fact that when the car rolled, you didn't hit any big trees, and the thick manuka scrub acted like a brake, stopping you from rolling farther and plunging over the edge into the sea. Go on with the story."

Sophie poured water into the glasses. "I went to the hospital with John and got a taxi to take him back to his hotel. When I discovered he'd lost any memory of the last few hours, naturally, I decided to stay and keep an eye on him—"

"And that had nothing to do with Ben, right?"

Sophie decided to ignore Nick's sardonic tone. "I rang Mom to get advice. She seemed to think staying was exactly the right thing to—"

"Mom is not a doctor."

Sophie gave Nick a very direct stare. She had learned at about the age of three that the only way to counter all of the macho dictatorial aggression of her brothers was to fight fire with fire. "Did I say she was? I think we both know she's a very experienced paramedic. Besides the other doctor, the one who saw John at the hospital, said I should stay, also."

Nick pinched his nose, then got up to pull out a chair for Francesca, who had just strolled in off the street. "Let's just stick with figuring out exactly what you were up to with Atraeus. You've treated him like the invisible man for the last couple of years. Pretty sure I've heard you describe him as boring as a post a couple of times."

Francesca sat down and gave Sophie an icy look before flipping open the drinks list with a small snap. "John Atraeus is not boring. He's...nice."

Sophie frowned at the way Francesca was behaving, but they couldn't have a conversation about it until Nick had gone.

Nick's gaze glinted with impatience. "Sophie, back to the conversation. Atraeus. I called him earlier. He said you were going to New York."

Sophie dragged her attention back to Nick. "To his mall opening in Manhattan, which I'm thinking will be great for *my* business. I don't know why this matters so much to you, unless you think it's going to somehow hurt your own precious deal."

"It matters because you're my sister."

Sophie's jaw locked. Every time one of her brothers tried to take the fatherly role with her, especially on matters of the heart, a stubbornness rose inside her and she found herself closing off. It had nothing to do with the age difference, which was negligible.

More probably it was because all four of her alpha, super-tycoon brothers were clueless when it came to relationships. Damian was still single, but Gabriel, Nick and Kyle were married. And the only reason that had happened was because each one of their wives had taken a hardline approach that had eventually delivered results.

She appreciated Nick's protective attitude, which meant he loved her. But Nick wanting to pry into her private life and imagining he could offer her relationship advice that she might actually take was, quite frankly, scary.

Nick's phone vibrated. He took it out of his pocket and checked the screen. "I've got to go."

Sophie suddenly remembered that Nick was scheduled to be at a business conference in Los Angeles. "I thought you were supposed to have left town yesterday. And that you were taking Elena with you?"

"We delayed the travel by a day. Elena felt she needed to see her doctor before she flew—"

"You didn't say she was sick!"

Francesca abandoned the drinks menu. "I was just talking to Elena. She's not sick."

The penny dropped. Sophie stared at Nick, who was now grinning. "You're having a baby?"

"In six months' time. Elena didn't want to say anything until she made sure the pregnancy was good to go."

Sophie was over the moon for Nick and Elena. They'd been trying for a family for a while, and there was nothing she would like better than another cute little niece or nephew to spoil. But as she congratulated Nick, an odd tension ran through her, a sense of time passing—and *bypassing*—her. It wasn't that she wanted to be a mother yet; it was just that seeing how happy they were made her aware of the emptiness of her own personal life.

For the past two-and-a half years she had been stalled, courtesy of her fixation on Ben. To date, he had been her only lover, and now she was beginning to wonder if she would ever find that special someone who would actually love her back.

A buzzing noise had Nick glancing at his phone again. He pushed to his feet as he did so. "It's Mom. We told her about the baby this morning, so now she's planning on visiting. This is going to take a while."

As Nick stepped out, a waitress delivered their lemonade and the tapas. The restaurant was starting to fill up with a steady trickle of the dinner crowd. There was a pleasant, relaxed buzz of conversation, which Sophie would have enjoyed if it wasn't for the unfamiliar tension that had sprung up between her and Francesca.

Sophie picked up a baby stuffed pepper, then froze as a lean, broad-shouldered guy walked out of the darkened interior of the restaurant. She caught the clean lines of his profile and jaw, the five-o'clock shadow and, for a disorienting moment, saw Ben.

Her heart jolted even as she recognized that it wasn't Ben. The man's smile was too easy, his features too smooth, nothing like Ben's rough-edged masculinity and air of command.

And right there was her problem, because it was a fact that she liked that Ben was so edgy and difficult. If Ben was more classically handsome and charming, like John Atraeus, she wouldn't have looked at him twice.

A little grimly, she sipped her lemonade, barely noticing the cool, sweet bite. Time to take the bull by the horns. "I know you can't possibly want to date Ben, which means he must have pressured you—"

"He didn't pressure me."

Sophie stared at Francesca. They had never, ever

been at odds over a guy, and she couldn't understand why it was happening now. Until just a few hours ago she would have bet her own business that Ben and Francesca had nothing in common. "I just don't understand why he asked you."

"When he could have asked you?" Francesca slapped a generous helping of pâté on a chunk of bread. "Maybe he finds me attractive?"

Sophie instantly rejected the idea that Ben was more attracted to Francesca than her. That logic would fly only if he hadn't slept with Sophie last week, then kissed her today.

None of it made any sense.

The bottom line for Sophie was that, no matter what Ben's reasons were, dating Francesca after what they had done in the past few days was crossing a line.

Francesca's gaze clashed with hers. She selected another slice of ciabatta bread and tore it in two. "If you must know, Ben asked me if I'd help him out. Apparently, he's having a problem with the daughter of one of his investors chasing after him. I said yes."

"Buffy Holt."

Francesca's head jerked up. "How did you know that?"

"Her social media accounts are practically wallpapered with pictures of Ben."

Buffy had a habit of cataloging her relationships from beginning to end on social media. She had an impressive list of exes, most of whom were involved in the music industry and sported multiple tattoos and piercings. Ben, who was older and in business, was a definite departure, which seemed to suggest that Buffy had finally reached the end of her rock-chick phase and had fixated on Ben as husband material.

A little bleakly, Sophie thought that someone should tell Buffy she was wasting her time, since Ben and the word *husband* did not belong in the same sentence.

"You've been following Ben online? Are you crazy? I told you not to do that!"

Francesca's outraged response surprised Sophie, but it was a good surprise, because she sounded more like the Francesca she knew. The Francesca who was not attracted to Ben and who didn't even like him very much. Sophie picked up her phone. "You can't date him."

Francesca's gaze was direct and distinctly chilly. "Why. Not?"

Sophie flicked through to Sally Parker's site and found the insulting headline from the other day that revealed what Ben really thought of them both: *Any Man Would Have to be Brain-Dead to Date Either of the Messena Twins*.

She slid the phone across the table so Francesca could read it. "That's why."

Francesca went red, then white, then red again. "So why on earth do *you* want to date him? Because that's what this is all about—" Her eyes widened. "You still want him."

Sophie stared bleakly at the tapas, her appetite suddenly gone. "It's more that I want to stop wanting him."

There was a brief, tense silence. "Is that why you slept with John?"

"I told you I didn't sleep with John."

"You didn't tell me that!"

Sophie felt her cheeks warming. From memory she had been upset enough with Francesca's conviction that she had slept with John one night after sleeping with Ben that she had deliberately left her thinking the worst. "I stayed the night in his hotel suite, but not in his bed.

Like I tried to tell you when you rang earlier, I was just helping him out."

Briefly she explained about the accident.

Francesca frowned. "Let me get this right. John's got *amnesia*?"

"Just involving a few hours." And then the devastated look on Francesca's face registered.

Suddenly a whole lot of disparate facts made sense. Francesca wanting to make herself over more radically than she'd ever done, her comment that maybe there was someone special. The fact that she had spent the night with someone on Saturday.

"You slept with John." Now Francesca's behavior over the last couple of days made perfect sense. She thought Sophie had poached her guy. "I didn't know. If I had I wouldn't have stayed the night in his suite. It was the accident thing. I just wanted to help."

"And that's why you phoned Mom. Not because he's a boyfriend, but for medical advice."

"If it helps, John only *just* likes me."

"He invited you to Manhattan—"

"Only so we can talk business. But in any case," Sophie said with sudden decisiveness, "I'm not going. You are."

Francesca's gaze was stark. "I can't. What if he doesn't *remember*?"

"Does it matter? If there's something special between you, that won't have gone away. Just…redo whatever you did the night you slept together."

There was a long pause during which the clink of plates and the buzz of conversation seemed deafening. Then Francesca's expression lightened. "Why didn't I think of that? Okay, I'll go to New York."

"Great. And I'll go on the date with Ben tomorrow."

Francesca frowned. "I don't see how Ben's going to agree to that."

"He's not going to know it's me." *Not until she felt like telling him.*

"You mean, do a switch? Now that you didn't steal my guy, I agree that you can date Ben. But I don't see how the twin-switch thing is going to work. For a start, you'll have to dye your hair blond. You *hate* blond hair."

Relief that Francesca had come around to the idea of the switch so quickly banished the horrible tension that had held her ever since she'd heard about the date. It was just such a huge relief that Francesca hadn't fallen under Ben's spell after all. "It'll only be for a short time, then I'll change back." Sophie stabbed another olive. "According to the media, Ben's got a thing for blondes."

Francesca looked suddenly defensive. "What's so wrong with that? A lot of men do. John does."

Which explained Francesca's decision to go blond. A decision that had worked out for Francesca, until John had lost his memory.

It dawned on Sophie that with Ben's well-publicized penchant for blondes, attracting his attention had always required something more than her usual low-key approach, which relied on…actually, nothing more than just being herself.

Sophie considered the fact that her conservative mind-set and hair color had meant the odds had been against her all along. No wonder it had taken eighteen agonizing months for Ben to respond to the attraction she had been certain had sizzled between them all along. And then, when he had finally responded, she could not forget that she had been the one who'd had to take the initiative to get him into bed.

It had been no different two nights ago. Somehow,

just like the first time, she had managed to convince herself that Ben wanted her, and then had taken charge and rushed him into her bed.

Twice she had seduced Ben, and twice he had ditched her. The only time he had credibly taken the initiative had been when he had followed her yesterday and kissed her out on the street. But she wasn't sure if that counted, since he had backed off fast afterward.

As if he had regretted kissing her.

She couldn't help thinking that, once her hair was blond, it would be interesting to find out if Ben treated her any differently.

Francesca dissected a piece of roasted eggplant. Absently Sophie noted that Francesca's nails were a deep, glossy pink that was far more eye-catching than the pale or clear polish Sophie usually wore. If she was going to succeed with Ben, clearly subtlety was out.

Francesca stopped torturing the eggplant. "Are you sure you're not secretly in love with Ben?"

"Why would I be in love with Ben? I just slept with him, that's all."

Heads spun. The conversation at nearby tables died. Sophie tried to look as if that kind of statement was no big deal, but she couldn't stop the hot color that warmed her cheeks.

Francesca lifted a brow. "Okay, whatever. But don't you think this is all just a little…obsessive?"

Sophie dragged her thoughts from Ben. Ben, looking edgily handsome in a suit with his tough jaw and broken nose; Ben, in faded jeans and a wet T-shirt. Ben, naked.

Ben, the rat.

"I am not in love with Ben." She stabbed at another olive. "And I am definitely not obsessed with him."

She was over him.

Any man would have to be brain-dead to date either of the Messena twins.

By the time Sophie was finished with Ben, he would be eating his words. He would, hopefully, have found some actual manners. And he would have an entirely new appreciation of why no one should ever try to date *both* of the Messena twins.

This was about revenge.

Ten

Sophie extracted her phone from her handbag as she left the restaurant, found the number of her hairdresser, who also happened to be Francesca's, and called him. As luck would have it, Rico's salon—which did regular late nights—was still open.

When Rico heard what she wanted—the exact same color he had put in Francesca's hair just days ago, which was called Britney Blonde Bombshell—he was so silent that, for a moment, she thought she'd lost the call.

She checked her watch. "If it's too late to come in now, no problem, I'll just buy some product and do it myself."

She heard a swift intake of breath. "You won't get Britney Blonde Bombshell off a *shelf*. It's a professional salon product. Besides, have you ever colored your hair?"

"I'm pretty sure you know the answer to that question." She had always been very firm with Rico that she liked her hair exactly as it was, and he was wasting his time talking to her about coloring it or adding any kind of artificial enhancement.

"Which is why you shouldn't be allowed to touch a bottle of hair dye. And most definitely not one off a supermarket shelf!"

Half an hour later she was seated in a comfortable chair while Rico worked his magic with her hair. She had to admit, as layer upon layer of foil went on, it became increasingly difficult to maintain the level of fury that had driven her into the salon in the first place.

It was a little too late to reflect that, when it came to Ben, she fell into the same trap every time. Her cool, controlled process dissolved and the passionate Messena emotions she normally kept tightly repressed catapulted her into situations like flinging water at Ben, sleeping with Ben and, now, coloring her hair for him.

Not that she was actually going blond *for* Ben. The only reason this was happening was to *fool* him.

Though the thought that Ben might like her better as a blonde made her go still inside for long, dizzying seconds.

Rico lowered a hair dryer over her head. "Looking good, babe."

The blast of hot air jolted her out of the disorienting feeling that in taking Francesca's place she was subtly sabotaging herself—that in her heart of hearts the reason she was doing it was because she still wanted Ben—and that this was a devious way to get him back!

One of Rico's assistants, a young man with bright blue hair called Antonio, who specialized in doing piercing and tattooing in a back room, handed her a frosted glass of lemonade. Feeling faintly sick because there was no going back now, Sophie sipped the lemonade and wondered at what point she had turned from Sophie to babe. Was it before or after Rico had applied Britney Blonde Bombshell?

As the color developed, she checked her phone, her annoyance levels skyrocketing when she saw a string of Buffy alerts. Since she couldn't afford to walk into the situation tomorrow unprepared, she clicked on the latest one. This time, something akin to compassion replaced the tension that usually gripped her when she checked Buffy's page, because she knew the gorgeous socialite was about to be Ben's latest discard.

The page opened. The message *B loves B*, delicately inked onto the golden tanned flesh of one slim upper arm, leaped out at Sophie, and her compassion died.

Buffy had gotten herself a tattoo.

In the grand scheme of things, maybe that didn't mean so much since Buffy had a number of tattoos. There was the dolphin on her left ankle, Asian writing on her left arm and the edgy, rock-chick pattern just above the base of her spine.

Feeling weirdly disoriented, because just seconds before she had been sure that Buffy was absolutely not Ben's type and had temporarily fixated on him because Ben and her father were in business together, she scrolled down a little farther. She found a close-up of the tattoo with a small caption. Apparently, Buffy had gotten the tattoo following a weekend party on her father's superyacht that Ben had flown in for a couple of weeks previously.

Cancel the pity party. Now she was just plain mad.

Buffy had also posted new photos of a charity dinner in New York for a wildlife preserve, which she had attended with Ben the night after he had slept with Sophie.

Sophie stared at pictures of Buffy clinging to Ben's arm and Buffy sitting next to him at an exquisitely set table, with a champagne bucket in the shot.

Now she knew exactly why Ben had been in such a hurry to leave her suite the night they had made love. He had gone directly from her bed to Buffy's.

She scrolled farther down to another set of snaps. Apparently, the event had included an auction, and Ben had bid on a number of items, which included a fluffy toy and a pair of extremely expensive diamond earrings. Buffy didn't have a picture of herself wearing the earrings, just one of the earrings nestled in their box. However, there was a close-up of her cuddling a small fluffy bear.

Sophie stared at the earrings, which had to be at least a carat each, and which were made and donated by Ambrosi, a high-end jeweler that had started out as a Pearl House on the Island of Medinos. Originally owned by the family which had given the Pearl House its name, Ambrosi was famous for its rare pearls. Now a global business, it was equally famous for its diamonds.

The earrings glittered with a soft fire. They were the kind of earrings a man gave to his wife or his lover: a gift of love and consideration. The kind of gift that, over the two-and-a-half years she had known Ben, had never been given to her.

With a stab of her finger, she closed the page.

On Rico's advice, after he had washed and blow-dried her hair, she had a makeup consultation with the salon's beautician. Apparently, with the change in hair color the low-key palette she normally used would make her look washed-out and tired. With the clock ticking, just fourteen hours before she needed to meet Ben, she also had her nails done. Since Francesca had gotten her nails done in Rico's salon, it was easy to get the exact shade of pink Francesca had chosen.

When the beautician was finished, she stared at herself in the mirror. The fact that she looked exactly like Francesca was something she was used to, just not with blond hair.

As she pushed to her feet and retrieved her handbag, her new blond locks swirled around her cheeks and her new, long glossy pink nails seemed to glow even brighter under the salon lights. When she extracted her card to pay, she snagged her nail on a zip pocket, making a deep scratch, although she disliked the color so much it was hard to care.

She noted that she would not make a good spy, because it was a fact that she did not adapt to change well. Ever since she was small, she had liked order and routine and was black-and-white in her tastes. If she liked something, such as her own hair color, she really liked it. If she disliked something, such as Britney Blonde Bombshell, then it was usually a complete and utter no for all time.

Making a determined effort to look happy for Rico's sake, and not shell-shocked because she hated her new hair color, she reminded herself that it was just for one day, and paid.

Before she left the salon, she made a second appointment for the following evening to change her hair back to its original color. Rico, who was clearly used to eccentric clients, made the appointment without blinking.

Before she left, she also had a word with Antonio, who headed up the tattooing department.

As she strolled out into the mall, Sophie registered

that her stomach felt distinctly hollow. She had skipped lunch and hadn't really eaten at Alfresco. Before she shopped for clothes, she needed to eat.

She made a beeline for a late-night street vendor stationed on the corner. Occasionally, when she was working late, she stopped by Big Mike's on the way home and bought a vegetarian taco and a diet soda. Normally, the transaction was quick and neutral, with minimal eye contact but, apparently, the blond hair changed everything, because now all Big Mike wanted to do was chat.

He took her money and winked. "Want a little hot sauce with that, babe?"

With calm deliberation, she dropped her purse into her handbag and fixed him with a level stare. "That would be no and no."

Big Mike froze. "I thought you were the other one."

The words *the sexy, more interesting twin* seemed to float in the air.

Holding the taco slightly away from herself so she wouldn't get grease on her clothing, Sophie strolled around a corner and back to the parking garage where she had left her car.

She told herself that she wasn't upset at Big Mike's reaction. No, she was glad about it, because it pointed out the flaw in her impersonation of Francesca: their wildly differing personalities.

Since acting was not her strong point, she would have to devise a strategy that would ensure that she and Ben had virtually no time alone together. The lunch itself would be a breeze, because he would be busy with guests. It was the initial meeting with Ben and the helicopter flight to and from Sail Fish Key that would be the problem.

She slid into the driver's seat of her car, locked the doors and sipped her drink, before taking a careful bite of the taco. Phase one of the operation was complete. Now she needed to buy Francesca clothes. She was tempted to drive across town, open up her own boutique and select some things. But she would also need makeup and a small bottle of Francesca's perfume, which meant she would have to shop elsewhere, anyway.

After she had finished eating, she drove to a nearby mall. Within minutes she found an upmarket boutique and bought a sheer jungle-print top and a pair of turquoise jeans. Half an hour later, she had shoes and accessories to match, along with a turquoise leather tote. Her final purchases were new makeup, since all of her eye shadows and lipsticks were on the neutral side, and a small vial of Francesca's favorite perfume. If she was going to carry this off, she needed to smell right.

By the time she made it back to her apartment, it was close on midnight, but she couldn't go to bed until she had figured out a way to fill her time alone with Ben so that there was virtually no opportunity for personal interaction.

The research she had done on Buffy in the salon had given her an idea.

Ben had bought Buffy gifts, and Sophie was meeting him at the Atraeus Mall so they could head out to Sail Fish Key together. Therefore, shopping seemed the perfect solution.

Making him buy her the same gifts Buffy had received would not only send a clear message; it would also turn the date into the kind of high-maintenance nightmare that would make Ben run a mile and dissuade him from ever coming near Francesca, or herself, ever again.

This was not just about her now: it was also about
Francesca.

Before tomorrow was over, Ben would discover that
the only person who was brain dead was the guy who
tried to date *both* the Messena twins.

The next morning, after a restless night, she drove
into the office—early so that no one she knew would
see her—in order to catch up on paperwork and reply to
emails. If everything went to plan, she would be able to
have the date with Ben and then get back to Rico's and
have her hair color restored before anyone other than
Francesca knew she'd had her hair dyed blond.

A good half an hour before anyone was due to arrive at the office or the boutique, she drove back to
her apartment and changed into her bright Francesca
clothes. She followed the instructions the beautician at
Rico's had given her the previous evening and made her
makeup a lot heavier than usual. She examined herself
in the mirror, then slid a stack of pretty bracelets onto
one wrist and stepped into the strappy turquoise shoes.
After a generous spray of perfume, she checked out the
effect in the mirror.

She looked like Francesca, but something was still
wrong. Francesca was vivacious, her features mobile.
In comparison, Sophie's gaze was too direct, her jaw
too set, and her face was way too calm.

Rummaging in a drawer, she found the largest pair
of sunglasses she owned and slid them on. The effect
was good but, if she was going to fool Ben, she would
need to keep them on all the time *and* avoid making
direct eye contact.

On impulse, she packed a pair of faded blue jeans, a
white sweater and sneakers into the bottom of her tote,

just in case the weather turned rainy as it seemed to do late afternoons and she didn't have time to drive home to change before her appointment at Rico's. She also packed a bottle of water, some protein bars, a bag of her favorite vegetable chips—which sounded revolting but were actually quite nice—and an apple, just in case she did have to miss dinner and go straight to the salon.

She checked her phone. According to the text Francesca had sent her, lunch was out on the island at the almost completed resort and was a full-on catered party with on-site chefs, a bar and waitstaff. Ben had chartered launches to transport staff. A number of investors and contractors were flying in and the Holts would be arriving by superyacht.

She checked her watch. It was five after eleven. She was supposed to meet Ben at the street entrance of the ultraexclusive waterfront Atraeus Mall. *Her* territory, she thought with a purr of satisfaction. Apparently, the helicopter he normally kept on the wild, marshy stretch of coastline where he lived would be waiting on the roof.

They were meant to meet at eleven sharp, which meant she was already late. But eleven was way before they were supposed to get to the lunch. Apparently, Ben needed time alone with her so he could brief her on her role as his fake girlfriend before they flew out to Sail Fish Key.

As if she was going to be some kind of robot drone who followed orders.

Sophie replaced her phone in the small, perfectly shaped pocket in her tote. She did not see why she needed a half-hour briefing when she already met the only criteria that counted.

She was blonde.

Eleven

Ben paced the glossy marble atrium of the large and luxurious Atraeus Mall. He checked his watch. But the fact that Sophie's twin was late wasn't what was praying on his mind.

He had made a mistake.

After an early-morning phone call with Atraeus that included the casually dropped information that Atraeus would be discussing a business partnership with Sophie when she came to New York to attend his opening, that mistake had come home to roost.

He knew how focused Sophie was on business and success.

He also knew just how much Atraeus could do to assist her in achieving her business goals. Goals that Ben could easily have helped with, if only he hadn't been so set against mixing business and relationships. An issue with which Atraeus clearly had no difficulty.

Yesterday's kiss replayed in his mind, literally stopping him in his tracks, and suddenly his decision was made. He wanted Sophie. His feelings for her were curiously black-and-white, and they weren't just sexual. He wanted her, period, despite the money issue: despite the risk that she could one day decide that he wasn't the kind of husband an heiress should marry and walk out on him.

He crossed his arms over his chest and stared at the shoppers drifting through the mall, abruptly annoyed at how wimpy that sounded, as if he wasn't good enough for Sophie, as if he was afraid to take a risk. If he had applied that kind of rationale to business, he would never have come back from near bankruptcy.

When push came to shove, he thrived on risk and challenge.

If he was honest, it was one of the key reasons he wanted Sophie. And after two and a half years, his desire hadn't gone away. If anything it had gotten stronger.

But if he didn't claim Sophie now, he was starkly aware that Atraeus would.

The plan had been to slow things down, to control the relationship. But the thought of Sophie, who had only ever been his, with another man made him go still inside. He couldn't allow that to happen.

For better or worse, Sophie Messena was his.

Ben checked his phone in case Francesca had sent him a text canceling the date. When he didn't see either a call or a text, he decided to call her and cancel the date. Now that he had decided he wanted to move on Sophie quickly, it would be a whole lot cleaner if Francesca did not come with him to Sail Fish Key. Buffy Holt was going to be a nuisance, but he had fended her off for the past few months. He could last another day.

As the call went through to voice mail, a flash of

turquoise turned Ben's head. Francesca, dressed in ul-
trabright colors and wearing a large pair of sunglasses
walked through the elegant marbled entrance of the
mall.

Ben terminated the call without leaving a message.
Gaze narrowed, he watched Francesca stroll toward
him. Not with quick, light strides, but with languid,
longer steps. The blond hair was confusing, but the
smooth walk, with the faint hitch to her stride—as if
she was favoring her right side—the tilt to her chin and
the instant buzz of arousal warming his loins were dead
giveaways. Along with the fact that the woman walking toward him hadn't answered her phone.

It wasn't Francesca. It was Sophie.

The disguise was more complete than the one she
had attempted yesterday, but once again he registered
that he would know Sophie Messena even if she had a
bag over her head.

There were additional giveaways, things he didn't
generally notice about other women but which he
couldn't help observing in her. The habit she had of always hitching her hair behind her right ear, which she
was doing right now. And, when she was up closer, he
was certain he would also see the small scar on her
wrist he had noticed a couple of days ago and the tiny
freckle at the base of her throat.

Just to confirm, he rang Francesca's number again
and had his confirmation. Both of the twins lived on
their phones. It was inconceivable that either Francesca
or Sophie would be without a phone during the day. If
the twin walking toward him had been Francesca, she
would have her phone in her hand now, checking on
who was calling even if she didn't bother answering.

The tension that had gripped him ever since the conversation with Atraeus dissolved and was replaced by relief and a familiar pulse of excitement.

The very fact that Sophie had taken Francesca's place, and had dyed her hair blond, when he knew from comments Nick had made that Sophie would never go blonde, meant something.

She wanted him.

Every muscle in his body tightened.

Yesterday, Sophie had literally said she would rather die a watery death in the Atlantic Ocean than go on a date with him.

Looked like she had changed her mind.

Even before she had strolled through the glossy, sliding doors of the mall, Sophie spotted Ben, looking lean and muscular in a pair of light cotton pants and a loose white gauzy shirt, the sleeves rolled up over tanned forearms. She tried to avoid staring at him, but once she'd spotted him, it was unexpectedly difficult to drag her gaze free, almost as if she was caught in the grip of some kind of weird magnetic force.

One slow second passed, then two. She noticed that his phone was glued to his ear and wondered who he was talking to, then he half turned and his gaze locked on hers through the lenses of her sunglasses. Her stomach clenched and a hot thrill shot down her spine. *Not* the right reaction.

As he started toward her, irritation clear in his gaze—probably because she was a good twenty minutes late—she had the sudden distinct sense that he could see clear through her disguise, that he knew exactly who she was, and panic gripped her.

She needed to calm down and think. Better still, she needed to do something that Francesca—who was skillfully adept at coping with her multitude of exes—would do. Like pretend she hadn't seen him.

After all, with her sunglasses on, and with the mall buzzing with shoppers, how could he possibly know that she had?

Keeping a pleasant Francesca smile on her face, she abruptly changed direction, as if she hadn't noticed Ben, and walked briskly toward a gorgeous café, with tables and chairs grouped outside the front door. Most of the tables were filled with women, designer bags grouped at their feet, but a lone guy was standing nearby, his back toward her, checking his phone.

He was far from an ideal choice, since he was at least three inches shorter than Ben, about forty pounds heavier, and his hair was thinning in patches. Unfortunately, he was also wearing a suit that looked a shade too small, but beggars couldn't be choosers, and how was she to know that Ben had dressed down for the beach?

As she made a beeline for the man, she could feel Ben's gaze drilling into her back, sense his long, ground-eating tread gaining on her with every step. Adrenaline zinged through her veins as she quickened her pace; she had the breathless, faintly panicked feeling of being hunted. Hitching the strap of her tote more firmly on her shoulder, she registered that she had wanted to feel pursued, but *not* because Ben thought she was Francesca.

Jaw taut, she sped up and waved at her quarry. When the guy in the suit realized she was headed straight for him, he gave her a startled look. Relieved that she hadn't had to resort to a Francesca-like hug, Sophie attempted a brilliant smile. "I'm sorry, but you look *exactly* like the person I'm supposed to be meeting—"

"Who happens to be right behind you," Ben growled. "But I'm pretty sure you already knew that."

Even though she was prepared for it, Ben's low, gravelly tones sent a little shock through her. Heart pounding, she turned toward him and tried to look surprised.

In that moment she shouldn't have felt anything but anger tempered by a dose of caution, but apparently her body wasn't connected to her brain, because awareness, sharp and heady, burned through her, tightening her breasts, pooling low in her belly and making her skin feel ultrasensitive.

She logged the sharpening of his gaze, as if he knew she was actually turned on by him, and tried to think. This date was going to be difficult enough to navigate. She could not afford for Ben to think that Francesca was attracted to him. She needed to do something to distract him.

Before she could change her mind, she closed the distance between them and gave him the brief Francesca-style hug she thought she might have had to give the stranger with the phone. She didn't intend any real body contact, just the social hug, but Ben didn't cooperate. He stood straight and unbending, as if he was carved from stone, which meant she had to take a half step closer than she'd planned and go up on her toes. In the process, she ended up brushing against him. That would have been okay, if she hadn't felt a part of him she shouldn't have felt.

Outrage poured through Sophie. Up until that point, she had not taken Ben's date with Francesca seriously because in her heart of hearts she had not thought he actually wanted Francesca.

Ben had not seemed to be even remotely interested in Francesca until yesterday when he had found out Sophie had spent the night with John. And for two-and-a-half years, every time Sophie and Ben had been in the same room the attraction that had flowed between them had been like an electrical current; it had gone both ways. Plus, if Ben had felt anything toward Francesca, Sophie would have known it, and Francesca would have told her, but for all this time there had been nothing. *Nada*.

After yesterday's kiss, and the fiery passion that had exploded between them, while Francesca had been kicking her heels inside the restaurant, the idea that Ben wanted her twin was utterly confusing.

Something was going on. She didn't know what, exactly, but she would find out.

For now, what she did know about Ben was that on a first date with her own twin—just two days after ditching Sophie—it was *not* okay for Ben to be aroused.

She was allowed to feel sexual arousal. After all, just three nights ago she had been having sex with Ben, and yesterday she'd had an unscripted sexual incident with him out in the street.

She wished she didn't feel anything for him. Unfortunately, she couldn't wipe her memory and reprogram herself, and she *did* feel something.

As Sophie stepped away from Ben, she stared at a pulse that was throbbing along the side of his jaw. She was off balance, her emotions all over the place. Normally she was very good at summing up character; it was the one area where she was genuinely intuitive. But with Ben she was distressingly blind. She still had difficulty grasping that she had been so wrong about him, that he was in no way white-knight material.

She drew a breath to ease the sudden tightness in her throat, her chest, because his sexual arousal—*for Francesca*—was hurtful in a way she could barely process. As if her twin was far more desirable to him than Sophie had ever been. As if Sophie had only ever been second-best.

Memories flickered. It had been so difficult for her to get Ben's attention in the first place. Eighteen months of agonizing over mixed signals before, in desperation, she'd had to make the first move. Looking back, she had to wonder if she hadn't taken the initiative, if he would have ever made a move on her.

He glanced at his watch. "You're late—"

"I'm here now." The words snapped out with more edge and force than she had planned.

Keeping her expression serene with difficulty, she noticed that a couple had just vacated a nearby table. "Since we don't have a lot of time before we fly out to the island, why don't we get down to business?"

Sophie realized she was being too take-charge, but in that moment she lost the capacity to care. She pulled out a chair and sat down. A waitress materialized and took their order. At the last minute, she remembered to ask for what Francesca drank: a kale smoothie. She only hoped she would be able to get at least some of it down.

Ben ordered a coffee, which irritated her because she was dying for one.

Rummaging in her tote, she pulled out the kind of bright, pretty notebook that Francesca loved. Flipping it open in a little shower of glitter, she detached the cute pencil and placed them precisely side by side on the table. "I've been doing a little research online with regard to Buffy Holt."

Ben stared at the notebook. "For a minute there, I forgot about Buffy, but it's coming back to me."

She just bet he had forgotten about Buffy. It had certainly felt that way.

"As I was saying, I've been doing some research online. Were you aware that Buffy is stalking you?"

"I wouldn't exactly call it—"

"I believe stalking is the correct word." Sophie reeled off three major social media sites, and a couple that were rapidly gaining in popularity. "Buffy has a lot of pictures. Think wallpaper. If we're going to discourage her, we're going to need to employ serious tactics."

Ben sat back in his chair, arms folded over his chest. "All I need is a date for the day. Once she sees I'm dating someone, she'll get the message."

Sophie drew a deep breath to try to douse another heated surge of outrage that Ben actually thought this was a real date. "First of all, this is not a 'date.'" She sketched quotation marks in the air. "And if Buffy was going to get the message, she would have got it Saturday night at the earliest, Sunday morning at the latest, because by then anyone on the planet who was interested, and who had access to social media, knew that you had kissed, uh, Sophie at Nick's launch party. And that you had very probably slept with her."

Ben stared at her for a long moment and, once again, Sophie began to get the horribly uncomfortable feeling that his steely blue gaze had somehow lasered through her disguise.

Thankfully, at that point their drinks arrived. Sophie stared at the deep green liquid and left it where it was.

Ben lifted a brow. "So, what are you proposing?"

She picked up the notebook and pencil, and made a production of looking at the first page, which contained just the three bullet points. She didn't think he would go for any of them, and maybe she was being passive-aggressive, but the way she saw it, the whole point was to heighten his awareness of his utter failure when it came to romantic gestures. Except, of course, when it came to Buffy.

Grimly she read the very short list, which included a gift of jewelry, a fluffy toy and that *he* needed to get a special tattoo. Because hell would freeze solid before she would get one.

"Not that you actually have to get tattooed," she said smoothly. She dug in her bag for the envelope that held the transfer that Rico's apprentice, Antonio, had made for her. "It's a transfer. The ink comes off in the shower." Eventually.

Ben took the envelope and slid out the transfer, which was along similar lines to the one Buffy had, but considerably larger. The silence seemed to stretch and deepen. She flipped the cover of the notebook closed. "I know the transfer looks a little large, but don't forget we're trying to send a message here."

Ben laid the transfer down on the table. Under the mall lights it seemed even larger and more garish. "What does the *S* stand for?"

A small shock froze her in place. She stared at the transfer. "B loves S" blazed up at her.

Sophie's heart jolted. She had been in such a hurry to collect the transfer she had barely looked at it, but there was no doubting that instead of an *F* the initial Antonio had used was an *S*.

Warmth flushed her cheeks and for a moment she felt disoriented and exposed. It was almost as if Antonio, in making the mistake, had revealed a guilty secret, because it was a fact that she had once wanted Ben to fall for her.

Desperate to control the embarrassed color in her cheeks, her chin came up and she met his gaze boldly.

"Antonio must have misunderstood when I ordered the tattoo. Probably, because you had such a well-publicized relationship with Sophie."

Smiling bleakly, she made the executive decision to rise to her feet and end what had been an unexpectedly awkward moment. She dropped the notebook and pencil back in her tote. "At the end of the day, I don't see that it really matters if it's an *S* or an *F*. The important point is that you've got someone."

Ben stood with a fluid muscularity she tried not to notice. His gaze glittered as he slipped the transfer back in the envelope. "I'm not wearing a tattoo, so you can forget that part. Once Buffy sees me with you, she'll get the message that I'm not interested in a relationship. In any event, I don't think she'll be too unhappy because I'm pretty sure it's her father who's pushing the relationship agenda."

Ben's flat statement abruptly made sense of the whole Buffy thing, since Ben was so far away from Buffy's usual type and Holt did have a reputation for thinking dynastically. He had two other daughters besides Buffy. One had married an oil baron, another a shipping tycoon, so why not add a real estate mogul to the family?

Even so, she could not forget that Ben had given gifts to Buffy. Expensive, thoughtful gifts. The kind a man gave to a woman he cared about and whom he wanted to please. The kind of gifts he had never given to her.

Ben paid for the drinks. When he came back, he indicated they should walk across the vast expanse of the mall. His helicopter was on the pad on top of Atraeus's building, so all they needed to do was take the elevator to the roof.

As they strolled past all the luxury shops, he checked

his watch. "If we're going shopping, we'd better get moving."

Sophie almost stopped in her tracks. She had pushed him over the tattoo and he had reacted true to form. But she had never in a million years expected him to agree to buy gifts, because she knew what he was like. Alpha males did not deal well with shopping lists, and they did not tamely follow their girls around malls. Her brothers were a case in point; according to their wives, they had to be dragged or blackmailed.

She threw a quick glance at Ben, who was altogether too chilled. Something was off. The plan had been to be so high-maintenance that he would run a mile and leave both Francesca and herself alone. She hadn't imagined that he would actually buy jewelry—*for Francesca*—especially since he had never, ever bought jewelry for her.

She drew a deep breath to ease the sudden tightness in her throat and chest. The long-ago words of her grandmother seemed to echo down the years. *The charm of a man is the kindness of his heart.* Her grandmother, who'd had a long and happy marriage, had known what she was talking about. So had Sophie's own mother, before she'd been widowed. As a child Sophie could still remember her father giving her mother gorgeous, personal gifts. Bracelets for birthdays, pendants and rings for anniversaries, perfume at Christmas. It wasn't the gifts themselves that had mattered; it had been the giving that had been so heartfelt and wonderful.

The mystifying thing was that she knew Ben was kind. Nick had mentioned how generous he was in supporting a distant cousin who had been left destitute with three young children. Ben had given her a house and helped her start her own business so that she no longer had any money worries. She knew he supported charities, especially those for sick and disabled children, and for animals. He had clearly been kind to Buffy Holt. But for reasons she could not fathom he had not been kind to her.

She stared at Ben, no longer caring about avoiding eye contact. "Let me get this straight. You're okay with buying me jewelry?"

Ben's gaze was frustratingly unreadable. "As long as we get it now." He indicated the closest jewelry store. "We've got ten minutes then we need to leave."

Sophie caught her breath at the familiar, very expensive name emblazoned on the glass frontage of the store. "You want to shop at Ambrosi?" They were the maker of the diamond earrings he had bid on at auction and given to Buffy. Ambrosi sold what she liked to refer to as "commitment jewelry," because there was nothing either cheap or fake behind those doors.

Ben's gaze shifted to the store next to Ambrosi, with its distinctive black-and-gold frontage. "I don't care where we shop," he said flatly, "as long as I'm not buying diamonds from Atraeus."

The mention of John Atraeus abruptly spun her back to the wet, steamy sidewalk yesterday, and Ben bluntly stating that he didn't want Atraeus sending her flowers, as if he had the right to an opinion.

Before she could think that through, Ben's hand landed briefly in the small of her back, sending another one of those small shocks through her as he urged her into the rich white-and-gilt interior of Ambrosi.

Twelve

Every cell in Sophie's body tingled. She was ultra-aware of Ben at her side, large and altogether too rough-edged and masculine for a store filled with delicate diamond and pearl creations.

With Ben so distractingly close, it was hard to stay in character and hard to think. If she had been shopping for herself, she would have gone for the more classical pieces, but she was supposed to be Francesca, so she headed for the counter that held Ambrosi's more modern, flamboyant designs.

She studied pendants and earrings made from flowerlike clusters of diamonds and pink pearls. Ben bent to look into the cabinet, the clean scent of his skin and a waft of some expensive cologne sending another fiery jolt of awareness through her.

Since time was of the essence, Sophie smiled at the assistant, a young well-dressed man who seemed pleasant enough until she indicated that she wanted to try the earrings on. Infuriatingly, he glanced at Ben, as if his approval was required before he would open the cabinet. Ben compounded the issue by nodding his head.

The sales associate, whose name was Henley according to his name tag, took the earrings out of the cabinet and placed them on a bed of lush black velvet on the counter, where they glittered in all of their showgirl splendor. Suddenly hating the whole idea of Ben buying the lushly beautiful earrings, which were too big and too garish, *and not for her*, Sophie nevertheless slipped the turquoise chandeliers she was already wearing out of her lobes and fitted the diamond-and-pearl earrings.

She could hardly bring herself to glance at her reflection in the mirror on the counter. In any case, with her sunglasses on, it was difficult to make out details, for which she was glad, because all she wanted to do was rip the earrings out and return them to Henley.

Before she could do that, Ben reached over and lifted the sunglasses off the bridge of her nose. "You'll see better without these."

Feeling suddenly naked and exposed, Sophie found herself caught in the net of Ben's gaze. Tension gripped her. Taking a deep breath, she forced herself to relax. Physically, her disguise was perfect.

Ben frowned. "Maybe you should try on something else."

Before she could protest, he directed Henley to open an adjoining cabinet. He pointed at a classic pair of diamond studs that occupied their own piece of plush black velvet real estate, and that didn't have a price tag.

Henley looked startled, which confirmed that the price was astronomical.

Feeling more and more miserable by the second, Sophie removed the showgirl earrings and fixed the diamond studs to her lobes. Each pear-shaped diamond was large and distractingly gorgeously beautiful, with a quiet, glimmering fire that she completely adored, even while she had to hate them because Ben wasn't buying them for her: he was buying them for Francesca. According to the salesman, the stones were flawless, which meant they were extremely expensive.

She shook her head. "They're beautiful, but—"

"We'll take them."

Sophie froze. Crazily, she found herself fixating on the way Ben had said "we" as if they were a couple. Then a fiery spurt of anger banished the weakening moment.

They were so not a couple, and never had been during all the time she had thought he was attracted to her. He had never once given her a gift, unless she counted the roses he'd had delivered to her suite, and she most definitely did not count them. They had been a cheap, cowardly way of fobbing her off after yet another convenient night of casual, meaningless sex. "I've changed my mind," she said flatly. "You were right, we don't need the earrings and, more to the point, *I* don't want them."

But Henley had already run Ben's platinum card through the machine and was in the process of handing it back to him. Ben dropped the small leather case that went with the diamond earrings, and which now contained her cheap turquoise earrings, in her tote.

His hand cupped her elbow, sending an electrical tingle through her as he steered her toward the door. "The earrings are yours."

The hurt she had felt when Ben had been aroused by the hug escalated. She stared at Ben's tough jaw, his cool blue eyes fringed by dark lashes, the intriguing nick on his cheekbone, but before she could say anything they were out of the store and stepping into a high-speed elevator with a group of Japanese businessmen.

Minutes later, she stepped out on a rooftop and saw the helicopter. Up until that moment she had been so busy focusing on Ben and the charade, she hadn't thought closely about the helicopter ride. One of the differences between her and Francesca was that Francesca adored flying and Sophie hated it.

She didn't know why. Francesca maintained it was because she was a control freak, and she had zero control over how an aircraft stayed up in the sky. Whatever. Since her accident, the most harrowing part of which had been the helicopter ride to the hospital, the phobia had gotten worse.

Mouth dry, heart pounding too fast, she climbed into the seat Ben indicated. Taking a deep breath, she concentrated on fastening the safety belt. When Ben swung into the pilot's seat, she realized that he was the pilot, which made sense since it was such a short hop and they would be on the island for several hours.

Still feeling tense and faintly sick, she fitted the headset he gave her.

Ben glanced at her as he flicked switches and started the engine. His voice came through the headset, unnaturally loud. "Are you all right? You've gone white as a sheet."

She stared straight ahead, which was a bad idea, because the helicopter was small, little more than a plastic bubble with a tail and rotors, and she was staring over the edge of the Atraeus building at a sheer drop to the street. She didn't know if, during the time Ben had worked with Nick, her brother had ever men-

tioned her fear of flying, but right now she didn't care.
"I hate flying."

"Don't worry, you're safe with me. I flew choppers
during my time in the military, so I've got a lot of hours.
You need to put your phone on flight mode."

She drew in another lungful of air and concentrated
on switching her phone over. As she did so, it occurred
to her that if Ben had flown combat helicopters that
meant he had flown under all sorts of adverse conditions, including at night. A small hop to Sail Fish Key
would barely register. She was so distracted by the notion that she almost missed takeoff.

Ben began pointing out landmarks along the coast,
the low timbre of his voice oddly soothing. She realized he was doing it to keep her mind off the fact that
the helicopter was skimming out to sea, and the tactic
was working. She wasn't loving being up so high, but
her heart had stopped pounding. It occurred to her that
she hadn't been able to trust Ben for a relationship, but
she trusted him to fly safe.

Lunch was served on a huge patio overlooking the
water. Sophie ate canapés, sipped iced water and chat-
ted with a number of people, most of whom she knew
through Nick. But only part of her brain was engaged
with social niceties.

Apart from the first ten minutes or so after their ar-
rival, when Buffy Holt had managed to practically glue
herself to Ben's side, so far Ben had spent most of his
time closeted in the resort office talking figures with his
business manager, Hannah, Malcom Holt and a couple
of other men Sophie recognized as subcontractors. Apparently, they were holding the meeting now instead of
after lunch because a summer storm was brewing, evi-

denced by dark clouds on the horizon. That also meant the party would have to be cut short.

Meantime, a string quartet was playing and the champagne was circulating. Included on the guest list were a number of rich and connected socialites, and the gorgeous wives and daughters of a number of Ben's business associates. There was also a media presence, which she hadn't expected. Buffy Holt, who was dressed in a pale blue pantsuit that highlighted her golden tan, had spent most of the party chatting with various media personalities and posing for photographs. She was presently with a woman Sophie recognized as the editor of a high-end lifestyle magazine.

Ben strolled out onto the patio and, despite wanting to stay cool and a little distant, Sophie locked gazes with him. As he started toward her, her heart sped up. Dragging her gaze free, she swallowed another mouthful of water and tried to ignore the hum of connection that had been her downfall all along.

The next time she looked at Ben, Buffy had both her arms around his neck and was doing a great impression of a clinging vine. The fiction that Buffy was being pressured by her father to go after Ben died. From where she was standing Buffy looked like the online version of herself as portrayed on her social media pages. Pretty, rich, entitled. Never heard the word *no*.

But all of that was mere detail. If Buffy had been Ben's date for the day, then she would be allowed to touch Ben. The problem was, Sophie was his date, and Buffy was trespassing.

Setting her glass down on the nearest table with a sharp click, Sophie started toward Ben and Buffy. A little dimly she noted that she was overreacting but suddenly she was over the charade. Clearly Buffy hadn't gotten the message that whatever she had shared with Ben was over, and now it was someone else's turn.

By the time she reached Ben, he had disentangled himself, but impervious as ever, Buffy didn't take the hint and move away.

Sophie kept a smooth, cool smile on her face as she strolled up to Ben and slipped her arm around his waist.

Ben gathered her in against his side in a possessive move that sent a small thrill down her spine. Another neat move and she found herself turned fully into his arms. Her palms ended up on his chest, preserving a small amount of distance between them, but she could feel the heat of his skin burning through the thin linen of his shirt, the steady thud of his heart. She stared at his jaw and tried not to remember what it had felt like to be kissed by Ben. "You should have worn the fake tattoo."

A glint of humor surfaced in his gaze. "And gotten the fluffy toy."

She blinked, still too annoyed to be amused. "Don't let her do that again."

Ben's gaze dropped to her mouth. "Or what?"

She drew a swift breath. "This." Lifting up on her toes, she cupped his face and kissed him on the mouth. She felt his brief tension, then his mouth softened and he pulled her close. Distantly, she heard shutters clicking as photos were snapped.

Her phone rang, breaking the spell. Ben's hold loosened and she released herself completely and slipped her phone out of her back pocket. It was Francesca. Turning and stepping away so Ben wouldn't hear, she answered the call.

"I think he knows you're not me."

Sophie froze. "How?"

"What time did you get to the Atraeus Mall?"

Sophie took another step away and stared out over the terrace at the sea. "Around twenty past eleven."

"That's around the time he first called. But he rang once more after that."

While she had been with him. "And my phone didn't ring."

There was a brief silence. "I'm sorry I didn't call earlier, but I've only just figured out why he would have rung twice like that."

Somehow, when he had seen her he had known, and the call was a confirmation. The breeze got up, whipping Sophie's hair around her face.

"Sophie, if you weren't answering the phone and he knew it was you all along, why did he continue with the date?"

The word that came to mind was *practicality*. He wanted to pick up where they'd left off the day before, and deal with Buffy's harassment. It was called killing two birds with one stone.

When Sophie hung up she found herself back at the table where she had left her glass of water. It had to be providence, because, peripherally, she was aware of Ben strolling toward her.

His gaze glittered into hers as he came to a halt beside her. "Babe—"

"Don't you mean *Sophie*?" Her fingers closed around the glass.

This time she wasn't quite so scientific about chucking the water. Most of it splashed harmlessly over his shoulder and onto the patio, but a fair amount hit his chest. Placing the glass on the table, she turned on her heel and threaded through a group of guests. One of them, she was embarrassed to see, was Hannah, Ben's business manager. She was also aware of a couple of media hounds who were tracking her with their phones, which were no doubt set on video.

Maybe walking out on Ben wasn't the smartest thing, because she was aware that he was right behind her, but if she was going to embarrass herself further, she would rather it was in private. She found the patio steps and made it down to the vast pool area, which was thankfully empty. Increasing her pace, she passed a newly planted garden, thick with palms and subtropical plants, and jogged down a set of steps to a white sand beach that was strewn with driftwood and seaweed. Taking her shoes off, she tossed them onto the ground and walked down to where the sand was hard packed, courtesy of the waves gliding smoothly back and forth.

Ben fell into step beside her as she strolled farther down the beach, but he didn't make the mistake of trying to touch her. The wind whipped her hair around her face. She sliced him a detached glance. "Why didn't you tell me you knew?"

"Because I wanted you with me. If you had known I'd seen through the disguise, you would have walked."

She stopped in her tracks. There was a definite relief in knowing that Ben had always known it was her, because it meant that everything that had happened had been for her; his arousal, the diamond earrings.

She had wanted to throw the earrings into the sea, but now that she knew he had always meant them for her, they were precious and she wouldn't part with them. "Would it have been so bad if I'd walked?"

"I knew if you walked, I wouldn't get you back."

She frowned. "Then why didn't you just ask me to be your date, instead of Francesca?"

"I was trying to avoid what happened just now."

A scene. But that wasn't all, because if Ben had only

confided in her, she would have handled things so much more smoothly. And suddenly the reason Ben had asked Francesca and not her was crystal clear. "You needed some time."

He caught her hands, drawing her close. "You have to know that if we're in an actual relationship, that means marriage."

Ben talking about marriage, as if it was a real possibility, somehow took the sting out of the fact that he had to think about it. She couldn't help loving that he was considering her in that way since it meant that he truly did value her, but the other half of her was offended that, after two-and-a-half years, he still had to weigh things in the balance.

But when it came to Ben, it was always terrifyingly difficult to think logically. And the reason for her lack of objectivity was suddenly blindingly clear.

She had never been just fatally attracted to Ben: she had fallen in love with him.

That was why she had slept with him in the first place, and why she hadn't been able to forget him or move on. That was why she had forgiven him and slept with him again.

She stared at the strong line of his profile, the faintly battered nose and mouthwatering cheekbones. His gaze locked with hers for an uncomplicated moment and out of the blue emotions swamped her, making her heart squeeze tight.

Ben's gaze rested on her mouth. "I'm sorry that I hurt you; dealing with emotion has never been my strong point. Can we start again?"

"What do you mean by 'start again'?"

"A relationship."

Her heart began to pound. They were talking relationships and marriage. A year ago, just a few days ago, she would have been over the moon. Now she wasn't quite sure what she felt. All she knew was that she couldn't say no. "Okay."

Abruptly Ben swung her into his arms and the surprise of it made her laugh. She was suddenly caught on a crazy, giddy high because, against all the odds, she and Ben were together. She wound her arms around his neck and hung on as he carried her up the beach. He set her down in a grassy hollow beneath a tree and sprawled beside her. Sophie propped herself on her elbow and kissed him. One kiss followed another, as they undressed each other and made love. And as they clung together, for the first time she felt they had a chance.

Thirteen

Ben's phone rang, rousing him from the doze he'd fallen into after making love. He dug it out of the pocket of his pants and connected the call. The conversation with Hannah was brief and to the point. She had kept the media and curious guests away from him and Sophie so they could have some privacy, but it was time to leave now.

The weather was deteriorating a lot more quickly than the forecast had predicted. Most of the guests were in the process of flying out and the catering crew were already cleaned up and boarding their launches.

Ben quickly dressed and roused Sophie, who had fallen asleep. He kissed her on the mouth. "We need to leave, now."

Grabbing her hand, he pulled her up from the sand. By the time she had dressed and found her tote, the clouds were building overhead and the wind was gusting.

He found his phone and checked the marine weather

forecast. It wasn't good. The forecast had been upgraded to a severe storm warning. They should have left an hour ago.

He hurried Sophie along the beach, up the steps and out to the parking lot. When they had arrived, they had landed in a small airfield a mile or so from the resort and driven to the resort using one of the contractor's trucks. The truck was parked where he'd left it.

Ben opened the passenger-side door of the truck for Sophie. As they drove along the dusty road to the airfield, he checked the resort's small marina. Hannah had managed the evacuation of the guests, so everyone had left in an orderly fashion, which was good news. The charter launches that had brought the catering people were just pulling out, and Holt's superyacht was nowhere to be seen.

He turned into the airfield and braked to a halt beside the hangar. He glanced at Sophie, who was checking her watch. She took out her phone and started texting.

When the text didn't send, she frowned. "We're late. I need to change my appointment with my hairdresser."

"I thought you'd just been to the hairdresser." The instant he said the words, he knew they were wrong. "What I mean to say is that your hair looks, uh, good as it is."

Her gaze narrowed on his. "Because it's blond?"

He frowned, suddenly wondering where this was going. "I liked it dark best. I don't know why you changed it, but it's okay blond, too."

Jaw tight, and feeling like he'd just negotiated a mine field, Ben hurried her toward the helicopter. "The point is, don't bother with the phone until we get back to Miami. You can get coverage down on the beach where the resort is, but this part of the island is a dead zone, courtesy of the mountain range."

Moving fast, Ben handed her into the helicopter, swung into the pilot's seat, switched on the engine and handed her a headset. By the time Sophie had strapped in, he had gone through his preflight checks.

He checked the weather again. If there was lightning, it would be an absolute no to flying, because helicopters didn't respond well to lightning strikes, but at this point the storm seemed to mostly be wind. There was rain coming, visible in the gray curtain out to sea, but it wasn't here yet.

He lifted up and skimmed out, keeping low as he skirted the base of the mountain ridge that gave Sail Fish Key its name. Minutes later, he rounded the eastern part of the range that thrust out into the sea, forming the "tail" of the fish, and the sky lit up.

He cursed and banked sharply. "We're going back to the resort. We can wait there until the storm passes."

He met Sophie's gaze briefly. He knew she hated flying; her knuckles were white, but that was the only evidence of it, and in that moment he saw a side of her he hadn't expected to see. He'd seen battle-scarred soldiers who had turned into gibbering wrecks on a flight, but true to form, Sophie was toughing it out. "Are you okay?"

"I'm fine. What happens if lightning strikes?"

"It won't because we'll be down in about five minutes."

As it turned out, he didn't have five minutes. By the time he'd turned the helicopter around, rain was sheeting down and a fork of lightning struck a tall pine tree off to the left, where it stuck out of a promontory. They were flying low, anyway, so he made the decision to set down on the beach. If they were going to sit the storm out, they could do it there as well as anywhere.

He was almost down, just hovering a couple of feet above the sand, when a gust of wind sent something, probably a branch from the trees, into the rear rotor. The helicopter shimmied a little and he corrected, but they landed with a thump.

Sophie muttered, "That's the third accident."

Ben turned the engines off. It wasn't a crash, more of a hard landing, but if the rear rotor had been damaged by flying debris, their steering was gone and they would be stuck here until they were rescued.

An hour later, Sophie tried her phone even though she knew it was useless. The storm had passed as quickly as it had arrived, leaving behind a beguilingly beautiful sky. Stars glimmered through drifting wisps of cloud, but there was no getting past the mountain range, which reared up, dark and brooding behind them.

Ben was busy with a tool set, trying to fix the rear rotor, which was bent. Apparently, the branch had hit it at just the right angle. It looked like they were going to be here for a while so Sophie set about checking on what they could use to make a campsite.

First things first. She dragged out her tote and decided that now was the perfect time to change into her real clothing. Once she had on her comfy jeans, white sweater and sneakers, she began collecting firewood. She managed to find a number of pieces of driftwood, which she stacked in a crisscross fashion so they would burn more easily.

She didn't know if Ben had anything like a lighter, but if not, she was sure, with his background, that he could rub some sticks together and, presto, they would have a fire.

If he needed paper to get the damp wood burning, she could help out there, too, since she had the little notebook and a small pack of tissues. She extracted those from her tote and lined them up beside the firewood.

Ben walked around the side of the helicopter, carrying the toolbox, just as she was inventorying the food she'd brought. Three protein bars, which meant she could have one and Ben could have two. A bottle of water, an apple and the pack of vegetable chips, which they could share.

Ben stared wordlessly at her neatly stacked pile of wood and the things she had lined up. He stowed the toolbox in a compartment behind the two front seats, and pulled out what looked like a fishing tackle box.

He placed the tackle box to one side of the kindling and began extracting items. The first was a lighter.

She drew her knees up and dropped her chin on them. "I'm disappointed."

He lifted a brow. "What did you expect me to do? Start the fire with a couple of sticks?"

Next he pulled out a small coffeepot, a tin mug and some grounds. "I always carry this stuff in the helicopter because sometimes I go fishing."

"I'm good at fishing. Nick hates it because I'm lucky."

Ben gave her a surprised look, which she met with equanimity. "I wasn't always a city girl, you know."

She realized that for the first time ever, there was a complete lack of tension between her and Ben. They were marooned on Sail Fish Key, and despite the drama of the storm, she was enjoying every minute of it. They were getting a chance to just be together.

Within seconds flames were licking over the pieces of wood she'd collected. Ben walked into the trees that bordered the beach and came back with sticks that he shaped into a frame. A few minutes later, he had the coffee brewing.

While they waited for the coffee, Sophie checked the interior of the helicopter and pulled out the cloth seat covers, which she spread out on the sand so they could sit in reasonable comfort.

Using a stick and a cloth, Ben retrieved the boiling coffeepot, which was giving off a mouthwatering aroma. While he poured coffee into their one cup, Sophie busied herself unwrapping the protein bars and opening the bag of chips. Ben produced a pocketknife to cut the apple, and they had a feast.

The first sip of coffee was bliss, the second almost as good.

Ben examined the protein bar as if it was an alien artifact from another planet. "What's in this?"

"Nuts and chocolate. They mostly make them so you can have chocolate and feel good."

Ben wound his arm around her waist and pulled her in close against him. "Cool. My turn for the coffee."

She handed the mug over and snuggled in, leaning her head on his shoulder while she munched chips and ate her protein bar in alternate mouthfuls to get the maximum flavor experience. The night had cooled, but enough heat radiated from Ben that she actually began to feel sleepy.

"Were you frightened when we came down?"

"A little bit, but mostly because I hate flying anyway." She shrugged. "I knew I was safe." She couldn't even quite explain it to herself, but in a weird way that did not compute, she had trusted Ben.

He handed her the coffee and she had another sip then ate her half of the apple. Smothering a yawn, she snuggled back into Ben. After a while, lulled by the glow of the fire and the sparks flying skyward, her eyes drooped and she drifted into a doze.

Ben's mouth grazed the top of her head. "I don't understand why you want me."

The words seemed to echo in her mind so that she wasn't sure if she had dreamed them or he had said them. "That would be because I love you."

A weird little stab of panic pulled her out of the downward plunge into sleep, and she knew with clarity that she had done the last thing on earth that she should do.

She had told Ben that she loved him.

The Messena resort helicopter landed on the beach just after dawn. Sophie's stomach dropped when she saw the pilot was Nick. She had hoped he would still be away, but someone must have called him when she and Ben hadn't returned. Probably Hannah.

Sophie met Nick's gaze and knew that he wasn't fooled for a minute by her blond hair. "You're not Francesca."

"We swapped places."

Nick sent Ben a narrowed, glittering look. "Did you know before you flew?"

Ben's gaze locked with Sophie's. "I knew the instant I saw her walking toward me. But you don't need to worry. We're engaged. When we get to Miami we're getting a ring."

The words sent a shock wave through Sophie. Giddy pleasure washed through her, but that was almost instantly diluted by the fact that Ben's declaration that they were engaged was so sudden. There had been no proposal, and, more importantly, Ben hadn't said he loved her.

And there was another issue. Last night, Ben had made it clear how he had finally realized that when they had made love the first time she had been a virgin. And that she had only ever slept with him.

She knew enough about the alpha male psyche, courtesy of having four brothers, to know that kind of thing mattered.

Then there was the fact that Ben was announcing their "engagement" while Nick was literally standing over him, as if he was more concerned with upholding some kind of unspoken masculine code, than about finding out if she wanted to be engaged.

Nick grinned and shook Ben's hand. "Why didn't you say so? Congratulations—"

Sophie eyed them both flatly. "I don't recall agreeing to an engagement."

Ben frowned. "I was going to wait until we got to Miami—"

"It would have been nice if you had actually asked."

Frustratingly, Nick had already backed off. The change in his demeanor spelled out loud and clear that he now saw them as a couple and didn't want to get caught in the middle of one of their arguments.

Feeling off balance because last night she had felt so close to Ben, Sophie helped pack up their rudimentary campsite. She didn't like it that Ben had announced an engagement she hadn't agreed to without any regard for her. She didn't like feeling manipulated and railroaded. However, she was in love with Ben, which he now knew, and that was a game changer.

An engagement, while not ideal, would give her the time she needed to unravel what exactly kept going wrong between them and, hopefully, allow Ben to finally fall for her.

Cancel that, she thought. To *make* Ben fall for her. And in terms of falling in love, there was a definite glimmer of hope because physically, at least, Ben couldn't resist her.

The flight back to Miami seemed even quicker than the flight out. Nick landed them at the Atraeus Mall, because, courtesy of Hannah, Ben's Jeep was parked there. After Nick offloaded them, he flew the chopper, which was normally booked up for tourist flights, back to his resort.

As soon as they landed, Ben's phone went crazy and he began fielding calls and texts. When they reached the parking lot, he unlocked the Jeep. Sophie dumped her bag on the floor, climbed into the seat and fastened her seat belt. She was still upset by the way Ben had announced their engagement—she hated being railroaded into anything. Plus, her back was stiff, a leftover from her injury and a sure sign that she needed to do some exercises.

Ben swung behind the wheel, a concerned look on his face. "Are you all right? You look like you're in pain."

"It's nothing. Just a little back problem I had before. I'll get some ibuprofen from the store later."

Ben pulled into traffic and drove into town, stopping at the first convenience store they saw. "I'll get you that ibuprofen now."

His phone beeped as a text arrived. He checked the text and, leaving the phone on the parcel tray, he swung out of the Jeep and walked into the store.

While Ben was gone, Sophie reached for her own

phone, which was also sitting in the parcel tray. As she did so, her fingers must have brushed the screen of Ben's because the phone lit up. The message Ben had just received was still open.

It was from Hannah —but that wasn't what made her freeze in place. Hannah's message was simple, declarative and clearly meant to be humorous. She wanted to know if the "aversion therapy" of taking the "other twin" to Sail Fish Key had worked.

The screen went blank again. Feeling numb, Sophie stared out at the parking lot. Suddenly everything that had gone wrong in her relationship with Ben now made a horrible kind of sense. His resistance to the attraction and the fact that she had been the one who had done the seducing. The way he had kept dropping her like a hot potato.

He didn't want to want her, to the point that he had used a number of different tactics to void the attraction.

Number one had been distance. Living half a world away had worked. The second tactic had coincided with the second time they had made love: she was pretty sure he had slept with her in order to gauge how he felt, and maybe even to get her out of his system. The third tactic had been the most insulting. He had used her own twin, for whom he felt nothing, as "aversion therapy," because if they became a couple, he then had to consider marriage.

Ben knew her brothers were, quite frankly, medieval when it came to relationships. He couldn't sleep with her, or even date her over an extended period of time, and not offer marriage. She had seen exactly how that dynamic had worked on the beach of Sail Fish Key less than an hour ago.

If Ben had failed to commit, Nick, despite liking

Ben, would have given him an ultimatum. If Ben had ignored that, things would very probably have gotten physical. Business ties would have been cut at the first opportunity.

When Ben came back to the Jeep, she simply closed her eyes and pretended to be asleep. Minutes later, he dropped her at her apartment. He gave her a searching look when she collected her things and didn't lean over to kiss him. His phone buzzed again. He ignored it, made a time to pick her up for dinner and drove away.

Feeling like an automaton, Sophie walked inside, had a quick shower and changed. She put her sandy clothes in the washing machine and walked through to her kitchen to get some iced water from the fridge.

Aversion therapy.

Humiliation flooded her. The fact that Ben hadn't said anything about love, just the engagement, now made perfect sense. His aim had been to resist her, but she had forced his hand by pretending to be Francesca and pushing them both together again.

He was marrying her because he thought he had to.

And, in that moment, her mind was made up.

There was no way she could marry Ben. She wanted a husband who would love and cherish her, who did not feel pressured into marrying.

It would hurt to walk away, but it would hurt more to stay.

Picking up her phone, she checked out flights. The urge to go back to New Zealand, and to the solitude and beauty of Dolphin Bay, was suddenly overwhelming. She couldn't be away for long, because she had a business to run, but she could go for a week and run the office remotely. Besides, Francesca was here to keep an eye on things.

There was a flight that left in a few hours. She checked her watch. Ben would be back to pick her up in two. The equation worked. She would have time to get on the flight, but the plane would leave quickly enough that if he thought to check the airport, he would be too late to stop her.

Ben knocked on Sophie's door. When there was no answer, he tried phoning her. The call went through to voice mail.

An older woman who occupied the next-door apartment opened her door, leaving it on the chain. "If you're looking for Sophie, she left. She's gone overseas."

Her door closed before Ben could ask a question. Not that he needed to ask, he realized. He had suspected something was wrong when she had gone so quiet in the Jeep. Added to that, she hadn't answered any of his calls. The fact that she had left confirmed it, and he was pretty sure he knew where she had gone.

He called Miami's international airport as he took the stairs two at a time. Sure enough, there was a flight leaving for New Zealand in an hour. When he reached his Jeep, he headed northwest toward the airport. As the crow flies it wasn't far from Sophie's apartment, around eight miles, but traffic was frustrating. While he drove, he called a contact he had who ran security at the airport and got the confirmation that Sophie was on a flight to New Zealand.

He pulled into the parking strip outside the departures building, went inside and studied the information boards. Sophie's flight hadn't yet left, but it was boarding.

He checked with the information desk and found out that the next flight to New Zealand left first thing in the morning. The stopovers would kill him, he would be hours behind Sophie, and he would miss a raft of meetings; but suddenly his business ceased to matter. He could take care of things by phone, and Hannah was more than capable of fielding any enquiries.

He picked up his phone to text Hannah and stared at the last message she had sent, the one about dating Francesca as aversion therapy. His heart almost stopped in his chest.

He remembered leaving the phone on the parcel tray, by Sophie's, as he had gone into the convenience store to get the ibuprofen. She must have seen the message. When he had come back to the Jeep, her eyes had been closed as if she had been tired. She had avoided making eye contact with him when he had dropped her off.

She had read the message.

Returning to his Jeep, he drove back to the city center. He had hurt her and there was no way he could take back the harm that he had done.

Somehow, he ended up back at Alfresco. He pulled into a parking spot and stared at couples as they walked into the restaurant.

When he thought back to the way he had behaved, it was no wonder Sophie had run. He had been arrogant and insensitive, and more concerned with preserving himself than considering what their relationship had been doing to her. Offhand he could not think of a reason why she would want him back.

But he had to try to get her back.

He drew a deep breath to ease the sudden tightness in his chest.

He had to get her back, because he loved her.

Fourteen

Francesca walked off her flight to New York and hailed a cab to the boutique hotel she had booked in Manhattan. Her hotel was near the Atraeus Mall, so once she had gotten dressed it was a matter of walking half a block and she was there.

She showered and dried her hair, then shook out the red dress she had worn the night she and John had slept together. She intended to look exactly the same, right down to her lingerie, so there was every chance that her appearance would jog his memory.

An hour later, she walked into the glossy new Atraeus Mall and accepted a flute of champagne from a waiter. She reviewed her strategy. It was fairly simple. She would do her best to replay the conversations and actions of the night she and John had spent together in Miami in the hope that he would remember. If that failed, she would resort to seduction.

She spotted John hugging an attractive blonde and

her stomach sank. Her fear that John would find some-one else before she had the opportunity to remind him they were perfect for each other seemed to be realized.

A tall, dark man who was instantly recognizable as Constantine Atraeus, John's cousin, joined them and re-lief flooded her as the blonde woman suddenly fell into context. She was Constantine's wife, Sienna Atraeus.

Taking a deep breath, Francesca continued walk-ing toward John. His gaze connected with hers and her pulse rate sped up, although she wasn't about to do anything silly and impulsive in front of everyone. In Miami, they had connected outside on the terrace, so somehow she had to lure John outside for some alone time in the hopes that he would remember.

By the time she reached John, Constantine and Si-enna had moved on to speak to someone else.

John stared at her for a perplexed moment. "You're not Sophie."

"Sophie couldn't make it, so she asked me to take her place."

A waiter drifted by, and she handed him her untasted flute of champagne.

John stared at her hair and shook his head. "I've just had the weirdest sense of déjà vu."

"Not déjà vu," Francesca said, feeling suddenly con-fident that everything was going to work out just fine. "It's a memory. Is there a terrace anywhere around here? You might remember better if we go outside."

"There's a hotel above the mall. I've booked the pent-house apartment for the night, which has access to a roof terrace."

Francesca calmly linked her fingers with his. "Can you leave your party for a few minutes?"

After taking an express elevator, John unlocked the

penthouse apartment and led the way to the roof terrace. It had a glittering view of the city and, more importantly, large potted trees similar to the ficus trees
at the Miami resort, Francesca started toward the largest of them. John stopped her in her tracks. "I've been
having dreams. Did we—?"

"Yes." Going up on her toes, Francesca cupped his
jaw and lightly kissed him. "We slept together, then
the next morning you gave Sophie a lift into town—"

"And we had the accident." His hands settled at her
waist, holding her close. "Memory has been coming
back in fragments. I guess I couldn't believe that I might
have slept with Sophie. I mean, I like her, but—"

"She's not your type."

He smiled, his teeth flashing white against his olive
skin. "And you are, but you've always been with someone."

Pure happiness flooded Francesca. "Not anymore."
She looped her arms around his neck. "Now I'm with
you."

Sophie, exhausted from the red-eye flight from
Miami to Auckland, which had been routed through
Venezuela, hired a rental car at Auckland airport and
drove to Dolphin Bay. By the time she pulled into the
cottage that was situated in a cove adjacent to Nick's
resort, and which he had said she could use for a few
days, she was practically dead on her feet. It was only
one in the afternoon, but she felt exhausted, probably
because she hadn't really slept on the flight.

She had stopped at a grocery store to get a few things
on the way, including some fresh fruit, so she wouldn't
starve. Not that she felt hungry. All she wanted to do

was crawl into bed and let the sound of the waves crashing on the beach lull her to sleep.

Hours later she woke up. She wasn't quite sure what had pulled her out of sleep. Then the sound came again, recognizable as the thunk of a car door closing. It sounded close enough to be in her drive, but it was also possible that the sound had carried across the water from the resort, which shared a common boundary with the cottage.

Tossing back the covers of the bed, she padded to the window but couldn't see the drive from her room because of a large, leafy oak.

Dragging her fingers through her hair, she walked down the stairs and caught a glimpse of a glossy black four-wheel-drive truck in the drive. She frowned. There was no logo on it, so it wasn't one of the resort vehicles, and her mother didn't own a truck; she had a bright red late-model SUV.

Sophie heard footsteps on her path, and a second later a dark shape became visible through the frosted glass of the front doors. By the time the knock came she felt as if she were having one of Francesca's feelings: she knew it was Ben.

Despite everything that had gone wrong, a pulse of hope went through her, which only went to show how difficult she found it to let go. After quickly pulling on jeans and a sweater, because unlike Miami, New Zealand was in the middle of a chilly winter, she walked down the stairs and unlocked the door. When she opened it, disorientingly, the glow of the setting sun flooded in, making her blink.

Ben stared at her for a long moment. "Thank God you're all right."

Abruptly aware of how scruffy she must look, with

her hair mussed and no makeup, she crossed her arms over her chest. Her only consolation was that Ben looked just as pale and tired as she felt. "What did you think could have gone wrong?"

"You could have had an accident of some kind. But of course if that ever happened, you would never tell me."

Her jaw tightened. "I rang you when I had the first one."

"And failed to tell me you were sitting in a crashed vehicle, down an embankment, with a sprained arm and a back injury. Nick filled me in on the details."

"It wasn't all that serious—"

"A helicopter extraction, two dislocated vertebrae and weeks of therapy. No wonder you're still limping."

Her brows jerked together. "I recovered. And, in any case, even if you had been in Dolphin Bay, I would hardly have asked you for help because you didn't want to know, remember?"

His hand landed on the doorjamb, and suddenly he was close enough that she could smell the clean, masculine scent of his skin. "You should have tried me."

"I did, if you'll recall, *three* times, and each time it didn't work out. I know your parents' marriage was horrible, I know your fiancée betrayed you. What I don't know is why you can't seem to understand that I'm not like them and that I'm worth a chance. Instead, you tried to get Francesca to go on a date with you because you wanted to cure yourself of wanting me. Do you know how much that hurt?"

Ben's gaze connected with hers for a long, tense moment. "I know how much I hurt you. If I could take it all back I would. I know it doesn't make up for it, but at that point I thought you'd spent the night with Atraeus. And there was another issue." He pulled off his shirt.

Golden afternoon light turned his skin to bronze and made the tattoo *B loves S* on his bicep pop.

For a long moment Sophie couldn't actually believe what she was seeing. "Is that the transfer?"

He dug in his pocket and handed her a familiar envelope. "No. It's ink. I got the tattooist to use the transfer as a guide."

Fingers shaking slightly, she opened the envelope and saw the unused transfer. Emotion welled, making her chest go tight. She tried to breathe. "You love me?"

"I'm in love with you. There's a difference. That was why I was so wary."

In terse sentences he relayed the facts about the mismatch that had been his parents' marriage and which had led to his father eventually committing suicide. His broken engagement had seemed to follow the same pattern, and then he had met Sophie. He shrugged. "I had gotten to the point where I no longer trusted wealthy women. I expected to be let down, then I fell for you. I couldn't believe it would work out, so I kept trying to control the relationship by ending it."

"And what about now? What if we get together and something goes wrong?"

He linked his fingers with hers. "When you walked out on me in Miami, that was a worst-case scenario. I don't want to lose you again, ever." He pulled her close enough that she could feel the warmth of his body, while still holding her loosely enough that she could pull away if she wanted.

"I love you," he said flatly, "and the way I see it, we're both strong enough to carry this relationship. What I need to know is, will you give me another chance. Will *you* trust me?"

Sophie stared at the stubbled line of Ben's jaw. She

knew he must have caught the next flight out after the one she had taken to get here so fast. But even so, he had made time to get the tattoo, which was permanent. Once again emotion welled in her chest. "Is that a proposal?"

"It is." He reached into his shirt pocket and brought out a jewelry box in Ambrosi's distinctive colors.

He opened the box, took out a diamond solitaire that glinted with white fire and went down on one knee. "Sophie Messena, will you marry me and be the love of my life, to have and to hold from this day forward?"

Sophie blinked back tears, then in the end just let them come. She held out her left hand. "Yes," she said as firmly as she could. "As long as you'll be the love of my life."

Ben slipped the ring onto the third finger of her left hand. "I will."

Ben rose to his feet and pulled her into his arms, and suddenly she was home.

* * * * *

COMING SOON!

We really hope you enjoyed reading this book. If you're looking for more romance, be sure to head to the shops when new books are available on

Thursday 12th December

To see which titles are coming soon, please visit
millsandboon.co.uk/nextmonth

MILLS & BOON
MEDICAL
Pulse-Racing Passion

Set your pulse racing with dedicated, delectable doctors in the high-pressure world of medicine, where emotions run high and passion, comfort and love are the best medicine.

MILLS & BOON

THE HEART OF ROMANCE

A ROMANCE FOR EVERY KIND OF READER

MODERN

Prepare to be swept off your feet by sophisticated, sexy and seductive heroes, in some of the world's most glamourous and romantic locations, where power and passion collide.
8 stories per month.

HISTORICAL

Escape with historical heroes from time gone by. Whether your passion is for wicked Regency Rakes, muscled Vikings or rugged Highlanders, awaken the romance of the past.
6 stories per month.

MEDICAL

Set your pulse racing with dedicated, delectable doctors in the high-pressure world of medicine, where emotions run high and passion, comfort and love are the best medicine.
6 stories per month.

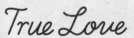

Celebrate true love with tender stories of heartfelt romance, from the rush of falling in love to the joy a new baby can bring, and a focus on the emotional heart of a relationship.
8 stories per month.

Indulge in secrets and scandal, intense drama and plenty of sizzling hot action with powerful and passionate heroes who have it all: wealth, status, good looks…everything but the right woman.
6 stories per month.

HEROES

Experience all the excitement of a gripping thriller, with an intense romance at its heart. Resourceful, true-to-life women and strong, fearless men face danger and desire - a killer combination!
8 stories per month.

DARE

Sensual love stories featuring smart, sassy heroines you'd want as a best friend, and compelling intense heroes who are worthy of them.
4 stories per month.

To see which titles are coming soon, please visit

millsandboon.co.uk/nextmonth

LET'S TALK
Romance

For exclusive extracts, competitions
and special offers, find us online:

 facebook.com/millsandboon

@MillsandBoon

@MillsandBoonUK

Get in touch on 01413 063232

For all the latest titles coming soon, visit
millsandboon.co.uk/nextmonth